I0525656

WHAT PEOPLE ARE SAYING ABOUT SHARON GERLACH

Praise for *Malakh*

"An intriguing debut from Gerlach that will keep you guessing until the final page." Kait Nolan, author of *Forsaken by Shadow* and *Devil's Eye*

"Ms. Gerlach is a masterful storyteller." The Romanceaholic

"It grabs you from the beginning and doesn't let you rest until the very last word."

Praise for *Office Politics*

"The delightful twists and turns, secondary and tertiary characters who are colorful and true to type make this story a laugh out loud experience." Taylor Lee, author of *Struck by Thunder* and *Race for Redemption*

"The exploits of Frannie Freeman and her office mates will have you laughing, crying, then laughing again."

Praise for *The Secret Dreams of Sarah-Jane Quinn*

"Gerlach's writing … always pulls you into the story. You feel for the characters and go through everything with them. I didn't want the book to end." Lauralynn Elliot, author of *The Haunted Lake* and *Starfane*

"This story was extraordinary. Ms. Gerlach's writing style is engrossing and descriptive, and some of her characters seem more real than people I actually know…you won't regret picking this one up."

"The story is masterfully crafted."

ALSO BY SHARON GERLACH

Harper & Lyttle Series

Office Politics
The Secret Dreams of Sarah-Jane Quinn

The Devil's Mansion Series

Malakh (novella)
The Wyckham House

Sharon Gerlach

condemned

A Devil's Mansion book

Running Ink Press, LLC

A Running Ink Press novel

This is a work of fiction. Names, characters, places, and incidents are products of the author's imagination or are used fictitiously and are not to be construed as real. Any resemblance to actual events, locales, organizations, or persons, living or dead, is entirely coincidental.

All rights are reserved. No part of this book may be reproduced in any manner whatsoever without written permission, except in the case of brief quotations embodied in critical articles and reviews.

Running Ink Press, LLC
1419 N Lee St
Spokane WA 99202

Condemned
Copyright 2012 Sharon Gerlach
ISBN: **0983291284**
ISBN13: 978-0-9832912-8-2
www.runninginkpress.com

Cover image ©2011 Joshua A. Gerlach

First Running Ink Press, LLC paperback print: August 2012

Printed in the U.S.A.

condemned

(Excerpt Kassandra Fotheringham's journal, appended by Pastor Hugh MacGregor through May of 2012)

June 5, 2009

Nothing, of course, ever begins the way you think it did.

I believe Lillian Hellman, the famous playwright, said that. She was right. I had thought I'd known where it all began: when Jonathan Fotheringham went on a murder spree through his house in 1945.

I have never been so wrong. But I'm not the only one; *everyone* had it wrong. But no one knew it until Geoffrey Windsor bought the house.

The house. Can a structure be evil? I don't think so, even considering what happened. But a structure can *shelter* evil, and since a structure can't fight back, can't seek exorcism, perhaps the distinction is not so important.

The Manor gave sanctuary to humans for decades; it might again, despite my warnings. I am comforted that no one will live in it while the present owner lives.

But when he is gone?

Ah, best not to dwell on *that*. You can only do what is within your power during your lifetime. After that, the gauntlet is taken up by God's chosen – or not at all. Will the evil claim more innocent lives? Perhaps.

It began with Rachael Payne—well, my part of the Manor's long history began with her, at any rate. The last I saw of Rachael, she was staggering away from Bayview Manor, reeking of gasoline, her hand blistered from the flame of the match she used to set fire to the mansion.

But Bayview Manor is still standing. I wonder sometimes ... Is Rachael

PANDORA'S BOX
Monday – February 16, 2009

He felt as though he'd handed over a portion of his soul when he gave Rachael Payne the down-payment check. It was due upon commencement of her work, however, which had already started. Despite the fact that he secretly thought the only thing Bayview Manor needed was a very large wrecking ball, Rachael was plainly enthralled as she scribbled notes in her plan book, tagging along behind him through the house.

Well, she trailed behind him, Geoffrey Windsor was forced to admit, but he held no illusions as to who was in charge of this expedition: Rachael Payne, the interior designer whose bid he had joyfully accepted despite the bottom-line cost that had made his bank account shriek in mortal agony. Of the three designers who had bid the job (and his mind still couldn't bend around the fact that only three had been interested), she was the only one who specialized in the restoration of Gothic Revival mansions.

Not that Bayview Manor had yet been identified as such. In fact, even Rachael was having a hard time pinpointing exactly into which period the mansion fit. While very much Gothic revival, it predated that era. From all history at hand, it post-dated Gothic. As the Manor had been discovered already built when a lumber baron named Nathan Fotheringham had cleared the forest around it in the late nineteenth century, it was doubtful anyone would ever be able to accurately define its architectural style or identify its builder.

Not one to look a gift horse in the mouth — or a gift house in the deed, as it were — the gentleman fancied it up and moved in his family. After all, it boasted a heavenly view of the Pacific Ocean near Perkins Reef. Forty years later, the last of the Fotheringhams lay dead in the Manor. Driven to jealous insanity by his wife's indiscretions, Jonathan Fotheringham had slaughtered his wife, the nanny, and his widowed sister who had been visiting before taking his own life.

It wasn't exactly a pristine history to entice a buyer. In fact, Geoffrey was the first to purchase the house in sixty-three years — sixty-three *unkind* years; the Manor had fallen into disgraceful ruin. Shutters and clapboard siding hung askew, the roof had sprung leaks, and most of the intricate stained glass windows in the ballroom had shattered, which in turn had let in the elements to ruin the hardwood floor. The mosaic patterns in various different hardwoods told him that restoring the ballroom floor would be a very expensive venture.

Although the upstairs windows had been boarded up (and he shuddered to think of *that* monumental job, installing sheets of plywood on the third story and attic windows), many of these windows had been broken as well — from the inside. He didn't know what kind of person would seek shelter in a huge, abandoned, and reputedly haunted mansion, but he *did* know that it took someone with immeasurably more courage than he himself possessed. He didn't even like walking through the house with an entourage of construction professionals in broad daylight.

It didn't matter; he wasn't going to live here himself. He'd purchased Bayview Manor for his mother, who had seen it from the sky while on an aerial coastal tour in a small aircraft. She could stay as long as she wanted, but he was going to make certain that sundown never found him inside. The house gave off a vibe that made his teeth ache and his nerve endings scream.

" —leaves the last seaside bedroom and the attic," Rachael concluded.

Belatedly tuning in, he discovered he had no clue what she meant. "Aahhh," he said, stalling for time, but he needn't have bothered. She sailed on as though not noticing his attention lapse.

"I think light and airy in the last bedroom. It's very small, and I'm concerned that dark wallpaper or paint will make it seem like a closet. There are some very nice gold-green toned reproduction wallpapers on the market now that would do nicely."

"I'm sure whatever you find will be suitable, Rachael." He was relieved she hadn't noticed his wandering attention. "Just get some samples, and we can look at them next time I'm on the Peninsula."

She juggled her graph pad and pencil to delve with one hand into the leather tote hanging from her shoulder. The hand came out with a daily planner bursting at the seams; it seemed that she carried her entire file cabinet of correspondence in it, attached to the pages with paperclips. She flipped through it to the current month and raised a brow at him expectantly.

"I should be back in a couple of weeks. First weekend in March," he clarified further.

She scribbled the information into the appropriate space. He was glad to see she had penciled it in; he couldn't guarantee he would make it, and less sure he wanted to oversee the progress on the Manor more than necessary—although he couldn't deny the prospect of spending more time with Rachael sent a completely inappropriate thrill through him.

"Now we should have a look at the attic. God only knows what's up there."

God could keep on being the only one who knew what was in the attic for all Geoffrey cared. He patted his pocket and made a face.

"I don't think I brought the key." He had deliberately removed it from his key ring and left it in his suitcase, to be perfectly honest.

"No worries," she said brightly, beaming a smile at him. She stuffed her daily planner and plan book back into the tote, and after a moment of rummaging produced a flashlight. "Harris gave me a set of keys."

He couldn't hide his dismay as she patted her jeans pocket, and made a mental note to whack his general contractor with the nearest two-by-four next time he saw him. Rachael didn't wait for him; she darted out into the hallway through the narrow beams of light slanting through the windows and open doors of the bedrooms; taking down the plywood coverings had been the first act of the construction crew. He followed reluctantly.

The attic entrance was at the end of the hallway, boasting the same style door and trim as the bedrooms. She had already slotted the key into the lock, grinning with excitement. It was no secret she was completely enamored of Bayview Manor. Her love of the mansion seemed to increase proportionately with his growing dislike of it.

She pushed the door open. The meager light from the hallway spilled into the entry, a murky pool of the golden radiance of a waning afternoon. Geoffrey reached forward automatically to stop her as she set down her bag and stepped out of the reach of the beams. Again, he needn't have bothered; her flashlight lit the stairs from top to bottom with a warm glow.

He joined her on the risers, and she pressed the flashlight into his hand with an understanding smile before dashing upward. So much energy, tied up in such a delicate package. "Petite" didn't come to mind when he looked at her; tall for a woman, she had slim curves that did wonderful things to the peg-leg jeans and pale yellow blouse she wore. With her dark hair pulled back into a claw-like clamp that looked more like a device of torture than a hair ornament, she appeared about sixteen years old. *Lecherous old man*, he chided himself, but that didn't stop him from enjoying the view.

His pace was slower as he came up after her. The general contractor had assured him that the stairs throughout the house were more or less sound, but Geoffrey was taking no chances. The moist sea air—not to mention the dozens of storms the house had weathered over the last six decades—was bound to have taken its toll on the integrity of the wood.

But he found no soft spots, no sagging treads, only a squeaky step midway. Rachael waited for him just out of reach of the beam of light, her impatience manifesting in the rhythmic tap of her foot. When he was within her reach, she grasped his wrist, aiming the flashlight into the room.

The blueprints had shown only an open expanse and supporting pillars. The plywood wall they now faced, with its equally cheap plywood door secured with an ancient but formidable padlock—he didn't have a key to *that* lock—had been added after the Fotheringhams had moved in. It appeared that they had been whitewashed long ago—*too* long ago—in an attempt to brighten the gloom.

Rachael turned, swinging him around with her. The beam

bounced a jagged course across the dingy walls. The light did not so much banish the shadows as it drove them into retreat, like sentient beings seeking anonymity in the darkness. The thought gave him no comfort.

"Oh, look!" Her eyes shone in the artificial glow as she stared down the dark hallway before them. "That must be the servants' quarters."

"I see Nathan Fotheringham spared no expense," Geoffrey muttered with barely veiled sarcasm.

Her grin widened. "It was a completely different era, Geoffrey. Servants were kept in their place – and in their poverty even while living in a splendiferous house."

He couldn't help his chuckle. "Splendiferous?"

"Exactly!"

She dragged him forward, and his tension ebbed as they moved away from the padlocked door. The servants quarters yielded nothing he found interesting, just several small iron bed frames, the mattresses long ago gone to whatever storage or dump site such things were relegated to back then. Plain tables with a single drawer stood between beds; one held an oil lamp, its hurricane shade long ago broken or repurposed.

Even Rachael couldn't find much to hold her interest, and it didn't take long for her to urge him back to the small entry room, her fingers resting lightly on his wrist to guide the flashlight. He imagined he could feel every cell of her skin pressing against his in that minimal, innocent contact.

He was startled when she yanked the flashlight from his hand and marched across the room to the padlocked door."What are you doing?"

"I'm breaking in. You obviously don't have a key – or don't want to admit you do – so I'm going to bust the lock."

"With the flashlight?" he asked dumbly, unable to think of anything else to say.

"I am nothing if not resourceful."

She knelt, raised the steel Eveready light, and brought it down on the lock. Geoffrey winced and backed a step toward the stairs when the light flickered.

"One more should do it," she muttered. Another smart whack separated the hasp from the plywood, and the lock clinked to the floor. Rusted screws, stripped from their moorings, scattered across the floor. "Excellent!" she cried.

"Yeah. Excellent," he echoed morosely. She sent him an amused glance over her shoulder. He opened his mouth to defend his reluctance, but she spoke first.

"I don't believe in ghosts, Geoffrey. I don't believe houses are haunted. This one has its history, its tragedies, but that's only to be expected with its age."

Her gaze held steady. He felt foolish for stubbornly holding onto his fear of Bayview Manor, but he could find nothing to say to convince her. Rachael was blind to the danger, and Geoffrey was unable to define it. He wanted to grab her and shake her and tell her —

Tell her what? That he had an acute case of the creeps, which grew unbearable near this door to the unknown? That the house had a history of swallowing people whole and never spitting them out? The list of the missing — or dead — stretched back to Nathan Fotheringham's occupation. Or he could *really* shoot himself in the foot by telling her that maybe ghosts didn't haunt the house, per se, but *something* dwelt here that gave off an aura of evil straight from the pit of hell.

And then what? Listen to her to tell him he read too much Chambers and Poe and that he needed to stop listening to the local rumors, no doubt.

"I know you don't want to go in here," she said evenly, her eyes sympathetic but determined. "I won't make you go in with me if you don't want to. But just think of all the things we might find in there."

Her eyes shone with excitement at the possibilities that awaited them in the attic — romantic possibilities, no doubt, born of her love of all things gothic and Victorian: chests of historic clothes and trinkets; antique furniture just begging to be restored; journals and diaries and letters tucked between the pages of old books. The possibilities were endless, which neatly explained his apprehension.

"All right, let's go." It wasn't what he intended to say, and it surprised him as much as it delighted her. She grinned so wide he feared the top of her head might fall off, and it was the joy in that grin that pulled him through the door after her.

The meager beam from the small Eveready wasn't nearly enough to cut the gloom in the enormous storage area. It appeared that everything the Fotheringhams had owned had been tucked up here, organized into more or less neat rows with wide paths between them. In some places, wooden crates and leather steamer trunks were stacked over their heads.

"Oh hey, that's handy," she remarked, shining the light on the wall to their right.

"Yeah. What is it?"

"A freight elevator, operated on a pulley system. No electricity, so nothing but brute strength." She caught his bicep between her thumb and forefinger and squeezed playfully. "Imagine how buff you'd be, Geoffrey, if you had to haul everything up here using that."

"Are you saying I'm not buff now?" he rejoined, affronted.

"You're put together very nicely, Windsor, but let's not kid ourselves. You're a businessman, and built like one."

"So hard-bodied laborers set you on fire, eh? Don't tell that to Harris's crew; you'll be fending them off with a baseball bat."

"Mmmm," she replied, distracted already. "I'm not much into body builders. We really need the electricians to get some light up here. It will take an age to explore."

"Which we don't have," he reminded her. "I have to meet with Harris and my accountant to go over some changes to the bid."

"Oh, that should only take you a couple of hours. You can come back when you're done. I should have found all kinds of interesting things by then."

He raised a brow. "You're not staying up here alone, Rachael. There will be plenty of time to explore the attic later."

"Don't be silly. I have a flashlight. I'll be fine." She flashed him a reassuring smile, which he did not return.

"It's not your wandering around in a dark attic that concerns me most, although that's reason enough, not only for me but for my insurers. You're the only woman on the job site, and it would be all too easy for someone to corner you, especially up here, and—" He broke off when she began to laugh.

"No one's going to rape me."

"Oh? You know all of those men downstairs?"

She shifted from foot to foot, uncomfortable. "Well, no, not exactly, but—"

"Then it's settled. No wandering around the house without a trusted chaperone."

"Trusted by you or by me?"

"Me. I'm the one paying the bills, remember?" His eyes gleamed at her crestfallen expression.

"I was afraid of that. Okay, let's go."

He was surprised that she gave in with such grace, but he offered no comment as she whirled around toward the exit. As the flashlight cut an arc through the blackness of the room, the beam illuminated the shadowy figure of a man. Geoffrey's heart stopped for a long moment, and then galloped out of control with panic. He grabbed her hand.

"Wait!"

"What is it?"

He didn't reply, just wrested the flashlight from her hand and shoved her roughly toward the door. "Go out, wait by the attic steps. I thought I saw something."

"Something?" she said, clearly thinking about the scads of *something* they had already seen just in the first few feet of the room.

But he was too preoccupied with jabbing the meager beam into the darkness, searching for something that might have presented a shadow like a human and finding nothing. There was no choice, really, but to make his way to the area where he'd seen…thought he'd seen…

"Where are you going?" Rachael asked sharply.

"Not far," he assured her absently. He wound between a couple of rows of leather- and canvas-covered flat top trunks where he'd seen the figure, his heart hammering painfully against his ribs, but there was nothing there. He shone the light around, searching for evidence that someone might be in the attic with them, and again found nothing. He stared into the gloom for a long moment, searching, and then sighed. Obviously his eyes had been playing tricks on him, producing images his overactive imagination expected to see. He turned to go back to Rachael.

The shadow-man stood right behind him, a coalescing darkness blacker than the rest of the gloom, almost a void in space. His heart leaped in his chest. He opened his mouth to draw breath to scream; there was no air, only a vacuum of nothingness. The shadow engulfed him; mind, body, and soul reeled from the contact and shrank in terror at the discordant chorus of inhuman jubilation that seemed to come from both around and within him.

He remembered nothing of his journey to the floor; he came to his senses to find Rachael crouching beside him, her hand on his forehead seeking evidence of illness.

"It's really stifling in here," she admitted. Her glance finally held what he thought was an appropriate amount of nervousness as she looked around them. The flashlight was wedged between two trunks, aimed at the floor. He stared at the small puddle of light until his vertigo passed.

"Come on," she said finally, her hand under his elbow to urge him upright. "Let's go get you a glass of water and some fresh air."

She led him to the door like she would a small child, and he offered no protest until they were outside the storage room and she remarked that perhaps they should leave the door open to air out the confined space.

"No, I'm closing it up," he disagreed vehemently. "No one needs to be coming up here." He was on his knees, ramming the screws back into the holes to secure the hasp to the plywood again, before she could protest. It wouldn't hold—a child would be able to break in—but it was the best he could do for the moment.

At last he followed her down the stairs and out into the third-floor hallway. As she closed the door and locked it, he swore he heard the screws dropping to the floor above.

(From the journal of Kimberly Owens Schaefer)

Monday, February 17, 2009

I wish the dreams would stop, wish they would go back to wherever they lay, dormant and benign, in the almost five years since the Circle scattered and the Wyckham House disappeared. I appreciate the blessings I've been given, but why does God not leave me in peace?

Dreams. Nightmares? Visions? Premonitions? I'm dreaming myself into a corner. How many more nights can I keep back the scream? Aaron already knows I have nightmares. How long until he realizes that something dreadful happened during those hours spent with Caleb in that infernal house — but not in the manner he's believed these past years?

He's there in Bayview Manor. Somehow, some way, Caleb Schaefer is there. Did he use this time for redemption, did he use Scott's sacrifice to change his life? I do wonder…I can't seem to help it. And how long until I have to tell Aaron about the Wyckham House — about Caleb's touch on my skin that keeps me awake nights, not in horror but in shame? Would he look at me differently, knowing what happened, knowing how close I was to giving in? Might I have thrown it all away for the momentary pleasure of physical relief? The question haunts me, because I see how easy it is to give in to sin. Not even "give in" really — because isn't it true that we sprint toward it, grasping it with our greedy hands, and the devil has only to sit back and reap the results of our own selfish actions?

And so I dream…and I worry…and I hide the events of the Wyckham House behind a façade of "nothing much happened, sweetheart" when he asks, but he knows I lie.

He knows.

THE WOMAN IN THE MIRROR
Friday – February 28, 2009

Kimberly Schaefer looked up from her laptop, her attention captured by the unseasonably warm March day beyond the sunroom windows. She didn't mind the interruption; it distracted her from the task at hand. The purging of events of four and a half years ago was long overdue, as her father kept reminding her, and dodge it as she tried, she couldn't fully escape the tenebrous grasp it held over her life. *Write it down,* he kept saying. *Write it down and get the poison out.*

Her husband didn't help matters, either. In spite of losing his brother and one of his best friends, Aaron had somehow managed to find the strength to put everything behind him. If he dreamed, he did it silently and didn't tell her about it. Kim suffered night terrors so acute she woke with a scream lodged in her throat, because in her dreams she fired the killing bullet too late.

But that was in dreams. In reality, Aaron had lived, and right there just past the deck and bare from the winter grew the angel trumpet vine that had served as a backdrop when they took their vows to one another. A miracle, their friend Taryn called it, because no one had ever believed Aaron would commit to another woman after his fiancée had vanished in 1993. They had been married almost four years now, and their children—fraternal twins of each gender—lay slumbering in their bassinettes under the ficus tree beside her desk. Another miracle, since the odds of Kimberly carrying a pregnancy to term were next to nonexistent.

She looked down from the window to her open laptop and stared at the words she had typed.

It happened in slow, surreal motion. Lightning rent the sky, and the wolf's lips curled back from its lethal fangs.

It hadn't seemed as simple as those two sentences. Writing

down the events of four years ago didn't ease the lingering effects of finding herself face to face with a werewolf, her only defense a silver bullet and the belief in an ancient legend.

A sleepy squawk beside her brought her head around. "Well, good afternoon, Miss Tia Schaefer." She bent and scooped up two-month old Tia, cradling the baby against her shoulder. Tia cooed in her ear.

One of the two miscarriages she'd suffered before becoming pregnant with the twins had almost been fatal. She'd vowed not to become pregnant again, for she couldn't bear to put Aaron through that agony. Fate had another plan in mind.

Kim thought she could pinpoint the exact night she'd become pregnant with the twins. There had been a strange quality to their lovemaking she'd only experienced when they kissed, the blending of their souls on a spiritual level. Aaron had seemed to be a reservoir of unplumbed passion, and his desire had driven them both to the brink of incapacitation. Afterward they'd lain together in silence, exhausted and stunned. Six weeks later her pregnancy was confirmed; she'd been confined to bed-rest immediately. The nine months passed free of complications; the twins were born three weeks early but completely healthy. She couldn't help but believe they'd had a little divine intervention boosting them along.

Kim realized Tia had fallen back asleep. She laid the baby in the bassinette, checked her son Evan, who still slumbered, and went back to her journal.

...the wolf's lip's curled back from its lethal fangs...

Her hands shook as they hovered uncertainly over the laptop keys.

...it sprang, snarling, jaws snapping and wide open for the kill...

Kimberly drew her hands away from the computer. She couldn't do this. It was hard enough to write about Tiana Michaels and Aaron's brother Scott, but this...

She glanced at her sleeping children but found no respite there; both Tia and Evan slept soundly, little bow-shaped mouths twitching as they suckled in their sleep. Both children had their father's dark blue eyes, but Evan looked as though he would be as blonde as Kim while Tia already sported a shock of raven hair. She didn't doubt they'd both have that Schaefer stamp of break-my-heart good looks and already they'd proven to be shameless charmers.

But none of that was writing this journal. She drew in a deep breath, saved the file, and closed the program. No more today; she'd progressed a little farther than she had yesterday, when she had barely been able to bring herself to remember the moment the wolf became airborne, aimed directly at Aaron like a bizarre missile. He bore the scars from the attack to this day, and frequently she caught him running his fingers over the ridged edges, relief etched sharply into his face. She completely understood the relief; the alternative to being scarred was being cursed.

A shiver raced down her spine and impatiently she shook off the memories. Enough! She had time to read the news and call her father in Forest Falls, California, before meeting Aaron for lunch at the greenhouse, but she didn't have time to resurrect the events at the Wyckham House. So with superhuman effort, she pushed the recollection of the Circle, its black magic, and its werewolf back into the crypt she was perhaps unwise to open, brought up an internet browser window to read the news, and went to get a cup of coffee while it loaded.

When she returned ten minutes later with coffee and a couple nicely toasted and buttered slices of banana bread, the page had fully loaded but for one stubborn graphic. The title of the article above the placeholder informed her HISTORIC BAYVIEW MANOR PURCHASED BY SEATTLE MILLIONAIRE GEOFFREY WINDSOR.

"Well, I'm glad for Seattle millionaire Geoffrey Windsor," Kim remarked, right-clicking on the graphic to force it to load. She scrolled down to read the article about the dilapidated Bayview Manor, located on the scenic Olympic Peninsula in Washington State, smiling a little at the obligatory mention of haunting. All creepy, abandoned mansions were haunted if they had any self-respect.

Her hand idly curled around her coffee and brought it to her lips for a sip as she scrolled back up to look at the picture. She was only vaguely aware of the mug shattering on the floor or of the splatter of hot coffee on her bare feet. Shock doused her like icewater.

The caption below the photograph read *Bayview Manor, circa 1944.* Kimberly knew the mansion intimately, had been held captive inside it for twelve agonizing hours...but she'd never been to the Olympic Peninsula. The mansion had been right here in Mills, Pennsylvania.

The Wyckham House.

She reached frantically for the phone, knocked it off the desk and into the puddle of coffee at her feet, and then fumbled with it for several precious seconds before managing to get a good grip on it. A speed dial code brought a familiar, soothing voice across the line.

"Kimberly? Is everything all right?"

The scent of coffee was strong in her nose; she thought for a horrible moment that she was going to be sick, but after a few seconds, the wave of nausea passed. "No, it's not. Cody, I found it — I found the Wyckham House!"

She paced the kitchen the next afternoon, arms crossed protectively over her chest. The sleeves of her sweater came to her fingertips and she worried the hem with her nails. Well, *her* sweater was a loose term; it had belonged to Scott. He had been wearing it one memorable day at the river when they'd discussed the town and its history of witchcraft, and for some reason it was the clearest memory she had of him — clearer even than Scott throwing himself in front of a fatal bullet to save her life. She'd filched it from the boxes in the attic that held his things, boxes her husband couldn't bring himself to get rid of.

Aaron had never said anything about the sweater, had just smiled slightly and nodded once. He had his own ways of feeling closer to his dead brother, such as "cleaning the attic." He'd "cleaned the attic" five times since they'd been married; Kim thought no one else in central Pennsylvania should have cleaner storage but truth be told, she couldn't see any difference in before and after. What he really did was go through the boxes and remember.

She pivoted, her teeth chewing on her lower lip, and found her path blocked by her father-in-law. Taller even than Aaron and still trim, Cody Schaefer presented an implacable front that was strongly reminiscent of a brick wall.

"Kim, honey, sit down. There's nothing that can be resolved immediately, and your anxiety is not good for you or the children." His arm around her shoulders, he guided her into a chair at the kitchen table next to his son.

"What do you know about the house in Seattle, Cody?" Aaron asked. His arm snaked around Kim's shoulders and kept her seated in her chair when otherwise she would have jumped up and started pacing again at the mention of the house.

"Ben Cummings called me several hours before Kimberly. He'd seen the article too." He tipped an ironic smile at Kim. "Bayview Manor has been known in Heron Bay since around 1850. There seems to be a bit of mystery shrouding its construction."

"No one remembers it being built, do they?" Kim interjected. "It's as though it just appeared—just like the Wyckham House."

Cody nodded reluctantly. She knew he didn't like her to dwell too much on her experience with the devil's mansion. He said looking backward at where you'd been meant you weren't looking at where you were headed. Aaron was already deeply concerned about her continuing nightmares. No longer were her dreams about future events; they now revolved around her hours spent in the Wyckham House with Caleb Schaefer, the events of which she had revealed to no one.

"It sits on a bluff overlooking a beach, but it's set far enough back that trees had to be cleared for a unobstructed view of the ocean. The mansion and its gardens were discovered when the forest around them was clear-cut."

"And so someone just moved in?" Aaron asked, barely suppressing his revulsion.

"Yes. The man who owned the land cleaned up the house, restored the gardens, and lived there for forty-some years, eventually passing it to his son. I haven't been able to find enough research to know what life was like inside Bayview Manor.

Everyone who's ever lived there is dead or not locatable."

Kimberly stared at him for a long moment. "You're going to go, aren't you?"

"Yes." He met her eyes without flinching. "My team was asked to intervene on Mr. Windsor's behalf."

"He's important then," she murmured.

"Everyone's important."

Renee had been quietly making coffee, and now she came back to the table with four mugs. One of them smelled strongly of brandy, which she set in front of Kimberly, who sniffed experimentally and sent her mother-in-law a speculative look. But she drank it, letting the conversation flow over her as the brandy filled her senses.

Renee's kiss on her cheek brought her out of her reverie, and she looked up in time to catch Cody's on her forehead.

"Don't worry, honey. We're professionals at what we do. I haven't lost a man yet and don't plan to start."

Her smile felt wrong on her face, and she knew it must not have been as reassuring as she'd meant it when the concern grew in his eyes.

"It just feels different, Cody. Worse than Mills. What if..." She chewed her lower lip for a moment and blurted out her worst fear. "What if Caleb's there?"

He couldn't hide his surprise. "Why would he be in Washington State?"

"He disappeared when the Wyckham House vanished. Did you honestly never consider the possibility that the house took him with it?"

Cody had no answer, but she heard him and Renee talking in low voices long after midnight and guessed the question had followed him to bed. She herself lay awake, staring at the moonbeams playing across the darkened ceiling, listening to Aaron's deep, even breathing. He didn't fool her; sleep eluded him too. Finally he rolled onto his back.

"Kim?"

"Mmmm?"

He found her hand in the darkness and twined their fingers

together. "What *did* happen in the Wyckham House with Caleb? You've never said."

"My time spent there was largely uneventful until you arrived," she replied softly, hoping he would leave it at that like he usually did.

"But not entirely?" he guessed. "Did he…"

She turned to look at him, wishing she could see his expression, but the moonlit windows were to his back and his face lay in shadow.

"Rape me? No—not that I could have stopped him had he decided to."

He sighed deeply and fell silent. When she felt certain he had abandoned the subject, he spoke again. "When you were changing into dry clothes at the cabin, I saw the bruises on your breast. They looked like finger marks."

"You were looking?" Kim replied, surprised. "I thought you were asleep."

"I faked it. I wanted to see how badly you were hurt and I knew you wouldn't tell me. Besides," and she could just make out the white flash of his teeth as he grinned, "I showed you mine."

"Lecher," she accused mildly. "What you saw was his warning to behave. That was the worst of it, other than leaving me with a painfully full bladder for hours on end."

Aaron was silent for a long time, then stretched across the bed to his night table and clicked on the lamp. The light chased away the shadows, and she wondered how he'd known she found it difficult to talk about his murderous uncle in the darkness. He rolled onto his side, facing her, and reached up to cup her cheek.

"If that was all he did, he wouldn't trouble your dreams so much." She opened her mouth to reply, and he pressed a finger over her lips. "You don't always keep back the scream, sweetheart."

She drew in an unsteady breath, her voice faint as she spoke. "He caught me at the cottage. He was hiding in the kitchen; I didn't see him. He threw me against the wall and twisted my arm up behind my back. I almost got out the back door, but he caught me and pulled me back in by my hair."

She paused, eying his clenched jaw nervously, but he motioned for her to continue.

"I started laughing. I don't know why, I just couldn't help it. I had one of those random thoughts that just strike you as funny. He was livid. I don't remember anything after he started choking me."

A muscle twitched in his cheek, and she had to force herself to continue.

"He asked me what made a woman like me fall in love with a man like you. When I said he didn't know what love is, he—he kissed me, as though lust and domination constitute emotion. Then he asked me why I'd said what I did when he'd been choking me in the cottage. I didn't remember saying anything, but he didn't believe me. He was...*so* angry."

She shuddered violently, but he didn't reach out to comfort her. Her need to tell him what had been done to her equaled his to hear it, so he could put those unknown hours out of his mind.

"He—he choked me again. I thought he was going to kill me this time, but finally he believed me when I said I didn't remember saying anything. Then he made me—" She closed her eyes, tears spilling from under her lids. "He made me lie down on the altar in Tiana Michaels' blood."

His work-roughened thumb scraped against her cheek, wiping her tears away. "What did he claim you said?"

"*Jesus still sees you.*" She opened her eyes, looking into her husband's solemn blue gaze. "I think...I think he almost killed me in the cottage. I had a dream about an angel who breathed air into me, and I woke up tethered to a bed in the Wyckham House. I've no idea how long I was out."

He stroked her cheek for a long time, staring at her silently as though committing her face to memory. His face was very white. "Sometimes I think about those hours he had you, and I want to break something. I have this overwhelming urge to kill him with my bare hands. I'm afraid I might do it if I ever come face-to-face with him again."

Kim rolled toward him, sliding into his arms with the ease of long practice. "But then you wouldn't be any better than him, Ron, and I know you are the better man."

"Only because of you," he whispered.

She moved the scant few inches separating them and pressed a soft kiss on his lips. When she would have drawn away, he held her pressed into his leisurely embrace as though their physical contact could erase what his uncle had done to her. It was almost enough to keep her nightmares at bay.

She walked down the middle of the gallery, placing one careful foot in front of the other to avoid tripping over debris. She'd never been in this part of the house before. Since the crew hadn't started renovations in this wing, no arrangements for heat had been made; she could see her breath drifting away each time she exhaled.

The portrait on her left caught her eye and she stopped, stuffing her hands into her sleeveless fleece jacket for warmth. The patriarch of Bayview Manor stared through the grime of the decades, dark eyes fixing her with a remote, haughty stare. His blond hair swept back from a cobwebbed forehead, the bones of his face strong, handsome.

A mirror hung on the wall across from Nathan Fotheringham's portrait, encased in an ornate, golf-leafed frame. She turned toward it and stared, astounded. It was not her own reflection in the mirror. Dark brown hair that brushed her shoulders, chocolate-brown eyes, ivory complexion...the woman was a stranger.

Now she realized the reflected eyes did not stare back at her; they studied the face, evaluating, considering — finding faults and flaws, judging from the woman's expression. They did not see what Kim saw in the background: movement from the portrait.

Horrorstruck, she watched as the canvas stretched outward, taking human shape. He stepped from the painting as though through a door, hand reaching toward the oblivious stranger. Malevolence and greed twisted the handsome features; now he looked cruel and demented, his fingers a bare inch from the woman's hair.

"He's behind you!" Kim shouted, but the woman didn't respond. Instead she leaned closer to the glass, brushing a long, slim finger over the freckles scattered across the bridge of her retroussé nose.

The man's hand hovered over the cascade of dark, glossy hair before him. The woman's eyes went wide and she whirled around, startled, as Kimberly's scream shattered the air.

"RACHAEL!"

The sound of her own scream jarred Kimberly into consciousness. A hand fell on her shoulder and she flailed away in a panic. When light flooded the room, she realized her husband was attempting to subdue her wild exodus from slumber.

"Oh God," Kim breathed, her stomach heaving. "Oh God..." She bolted from the bed and into the bathroom, shoving the door closed behind her and skidding on her knees to the toilet...just in time.

He waited politely until she shut off the tap after brushing her teeth, then opened the door, hesitantly peering around it.

"Honey?" When he saw her leaning against the wall, a cool washcloth over her face, he stepped inside. "Are you all right?"

"Yeah, just a bad dream, probably because my stomach's upset." But her voice quavered and she knew she hadn't convinced him. Beyond him in the bedroom, she heard Cody and Renée murmuring in quiet conversation. Her cheeks burned in embarrassment.

"Who is Rachael? You screamed her name."

"I...don't know." But she didn't quite meet his eyes. She tried to slide her arms around him, but he held her at bay, scanning her face with concern.

"What *kind* of nightmare? One of...one of *those* dreams?"

She could lie and tell him it was nothing serious; he wouldn't buy it, especially since she trembled violently and had just made a mad dash to empty her stomach. She might even be able to get him to drop it. But the nature of the nightmare frightened her too deeply to make light of it. Her precognitive dreams had mostly ended after her ordeal at the Wyckham House; she hadn't had one in four years.

So she nodded, because this dark ride had already started and there was no getting off until the bitter end.

He slid an arm around her, supporting her, and led her back into the bedroom, where Cody and Renée waited anxiously by the door. Cody watched as she sank down onto the bed and drew a blanket over her knees, his expression as cool and unruffled as ever. Annoyance and frustration slammed through her like a flash flood. Did no one else sense the danger? It was as though she was screaming "Fire!" in a room full of deaf people.

"He *is* there, in Bayview Manor," she said. Her voice shook, but her gaze was steady on his. "I saw him in my dream."

"Who?" He didn't move even a fraction of an inch, but his posture suddenly spoke of tension.

The name fell from her mouth and lay in the room like the unspeakable offspring of some foul being.

"Caleb."

(From the journal of Kassandra Fotheringham)

August 16, 1944

I come ever closer to contacting my precious Regina. Boldo says it will be any day now; he says I have made tremendous progress and could be a spirit-seeker myself one day. I only smile at him when he says this; I know that Jon would never allow it. I must hide my crystals and the planchette daily, or he will throw them into the fireplace. His intolerance is confusing to me, for he is the one who found Boldo and engaged his live-in services specifically for such things. I have abandoned all hope of understanding him and seek only to contact Regina.

I see things in the Manor now, things that lurk in shadows and hide their faces from the light. They seem eager for our séances, for our tarot readings, for the Ouija. I do not know what they are, but they no longer frighten me. Boldo says they are spirit guides. I glimpse them from the corner of my eye and they appear to be lovely beings bathed in darkness.

Jonathan has engaged a nanny to care for Rebecca and Joshua. I must admit to a certain relief; caring for their daily needs takes so much of the time I have in which to contact Regina. I believe Jon is smitten with Miss Emily Matthews; I must encourage that so he will leave me be. If he is otherwise occupied, he will stop interfering in my activities.

I must go. I hear Jonathan on the stairs…

BATS
Saturday, March 7, 2009

It didn't escape Rachael's attention that Geoffrey did everything humanly possible to avoid the third floor of Bayview Manor over the weekend. She didn't press him to take her into the attic again; she thought if she gave him enough time, he would eventually realize how silly he was being and would relent. She didn't mind waiting.

The man in question was, even as she thought of him, wandering the ballroom or the kitchens, perhaps even the cellar — although he seemed to have an aversion to that floor as well — anywhere but where she needed him right now: the third floor bathroom. Her notepad had grown to be her constant companion; she jotted her thoughts feverishly, her hand barely able to keep up with her mind, the graphite sketching out grand ideas she would have to try to articulate to him later. It would be much easier if he were in the room; he would be able to visualize the space much easier.

When she finally tucked her pencil behind her ear, her disposition was as cramped as her hand. She stopped by a window looking into the side yard in time to see debris falling into a strategically-placed Dumpster: the remains of the roof. From the cellar below she could hear an occasional screech of metal as the boiler company wrangled a brand-spanking new piece of machinery into place.

Rachael flipped backward in the notebook to a list she had made a couple of weeks ago, retrieved her pencil, and placed a checkmark beside "Boilers." Similar marks were noted by other steps completed, giving her an idea of where she could begin her own work, although the foreman on the site seemed to believe she thought her job was telling everyone else what to do.

Frowning thoughtfully, she tucked the pencil behind her ear again. She was dying to start ordering tile and wallpaper, but presently there was simply nowhere to store them. Harris, the foreman, had adamantly refused to have another POD storage unit delivered to the site, claiming she was driving him into bankruptcy.

A sound behind her brought her out of her thoughts. She turned to see the foreman himself hovering in the hallway outside the bathroom. He removed his hard-hat as he stopped in front of her.

"Miz Payne, we've a problem," he declared without preamble.

"What is it?" Rachael cast a glance toward the back stairs, which would take her directly to the kitchen, but he was standing in her path and didn't look as though he planned to move any time soon.

He raked a hand through his grey hair. "Two of my four-man demolition crew just walked off the job."

"And they were working where?" She raised a brow inquiringly.

"Kitchen." He shifted his weight from foot to foot nervously, and she stifled the impulse to ask him if he needed to use the facilities.

"Did they state the reason they quit?" Mentally, she was saying a lot of words she rarely said aloud and was frantically trying to recall just when she had penciled in the kitchen's completion.

"Oh, you betcha." But he didn't seem to want to tell her.

A cross frown of irritation creased her brow. "Well then, I suggest you spit it out."

"Really, I think I should talk to Mr. Windsor. I thought he might be up here with you."

Rachael's foot tapped impatiently on the ruined oak floor. "I'm not even positive he's on the Peninsula, Mr. Harris," she muttered, still vexed that Geoffrey seemed to be going out of his way to be inconvenient. "Just spit it out."

"Yes'm," Harris muttered, looking both chagrined and a little peeved that he was being forced to confide in her. It wasn't that he didn't like her; she got along with everyone. It was just that she didn't share the viewpoint of most of the crew that Bayview Manor was haunted.

"Anytime, Mr. Harris," she prompted, a smirk taking the sting from her words. "I haven't time to find a psychic who isn't a fake, so I suggest you start talking. Or do I need to find my thumbscrews?"

Harris smiled sheepishly. "The thing is...well, they both claim they've seen and heard things in the house. Bad things. Tools go missing and end up in odd places. And when they were working in the kitchen a while ago..." He trailed off uneasily.

"Go on," she invited dryly.

"They said they saw some bat-like creatures—"

"Could they have been...bats?" Rachael suggested pointedly. She was sure the attic was full of them, and the manually powered freight elevator ran from kitchen to attic. No stretch there to imagine the bats traveling from one floor to another via the elevator shaft.

"Man-sized?" he asked, arching a brow.

Rachael's mouth opened, but for a long moment nothing came out. At last her chaotic thoughts formed into a coherent sentence. "And you believe them?"

His spine straightened. "I'm a pretty good judge of character, Miz Payne."

"I didn't mean to imply otherwise," she assured him. "I'm just surprised."

"Well, ma'am," Harris went on, his face turning the approximate shade of a boiled beet. Rachael was rather alarmed at the sudden high color and began refreshing her mind on current resuscitation methods. "I can't say I'm awfully comfortable working in this house myself. I always feel like there's someone looking over my shoulder. At first I thought it was just you—" He shot her a sidelong glance and they both laughed— "but you're never around when I have that feeling. And sometimes I'll lay something down, and when I go to pick it up it isn't there. I put my hammer down on the kitchen counter yesterday, and I found it in the ballroom an hour later."

"Could someone have borrowed it?"

"Doubtful but not impossible. We finished the demolition in the ballroom last week but are waiting on the flooring expert, so I don't see why anyone would need it in there."

Rachael pressed her fingers against her temple, trying valiantly to quell her impatience. "All right," she said finally. "The men are gone. How soon can we replace them?"

He didn't reply right away, and when she looked up suspiciously, he was even redder than before.

"No," she said disbelievingly. "Don't tell me you *can't* replace them!"

"Well, all right, I won't tell you. I'll just let you figure it out for yourself."

"You're not *serious*?"

"I suppose with some searching we might be able to hunt up with some men to round out the crew. The thing is…well, this house is pretty well known, even as far south as Hoquiam."

"What about some local guys?"

Harris seemed extremely ill at ease now. "Rachael, no one wants to work here. Didn't you ever ask yourself why Windsor had to hire a contractor from Hoquiam, why none of the local companies even came out to bid this?"

"Well, no," she admitted slowly. "They were all booked solid, and Geoffrey wanted to start right away."

"Every local contractor, in a depressed economy, in the off-season, and they were all booked solid," Harris mused thoughtfully. "Perhaps I should be living up here, seeing how the work is so much better."

Rachael gave him a considering look. "You aren't suggesting they blew him off because they didn't want to work on this house, are you?"

Harris cast a glance over his shoulder, and his voice lowered. "That is exactly what I'm saying. I had a hard enough time getting a full crew, and I ended up with a crew of out-of-towners."

"No locals?"

"Half are from the Spokane area. The other half is made up of guys from Portland and Salem, and a few from up north—Bellingham and Lynden. No one in my company was willing to work on Bayview Manor except me."

Rachael was at a loss. "So what do we do, Harris? Go on with half a crew?"

"I can pull a man off removal of the debris." He frowned, making it obvious that while he could do it, he didn't want to. "It will slow down that end of things, but we can manage, I suppose. But I have to tell you, if we lose another guy, we're pretty well screwed."

"Yes. Yes, I see."

Harris watched her struggle for a solution for a full minute before he cleared his throat. "I'll try to find someone to replace them, but I have to be honest with you: I just don't think we're going to."

He reached up to tip his hat, realized it was in his hand, dipped his head respectfully instead, and scurried away.

Rachael watched him go, thinking he strongly resembled the mice about which he was always complaining as he shuffled down the hallway to the stairs, darting nervous looks over his shoulder. She shook her head, making a mental note to look up "mass hysteria" on Wikipedia; it was bound to have a picture of this construction crew.

The feeling of being watched slowly overcame her amusement. Wouldn't it be just like Geoffrey to sneak up on her and scare her, thus proving his stubborn belief that she should be alone nowhere in the house?

"All right, you've made your point." She spun around. The room behind her was empty, and she laughed at herself, a little embarrassed. Silly.

She reached up to retrieve the pencil from behind her ear, patting halfway around her head when she couldn't immediately find it. A quick search of the floor turned up nothing but sawdust and dust bunnies, the latter liberally sprinkled with the former, so she spent a few moments fumbling, and her fingers closed around a cylindrical object.

"Aha!" she cried, whipping it out of the bag.

A ballpoint pen, not a pencil. Rachael stared at it for an uneasy moment.

Man-sized bat-like creatures, Harris had said.

Suddenly, vacating the mostly abandoned third floor in search of Geoffrey seemed like a great idea.

Love raises the problem of a ricocheted spell. Should your target have found his or her true love, your spell will ricochet back onto you. There is no dodging a ricochet; therefore it is vitally important to have a contingency plan in place that will allow for immediate quarantine while the spell runs its course.

In coming between two people who share real love, magic is not an asset. It is better to use stealth, cunning, and devious tactics. Better to plant a misleading seed of doubt than to waste Power. Sometimes a lie works more efficiently than any magic ever could.

WITH THIS RING
Friday, March 20, 2009

The little town of Forks, Washington boasted two motels on the main drag, across the street from each other. Cody chose one at random, checked in, and called Denny Wallace from his cell phone. He had stationed his underling in Heron Bay proper while staying a safe distance from the town himself. If Caleb truly was in Heron Bay, Denny's presence would be less noticeable — and less alarming — than Cody's.

"Where are you?" he asked without preamble.

"Trying to convince the local Historical Society that my badge gives me the right to delve into their restricted archives," Denny replied. If he felt impatient with the Society, he didn't show it; he had the tolerance of a saint, which was why Cody had placed him at his right hand.

"Great. When do you estimate they'll cave?"

"The Twelfth of Never."

"Ah," Cody said in understanding. "You want me to come down and handle it personally?"

"Nah, it's all good. I'll just be my usual charming self, and they'll relent."

"Perhaps you should be your usual charming self in Mills if it works so well on blue-haired ladies." The note of censure in Cody's voice was unmistakable. He didn't often poke his nose into others' affairs...ah, who was he kidding? He poked his nose into other people's affairs all the time.

"Yes, well... Blue-haired ladies are a lot less demanding," said his subordinate coolly.

"A lot less fun, too." Cody rolled his eyes at the motel room wall, sat down on the end of the bed and slipped off his shoes, flexing his toes with relief. "Have you been able to look at any records?"

"Transfers of title, marriage and death certificates of the previous owners. Some old articles, some of them a bit weird."

"Weird? How?"

"They just don't seem to be related to anything about the house, yet they're indexed under Bayview Manor." Denny seemed relieved to be moving on to subjects less personal. "I'll have to dig a little deeper. This may take some time, Cody. You don't have to stay here indefinitely."

"Neither do you," Cody pointed out. "You can go back and forth."

"Cheaper to stay."

"Coward."

"Says you. Gotta run; I have a meeting with the Directory of Library Services for the Historical Society. We'll see where that goes. What are you gonna do while I'm handling all the hard work?"

"You're a riot. I'm going to track down Geoffrey Windsor in Seattle and see if he'll talk to me about the house."

"You think things are already happening to him?"

"I don't know. He bought the house in early November; work began in February. If this house is connected at all to the Wyckham House, things were happening before anyone arrived."

"All right. Have fun with that."

"Come up to Forks tomorrow and we can compare notes."

"All right. I'll call first to make sure you're back; it's a long drive to Seattle. Oh, and be careful not to trip over all my dirty laundry while you're cleaning my house."

Cody wasn't stupid by any means. "Okay, point taken. I'll try to mind my own business."

"I'm a federal agent; don't think I didn't notice the use of the qualifier 'try,' Cody." But he chuckled as he hung up, and Cody knew he hadn't taken offense.

He stared at his socked feet, lamenting his short-lived relief, and finally moved to change out of his jeans and sweatshirt and into a suit. Something told him Geoffrey Windsor would not turn away a federal badge wielded by a sharp-dressed man.

☙

A cloud of dust coming up the driveway heralded the arrival of a guest, and Kimberly groaned inwardly when she saw whose car approached. Trouble personified, Melody Olmstead had been making a name for herself around town with her increasingly odd behavior and blatant crossings of boundaries when it came to married men. Melody flirted shamelessly with Aaron, and he had become uncomfortable to the point of making sure he never found himself alone with her.

Kim cast a glance at the bassinettes where both babies napped to be sure they still slept and slipped out the door to wait on the porch. She didn't want that woman in her house.

The aging Oldsmobile's motor groaned and clattered as Melody parked beside Kim's Explorer and climbed out of the car. Kim couldn't help but admit she was attractive: dark auburn hair, alabaster skin, brown eyes framed with long, black lashes. Oh, she was a walking missile aimed at any marriage in her painted-on jeans and clinging low-cut t-shirt, cleavage visible through the gaping flaps of her unzipped jacket—a missile apparently now aimed at the Schaefers.

"Kim, can we talk for a minute?"

"Sure." Hiding her trepidation, Kim motioned her guest to a cluster of wicker chairs on the opposite side of the porch from her treasured porch swing. No way would she have this woman in her and Aaron's favorite spot.

Melody shot a look at the closed front door; the March day was crisp and cool, intermittent clouds stealing the meager warmth of the sun, but Kim made no move to take them inside. The implication was obvious that Melody was not welcome inside the Schaefer abode.

"I debated coming—"

"Then perhaps you shouldn't have."

Melody's ruby-painted lips puckered in irritation. "We need to have this out in the open."

"*What*, exactly, out in the open?" But a sick feeling uncoiled in Kim's stomach, and she wished she had decided to go shopping in

Scranton today, scheduled a root canal, gone in for a pelvic exam – anything to not be here for this.

Silently, Melody reached into her jacket pocket and held out her treasure for Kim to see.

Kimberly's hand seemed disconnected from her body; she watched her fingers grip the smooth gold circle. A wedding band – her husband's wedding band. Her body went completely numb. The ring undoubtedly belonged to Aaron: the gold band with its platinum channel holding one large diamond in the center and a series of smaller diamonds and sapphires had been purchased from a local artist who had made a limited quantity – not exactly unique but close enough.

"Where did you find this?"

Melody Olmstead managed, just barely, to keep her expression solemn and compassionate, but Kim had seen the malicious gleam in the other woman's eyes. *The other woman...* She couldn't bear thinking it.

"Beside my bed."

The words fell between the two women, resounding in the golden light of the waning day.

"I see," Kimberly said faintly. "And you're returning it to me and not Aaron because...?"

"Let's not mince words, Kimberly. Did you really think a man like Aaron Schaefer would be satisfied with the happy little family scene?"

"He seems happy enough."

"Happy enough," Melody echoed softly. "Is that what you want – *happy enough*?"

Kim swallowed hard, but managed to say levelly, "And what is it that *you* want, Melody? Other than my husband, I mean."

"I just think that you should be aware of the situation. That way there are no awkward fights and sleepless nights when he doesn't come home."

A muffled squawk reached Kim's ears; one of the twins had awakened. Melody flicked an impatient glance at the door.

"I think it's time you left, Melody." Kim silently prayed, even as the words left her mouth, that the dust cloud from the woman's departure would dissipate before her tears came. She wanted nothing more than to collapse to the porch floor and wail her shock and misery to the sky, but she would rather die than let Melody see her devastation.

Melody gave her a considering look, and finally allowed the smirk to twist her lips. "There are no such things as fairy-tales, Kimberly. There are no white knights on fearless steeds, there are no dragons—"

Kim narrowed her eyes. "Oh, there are dragons, all right."

"—and there are no fair maidens who win the everlasting love of the charming princes. The charming princes dally with the willing village maidens while the princesses are incapacitated due to pregnancy."

"Ah, how convenient. Since I slept through a good part of my pregnancy, it's very easy for you to make your claims. I wouldn't know sometimes if he'd come home or not. How charming you would use that to convince me my husband's having an affair with you."

"You think he's a devoted husband and father? If so, why did he need me while you were confined to bed-rest? And quite a need, too. It's a very...*interesting* phenomenon when he kisses, isn't it? Kind of like...oh, the blending of our spirits. Very powerful."

Kimberly clenched her jaw and held a hand in invitation toward the Oldsmobile. Still smirking, Melody went slowly down the steps. She paused before getting in the car, but Kim closed the door on her savagely triumphant smirk.

When the dust—and the babies—had settled, Kimberly returned to the porch. She rocked herself on the swing, the lifeblood of her shattered dreams running in silver rivers down her cheeks.

CR

"Are you *sure* you put it in the cash drawer?" Taryn, red-faced and sweating in the close, humid air of the greenhouse, pushed her damp hair off her cheek, leaving behind a streak of potting soil.

"Yes. I put it in there before I went out to the cutting field. I didn't want to get manure on it." Ron raked a hand through his already disheveled hair. His missing wedding ring normally covered the pale strip of flesh on his ring finger, which now glowed through his raven hair like a beacon. He dropped his hand and hit the counter in frustration.

"We've been looking for two hours, Ron. If it were here, we would have found it. We've torn apart the greenhouse." She paused, blowing her auburn bangs off her forehead. "Is Kim going to be very angry at you for being so late?"

He glanced at the clock. "No more so than for losing my wedding ring. Let's look a little more; might as well be hanged for a dollar as for a dime."

And so they looked, to no avail, and only when Ron was seriously late going home did Taryn call a halt to their search.

"It's not here," she said impatiently. "Go home! I'll lock up." And she all but shoved him out the door.

Most days—at least in fair weather—Ron walked from the house to the nursery through the adjoining fields. A locking gate at the edge of their private garden kept intruders out of their personal space, and as he let himself through it he noticed the only light came from the solar lights along the cobblestone paths. The house sat in the distance, dark and brooding.

The motion-sensor light came on over the back door as he crossed the deck. He tried the knob and found it unlocked, an unusual event. Kimberly always locked the doors at dusk; her experience with this town had left her with a healthy suspicion.

"Kim? Are you home?" The flick of a switch threw bright light down the hallway. He checked the rooms as he passed: the laundry room on the right, her small den on the left that she didn't use except to store her research books and computer equipment. The sun room that overlooked the deck and the gardens, the spare bedroom.

He entered the kitchen with trepidation; the last time he had come home to a dark house, he had found Kimberly unconscious on the kitchen floor in a pool of blood, the miscarriage too far advanced to save the pregnancy. But that had been two years ago, and since the twins were only three months old and they'd barely resumed their marital activities, he rather doubted she was pregnant again. It didn't come easily for them.

Ron palmed the switch and let out a relieved breath. No

Kimberly. No evidence of dinner, either. His stomach loudly protested this omission.

"Kim?" he called again. The silence in the empty house seemed to mock him. His skin prickled into gooseflesh.

Out of the kitchen and into the living room, where the babies slept in their matching bassinets, warm under thick fleece blankets. The front door stood open, and the creak of the porch swing pinpointed her location. He stepped out, clicking on the porch light as he went. The early April night was chilly, but she sat in only capris and a tee-shirt, her feet bare.

"Honey? Is everything all right?"

"I don't know. Why don't *you* tell *me*?" Her voice was husky, as though she'd been crying, her expression carefully blank.

"What happened? Is it one of the parents?"

"You're late," she said as though he hadn't spoken. "I didn't make any dinner."

"Have you eaten? We can go to Sutter's Inn. You should have something before bed."

The swing filled the ensuing silence. *Creak. Creak. Creak.*

"I'm not hungry."

He sighed resignedly. "I know I'm late. Taryn and I were tearing apart the greenhouse looking for—" Another sigh. He pulled a patio chair closer and sat down facing her. "Before I went out to the cutting field to fertilize, I put my wedding ring in the cash drawer. Now I can't find it."

Her teeth chewed into her lower lip, and when she looked up he could see the ghostly tracks of tears on her face. She *had* been crying.

"I'm sorry I didn't call. I know you worry."

Creak creak.

Just when he thought the sound might drive him insane, Kim stopped the swing and leaned forward, holding out her fisted hand. Ron took what she offered without hesitation, and stared down in shock at his wedding band, glittering in the palm of his hand.

"Where did you find this?"

"I didn't. Melody Olmstead did."

"Where did *she* find it?" His voice took on an edge.

Perfect. Just perfect. Melody Olmstead, the typhoon of Mills. He should have known. He'd been uneasily side-stepping her implied advances since Kimberly had been put on bed-rest seven weeks into her pregnancy.

She set the swing in motion again, and he thought its creaking might make him lose his mind. He had the insane urge to reach out and stop it, thereby stopping what he instinctively knew approached like a meteor of doom: the Hiroshima of any marriage, what Denny called The Mother of All Accusations.

"Beside. Her. Bed."

For a long moment, he could find no words. He was stunned that she would believe anything Melody said. No one else did; she had, as Taryn colorfully termed it, gone round the twist since the deaths of her husband and son, for which she held the entire Schaefer family largely responsible.

"She said *what*?"

"You heard me."

"And you *believed* her?"

"About your ring? Of course not. I've told you a million times to put it in the safe in your office, not in the cash drawer. It's too easy for someone — Melody, for example — to slip it out when the cashier's distracted."

Ron, fighting the surreal sense that he'd fallen down the rabbit hole after Alice, unwisely voiced his next question aloud: "So why are you angry with me?"

She gritted her teeth and visibly fought the urge to shout at him. "How did she know what happens when you kiss me?"

"I have no idea, Kim. I've only ever told one person about it, and she wasn't it."

"You *told* someone?" She looked truly aghast; it was tantamount to divulging the intimate details of their sex life. Telling Taryn hadn't been easy; he'd blushed so much he thought his face would burst into flame. But she hadn't laughed, and she had desperate need of his advice.

"Only Taryn, and only because she needed to know. She was devastated when Denny went back to Philadelphia instead of staying here with her. She wanted to understand how we knew we were right for each other."

Kim chewed her lip a little more. "Regardless, it doesn't explain how Melody knew...unless she had firsthand knowledge."

The silence between them seemed a living thing. Ron could feel it coiling around them, wrapping them in strangleholds with its rubbery tentacles. Appalled at this turn of events, he could only stare at his wife, his mute plea for trust deflected by her dead gaze.

"I've never—*never*—experienced that with anyone else. And I've *never* touched Melody Olmstead. I've been with no one but you in the last nine years."

And they'd been together for only the last five of those years. His celibacy preceding their relationship should have been enough to assure her that sex wasn't the driving force in his life, that he would have no need to turn to another woman to assuage any pent-up desire lurking inside him. Even during their forced abstinence while she was pregnant, he had felt no temptation to step out on his wife. How could she even *think* it of him?

Kimberly bit her lip again, uncertain, but in the end she turned her face away. Anger blazed through him at the hideous injustice, igniting his temper. He stood up abruptly, sending his chair skidding backward into the wall. She whipped her head around, alarmed.

"Accused, tried, and convicted, all before I even got home. Well, thanks a lot for your vote of confidence, Kimberly. I rather thought this was a marriage, not a high school rumor mill."

Her face went white, but she stood too, facing him fearlessly. "She *knew*, Aaron! How can you even refute it when she described what it's like?"

"*I DON'T KNOW HOW SHE KNEW, BUT YOU'RE DAMN RIGHT I'M REFUTING IT!*" He reached out, snagged her hand, and slapped his wedding ring into it. "When you're ready to grow up and start acting like a wife, let me know. Maybe it will still fit."

He slammed the door behind him, waking the babies, but Kim left their care to him, the smart thing to do, he had to admit, considering her current emotional state. And sure enough, within a short amount of time the children had stopped crying. He carried them, one by one, upstairs to the nursery, tucked them in, and stood with a hand on each crib rail, wondering what had just happened to his ideal life.

Kimberly sat in the growing darkness, not feeling the cold night pressing in on her, not noticing her breath leaving her in silvery clouds, only feeling the wintry chill in her heart. She was smart enough to know she had just dealt her marriage a fatal blow.

It was after midnight when she dragged herself upstairs. She approached her bedroom door with trepidation, wondering if the argument was about to continue and wondering how she could bear it. Her head ached fiercely and her eyes burned; all she wanted was to fall into a slumber so deep she couldn't dream.

The light on her night table sent a soft glow across the bed; the empty bed. Aaron, ever courteous, had made sure she didn't have to fumble her way through the dark, but he had already made his own bed on the window seat, his back to the room. She doubted he slept, judging by the resolute set of his shoulders, but she didn't challenge him.

Kim lay in their king-sized bed alone, muffling her tears with her pillow. Exhaustion finally granted her respite from the waking nightmare that had begun when Melody Olmstead wrecked her world, but the nightmare followed her into slumber, an ever-present menace of anxiety and despair.

(From the journal of Kassandra Fotheringham)

October 23, 1944

Jonathan has suggested we leave Bayview Manor. He says he fears for my emotional state and for the welfare of the children. He acts the concerned husband and father, as though he is not dallying with Emily Matthews and making her raise our children. What a happy little family they are. He wants to sell Bayview Manor; he says there are evil things here, dark things lurking in the shadows, whispering in our ears to push us to commit the atrocious deeds he claims we are committing.

Boldo worries, but I don't believe Jonathan really knows anything. We are a group now. It is so exciting! Every Saturday night they come, and we hold our séance in the secret room in the attic. There are passageways throughout the Manor, and one leads to the attic and another to the cellar. That is very convenient to our activities. I hide my journals in the passageway now; I don't think Jonathan knows of the secret corridors, so they should be safe. And since the passages are the only route to the altar room below the cellar, he should not find that, either. It's not what he thinks, but I doubt he would understand.

SUMMONING
Wednesday, March 25, 2009

It figured that when he finally made it back to the Manor after a barrage of problem-solving meetings the day before, Rachael Payne was nowhere to be found inside the sprawling mansion. Geoffrey wandered through its capacious depths, trying to overcome the sensation that the house — still gloomy inside while the electricians were fightning no end of setbacks in modernizing the wiring — was swallowing him.

On the third story, he paused at the end of hallway of the west wing, staring resignedly at the closed attic door. She wouldn't...would she? His shoulders slumped. Yes, she would. He stepped forward and grasped the knob, gratified when it refused to turn. She would...but she couldn't because he'd taken her key on his last visit so she couldn't make any solo explorations of the attic storage room. If he could fire-bomb that room and not set the rest of the damned house ablaze — oh hell, who was he fooling? The rest of the house could burn to a pile of godforsaken rubble for all he cared. He wouldn't turn a hair or shed a tear.

Still ... If she wasn't in the house, where *was* she?

He paced away from the door and into the nearest bedroom facing the ruined gardens and the bluff. From up here, the disorderly jungle of growth and haphazard layout of flagstone paths seemed to have a pattern, but its significance eluded him.

The garden yielded the solution to the mystery of paramount importance: from here he could see Rachael struggling in a tangle of junipers into which she had — somehow — fallen. He watched her for a moment as she ripped one leg free of the prickly shrubs, placed it into the center of a grossly overgrown specimen, and rocked her weight onto that leg. He knew it was a mistake before she went over, but the sight of her toppling sideways, her arms spinning wildly like an out-of-control windmill, brought a snort of laughter.

He watched her flail in the junipers for a moment, then pushed aside his sense of humor in favor of a sense of mercy—she was going to itch like mad for the rest of the day, because the crazy woman was wearing only a short-sleeved tee-shirt and capris despite the chill of the day. He'd buy her some calamine lotion and take her to lunch, getting as far from the Manor as was possible without having to leave her as well.

He grimaced, stifling that dangerous thought. Lunch probably wasn't the wisest decision—an hour or two in the sole company of his captivating interior designer—but it wasn't like she had anything else to do, hence her trouble with the shrubbery. She'd been exiled from the house late yesterday afternoon when Harris had attempted to explain the reasons her design for the kitchen would not work.

Geoffrey had faded into the background, distancing himself physically from the area and verbally from the argument, and watched in fascination as Rachael Payne came extremely close to losing her temper. He had stepped forward when it became obvious Rachael's stubbornness would not lend itself to admitting Harris was right, taken her by the arm, and guided her out the back door even as she was grumbling that testosterone was poisoning the male of the species. Harris had hollered after them that he didn't want to see her until she'd found some common sense and logic. Geoffrey wasn't all that sure she would ever be let back in.

The reason for her attempt to cross the sea of junipers became evident when he reached the garden. The shrubs and weeds had spilled over their raised boundaries and had, insofar as neglect would allow, made a creditable attempt to take over the flagstone paths. Here and there the raised beds had eroded and a spill of jagged lava rock littered the stones, making the journey treacherous.

At last he reached her—or as close as he could get, anyway—after much leaping, stumbling, and wading through weeds. His jeans were thorny with foxtails and sticky cleavers seeds, but she had fared no better; already she was scratching her arms, which had broken out in a blazing red rash.

"Need a hand?" he asked, tongue firmly in cheek.

"And two new arms," she said ruefully. She accepted his offered hand, but the distance was too great for her to leap. "If I just put my foot in the center of this ginormous shrub — don't look at me that way; it's sturdy — then I can leap from there."

"Isn't that how you took a tumble in the first place?"

But she had already shoved her foot through the dried husk of shrubbery and pivoted her weight onto its center. An ominous creak gave him a second's warning before the trunk of the juniper cracked in two. He gave her arm an almighty yank. Already off balance and struggling to remain upright, Rachael flew out of the shrubs like a landed trout and hit Geoffrey squarely in the shoulder. They crashed to the broken flagstones with bone-bruising force.

"Aaaaaaah," he groaned after a moment, rolling onto his knees. Pain flared through the arm that had taken the brunt of their impact, and he hissed in a breath, which made the ribs on his other side lodge their protest. She looked light, but a hundred and thirty-odd pounds of woman with considerable momentum behind her took a toll on a man's body.

"Are you all right?" she asked with concern, bending over him. Her curtain of hair brushed his cheek, leaving behind a tantalizing scent he couldn't quite identify.

"I don't think anything is broken. I won't be dancing the tango anytime soon, though." He slanted her a sidelong look. "Are you one of those people around whom bad things tend to happen?"

That startled a laugh out of her. "Come to think of it... I'm not particularly clumsy or accident-prone myself, but I've witnessed many a friend take a tumble." She straightened and extended her hand down to him, returning his favor.

"I actually came to take you to lunch and talk about how the delays in the electrical change-out are going to affect the rest of the renovation," he said when he had regained his feet. The foxtails stuck stubbornly in the fibers of his jeans and he had to pinch them to pull them out. The cleavers relinquished their hold easily, happy to stick to his palms instead.

"Maybe I should take you to the emergency room instead," she said critically, eying the red, irritated patches the cleavers seeds had left on his hands.

"A quick trip through the pharmacy for some calamine lotion will do us both good," he replied jovially, in turn eying her own rash. "Let's go. I'm starving. And I'm itching like crazy."

"When we're done with lunch, maybe we can check out that mausoleum in the middle of the gardens. I can't get past the gate — the lock's not rusted enough to break it — but I saw a hole in the middle of the floor. I'm almost positive it's a staircase. I want to see where it leads."

"What mausoleum?"

She sighed impatiently. "You know, that small marble structure behind me."

He looked, just now taking notice of the little building. "It's not a mausoleum, it's a memorial. And that's granite, not marble. The realtor mentioned it when I came to look at the house. I have a key to it. She didn't say anything about a hole in the floor or a staircase, though."

"I doubt she knew; after all, it's difficult to get to the stupid thing and there are vines growing over the roof, so she probably wanted nothing to do with it."

Geoffrey squinted at the small granite building, then frowned at her. "I don't think we should explore it yet, Rachael. You should probably let the crew go first. You never know what you'll come across."

"Like what?"

"Structural damage or weaknesses. Spiders. Snakes."

Rachael made a face at him. "And you think they're better equipped to handle those, I suppose."

He lifted one shoulder in a shrug. "Well...yes. I do." He ignored her scowl and took her by the arm, leading her away from the gardens. He thought she might be contemplating resistance, but then she acquiesced with grace, shrugged philosophically, and followed him to his car.

"Where's your jacket?" he asked belatedly, noticing her trying to hide a shiver as they rounded the Manor.

She smiled sheepishly. "On the other side of that graveyard of juniper shrubs," she admitted. "It was hard work getting over to that memorial. I was hot. So you see, we have to go investigate when we get back."

"I fail to see how you came to that conclusion."

They both stumbled off the raised edge of dry, crisp grass and onto the gravel driveway, which was nothing more than a rutted dirt track with a few tenacious, scrubby weeds between potholes. The gravel had disappeared, hammered into the ground by the harsh coastal winter storms.

"Since we'll be there already to get my jacket, there's no sense in wasting the opportunity to explore, is there?" she explained, her tone reasonable.

"I could simply buy you a new jacket."

"Hush," she said. "That's my favorite jacket."

He paused by the car, but she was already climbing into the passenger seat. When he got in, her eyes were closed and her expression was blissful as she drank in the solar heat. He let the subject go, because both of them knew he would give in. This wasn't like the attic; the memorial wasn't connected to the house. He doubted he would have much trouble sharing her enthusiasm, although the hole she had seen would probably turn out to be nothing more than a built-in storage space whose cover had long ago vanished.

Famous last words.

Two hours later, his clam chowder roiling in his stomach and threatening rebellion at the stench wafting from the open hole in the middle of the memorial floor, he saw it was obviously a staircase leading downward. So much for luck. He had the distinct feeling that luck had fled with undue haste when he'd signed the mortgage papers and hung this albatross around his neck.

He had borrowed a flashlight from Harris, who had been more than happy to supply Geoffrey with anything that would keep Rachael out of the Manor. While she had been right about the hole being a stairwell, he had been right about the spiders. He knocked down a web as they descended; no way was he walking through one the size of *that* hummer. It probably housed an arachnid the size of a terrier.

The smell of damp dirt, seaweed, and dead fish was almost a

physical assault. He breathed shallowly through his nose and grinned a little when Rachael said "Eeeew!" in a tone that squelched some of her enthusiasm.

"Twenty-five steps down, now, Rach," he sang out. "Are you sure this isn't a mine shaft?"

"Bet it comes out on the beach, judging from the smell of seaweed and dead fish. There are some caves you can get to only when the tide is out; no one knows how deep they go because they eventually lead upward. Too hard to climb up."

Seven more steps and the rough stone stairs ended in a small chamber no more than five feet by five feet, its smooth black walls of volcanic rock glimmering in the glow of the flashlight. He reached out a finger and touched one, grimacing, but it was only water.

"This looks like a natural chamber and tunnel," he remarked, studying the weirdly smooth, flowing contours of the chamber, which stretched to the left and right of the stairs. "I forget what they call them, but diamonds are often found in them."

"You're thinking of diatremes or pipes. This would be a lava tube."

"Ah. You're right. Which way, then, Madame Geologist?"

She considered, looking each way. A breath of wind came from the right, carrying a briny scent. "That way is the ocean," she said. "Tide's in, so we definitely don't want to go that way. To the left, Intrepid Explorer."

He grinned over his shoulder and led the way. The tube curved gently but had no radical switchbacks or abrupt changes in direction, so the air stayed fairly fresh. The sensation of being swallowed alive by the ground was impossible to shake, however, and he wondered why this land and its dwelling had that particular, unsettling effect on him. He wasn't particularly claustrophobic. Heebie-jeebies, that was why. He'd had the heebie-jeebies since the first time he'd set foot on the property.

Further on, the passage had been carved by hand when the smooth, natural walls of the tunnel arced upward and became unusable. He didn't need to guess that previous occupants had wanted to connect the memorial to the house, for he was sure that was the direction in which they were headed. He heaved a mental sigh; there was no escaping his albatross.

"This is really kind of exciting, Geoffrey," Rachael said, breaking the comfortable silence that had fallen between them the longer they walked. "No one knows this is down here."

Exciting. The words he would have used were "creepy," "dreadful," and "claustrophobic." But if he pushed aside his natural revulsion, he could see her point. If this tunnel had been anywhere other than on Bayview Manor property, he would have been as enthused as she, claustrophobic or not.

"I wonder how long it took whoever did this to tunnel from here to the house."

"The house?" she repeated, bewildered, and he realized she hadn't been following his train of thought at all. That the tunnel led to the house had seemed a natural conclusion to him.

"Where else would it go? I wonder if it was an escape route — maybe the other direction leads out above the tide line. The house was occupied in a less civilized time, after all."

"That's a clever thought, Geoffrey." She paused as though trying to decide whether to move forward or go back and explore the tunnel in the opposite direction.

"Don't even think about it, woman," he warned. "We've come too far to go back now." When she still wavered, he said, his tone sharper than he had intended, "Don't you want to see what's at this end? I think we're almost there."

And they were. Ahead of the meager reach of the flashlight beam, he could sense a larger space looming. *A stomach,* his mind supplied with gruesome pessimism; he couldn't deny that this parcel of land seemed like a living entity. *We're in the gullet right now, heading to the stomach.*

Perhaps they were going the best direction, after all, for if they were heading for the stomach now, the other direction led to the arse. That didn't bear thinking about.

The slight air current wafted a noxious scent toward them, an odor he had always referred to mentally as Eau du Grave. When he had purchased two historic buildings side by side on a downtown block in Seattle and began restoring them to use as his offices, a sealed passageway between the two buildings' cellars had been discovered. When the bricked-up, arched doorways had been reopened, an appalling stink had rushed out, sending most of the crew home for the rest of the day prone to violent bouts of vomiting. The sealed passageway had become the tomb for countless mice and rats that had found their way in through a breach in the foundation four feet off the ground and had been unable to get back out. The death-stink had hung in the stagnant air long after the flesh rotted away and only tiny skeletons remained, heaped on the cobblestone floor. Eau du Grave.

As predicted, the narrow tunnel opened to a large chamber. The flashlight beam skittered around it, and they both halted, dumfounded.

"A graveyard!" Rachel breathed at last. The manic gleam of the adventuress had returned to her eyes. Geoffrey noted it with some dismay. She snatched the light from his hand — damn, the woman had boundary issues — and rushed into the chamber. He had no choice but to follow or be left in the dark.

A graveyard it was, too. The size of a small church cemetery, the crypt was lined with neat rows of enormous stone boxes engraved with epitaphs and what looked in the flashlight beam like intricate faces. *Sarcophagi*, he thought, and shuddered.

Rachael was now winding her way among them, reading out some of the more amusing ones. Her voice echoed off the lava stone walls, the S sounds trailing away in hisses that made it seem as though a dozen people were in the room, all whispering.

"Geoffrey, this is even more astonishing than the tunnel. No one knows this is here — this is a huge historical find!"

He shrugged uncomfortably. He didn't care about huge historical finds. He was, in truth, wondering if it was possible for evil to exist in concentrated form on a particular plot of land. Just look at the carvings on these crypts – not the faces of cherubim, as had been the style when these people died, but faces of extraordinary, alien beauty. His gut twisted uneasily, as though he'd seen faces like these before in unpleasant circumstances, but couldn't quite recall the memory.

"Oh, look! The tunnel continues over there!" She aimed the

flashlight to a rectangle of darkness of the opposite wall.

"Great. The fun just ever ends."

She shot him a disparaging look. "Stop being so stuffy. You've quite obviously had your head buried far too long in the too-ordered and logical world of financial affairs."

As he owned a very successful financial advisory firm, which he had built into a multimillion-dollar money-machine, he could hardly argue with that assessment. And since Rachael seemed so fearless, Geoffrey felt his male pride bristling, pushing him to set aside those heebie-jeebies and match her courage.

Testosterone poisoning, without a doubt.

She swung the flashlight to the left of the new tunnel, passing across a wall sconce. A crude torch made of a stout wood branch and a rag wrapped around the end was wedged firmly into the sconce.

"Oh, *hey!*" Rachael exclaimed in delight, and Geoffrey groaned inwardly. Of *course* she was delighted. How could he have expected anything else? Now she stalked across the room to the wall sconce, and he was obligated to follow her with the light. She struggled with the torch for a few minutes before managing to wrest it out of its rusty confines, and held it under her nose experimentally.

"What do you know! It still smells of oil. Maybe kerosene; I can't tell the difference." She tucked the flashlight under her arm and began rummaging in her pocket.

"What are you looking for?" He started across the room, strongly suspecting she was checking her pockets for matches. And look at that, she was pulling a plastic Bic lighter out of her jacket. He shook his head disbelievingly.

"You wouldn't happen to have a ham and cheese sandwich in there, would you?" he asked, only half joking.

She grinned, thumbed the wheel of the lighter and held it to the rag to see if it would catch.

"I believe in being prepared," she explained as she pocketed the lighter, only marginally disappointed that the torch had burned for only a brief second before the flame guttered out. "I often need one, so I keep it handy. It's like my American Express card; I don't leave home without it."

He was secretly grateful the torch had had spent too many years in these damp confines to burn. Had it ignited, no doubt she would have wanted to shut off the flashlight and explore by torchlight.

"Let's go, Rach. It really stinks down here." So much so, in fact, that his lunchtime clam chowder was now staging a full-fledged rebellion.

She gave him a speculative look. "You're completely creeped out, aren't you?"

"Thoroughly. And I'm getting claustrophobic."

"You're claustrophobic, and you still came down here with me? That's really sweet, Geoffrey."

Bathed in the warmth of her smile, Geoffrey would gladly have explored a hundred tunnels with only an aging torch for light.

The next tunnel was much shorter and ended in a tiny chamber with a wood-planked door crossed with iron strap hinges, which Rachael proclaimed belonged to the Elizabethan period. She frowned at the old copper doorknob, and informed him that the doorknob first made its appearance in history in the 1800s. The mismatching of hardware made her job of pinpointing the Manor's time period almost impossible.

The knob was tarnished and slimed with moss and mold from its decades in the cold, dank cave. He reached around her and grasped it—more testosterone poisoning—and grimaced as his hand slid off, slimed with muck.

"Oh, gross," he said fervently. He manfully grasped the knob again, got a firm hold, and wrestled with it for a few minutes. Mechanisms long unused grated against each other, and the keyhole emitted a puff of rust flakes.

"Looks like we might be going back the long way, Geoffrey."

"Not if I can help it."

He worked the knob for a few minutes longer until he felt the latch let go. The door was swollen shut but not so badly that he couldn't free it by shouldering it a few times. Pain splintered through his arm where he'd landed on it in the garden, but he didn't care. He wanted out of this underground mausoleum, and *now.*

The door swung inward with a rusty creak, leading into a subcellar that looked as though it had served as a wine cellar. He wondered if the first Fotheringhams had planned to use the caves as an expanded wine cellar and ended up using it to bury their dead as sickness and old age claimed them.

"Well, it's better than the tunnels, I suppose," she said uncertainly as they advanced a few steps into the room. "At least it's fairly dry."

It was in truth the only good thing he could say about the small room. A dilapidated set of simple wooden stairs hung precariously on the wall to the left, leading up to a door that hung crooked in its frame. He didn't see the ramshackle construction; he only saw escape.

He reached back to pull the wooden door closed behind them, closing off the tunnel. As he followed her to the steps, he felt eyes boring into his back, so intently he could almost feel scorch marks in his flesh. He forced his concentration to the task at hand: the steps, some of which were nothing more than slivers of wood, the rest having rotted away or been chewed by termites.

They reached the door at the top without mishap; this one opened easily, if noisily, letting them into the spacious root cellar. Wooden shelving had long since crumbled from the walls and littered the floor. As they picked their way around and over it, he could sense the eyes following him. He paused, searching the inky darkness of the subcellar behind him. Finally deciding it must have just been a case of overactive imagination and nerves, he pulled the door closed with a bang that made Rachael jump. A draft chilled the back of his neck.

"Geoffrey."

Less than a whisper, barely audible, almost like a thought so clear and precise he assumed he heard it out loud. Geoffrey stopped cold, head cocked, heart pumping frantically.

Imagination, he reassured himself. *That's what Rachael would say. Imagination, that's all. Because I don't believe in ghosts, Geoffrey. You probably just heard an echo from upstairs. Sound carries in old houses; you can be in the second floor bath and hear a conversation clear as a bell in the kitchen. Echoes. Imagina –*

"Geeoofffreeee."

Like a sigh on the wind, the whisper floated in the still air, quiet, private, audible only to him. A summoning.

The saliva in his mouth vanished abruptly. Adrenaline flooded his veins; the instinct of fight warred with that of flight and momentarily paralyzed him. Rachael, oblivious to the drama playing out behind her, was climbing a set of stairs that were slightly less dilapidated than the ones they'd just come up.

A lazy chuckle shivered through the silence. The door he had just closed sprang its catch and creaked open.

Geoffrey ran, pushing past Rachael as carefully as his panic allowed, clattering up the stairs to the main floor. He burst through the door and into the kitchen, startling the work crew.

"Geoffrey!" Rachael scampered up the last stairs and banged the pantry door shut behind her, trying to catch up.

The electrician and the remaining members of the demolition crew exchanged uneasy glances, but he was so desperate to vacate the house that he didn't care how his hasty exodus appeared to the onlookers. He rather thought their expressions were sympathetic.

Rachael Payne might not believe in ghosts, but there were plenty of others who did.

(Correspondence from Dennis Wallace to Taryn Ackerlin)

March 21, 2009

My Dearest Taryn,

I've stationed myself in Heron Bay, Washington, with no undue notice by the locals. The Washington peninsula is beautiful, with many beaches and forests. The Hoh Rainforest is exceptional; I took dozens of pictures that I'll send to you via e-mail.

I write this letter not knowing if I will ever even send it — and not knowing if you will read it if I do send it. Where did it go wrong? Is my refusal to stay in Mills reason to sever all ties? You refused — on several occasions — to move to Philadelphia, and I always understood. I accepted what you could offer. So why haven't we spoken since I refused to quit the team and move home? I've tried to call you; does your finger even hesitate as it hovers over the button that sends my call to voicemail?

Taryn, I love you. And I love the work I do. It is my calling; who am I to say God chose the wrong man? I will do "the job" until I am certain it is not my calling any longer, but it is lonely work with no one to come home to. Why does it have to be one or the other?

Please — answer my calls. I'm not a begging man, but I'm pleading with you now. The world is a cold, unforgiving place — I see its cruelty every day. Please don't turn away from me.

All my love,

Denny

YOU AIN'T THE FIRST ONE
Sunday – March 29, 2009

The Heron Bay Historical Society proved to be no match against the charm of one sandy-haired, grey-eyed man with a lopsided grin and a decidedly flirtatious manner.

Anne Quequesah, the current Director of Library Services, wavered only fifteen minutes before caving to the beguiling smile directed at her. An attractive Native American woman with glossy black hair cascading to her waist, Anne did not appear to be immune to the appeal of a charismatic man despite the fact she wore a wedding ring with a rock the size of Gibraltar.

She led the way to the restricted access section of the Society's library, and he followed her trim, suited figure with a slightly ironic twist to his lips, perfectly aware that this was precisely the reason Cody had sent him. Denny Wallace didn't doubt that Cody could have gained access within the same amount of time – after all, the director of the Omega Team was himself a handsome man with considerable charm – but they both knew Anne Quequesah would have caved to Cody only because he was a powerful, dangerous man, and her capitulation would have been tainted with resentment. Resentment led to uncooperative behavior and loose lips, both of which the team wanted to avoid.

"Here's the section on Bayview Manor. Top two shelves of the first section." Anne stopped at the head of an aisle and motioned to the books on one side. She reminded Denny of a flight attendant indicating an airplane's exits. "Please let me know if you need anything, Agent Wallace."

"I'll be sure to."

He watched her leave, his frank appreciation of her attractiveness leaving behind a residue of guilt. More than a residue, he thought ruefully; more like sediment. But he hadn't been the one who stubbornly refused to leave that hole-in-the-wall town, who chose the familiar instead of him. He wondered if the familiar was adequate to meet Taryn's needs; it sure wasn't enough for him. He wanted a lifetime mate; a woman not afraid to trek out of the tiny town where she'd been born and into the great, wide world. A woman who understood his work may take his presence from home but not his heart or his loyalty, and he wanted that woman to be Taryn Ackerlin.

Too bad she didn't share that sentiment.

Denny pushed away the thought with monumental effort, stepped into the aisle and ran a practiced eye over the books lining the shelves. Selecting a couple of likely prospects, he took them to a small table nearby and slid a notebook out of his briefcase, ready to take notes.

The task at hand might seem huge to one not used to searching for information without knowing what that information might be, but Denny was undaunted. He had an eye for strange information and an intuition for how it fit into the case at hand — another reason Cody had chosen him.

Two hours later, he turned a page and his breath left him in a rush. After a shocked moment, he realized he had pushed himself several feet away from the table.

Staring up at him from the pages of a book written twenty-three years ago was an expertly-drawn portrait of a familiar face, a face he saw when his dreams were particularly bad. A face that should not have been known in Heron Bay because twenty-three years ago, this man lived in Mills, Pennsylvania.

Denny slid his phone out of his pocket, surreptitiously checked the room to be sure he was alone, and pressed a button to speed-dial Cody.

"You aren't going to believe this," he said without greeting as soon as his boss answered. "I found a drawing in a book written twenty-three years ago. The drawing was an artist's rendition of a supposed spirit seen by a realtor at Bayview Manor in 1979. When the author wrote this book, she commissioned an artist to do a sketch based on the realtor's description of the ghost, much like a police sketch."

"The point, Dennis?"

"It's Caleb." Complete silence met his statement, and Denny worried he might have given his employer a heart attack; Cody was not a young man anymore and had worked in this stressful field for decades.

"Impossible. It must just be a strong resemblance."

"It's not," Denny replied evenly. "It's an exact likeness. I'll take a picture of it with my phone; I doubt Anne Quequesah will let me out of here with the book."

"What's the title? I'll see if I can purchase it somewhere. I'm still in Forks, by the way. Geoffrey Windsor is on the Peninsula, so maybe I can catch up with him here. His assistant said he would relay the request."

Denny gave him the information, hesitated, and then decided he might as well ask. When Cody had arranged this assignment and drafted Denny to handle the research, he'd not given a reason for his interest in Bayview Manor. Denny simply assumed that the government needed to keep Geoffrey Windsor from some suspected harm; Windsor was, after all, a prominent citizen in Washington State. Now he wondered if there was more to it.

"Cody—is Kimberly dreaming again? Is that why we're here? It's entirely too coincidental that you take a sudden interest in this house, and I find a drawing of your brother in an old book about the same house. Did she see Caleb in her dreams?"

Cody inhaled sharply, let out the breath wearily. "Yes."

Denny sighed himself. "Okay. As long as I know what I'm working with. But you know what? You should try trusting me a little more. You could have told me."

"I needed you to be completely objective. If I had told you and you found him, you would always think it was because you were looking for him—in which case you would doubt the drawing is Caleb—and you would always wonder if I'd known all along where he'd gone."

"Are you forgetting that this book was written two decades ago? And the sighting was nearly *three* decades ago?"

"No, I'm not forgetting. Are *you* forgetting what house we're dealing with, Dennis?"

The question poked at him all day. He took a picture of the drawing with his phone's camera, wrote some extensive notes about the particular incident the drawing illustrated, and left the books on the table on his way out. He stopped at the door of Anne Quequesah's office to let her know he was leaving.

"I left the books on the table so someone could put them back where they belong; I'd probably mess it all up," he said with a grin, although he knew he could take every item off the shelves and put them back in precisely the same order. "Thank you for allowing me to look at them. Will you let me return?"

Anne Quequesah hesitated only a fraction of a second before smiling warmly. "Of course, Agent Wallace. When you come in, just ask for me and I'll escort you."

"I appreciate it." He left her with a warm smile of his own, which faded as soon as he reached the relative privacy of his car. His hands shook as he forwarded the picture of the drawing to Cody. He closed his phone and tossed it on the seat beside him, leaned his forehead against the steering wheel, and drew a shaky breath.

"Oh God, don't let it happen again," he whispered. "Don't let him have started another Circle."

A long while later, when the shakes had subsided, Denny started the car and headed toward Bayview Manor.

No one seemed to notice him as he slipped through the open front door and walked through the frenetic activity in the Manor. Steady hammering in the kitchen masked his footsteps through the foyer. He paused, giving way to two workers carrying several sheets of drywall. One nodded cordially at him, and he returned the nod, shoving his hands into his jeans pocket and trying to appear as though he belonged as he followed them out of the room.

A shrewd judge of character, it didn't take him long to identify the leader of the crew: he leaned on a makeshift worktable, poring over blueprints, his yellow hardhat pushed up off his forehead. He wore a perplexed frown, and as Denny made his way across the debris-laden room, the man swept the hardhat from his head and tossed it on the table, scratching his head in bewilderment.

"I'm an old hand at blueprints, if you need help," he offered.

The foreman looked up in surprise and not a little irritation, which he suppressed immediately. Although he was not as physically intimidating as Cody, Denny exuded a sense of power, and people seemed to instinctively sense he was a man who could make things happen — good or bad things.

"I hope you're a math whiz as well." The foreman came forward, hand extended. Denny shook it firmly. "Lon Harris. I'm the foreman for the general contractor, Carson Construction. If I'm not mistaken, you're not one of the replacement workers I sent for?"

"Afraid not," Denny replied, chuckling. His gaze swept Harris's face, gauging how much he should divulge. Before he could decide, Harris went back to the blueprints and was motioning with a blunt, calloused finger.

"See right here? These measurements on the original prints are *not* what I'm measuring now. Of course, our plans were drawn on the actual measurements we took ourselves before beginning work, so it won't mess us up. It's just a puzzle, is all, and I can't leave a puzzle alone until it's solved."

"I understand." Denny moved closer and peered closely at the prints. "Do you have an idea of how far the anomaly extends?"

"Sure. I lined it out on tracing paper." He unrolled a scroll of thin, see-through paper and arranged it over the blueprints. Denny could clearly see a pattern and was surprised the foreman had not.

"Hidden passages," he said. He pointed to what appeared to be a dead-end. "It looks like they travel throughout the interior walls. Right there — I bet you'll find a spring-latched pocket door that lets you inside."

Harris grinned. "I'd take the wager, but it would be entirely unethical since I have intimate knowledge of the house. That's solid wall right there, my nameless friend. But I don't doubt your theory of hidden passages. I'm wondering, though, why they aren't noted on the original prints."

"Then they wouldn't be secret."

"Good point. Perhaps they were added after the original construction, or in secret at the time the house was originally built." He let go of the tracing paper and it coiled into a loose scroll again. Harris swept it aside. "But that's not the weirdest thing about this house."

"Oh? Are you saying it's haunted?"

Harris sent him a narrow-eyed look. "Perhaps you should talk to the owner, Geoffrey Windsor, Mr. — ?"

Denny sighed inwardly; he had hoped to keep his federal identity under wraps for a while. He flipped out his credentials wallet and flashed his identification. "Dennis Wallace. I'm with a branch of the FBI."

"And your business here is – ?"

Denny slid a photograph of Caleb from behind his federal I.D. "We've been looking for this man for nearly five years now. Have been trying to bust him for even longer. Our last intelligence indicated he might be here in Heron Bay. He is fond of old mansions like this, so I thought I'd check."

Lon Harris studied the photograph carefully, and finally satisfied himself that not only had he not seen the man before, he had also not employed him. "Afraid I can't help you, Agent Wallace. Never seen him before."

"If you do, please call me at once. Don't let on that you know who he is—I don't think I need to stress the danger in which you would find yourself."

"Spoken like a true federal agent," replied Harris with an ironic smile. "In the meantime, I'm late for a lunch meeting, so I'll have to cut this short. But if you'd like to come back later, perhaps you can help me hunt for an entrance to the passages."

"I'd love it. Do you mind if I poke around and talk to some of your crew?"

Harris's smile widened, as did its irony. They both knew Denny Wallace could, within reason, do just about whatever he pleased. Asking for Harris's approval was nothing more than a goodwill gesture designed to elicit cooperation.

"Knock yourself out. My meeting is with the owner, so perhaps you can pin him down when he comes back."

"Perhaps," Denny said noncommittally. With a nod of farewell, he wandered off into the house, and Harris headed out the door.

If Caleb was indeed in this house, the only refuge he would have while the construction crew was present was the attic.

Denny's steps took him up the grand horseshoe staircase to the second level, and on up to the third. The frenzied activity of the main floor was noticeably absent. While he ran into workers here and there—mostly electricians—it was quiet and subdued and no one paid him any mind as he slipped into the attic. A flashlight surreptitiously requisitioned from a toolbox he passed on the second floor lit the way for him as he picked his way through stacks of boxes, wooden crates, and clusters of antique furniture. The air smelled of decades of dust and rodent feces and decay, and was almost a physical presence.

Deeper he went, marveling at the sheer enormity of the warehouse-sized attic. Farther and farther, and then an abrupt end. Something didn't seem right; he remembered the other end of the room and how the low ceiling dipped so far toward the floor he had to duck-walk. At this end he could stand upright. He studied the wall for a long moment, then ran his hands over it, searching for a hidden spring.

"I don't know what you're trying to find, but you could search forever up here and never come across it."

Denny spun around at the unexpected voice behind him, shocked that someone had gotten the drop on him. She leaned against a support pillar a few yards from him, her print dress flirting with her shins, its style bringing to mind the 1940s. She scuffed the toe of one white pump against the worn, bare boards of the floor and toyed with the thick blonde braid that lay over her shoulder.

"Who are you? What are you doing up here?" he asked sharply. He took a couple of steps toward her and she straightened although she didn't seem alarmed.

"I could ask the same of you," she replied. "I'm certain the work has not extended to this floor."

"I'm not with the work crew."

"Oh, without a doubt."

"And you are—?"

"Uninvited," she said, "but extraordinarily curious. So, like you, I snuck in."

Denny sent a pointed look at her shoes. "I didn't hear you

coming."

Her smile widened, and she leaned down to slip her shoes off her feet, then tiptoed a few silent steps toward him.

"I see," he said, still wary.

"So are you one of those abysmal ghost hunters from town?" she asked, slipping her shoes back on.

"No." Denny came another couple steps toward her. She held her ground, her gaze inquisitive but not frightened. "I still didn't get your name."

"I didn't offer it. But if it makes you feel more at ease, you can call me Emily."

"Is that your name?"

She grinned again. "I *did* say you could call me that."

"Yes, well," he replied dryly, "in my line of business I've learned not to swallow every line I'm handed." He glanced at his watch; Geoffrey Windsor should be finished with his lunch and on his way back to the Manor soon. Denny didn't want to be there when he arrived; he wanted to let Cody handle the owner of the Manor.

"Why don't we move this conversation to more pleasant surroundings?" he suggested.

"Care to buy a girl lunch?" Coquettishly, she batted her lashes at him.

"Not when I don't know her name."

"Emily," she reminded him, a trace of reproval in her voice.

His eyes narrowed on her face. "I meant her real name, but all right, *Emily*. Shall we?"

She led the way down the narrow staircase, chattering animatedly. When they reached the third floor landing, voices echoed down the empty hallway, coming toward them; more workers, making their way through the house. Emily let him pass her, taking refuge behind his broad shoulders as the crew came into view.

"What's the matter?" Denny asked.

One of the electricians looked up, glanced at his partner, and looked back at Denny with a perplexed frown.

"Nothin'. What's the matter with *you*?"

"I wasn't talking to you," Denny replied patiently.

The men exchanged another surprised look. "There's no one here but us."

"Em—" His voice trailed off as he turned and saw he walked alone. Emily had vanished. "Oh. I—uh—"

The first man nodded in understanding. "Don't sweat it, brother. You ain't the first one to see things in this house."

"But—she was right there!"

"Yeah," the second man agreed. "We know what you mean."

With one last perplexed glance up the attic stairs, Denny moved rapidly past them, expecting at any moment to hear their laughter behind him.

It never came.

(From the diary of Emily Matthews – classified TOP SECRET in the Schindler Project's Omega Team archives)

October 31, 1944

Something is happening at the Manor tonight. I have seen no less than six cars arrive, but they leave without waiting for their guests. I would have thought the Fotheringhams were hosting a party except the lady of the Manor has been conspicuously absent. It is my belief Kassandra is readying her secret room where she meets with Boldo and the others who participate in their activities. Jonathan says she is holding séances in her secret place; even he does not know where the room is. He tried to follow her, but she realized it and went into the library, pretending to read. Jonathan has confided his plans to take the children and leave the Manor; the plans go slowly because he is arranging custody of the children with his attorneys. He is quite frightened of Kassandra's mental state, and I believe he fears Bayview Manor just as much.

Bayview Manor...do I tell Jonathan that I am too frightened to leave my room in the dark? I have moved the children into my room. Joshua dreams poorly, and stands guard over his little sister's bed with a solemn determination he should not possess at the tender age of six. Sometimes I catch him staring intently at nothing, his expression one of warning, and I wonder...does Joshua see the vile beings I am sure roam the Manor — the beings his mother invited into the house with Boldo?

Ghosts, the town calls them. Demons, I say. Dark powers. Hell walks in this house, whispering temptation in our ears. I am frightened for my life, and terrified for my soul.

We are not alone.

WE ARE NOT ALONE
Thursday, April 2, 2009

Rachael was allowed back into the house after redrawing the kitchen design and receiving Harris's seal of approval. She dropped the new plans off to the architect, who blanched at first and then relaxed when he realized he wouldn't have to visit the mansion to make the changes to the blueprints. He was fantastic at his job, but he had relied solely on Rachael's and Lon Harris's measurements and diagrams because, as a lifelong resident of Heron Bay, he absolutely refused to be inside Bayview Manor. She had heard he wanted this job to be done so he never had to think about the Manor again and could cease to live in fear of being forced into an up-front and personal inspection of mansion's innards.

Silly.

When she returned to the Manor , she found Lon Harris poking at the parlor walls.

"What's going on?"

"Unaccounted square footage. Someone agreed with me that there are probably secret passages. Since Mr. Windsor postponed our meeting, I thought I would look for an entrance."

"Secret passages," Rachael repeated softly. "A lot of the larger houses from this era had secret hallways between rooms to keep the servants out of sight and their service unobtrusive. They moved through these passages with soiled linen and other laundry, trays of food and drink. I'm sure if you check the walls carefully in the rooms that would be most used, you'll find panels that slide open or swing inward to give access to the passageways."

Harris blinked at her in surprise, speechless, and she smiled. "This is my favorite era of architecture. I positively love the style of the Victorians...so gothic and brooding and elegant. I made a year-long study of it in college."

"No kidding," he marveled.

"No kidding. Although it's true this house really doesn't completely fit into either Gothic, Victorian, or Gothic Revival. It's strange." Turning her attention to the parlor, Rachael could almost see an overlap of the past imposing itself on the present: ghostly draperies, stunning Aubusson carpets, graceful Louis XIV settees and arm chairs, tapestries and graceful oil lamps placed strategically for maximum illumination. And where would one design a discreet access to a passageway in this room?

"Beside the fireplace," she announced aloud, startling Lon Harris. She paced to the fireplace, which had was graced with a mantle that had once been nothing less than a work of art, hand-carved roses and vines polished to a high shine. Now it was dull and bedraggled, the wood water-stained, gouged, and greying from exposure to years of dust and grime.

Rachael looked up at the ceiling, at least three and a half feet above her head. Hooks in the soffits on either side of the fireplace had once held tapestries that hung eighteen inches from the wall, leaving adequate space for a servant to move from passageway to the room unobserved.

She frowned toughtfully and moved to the left of the fireplace, scanning the wall, and then pressed and prodded the area, to no avail. She was vaguely aware of Lon Harris at her elbow, poking and prodding alongside her. Finally Lon hit upon the solution: a button in the center of a rosette on the side of the mantle near the wall. He pressed it, and they heard an audible click as a latch released. Now a half-inch crack in the wall appeared. Rachael inserted her fingers and pushed aside a cleverly hidden pocket door. She flashed a delighted grin at Harris, snatched his flashlight, and ducked into the passageway before he could stop her.

ᙘ

Geoffrey had been unable to think of much else over the last week except the ghostly voice in the cellar, calling his name, and the men who had quit after seeing bat-like creatures in the kitchen.

Determined to get the story from the horse's mouth, he finally ran his man to ground in the O'Shaughnessy's Irish Pub in Ocean

Shores, just where Greg Flanders' wife had told him to look. It was a popular hangout for contractors, and if one happened to be a man short and knew you were a working joe, your chances of gaining some extra cash were good. Being currently unemployed, Flanders had figured it was his best bet for finding work as far away from Bayview Manor as possible.

No one else in the place possessed a complexion the color of paste and spent more time peeling the mangled label from a barely touched bottle of beer, but Flanders was easily identifiable from his wife's description.

"He looks like someone plucked him off a San Diego beach, stripped him of his surfboard, and gave him a hammer in its place," Nanette Flanders had said. And then she had flatly refused to say anything more, briskly closing the door in his face.

Flanders' expression changed to one of sick dread when Geoffrey claimed a seat at his table and signalled for the server. A pro, she sized him up in a glance, determined that he might be worth a hefty tip, and immediately altered her course to cruise by his table before continuing on to her original destination.

"Whatcha havin'?" She rested a hand on one hip, her lively eyes darting between the two men.

"Coffee," Geoffrey said before Greg Flanders could reply. He laid a fifty-dollar bill on the table. "Keep it coming, and this will be yours."

She flicked a glance at the bill, the bottle clutched convulsively in Flanders' hand, and at Geoffrey's impassive but perfectly sincere expression, and nodded. "You got it." She nodded at the mutilated bottle of beer. "You gonna drink that, honey, or peel it 'til your fingernails fall off?"

Flanders jerked as though she'd poked him with a cattle prod, but he willingly relinquished the warm beer with no sign of regret.

"So your wife was right; you're not a drinker."

"You spoke to Nan?"

"Briefly," Geoffrey allowed coolly. "She would tell me nothing except where to find you and that you weren't a drinker, just looking for work."

"I'm *not* a drinker. Even now I can't manage to be a drinker."

He paused, then muttered, "It would be much easier if I could for once get blind stinking drunk."

"I'm not a drinker either. It clouds the issue."

"Ah yes, the issue. The issue being that I took a two thousand dollar draw, worked about five hundred bucks worth, and owe Harris fifteen hundred. I'll tell you now, Mr. Windsor, suing me would be worthless; Nan and I don't have anything. We rent the house we live in, my truck is so old it's held together by the paint, and I have no investments. I'll pay him back, but it may take some time. Like years."

Geoffrey reserved comment as the barmaid unceremoniously plunked down two sturdy mugs of coffee, cast a glance at the fifty-dollar bill, and gave him a cursory nod. "Be checkin' on ya in a minute."

"Make it at least ten," Geoffrey advised. For a long moment, he studied the non-drinking, surfer-turned-carpenter with no investments. Nanette Flanders had been right; her husband's hair was a trifle too long, and shaggy, streaks of blonde bleached to white winding through it. His skin was permanently tanned, and squint lines were just starting to form at the corners or his sky-blue eyes. He'd probably broken more than one young girl's heart in his heyday; Geoffrey judged him to be closing in on thirty-five, long past his young surfer days. Nothing seemed to signify that he had a screw loose or that he was a con man.

"I'll make you a deal, Flanders. You tell me what happened at my house to make you walk off the job, and I'll take care of Harris and the draw."

Dark eyes regarded him suspiciously; Flanders was by no means stupid. "Could I have that in writing?"

Geoffrey grinned. "Sure."

Flanders stared at him silently, then said, "Now?"

Geoffrey blinked, then grinned again, taking his pen from his shirt pocket and reaching for the paper drink coaster that had been under Flanders' beer. He turned it over and scribbled a note exonerating Greg Flanders from any debt incurred to him. The coaster vanished into Flanders own shirt pocket.

"What do you know about your house, Mr. Windsor?"

Geoffrey leaned back in his chair, regarding his coffee cup thoughtfully. "Built in 1850 by the Fotheringham family. In 1945 Jonathan Fotheringham murdered his wife, his sister, and the children's nanny before turning the knife on himself. The children were four and six years old at the time, and I believe went to live with a maternal relative somewhere back east – Boston was the popular rumor. They never returned to claim the house. The house sold in 1951, for the first time belonging to someone outside the Fotheringham family. It went up for sale again three months later. A couple from California bought it in 1956, opened it as a boarding house, closed it again less than a month later. I purchased it from their grandson, who inherited it when his parents were killed in a boating accident in 1979. The house had been up for sale since they closed the boarding house."

Greg Flanders made no comment for long a moment, then said very clearly and deliberately, "Yes, but what do you *know* about your house, Mr. Windsor?"

For a long moment Geoffrey was silent. "I know when people lay something down, it sometimes disappears and reappears elsewhere. I know sometimes I feel like I'm being watched. Sometimes I think … sometimes I think I see things from the corner of my eye or hear voices when no one's around. And the attic …"

Flanders gulped his coffee down as though it was bourbon and gasped as the hot liquid burned a trail from throat to stomach.

"Yes!" His heartfelt agreement came in a strangled squawk that turned heads their way. He lowered his voice, leaning across the table closer to his companion. "I keep losing things too, only they don't always turn up. I've heard things, too, like whispers. Once I heard my name said, really clearly, just like someone was behind me, but no one was there. And I've been seeing things."

"That's what brought me here. Lon Harris told me about what you saw in the kitchen." Not quite the truth, but no need to bring Rachael into this. Rachael, who didn't believe in ghosts. But what if it wasn't ghosts? What if it was worse than ghosts?

Greg Flanders' mouth twisted in bitter semblance of a smile. "At least you didn't word it the way he did."

"He didn't believe you?"

"He didn't appear to, no. I've seen more things than...that, but that was the deal-breaker."

Geoffrey rubbed a finger over his upper lip. Interesting. He thought Rachael had said—no, he was *sure* Rachael had said Lon Harris admitted to things relocating by themselves and the feeling of being watched. And he was the one who had defended the men, saying they weren't prone to will-o'-the-wisps.

"I believe you. Tell me exactly what you saw, Greg. I need to know."

Flanders stared at him so long and so hard that Geoffrey became uncomfortable. Then he nodded as though he'd seen what he'd been looking for in Geoffrey's eyes, and began to tell his story. At first his voice was halting, uncertain, but when no skepticism or derision showed in his listener's expression, his voice came stronger, surer, but still pitched at a whisper that only Geoffrey could hear.

It had been a stealthy, secretive footstep, sliding across the floorboards, that first indicated they were not alone.

"Rats," said Pete, nodding his head in a knowing way. Greg, who doubted that Pete Corvalis had ever seen a rat in his entire life, went back to gathering the flooring Pete had pried up. He lifted a huge stack of ruined jagged pieces and stepped out the kitchen door, tossing the stack off the porch and onto a huge pile of like debris in the yard. When he stepped back in, Pete was scowling.

"Did you take my crowbar?"

Greg scowled himself. "Why would I take your crowbar? You're peelin', I'm cleanin'. We had an agreement."

"I know that. But I laid my crowbar down, you picked up a pile of the flooring, and now my crowbar is gone."

"You had the crowbar in your hand when I took the junk outside."

Pete looked uncertain. "I did?"

Now Greg wasn't sure. "I don't know. I thought you did."

Both men started out the kitchen door at the same time. Greg lifted away pieces of discarded oak flooring as Pete poked around underneath for his crowbar. After a few minutes it became obvious that wherever the crowbar had gone, it had not ended up in the debris pile. It was also very obvious that if Pete wanted to delve any farther down in the pile, he was going to do so without the help of his good buddy Greg Flanders.

Pete swore and stomped irritably back into the house. Greg followed him, coming in just in time to hear a loud clank and thump from the pantry. He exchanged a look with Pete and they both swallowed. Neither of them wanted to investigate; too many weird things had happened since they started this job. Nevertheless, Pete started toward the small storage room, and not about to be outdone by his friend, Greg followed. Courage under fire. Yes, that was it. Courage under—

The thought ended abruptly. Pete had pushed open the pocket door of the storeroom and now sucked in a breath to scream. Greg moved by instinct, leaping across the four feet that separated them to clap his hand over Pete's mouth. If Pete's terror became public knowledge, the humiliation would be unbearable.

The hunched, scaly creature crouching in the pantry, grinning with sharp pointed teeth as it held Pete's crowbar from one taloned claw, halfheartedly flapped its leathery wings. It tapped the crowbar on the worn wooden planks of the floor and beckoned with its bony claw for them to come closer.

Greg felt his own scream welling up in his throat, pushing frantically and relentlessly at his closed lips as Lon Harris came into the room, muttering something unflattering about interior designers as he spread the blueprints out on the work table he'd made from a sheet of plywood laid across two battered sawhorses.

"You guys ain't getting the floor done by staring at the storeroom all day," he bellowed without looking at them. Pete clawed Greg's hand away from his mouth and drew in a gasping breath that made Harris turn to look at them. "What's wrong with you?"

"Asthma attack," Greg replied weakly. He reached out a hand that shook violently to tug the pocket door closed—a move he dreaded because it brought him within reach of the human-sized bat-creature—although he was strangely sure Lon Harris would be unable to see it.

"Asthma?" Harris bit out impatiently. "Pete doesn't have

asthma."

"Asthma," Greg insisted, staring defiantly at Harris as he gripped Pete by the arm.

Black spots danced before his eyes and he knew it was a toss-up at to what would happen first: him passing out or Pete completely caving in to hysteria. He managed to get his friend outside, and they both collapsed haphazardly on the dilapidated steps.

"Sweet Jesus!" Pete gasped, reflexively crossing himself. Born and raised a Catholic, he was completely unaware of doing so. "Did we really see that? Did we really see that...*thing*?"

"Yeah," Greg confirmed, breathless himself. He abruptly leaned over, putting his head between his knees as waves of darkness threatened to engulf him. Without warning, he felt his bile rise and barely made it off the porch steps to the weedy flowerbeds lining the length of the house. When he rose from the crispy brown lawn, it was to find Lon Harris in the doorway, watching the festivities with stunned disapproval.

"We didn't go back in the house again. We explained to Harris—at a distance, mind you—what we had seen. He searched the pantry, but of course saw nothing."

"I can see why he might have trouble believing you if he didn't find anything."

"He didn't give us any more flak about it. What clinched it, I think, is Pete telling Lon he'd pick up his tools in Hoquiam whenever Lon got around to gathering them up. In this trade, a man's tools are his livelihood." Flanders paused, then confided, "It's like a curtain opened between this world and the unseen one, and allowed us to see what walks among us. A demon, Mr. Windsor, that's what I saw. You can't convince me otherwise."

Geoffrey gaped at him. "A demon?"

"You act surprised. This *is* Bayview Manor."

"Did you know about this house before you came to work on it?"

Flanders shrugged. "I'd heard a thing or two about a house here, but I didn't realize it was this one until after Harris drafted us for the crew. I've worked with him before, see, so I was surprised he wasn't using his regular crew. But when I asked about it, he just smiled and brushed it off. Now that I think about it, that was kind of an odd smile. Tense, maybe."

The barmaid appeared at their elbow, and Greg paused as she topped off their coffee and moved away.

"Some old guy approached me about a week before we started work. We were reloading the rigs with only the things we'd need. The others were gone to lunch, but I'd come in late because Nan was sick and I had to get the kids breakfast. This guy told me all about the house and said I shouldn't go. I just kind of laughed it off." He paused, grasping his coffee mug and staring thoughtfully into its murky depths. "I'm not laughing now."

"No, I don't imagine there's anything funny about it," Geoffrey agreed. "You've seen other things? Lon said—"

"Lon sure opens his big mouth sometimes," Greg grumbled. "Yeah, I've seen other things, but that was the worst. Mostly I just catch something out of the corner of my eye, like a glimpse of someone leaving the room or something. Or I'll go into a room and there will be a tool or something there, and I blink and it's gone. That wasn't so bad—I just chalked it up to this being a big house and all, and getting my rooms confused."

"Easy to do."

"I started to get a clue that something was definitely not right in that house when I saw the girl in the attic."

Geoffrey went still, his back straightening slightly. "A girl? In the attic?"

"Well, a woman, I guess. But very young in her mannerisms, you know what I mean?"

"I do. Did you talk to her?"

Flanders shrugged. "I tried. I was upstairs on the third floor in one of the back rooms near the attic and saw her in the doorway. I told her she shouldn't be on the grounds, did she want to get hurt? I mean, it's a construction site, anything can happen." He shrugged, the movement odd, as though he was shifting an invisible burden.

"Then Pete came in and asked who was I talking to. I turned to point her out, and she was gone, but I'd heard no footsteps going up the stairs to the attic, and there was nowhere else for her to go. Pete said he hadn't seen anyone as he came up behind me, just me talking to myself. " He spun his mug between his hands, and they both watched as centrifugal force brought the dark liquid close to the lip of the cup.

Flanders stopped the mug's spirals and speared him with a burning, haunted look. "How could she have just vanished?"

"How indeed," Geoffrey murmured.

"She couldn't have. Not if she were human. So I came to the conclusion that she wasn't, that maybe Mi — that maybe the guy had been right about the house."

"'Mi —' as in Mike?" Geoffrey tried.

Flanders looked trapped. "I can't say anymore than I already have, Mr. Windsor."

"You've been puking-scared by my house, Greg. I think you can call me Geoff now."

"He won't talk to you anyway," Greg went on as though Geoffrey hadn't spoken. "He thinks you must have a screw loose to have bought the house. The fact that you're renovating with the intent of habitating has him convinced that you're totally wacko."

Geoffrey closed his eyes, feeling a headache beginning to throb at his temples. When he opened them again, he pushed his coffee away.

"My mother will want to live a good part of the year in that house. Unless I can find enough information about it to convince her otherwise, she will begin moving in the day the renovations are completed."

Flanders blanched. "But she *can't!*" he blurted with some urgency. "It's haunted!"

There, Geoffrey thought, *the word's finally been said. Haunted. The two million dollar house I just bought is haunted.*

I don't believe in ghosts, Rachael's voice reminded him. *I don't believe houses are haunted.*

And could he sit across from her at dinner tonight and tell her that he did, and be able to bear seeing her opinion of him visibly slip a notch? And why, now that he thought it over, did he care so much what Rachael Payne thought of him anyway?

Best not touch on that one, pal, he cautioned himself. *That one's trouble. And how do you spell trouble, Geoff old boy? Easy: S-O-N-I-A.*

"Mr — er — Geoff?"

Geoffrey gave himself a shake. "Who is Mike, Greg? I can get his name from you, or I can go through Lon Harris and find him myself. Either way, I *will* speak with him, I can guarantee that."

An expression of total dismay claimed Greg Flanders' face. "I wish you wouldn't —"

"I wish you wouldn't make me."

Greg sighed. "Fine. It's Michael, not Mike. Michael St. Claire. He's originally from Louisiana. New Orleans, I think. His mother was some sort of voodoo queen or something, and he's very superstitious. That could account for some of the things he told me. But I've seen things myself, Geoff, so it isn't just the influence of someone who grew up with superstitions."

"Thank you." With a quick glance at his watch, Geoff pushed his chair back. "Now I really have to go."

Panic edged Greg Flanders' voice. "You're going to see St. Claire *now*?"

"No. I have a meeting with Rachael."

Flanders' expression was troubled, and when he said "I really like Rachael a lot, Geoff," Geoffrey sensed a what-are-your-intentions talk coming. But Greg veered so far from that topic that it took him a moment to understand what he actually did say.

"I believe to the bottom of my soul that you should keep her out of that house at all costs."

"Because of the demons," Geoff said.

"Yes."

"But she's a Christian. Isn't she...protected from all of that?"

"No one's immune, even Christians," Flanders replied, staring into his coffee cup. He swirled the contents and then set it aside. "Have you noticed how everyone hates that house, can't stand to be in it unless they have to be — except Rachael?"

"Do you think her faith protects her from what's in the Manor?"

"I think it blinds her to it."

The words hung heavy between them, and neither moved for a long moment. Then Greg Flanders scooped up his discarded coffee mug, drained its contents, and muttered to himself, "God, I wish I could get drunk."

Date: March 30, 2009
To: Cody Schaefer [encrypted]
From: Todd Garrett [tgarrett@garrettresearch.com]
Subject: Wyckham House

I arrived in Koblenz, Germany two days ago, and while touring Schloss Stolzenfels, I overheard a conversation between two others in the touring party about another castle near the Rhein not on the tourist scene. It is spoken of in hushed tones and is regarded as a malevolent place. They call it *Teufelhaus*, which means "devil house", or sometimes *Haus des Teufels,* or "house of the devils."

You know me — I couldn't resist tracking down this castle. It is not easy to get to; there is no clear path, no clear directions. But I persevered, much as I did in Mills. And I found it. It is identical to the Wyckham House. I took a picture with my camera, but my battery is dead and I misplaced my charger. I will send it to you as soon as I can.

I dislike dredging up the past. Of the people I have known who have had anything to do with that house, the cost has been exorbitant — you and Renée, Aaron, Kimberly, Tiana, Scott, and myself have paid a heavy price for our brush with hell. But I'm compelled to search, to look over my shoulder, and when I spill the salt shaker, I throw the spilled salt over my left shoulder these days. One can't be too careful, eh?

Todd

THE WEIGHT OF THE WORLD
Thursday, April 2, 2009

"Thank you for your return call, Riley. Next Tuesday will be just fine. Please just send me an e-mail with the details."

Cody relayed his e-mail address to Geoffrey Windsor's personal assistant, thanked him again, and disconnected the call so that he could make another. It went to voicemail, as he knew it would; Renée had already told him she planned to go to a church potluck.

"Honey, I'm not going to be home on Tuesday like I expected. I can't meet with Windsor until then. I'll try to get on standby to come home Wednesday. I love you."

He never hung up without saying those last three words, because he never knew which time would be the last. He'd had a close encounter with death in Illinois fifteen years ago that had driven deep a few home truths.

He'd never been an inattentive husband or father, but he'd given his job equal status to his family. When he had come out of surgery to find his white-faced wife standing beside his bed, he knew something had to change. His oldest son remained institutionalized in a catatonic state—a tremendous worry for Renée—and now Cody himself lay near death, leaving this extraordinary woman to shoulder the weight of the world into which he'd enticed her.

He'd vowed then to alleviate as much stress as he could. Granted, it was a small amount, but she recognized the effort and knew he'd done the absolute most he could short of quitting the agency.

His immediate tasks completed, Cody set up his laptop on the small table by the window to begin an exhaustive search on Bayview Manor. While the search engine located matches to his specified criteria, he opened a second tab in the browser window and began another search, this one for a house in Koblenz, Germany, that his daughter-in-law's father had told him about.

While the search engines crunched relevant information, he opened his favorite news website. This was his daily ritual: begin research for the current project at hand, read e-mail, read the news, analyze the search engine results. Cody was nothing if not methodical and thorough, which was what made him so good at his work.

A headline caught his eye: *Search called off for missing heir to Talbot Software fortune.* He clicked the link and skimmed the article, his mind sifting out the most pertinent details. Harold Talbot and his wife Mia had bought an estate called Blessing House near Stamford, Connecticut just last October, and had only occupied it just over a week when they vanished. There was no sign of foul play; the police were mystified.

He opened a third tab, starting a search on Blessing House in Connecticut. He waited for the results of this search, clicking on the most relevant result. The picture that loaded on his screen made his stomach turn a slow somersault. He knew exactly what the Talbots had come up against. The soaring towers and grey stone façade might be hidden under pristine driftwood-grey siding and charcoal shingled roofs, but the design and mass of the house were unmistakable.

An e-mail notification popped onto the screen: his boss, e-mailing the very article he had just read and asking if Cody wanted to investigate. He rubbed a finger over his upper lip, weighing the need of the Talbots in Connecticut against the situation in Heron Bay. He doubted anything would be happening here in the immediate future; yet the Talbots were already missing, undoubtedly dead if his experience with the devil's mansion was anything to go by.

A tap of his finger on his phone screen brought up the photograph of the drawing Denny Wallace had sent him. He stared down at a penciled lines Denny had not been exaggerating; the drawing really was an exact likeness of Caleb. It was impossible, but he couldn't refute the evidence staring him in the face.

If Caleb was here, he had to stay. He owed it to Scott, and to Kimberly, to bring his brother to justice. The look of dread and fear in Kimberly's eyes when she had confessed her fear that Caleb was at Bayview Manor made it clear he couldn't abandon this mission and go to Connecticut.

He sent a message back to his supervisor, saying the need in Heron Bay was greater and that he would make a trip to Connecticut when he was done, unless Ben Cummings — his former second-in-command — could be coaxed out of retirement to handle it.

Cody turned his attention to the search he'd done on Bayview Manor. The engine had returned numerous pages of results, mostly to do with the 1945 murders. He chose one that gave the most information, and after reading it four times, sat back in his chair, the temple tip of his gold-rimmed glasses clenched between his teeth, his finger rubbing his upper lip again.

Had the case made as little sense to the investigating officers sixty-three years ago as it did to him now? The facts themselves were bizarre, and to order them in his mind, he wrote out a list:

*Eleven guests at the Manor that night, none ever seen again

*Boldo Pattin, the gypsy seer who had been Kassandra Fotheringham's constant companion, also missing

*Kassandra's mysterious companion Alexander vanished without a trace — and no one reported him missing

*Kassandra's body found in the gallery, bled out

*Jonathan's sister Charlotte found dead in her bed, a silver dagger through her heart

*Emily Matthews, the children's nanny, killed in the kitchen, throat slashed so deeply she had nearly been decapitated

*Jonathan Fotheringham dead beside her, both arms slashed from forearm to wrist (classic suicide method)

*Fotheringham children found cowering in pantry where Emily had hidden them — and apparently defended them

*Rumors of extramarital affair between Jonathan and Emily Matthews

*Jonathan was making arrangements with his attorneys to divorce Kassandra and take the children

Cody jotted a reminder to himself to check who had served as Jonathan Fotheringham's legal counsel. Perhaps the records could be located. He made notes for the next half an hour and then did what he called a murder sketch—outlining the murder from the viewpoint of the alleged perpetrator based on the surmised motive.

And it made no sense. A man makes arrangements with his attorneys to divorce his wife and take the children, supposedly instigated by his wife's descent into insanity and his affair with the children's nanny...and he murders the wife, the nanny, *and* his sister, who had come to help him with the children? And then he commits suicide not five feet from where his children hid?

He didn't do it. Cody could come to no other conclusion. How many years had Jonathan Fotheringham unfairly carried the label *murderer*?

There was no answer - and none would be forthcoming any time soon - so he stowed his notepad in his briefcase, which he locked in the trunk of his car, and headed south to find answers to other questions.

It didn't take him long to track down the realtor who had seen the spirit in Bayview Manor twenty-nine years ago. While the fellow had been understandably alarmed to see what he kept calling "a physical manifestation of a ghostly presence" in a structure that had been uninhabited for decades, it apparently had not frightened him enough to move from the area. He resided in a town with the unlikely name of Humptulips and still represented properties from Pacific Beach to as far north as La Push.

"And so there I was in the gallery—and a spookier room I've never been in, I must say—when this gentleman comes up behind me and taps me on the shoulder. I about had a heart attack."

"I can well imagine."

Herb Lester of Lester Property Management lifted his hat, swept his hand over his mostly bald head, and replaced the cap, trapping the few wispy strands of hair that had been blowing into his eyes.

Cody had arrived at Lester's home just as the elderly gentleman had been about to indulge in a walk on the beach. "A walk" appeared to be a relative term, for Herb Lester had made for a pile of driftwood, settled himself on a low log, and began to tamp the handsomely carved bowl of a briar pipe. He motioned for Cody to sit beside him.

"I'm not a superstitious fellow, mind you." Lester waved the stem of his pipe at Cody in caution. "Never had a moment's qualm about going into Bayview Manor despite the stories. And I'd been in it no less than a dozen times before that day and never had even a tiny case of the creeps."

"What was different about that day?" Cody zipped his jacket higher and eyed the tide-line with trepidation. It had been a winter of storms on the Washington coastline, and much of this stretch of the Peninsula had been without power for weeks in late November and early December. The wind now swept along the beach and whipped the waves into frothy whitecaps that crashed onto the sand with furious power.

Lester had managed to get his pipe lit, although Cody had no idea how he managed to keep the gusts from stealing the flame. "I went in the gallery that day." A cloud of aromatic pipe smoke hit Cody full in the face, and Lester waved it away apologetically. "Sorry about that. I shoulda sat downwind from you."

"I don't mind. What's wrong with the gallery, Mr. Lester?"

"What's *right* with it is a better question, Agent Schaefer. Rumor says Kassandra Fotheringham and her lover, Alexander, met in the gallery frequently."

"And Alexander is dead as well?"

Herb Lester sucked on his pipe, mulling over the question. "I can't rightly say. It's always been a great mystery, mind you. The official story is that Jonathan killed his sister, then Kassandra, Emily, and himself. Another version says he found Emily Matthews dead in the kitchen and believed Kassandra had murdered her. He then supposedly hunted his wife through the house and cornered her in the gallery where he managed to kill her after a violent struggle, and then killed himself in the kitchen beside his dead lover—if you believe that he was involved with Emily Matthews – though when exactly he killed his sister is unexplained. Yet another version has all three murdered by the gypsy seer Boldo Pattin. The truth lays somewhere amongst the rumors."

"I guess we'll never know. Is it true Jonathan Fotheringham was taking the children from Kassandra? Do you believe he was involved with Emily?"

"Oh, he was taking the children from his wife, all right. The Fotheringham attorneys had it all set up. But I don't believe he ever laid a hand on Emily Matthews, although I do think she might have been an ally in removing the children from Bayview Manor."

"Which version of the murders do you believe?"

"I've always thought it was Boldo Pattin. My father said that man walked hand-in-hand with Lucifer. And then there was Alexander, who was always in attendance at Kassandra's séances, although no one seems to remember what his surname was. He's never been found. In fact, no one can really say where he came from to begin with. He didn't seem to be a local; he just seemed to appear at the Manor one day."

"Alexander." Cody clenched his jaw. "Back to the man you saw in the Manor —"

"The spirit, you mean," Herb Lester corrected. He tucked the stem of his pipe into the corner of his mouth, speaking around it. "Handsome fellow. Very polite. But I got the feeling I shouldn't cross him, you see. He had a way about him that said he had been a dangerous man." The realtor slanted a look at Cody from the corner of his eye. "You remind me of him, in fact."

"Oh? How so?"

"You have the same demeanor. You look like him, too."

"Swell," Cody muttered. "What exactly did he say to you?"

"He told me I was trespassing and asked me to leave." Lester chuckled a little. "So I told him who I was and why I was there, and that as the realtor representing the property I had unlimited access to the house. He just laughed and told me I should leave immediately and not return. He said that nothing good would ever come of the Manor."

Cody digested this silently, huddled against the chilly March winds, his collar turned up to shield his ears. "And *has* anything good come of it?"

"Before February, I'd have said no. Geoffrey Windsor isn't the only wealthy man who's looked at the estate over the decades. The last sale was in 1946. Agent Schaefer, you can't tell me *no one's* wanted Bayview Manor in sixty-two years without there being a reason for it."

"You think it's haunted."

"Haunted, possessed, whatever." Lester waved away any difference between the two. "There's *something* there; I've come face-to-face with it, but at least it put on a pleasant face for me. I've not gone back. I refused to renew my contract to represent the property and thankfully it passed to other hands."

"And I'm sure you passed on the history and your experience with the house to the new real estate agent."

"My experience is recorded in a book. If the new realtor does not bother to investigate his clients' properties, that's no affair of mine."

Which Cody correctly read to mean Herb Lester did not want to give the new realtor any reason to think he was not firing on all cylinders. Not precisely ethical, but not exactly stupid either.

"But you did tell *someone*, didn't you? Windsor's interior designer told me that the gallery wing has been sealed off and won't be renovated for some time yet. She said the general contractor's foreman papered over the panes in the French doors and locked them."

"Well, Lon Harris and I go way back. I just passed on a little information for the sake of professional courtesy, that's all." Lester sucked on his pipe, his gaze holding Cody's steadily — or as steadily as the gusting wind would allow.

"How altruistic of you," Cody murmured.

"Let me level with you, Agent Schaefer." The realtor scooted around on the log to face Cody and took the pipe from his mouth. "There is something in that house. Whether it manifests itself as a handsome man or as a man-sized, bat-like creature — yes, rumors make it all the way down here to Pacific Beach — doesn't make any difference. Deciding whether it's haunted or possessed, whether it's demons or ghosts — none of it matters. The house should be razed to the ground, the debris burned, and the ground salted over. The property should be blessed, and the town should include it in its prayers.

"But that isn't going to happen, and I'll tell you why. Drive slowly through Heron Bay and take a look at the businesses. Tot up how many psychic parlors there are, and then compare it to the number of churches. The playing field isn't level; it's tipped in favor of the devil. You could not pay me enough to go into Bayview Manor or the town of Heron Bay itself. Open your eyes; can't you see the darkness? Can't you see the oppression?"

Cody cast a glance at the darkening sky and lifted a brow. Herb Lester cracked a self-deprecating smile.

"Yeah, and here I was waxing eloquent. But I'm serious. Take a drive; you'll see. And now, Agent Schaefer, I'm chilled to the bone and would like nothing more than to be home in my den with a cozy fire, a good book, and a glass of brandy to chase away the ghosts."

He stood and tapped the pipe bowl against the driftwood log, knocking the tobacco into the sand. He crushed it under his heel until he was satisfied all embers were out, then held out his hand. Taken aback by the obvious dismissal, Cody shook automatically.

"Stay a while, Agent Schaefer. Think things over. The sea has a way of making complicated situations seem much clearer."

Herb Lester was long gone and the wind had deposited hundreds of salty diamonds in his hair before Cody moved from his perch. The next day his cheeks and lips would be chapped and his sinuses achingly, bitterly cleansed—but the time on the beach, braving the elements, had been well spent. He felt calmer, more connected, more focused.

He was ready to go to Bayview Manor—and ready to level the playing field.

(From Rachael Payne's DayPlanner)

Week of March 30 – April 3, 2009

March 31
9:30 AM Delivery: Boiler – Thurman Heating & AC
11:00 AM Kingston Ferry - pick up wallpaper samples in Edmonds

April 2
7:00 PM   Dinner w/Geoffrey @ Catch of the Day Diner – go over wallpaper samples (pages flagged)

April 3
8:30 AM   Stained glass artist for ballroom windows @ Bayview

NOTES:
*Boiler was not delivered until April 3 due to staffing issue @ Thurman – shift work in rooms scheduled for radiator replacement to April 13 – 17

*Reschedule flooring appt for ballroom to early May due to delays in demo (attrition of demo crew)
*Ask Harris if he borrowed my attic key; can't find it anywhere. Also, has he or anyone else found an unclaimed cell phone? Mine is missing.

*Is someone staying overnight in Manor? Saw lights in forbidden wing, main floor, last night. Remember to ask Geoffrey at dinner Thursday evening.

I KNOW YOU'RE HERE
Thursday, April 2, 2009

"I wouldn't do that if I were you," said an unfamiliar voice behind them. Lon Harris jumped as though goosed, and Rachael popped her head back out the passage door in surprise. "You never know where such things might lead. There could be structural defects you don't know about."

The stranger leaned casually against the parlor doorjamb, surveying them with dark blue eyes that were at once friendly and secretive. The wind had swept his raven hair across his forehead, making him look younger than the silver streaks in his hair said he was.

"And who the hell are you?" Lon Harris demanded, moving to stand between Rachael and the stranger.

"Cody Schaefer." The man reached into the breast pocket of his leather jacket and flashed a government ID at them. "I actually was on my way to speak with Geoffrey Windsor when his personal assistant called and told me he is unavailable today. I thought I would stop in anyway and see the house."

"The government is interested in Bayview Manor?" Rachael asked in surprise. She stepped out from behind Lon Harris to stand beside him. "Is something wrong?"

"Not really. We're looking for someone, and this person has a fondness for old mansions. We thought perhaps he'd been seen here."

"No one's lived here in more than sixty years," Harris said. "I sincerely doubt he'd have come here. The house is not in great shape, and up 'til now didn't even have electricity."

"Nevertheless," Schaefer said inexorably. "Our intelligence places him here at some point in time. We'd just like to check it out."

Harris took a step forward, giving the illusion he was in front of Rachael again. She sighed in exasperation. "Is this man dangerous?"

"Extremely." Schaefer slid a photograph from behind his ID, arched a brow at Harris, and at the foreman's nod closed the distance between them. Rachael took the picture from his outstretched hand, studied it for a moment, then scrutinized him carefully. The family resemblance did not escape her notice.

"He's a relation of yours," she said, with a slightly interrogative lilt.

"My brother."

Harris peered at the photograph and shook his head. "You're the second person to ask about him. He's not here. I've seen every man-jack, and he isn't one of them. I'm assuming we should call you if we do see him."

He clearly meant it as a dismissal, but Cody Schaefer didn't seem ruffled by it. Neither did he seem to perceive Harris as any particular threat. Other than a slight tug at the corner of his mouth, suggesting a knowing smile, he gave no indication that Harris had done anything other than make a statement.

"His name is Caleb Schaefer. He is extraordinarily dangerous. It would be very unwise to approach him or try to apprehend him, so yes, you should call if you see him." He handed them both a business card. Harris put his into his jeans pocket — it probably would end up going through the washing machine tonight and would be summarily discarded once its remains had littered the dryer — but Rachael read hers and stowed it carefully in her back pocket.

"If one of you has a few moments, I'd like to see some more of the house." Cody's eyes bounced from one to the other of them, gauging the one most willing as compared to the one most knowledgeable. The decision was taken out of his hands by the appearance of one of the work crew.

"Harris, sorry to interrupt, but we got a problem with the supplies that were delivered today."

The foreman breathed in sharply through his nose. "All right. I'll be right there." He seemed reluctant to leave her with the federal agent.

"Harris, it's fine. I don't mind showing the house."

"If you don't mind, Agent Schaefer, I would feel much better about this if I could see that ID again, and perhaps your badge."

Schaefer's smile widened. "I see you're not the trusting sort. But that's not a bad thing." He handed his credentials wallet to the other man, who perused the enclosed identification and the gold federal badge with paranoid concentration. Finally satisfied with Cody Schaefer's *bona fides*, he handed back the wallet.

"I'm sorry for that, but if I'd let Miss Payne wander off with a stranger and something happened to her, Geoffrey Windsor would have my hide. Not to mention I would feel terrible."

"No offense taken. It's better to be safe than sorry. I promise she will be safe as a lamb."

"Says the wolf," Harris muttered.

Cody held up his hands with a gleaming smile. "Look, no claws. Miss Payne...?"

At Schaefer's offered arm, Rachael stepped around Harris, impulsively stopping to kiss his cheek. "You worry too much, but you're awfully sweet, Harris."

His face flamed scarlet. "Be safe, Rach."

"Of course I will," she assured him. Lon Harris hurried off to handle his supply problem with a slightly uneasy glance as she left with Cody Schaefer.

"Where did you want to start?" Rachael asked Cody.

"The floor we're on is fine," he assured her. She noticed his eyes went everywhere, not seeming to rest on anything for any particular amount of time, but taking in every detail of what he saw. He had definitely honed his skills to a sharp-edged talent.

"All right." She paused in the large foyer, standing precisely between the feet of each section of the horseshoe staircase. She pointed to a double set of French doors at the left end of the foyer. "That wing isn't being worked on right now. I hear there's a gallery and a fantastic library, but I've little chance of ever seeing them."

"Oh?"

"Geoffrey intends to work on the main section and the south wing first. He said he won't have anything done with the north wing for a number of years. The doors are kept locked, and Harris covered the inside of the French doors with brown paper so no one can see in, so we won't be tempted to go in. He said there's a lot of debris and structural damage there."

She led the way up the left staircase, Cody Schaefer tagging at her heels. Rather quiet, he didn't ask many questions or offer many comments; instead he seemed to absorb all she told him, feeding it into some internal computer and coming up with God knew what conclusions. When they reached the third floor attic door, Rachael paused, frowning at it as she remembered Geoffrey's odd reaction to the storage room. Cody, more alert than ever, seemed to finally find his tongue. Some of his questions were odd and a little probing, and finally Rachael stopped him.

"If you're hinting that the house is haunted, Agent Schaefer, I'm afraid you've been misled. There are no ghosts here."

"What *is* here then?" he countered, his blue-eyed stare never wavering.

Rachael sighed and lowered herself to sit on the steps. "I don't know, to tell you the truth. Between Harris's crew quitting over imaginary visions, Geoffrey's screaming meemies, and now your interest in the house, I'm beginning to wonder if we shouldn't just torch it and have done with it."

"Well, if you think it will help…" he remarked noncommittally.

She couldn't think of a reply for a surprised moment. Was a federal agent really agreeing she should commit arson? "I don't believe it will. Why don't you try telling me why you're really here?"

"I really am here to find my brother."

"Mmm," she said. "But I'm not naïve enough to think you came here to arrest him, Agent Schaefer, because I know it would be considered a conflict of interest. Perhaps you do want to find him and thought the house might have attracted him, but that isn't the real reason."

"You're very perceptive," Cody replied approvingly. "Let me level with you, Miss Payne."

"Rachael," she insisted.

"Rachael, then. Please just call me Cody."

"You have a deal."

"I *am* looking for my brother, but you're wrong. I *can* arrest him, given the purview of my agency. I've led the investigation against him for more than a decade. But I'm mostly here because this house is identical in design to one in my home state."

"Which is?"

"Pennsylvania." Cody lowered himself onto the step beside her, keeping an appropriate distance between them. "Nearly five years ago we disbanded a black magic cult responsible for numerous deaths and disappearances. My son Scott was one of their victims; my brother shot him. Caleb served as this cult's high priest. They practiced their craft in a ruined stone mansion deep in the woods, identical in design to this one. My older son's wife saw a picture of Bayview Manor on the internet and recognized it, even though Bayview has siding and the Wyckham House did not."

"I think I saw something about that on the news," Rachael murmured, thinking back in time. She had been finishing up her degree around then and hadn't paid much attention to what had been going on in the world, so she couldn't recall the details. She had mostly noticed the house and its Gothic elements – flying buttresses, lancet windows, ribbed vaults, and crenellated turrets – from the old, grainy photograph the news clip had shown.

"No doubt," Cody replied. "It made the national news wires. It was a huge bust. It is estimated that Caleb and his cult are responsible for several dozen murders and/or disappearances."

He fell silent for a moment, staring at his hands held clasped between his knees. "Do you believe that some people are just wired to be evil?"

Rachael considered. "Yes. I believe your profession calls them sociopaths."

"Indeed we do," he agreed with a quick, sideways glance at her. "And what does Rachael Payne call them?"

"Possessed," she said simply. She turned slightly toward him. "Look, Cody, I don't believe in ghosts or hauntings, but I *do* believe in demons. I believe they attach themselves to people...and sometimes places."

Cody stared at her for a full minute.

"I'm sorry if I sound like a crackpot to you. I'm a firm believer in angels and demons, heaven and hell, God and Satan."

"You're preaching to the choir, Rachael. I've been a tried-and-true believer since junior high school."

"And yet you wonder if people are wired to be evil?" she queried, raising a brow. "I think it's more like some people are more susceptible to evil, to the whisperings of demons. It could be your brother is one of them. Has he always acted like this?"

"As long as I can remember. Caleb is only five years older than me, but I still grew up alone. I don't remember him any other way."

Rachael nodded. "I see. And why do you think he has been here at the Manor?"

Cody took his cell phone out of his jacket pocket, opened it and began scrolling through his menus. Finally he held it out to her. The display screen held a penciled portrait of a handsome man bearing a strong resemblance to the one beside her. She sent him a quizzical look.

"I don't understand."

Cody Schaefer smiled wryly. "I don't either. That picture is in a book written more than twenty years ago. This is a drawing, much like a police sketch, of a spirit a realtor supposedly saw almost thirty years ago."

"But that's impossible," Rachael said. "It looks exactly like the photograph of your brother."

"Now you see why I'm so interested in the Manor."

"Is that what prompted you to come to Heron Bay?"

Cody shook his head. "No. The house is what brought me here. My daughter-in-law saw it in an online article about Geoffrey Windsor, and then she had a dream that Caleb was in this house."

"A prophetic dream?"

"Yes. She's known for them. In fact, it's how she met my son. She dreamed of him while living in California."

Rachael gaped. "That's incredible."

"What's more incredible is when she dreamed of Bayview Manor and Caleb, she woke up screaming your name."

If nothing else had rendered her speechless, this certainly did. Rachael had never expected anyone to have prophetic dreams about her. And another thing she would never have expected was a federal agent as cautious as Cody Schaefer confiding so unreservedly in a total stranger.

And so she asked, "Why are you telling me all this? I'm virtually a stranger. Aren't you afraid of compromising your investigation?"

"I'm not afraid. I trust you."

"You knew who I was before you even came here, didn't you?"

Without answering, Cody pushed to his feet and held a hand down to assist her. His grip was warm and firm but not overly personal. "I would like to see the attic. My colleague was here earlier, asking some questions and poking around the house. He had an...experience there."

"Let me guess. He saw a ghost." Rachael smirked.

"Or a demon," Cody replied, unperturbed.

Her smirk faded. "We need a flashlight."

Cody produced one from his pocket. He had come prepared, and she understood—belatedly—that when he had said he wanted to see the house, he had really meant he wanted to see the attic.

"Well, I guess we're set." She started up the stairs.

The door to the storage area stood ajar. She eyed it with troubled curiosity. She doubted anyone had been up here—no one seemed to share her desire to unearth the treasures stored for decades within—and yet the screws that Geoffrey had pushed back into place were nowhere to be found.

Cody Schaefer seemed as impervious to the stifling, stuffy attic-odors as he did to the shadows and eerie creaking of the rafters. He strolled through the haphazardly stored furniture of the last residents of the Manor as though perusing through an antique shop. The messy storage soon gave way to neatly organized rows of trunks, crates, and furniture. Rachael followed close behind him, loathe to wander too far from the light, her eyes shining in wonderment at the treasures the attic held, her enthusiasm unabated despite Geoffrey's experience and the rest of the crew's aversion.

They chased the beam of light through the debris of decades. Rachael longed the stop and fling open trunks of all sorts: steamers and camel backs, Jenny Lind keyholes and oak-slatted Excelsiors. But Cody didn't pause, and she faithfully followed the light. The trunks would have to wait.

Their forward progress was impeded by solid wall. Cody didn't seem disappointed. He shone the light carefully over the wall, but Rachael couldn't have said why. Finally he stepped back several feet so he could take in the wall as a whole, crossed his arms over his chest, and frowned pensively. The brooding expression on his face troubled Rachael.

"What is it you're looking for, exactly?"

He didn't seem to hear her. He paced from one side to the other, all the while surveying the blank wall before them. The joint where the wall met the ceiling seemed to be of great interest to him. When she thought he had forgotten her, he whirled around and joined her.

"See where the wall meets the ceiling? It's much higher at this end than at the other."

"I wonder why."

"Hidden room. I just can't find the way in. I need better light to examine it."

"Any idea what's in there?"

Cody shrugged. "Knowing the nature of the house, it's probably nothing good. I think we're done for the day."

He took her by the elbow and guided them back toward the door. Rachael sent a sorrowful look at the trunks they passed. She didn't ask Cody to stop, but he did so on his own, eyeing the layer of dust coating the flat surface of a leather steamer trunk. He moved decisively toward it, his finger etching letters into years of grime.

At last he stepped back, shining the flashlight on his handiwork. Rachael peered around him to see. In the dust he had carved the words CALEB, I KNOW YOU'RE HERE. CODY.

"You think your brother is living in the attic?"

"I don't know what I think, Rachael. Come on, let's get out of here. This place gives me the creeps." Cody took her by the elbow again and led her through the history of the previous owners. Once they had gained the third floor hallway, he stopped to close the door to the attic steps.

"I think that should remain closed. In fact, I think it should remain locked. And I *really* think you should not be alone in this house."

She rolled her eyes. "Geoffrey says the same thing."

"Then Geoffrey Windsor is a wise man. Now if you'll guide me out of this maze of rooms, I'll leave you to your work. Speaking of... I wouldn't explore those passageways alone, either."

"Yes, sir." Rachael smartly saluted him, surprised by the boyish grin that curved his mouth and made him look about thirty. The grin faded quickly.

"Seriously, Rachael. Caleb has a penchant for young, beautiful women."

"I'm not susceptible to men who are that much older than me."

"It won't matter if you're susceptible. He will take you willing or take you by force, and it never ends well. Please be careful."

Rachael returned his look solemnly. "I promise."

"Then I feel much more comfortable leaving." He started walking again, and when they reached the front entry, he stopped and shook her hand.

"It's been a pleasure meeting you, Rachael."

"Likewise, Cody."

"I'm sure we'll meet again. Good day."

She watched him make his way to his rental sedan, as unaffected by the rain as he seemed to be by everything else. Closing the door as she turned, she cast a speculative glance up the stairs. She didn't think twice; she hunted down Harris, borrowed a flashlight, and made her way back to the attic.

The storage room door creaked as she pushed it open. As she made her way through to the steamer trunk, her heart pounded frantically and she tried not to think about how quickly she had broken her promise to Cody. But after all the talk about the house...she had to see if Cody's message had been answered, just to satisfy her skepticism. She knew she would find nothing but Cody's words etched into the dust.

And she wasn't disappointed. Only Cody's note waited for her: *CALEB, I KNOW YOU'RE HERE.* Rachael heaved a sigh of relief and, laughing at herself, made her way back to the door. She closed it behind her without a backward glance.

The man stepped from the shadows, his ice-blue eyes watching to make sure she didn't come back. He made his way unerringly to the steamer trunk and read the message. He stared down at the words for a long time, his lips compressed into a tight line, and at last moved to leave his reply.

April 2009

The book was hidden under the loose floorboards in the house where I'd lived with my husband and son. That was in a different life, when I'd lived in fear of the next blow from my husband's drunken hand, when I'd been the mother of a teenage son who'd wanted only to be nothing like his waste of an old man. The years since the property was taken from me have not been kind; no one knows who owns the house now. No one sees to its upkeep. Yellow plastic tape emblazoned with CRIME SCENE DO NOT CROSS in stark black letters still encircles the house. You'd think it would be tattered and shredded from the elements after five years, but I think someone comes to replace it, although I've never seen anyone. And I've been watching for a long, long time.

The cellar has an outside entrance, as well as one from the kitchen. No tape has sealed this; a padlock secures it, and I rather suspect they thought it was enough. But the hasp is loose, and the wood door is rotting; a few hard tugs allowed me entrance to my former home.

That was the easy part; I'd known Fred kept his grimoire somewhere in his den, but I hadn't found it while packing up the house after the foreclosure. He had hidden it well, after all; it would have been the height of foolishness to shelve it amongst the standard trade paperbacks I purchased from the local secondhand shop, where Cody Schaefer and his damnable government goons could find it.

And I wouldn't have found it at all had I not walked on the very edge of a loose floorboard just so, making it lift slightly above the others. Quick work with a utility knife and a screwdriver popped it completely out of place, and from there I was able to lift the next two, revealing the roomy storage compartment that held the three Books of Shadows in which Fred had recorded his instructions.

I've been approached over the last couple of years by several former members of the Circle who are dissatisfied with hiding behind a respectable front. Their questions boil down to the same one, worded differently but all meaning the same thing: don't I want vengeance? My husband and son are both dead by a series of events set into motion by the Schaefer family.

And although I refused to talk about it for the longest time — because secretly I didn't believe Ron and Kimberly Schaefer's marriage would last — Aaron's increasing avoidance and caution of me chafes my heart. He ceased to see me — *really* see me — from the first moment his eyes rested on *her*.

And slowly, perhaps unavoidably, my hopes that she would tire of small town life and head back to the bright lights of her city soured in my heart. Can I pinpoint exactly when unrequited love turned to bitter resentment and hatred? Not really. It was a slow metamorphosis, an evolution that ground away at my love so slowly that even I was surprised the day I looked at him and felt my stomach twist with rage and loathing.

I sat for long hours amongst the ruins of my life, and as I turned page after page, I let go my tenuous grasp on forgiveness and accountability, let go my sufferance and my respectability. For somewhere in these pages, I knew, lay the secret path around the ricochet. Somehow there was a way to ensnare Aaron Schaefer despite his utter devotion to his wife, and I was determined to find it.

And find it I did.

My heart no longer harbors unrequited love; its only child is revenge, born of bitterness and malice and birthed in the pages of my dead husband's unholy bible. To the victor belong the spoils, and God help Aaron Schaefer now.

TOO LATE FOR ME
Monday, March 30, 2009

The queasy feeling he usually had when riding a rollercoaster swelled uncontrollably as Melody Olmstead came through the door of the greenhouse. Aaron moved casually toward Taryn and grasped her elbow as she started to move away to straighten a display of seed packets.

"Stay close," he muttered.

She caught a glimpse of Melody from the corner of her eye. "Ah. No problem."

He watched as Melody wound her way through the aisles. His expression must have seemed formidable, for as she closed the last ten feet between them her confident stride faltered, and she cast a dismissive glance at Taryn, who appeared to have gone temporarily blind.

"May I have a word with you?" Melody asked Ron. She seemed to have gone blind as well, because she didn't appear to see the blooming anger on his face.

"After what you said to my wife, do you honestly think I have anything civil to say to you?"

She flicked another glance at Taryn, who was arranging garden gloves on a rack on the check-out counter—and who also was making no attempt to disguise the fact that she was listening to every word.

"You don't have to say anything," she said evenly. "Just listen."

"Another request that takes considerable gall to ask."

"Please, Aaron. Call off your watchdog; we need to have a tête-à-tête."

"I can't see any reason for us to speak at all. If you'll please remove yourself from my place of business, I can get back to the important things in my life."

"After we talk."

"Taryn, please call the—" He stopped abruptly, belatedly remembering that Mills' most recent constable had been gone since November.

Melody smirked. Aaron realized they had reached an impasse. Taryn sent him a helpless look; there was nothing she could do short of forcibly removing Melody, which would cause a scene in front of the customers. He refused to have any sort of discussion with her whatsoever, but he also refused to cause such a scene. While retreat went against every fiber of his being, there was no other choice left to him.

He sent Taryn his own eloquent look, spun on his heel, and made for his office at a casual speed that belied his desire to put as much distance as he could—and as quickly as possible—between himself and Fred's widow.

Taryn didn't come in for more than fifteen minutes, and when she did, worry creased her brow.

"Ron—"

"What did she say?" he interrupted.

"She said she noticed you weren't wearing your wedding ring." She swallowed hard. "I noticed as well—which means you never found it. What's going on?"

"It's best if you stay out of it, Taryn."

"Are you and Kim having trouble?"

"I said—"

"Yeah, I heard you. You want me to stay out of it. But both you and Kim are my friends, and I worry about you. Does this have something to do with last week when you went home late—when you lost your wedding ring?"

Ron heaved a sigh from the depths of his soul. Weariness pressed heavily upon him and he thought he couldn't stand another moment of it. But he had no choice. The situation was what it was: a nightmare from which he could not wake.

"I didn't lose it; it was stolen out of the cash drawer. I don't know how she managed it."

"Who? Melody?" He nodded. "Wasn't Anna running the till that day? I swear, I don't know where that girl's head is some days."

"College boys and parties," he answered in the tones of a disapproving uncle. Anna Malone was his honorary niece, and she had not been making good choices since her ordeal four and a half years ago. "Anna said she remembered Melody being in the greenhouse that day. She didn't remember her being near the till, though."

"No, but that Palmer kid you hired last month remembered her being in the cutting field. He said she was out there while we were." His head came up and he fixed her with a piercing stare that made her squirm. "What?"

"So it's possible she overheard what we were talking about?"

"Sure, I suppose so." Taryn shrugged. "Why?"

"Melody went to visit Kim that afternoon. She had my ring, and she told Kim I'd left it on her bedside table." Taryn's mouth fell open in shock. "The only reason Kimberly believed her is somehow Melody knew what happens when I kiss her. I've told no one about it but you—yet she knew."

Taryn's mouth still hung open most unattractively. When she realized it, she snapped it shut. After a moment she ventured, "So Kim thinks you're having an affair with Melody."

"Yes."

"Are you?" his friend asked candidly, watching him closely.

Ron felt angry color flood his cheeks. "Are you *serious*? After everything I've been through, why would I screw up the best thing that's ever happened to me? I've never laid a hand on Melody Olmstead—or any other woman, for that matter—and I never will. I can't believe you would even ask."

"You're married, Ron, you're not dead. I know you watch attractive women."

"So does every other red-blooded, heterosexual man with a pulse. An attractive woman is a fine thing to see, but it doesn't mean I have any desire to be unfaithful to my wife."

He scooted his chair around the desk and grasped her hands. "Taryn, don't you see what's happening? She drives a wedge between me and Kim, believing we'll divorce over it. She's been making moves on me since Kim became pregnant with the twins."

"Ah, I see," Taryn replied, still playing devil's advocate in spite of the risk of incurring his considerable wrath. "She just can't stay away from a hot number like Aaron Schaefer."

Ron glared at her. "I'm just telling you how it seems, all right? I could use a little help here."

"What can *I* do? I try to stay away from crazy people, Ron."

He grinned. "Yeah? Why are you here, then?"

"Ha ha, funny. You're a riot."

"*Please*, Taryn. Will you help me?"

"Again I ask…"

"What can you do?" he finished for her. "You can be with Kim, just until this blows over. I'll pay you the same as you would make here. I don't want to leave her to the mercy of a woman like Melody, and the busy season is just starting; I have to work long hours."

She frowned at him, sending him a censorious glare down the length of her nose. "I can work the long hours, Ron. You should be home with your wife."

Ron raked a hand through his hair, closing his eyes for a brief moment. "I doubt I'd be much help. It's better if I'm out of the way right now."

"It's better if you just go home and talk to Kim," she said sharply.

"I already tried that. Might as well have cut my own throat. Will you help me or not? I can send Anna instead."

Taryn blew out an impatient breath. "All right, I'll help. But you'd better straighten this out fast, Aaron. Your marriage is nothing to mess around with."

"I will. I promise. Thank you," he added fervently, and let go of her hands.

Taryn sighed heavily, obviously wondering when she'd ever learn her lesson and harden her heart against good-looking men with charm. Ron hoped never; he'd been at a loss as to how he'd be able to both guard Kimberly and run the greenhouse, but now he had a solution he felt comfortable with. It wasn't the ideal situation; he'd rather none of this had ever happened, and he blamed himself for not being more cognizant of Melody's mental state and more careful with her fragile emotions.

None of that meant he planned to treat her with kid gloves when he ruthlessly squashed her sabotage.

He went home early that afternoon, hoping that Melody had not paid Kimberly another visit. After the last one, however, he rather doubted Kim would open the door when she saw who stood on the other side.

It was no secret that his wife had never cared much for Fred Olmstead's widow, believing her reliance on and interest in Aaron went deeper than anyone suspected, but Ron had shrugged it off. Fred's life insurance—more than likely purchased by Caleb, or at least at his insistence—ensured Melody could take care of herself. Ron no longer felt the need to help out when her husband drank the rent money, and he had relinquished that charitable act with relief, secretly thinking the best thing Fred had ever done for his wife was die.

Kimberly had the twins down for a nap and was taking advantage of the free time to indulge in one herself. She lay curled like a comma on her side of their bed, covered with a thick velour blanket, one shoulder poking from beneath the blanket's edge. He smiled wistfully, feeling a desperate urge to lay down beside her, wake her with a gentle hand against her cheek as he so often had, and let his lips show her the truth without words.

But his anger and hurt at being unjustly tried and convicted still rankled. Why should he be the one to fix it? She believed he had cheated on her and had displayed no trust in him. That made her the faithless one.

And so he simply stared down at her for a long moment before moving to the window. From here he could see the trumpet vine, just beginning to show signs of bud swells. The burnt orange blooms had been huge, hanging over them as they vowed to honor and obey, for better or worse. Ron didn't think it got much worse than this.

He cast a look over his shoulder at Kim, thinking back to the warm July day they'd married. The amber rays of the waning sun had slanted across the room, setting glorious fire to her summer-wheat hair. He had found his slice of heaven on earth that day as Kimberly's gold wedding gown whispered to the floor and beams of sunlight bronzed her skin. The scar on her arm from Caleb's knife glowed silver in the light, a silent testament to their ordeal the year previous. Her badge of courage. He'd known in that frozen, golden moment that no other woman could match her valor, no other woman could love him as fearlessly, recklessly, and completely as Kimberly Owens.

The thought hurt too much to bear, and he whirled on his heel and exited the room as silently as he had entered, leaving his wife to her troubled slumber.

CR

He stepped from the shadows, following a weak beam of light through the cramped aisles of forgotten riches belonging to a family long dead. Stopping at a pair of leather steamer trunks stacked one upon the other, he shone the light onto the surface of the uppermost one. It reflected off the dusty leather, throwing his careworn face into sharp relief. Stress lines fanned out from his eyes and mouth. No emotion showed on his face as he read the message left for him in the dust of the decades.

Finally he raised his hand, a long, elegant finger cutting through the grime to leave his mark.

Her dream-self read his message with surprise. It seemed she could see emotions rising from the words where she could not see them in his impassive expression. Regret, despair, wretched longing. She inhaled sharply as each seemed to pierce her to her soul, and the clean woodsy scent of his aftershave filled her nostrils.

Her hand reached out of its own volition, offering comfort to the man who would have despoiled her body and stolen her life. Her reaching fingers passed through him as though he were made of no more than smoke. He jolted, his breath catching, his own hand reaching through her.

"Kimberly?" he whispered. His grasping fingers found the solidity of her soul, catching in its diaphanous strands, and she fled.

She didn't so much awaken as she frantically exploded from sleep. She had backed herself off the edge of the bed escaping from his clutching hand, and came to consciousness squatting by her bedside table, her blanket tangled around her legs.

Kim rose, trembling, fumbled to free herself from the blanket, and collapsed in the wingback chair on the other side of her night table.

"No," she said firmly, shaking her head. She cast a glance heavenward. "No way. I don't believe it for a minute."

Her terror of Caleb Schaefer had not been diminished by the years of his absence, and some fanciful dream in which he felt remorse for his horrific deeds could not erase the scars he'd left on her psyche. Kimberly didn't believe a man so steeped in the malevolence in which he'd joyfully wrapped himself could ever feel guilt or shame.

A long while later, the plaintive cry of one of her children called her out of her daze. With monumental effort, Kimberly swung closed the crypt in her mind that held Caleb Schaefer, and went in search of a bit of sanity.

Three thousand miles away in a house with no doors or windows, ensnared by the very power he'd once sought to harness, a raven-haired man with wintry blue eyes stared down at his hand in shock. Slowly he raised it to his nose; he could just catch the scent of fresh lilacs left in the hot sun—the scent of the woman who had haunted him for nearly five years.

He looked at the top of the steamer trunk. A film of fine dust lay in the letters his brother had scrawled, but every day he came and refreshed his own so they would not be lost to time: *TOO LATE FOR ME. GO HOME.*

Today he added one more word, sure that Cody would never see it but driven to write it nonetheless: *PLEASE.*

(Correspondence from Jonathan Fotheringham to his sister, Charlotte)

February 17, 1945

My dearest Charlotte,

I write to you with a heaviness of spirit, hat in hand to beg your assistance. I've no time to explain the sordid details of the situation, but ask only that you provide refuge for my children. I fear my wife has lost reality, and don't wish Rebecca and Joshua to witness the complete collapse of their mother's mental state.

I ask your help only for a short time, to show them kindness and perhaps ease them into Boston society. Of course, this favor is not asked without promise of recompense; the children's every expense shall be met by a trust fund I have already arranged, and you will be provided a modest stipend. I shall be joining the children once I have cleared away all the legal affairs.

If you are agreeable, please contact Sir Hubert Landry, Attorney, at 125 Summer Street, Boston MA.

Your loving brother,
Jonathan

WHAT IF IT'S WORSE?
Friday, April 10, 2009

He thought that she was a pixie — or was that piskie? — or some other fey creature. Her platinum hair shimmered in the fluorescents like sunlight on water, framing a heart-shaped face so stunning it stopped his breath and flushed him with sudden heat. Her skin was flawless porcelain, a blush of rose on her cheekbones. Graceful brows swept upward from the inner corners of her eyes and arched back down in a perfect curve. He couldn't see the color of those eyes; her lashes were swept down, shielding them, as she read the label on the jar of peanut butter she held.

"Ahem."

The discreet clearing of a throat from beside him made him start, and he came back to reality with a crash and a flash of irritation. The woman next to him raised her brows silently, but amusement showed plainly on her face. A passing man, clearly old enough to be the pixie's father, did a double-take and nearly ran into a support pillar. A younger man, trying to summon the courage to speak to the ethereal creature three feet from him, blindly reached for a jar on the shelf and knocked four onto the floor.

The young woman didn't appear to notice. She made her selection, popped it into the small shopping basket she carried on her arm, and turned without even a glance at her unfortunate would-be suitor. Now he could see her eyes — clear blue like the sky in August, fringed with dark lashes.

And they were looking right at him.

She came toward him, a smile of recognition on her lips, and he squirmed uncomfortably as his companion's amused tolerance waned.

"Geoffrey Windsor, right?" She pitched her sweet, clear voice soft, and he caught himself leaning toward her to catch her every syllable.

"Do I know you?" The fingers resting lightly on his arm tightened painfully, but he hardly noticed. His eyes were glued to her perfect lips; a pouty lower lip topped by an exquisite bow-shaped upper lip, painted a deep, vibrant red.

"Not officially." Her smile widened, and she allowed it to crinkle the corners of her eyes, breaking the spell of fragile, otherworldly beauty. "I'm Rachael Payne's roommate, Sabrina. Sabrina Kettrick."

She extended her hand and he took it. His engulfed her delicate bones, and he suddenly felt enormous although he was not a particularly large man. He released her reluctantly, and she offered her hand to his companion.

"Sonia Stockwell," Sonia murmured. Her amusement had returned; he could hear its unmistakable tones in her voice although he dared not look at her.

"Very pleased to meet you both. Rachael has been telling me all about the Manor." Her windchime voice fell flat on the last word, and something tightened in her expression although her smile never wavered.

"Yes, she loves her mansions, does Rachael. Her wallpaper, too," he muttered inanely. "I believe she would be there round the clock if I allowed it."

"Yes, well, please don't. We share the household chores, you see." Her gaze swept down. "You're dripping."

He belatedly remembered the bouquet of roses in his hand; he'd stuck the stems into a plastic bag he'd acquired in the produce aisle to catch the drips. Now he held it by the stems, allowing the water to run out of the bag and onto the tile floor. With an elegant snort, Sonia rescued the bouquet.

"Perhaps you could help us, Miss Kettrick," she said, her voice like a deep cat's purr in comparison to Sabrina's tinkling crystal tones. "We were unsure of Miss Payne's favorite flowers. Should we rethink our selection?"

Sabrina's gaze swept from Sonia's face to the bouquet in her hands. "She'd love whatever you gave her," she assured them. "But she's more of a wildflower kind of girl. Or daffodils. She adores daffodils. She planted so many around the grounds of our apartment that our landlord finally begged her to stop."

Geoffrey felt his smile sag. "No roses?"

Her smile widened again, but this time her eyes didn't crinkle. He rather thought they'd taken on the chill of a Nordic fjord. "No roses."

Sonia gave his arm a gentle tug. "Let's go correct our mistake, and then we'd better go or we'll be late."

"She'll understand." He couldn't shake a trace of annoyance every time she used the pronoun "we." It was unreasonable and unfair, but logic had nothing to do with it.

As though sensing his discomfort, Sabrina bobbed her head, bestowing on each of them one last smile. "I'd best be getting home. My half of the chores, you know. Enjoy your evening."

She was walking—gliding? floating?—away before Geoffrey could think of a suitable reply. Sonia was laughing a little as she led him away to the floral department.

"She kind of takes one by surprise, doesn't she?"

"Yeah. I thought maybe she was a faery." He chuckled at his fanciful thoughts, but his insides were squirming uneasily. Their encounter with Sabrina had taken only a few moments, but he wondered how much she had guessed.

And he wondered how much she would tell Rachael.

࿇

"Off with the aqua skirt suit, and on with the plum silk pantsuit," Sabrina ordered. Geoffrey Windsor would not have recognized her voice; gone were the windchimes, replaced with the steely tones of a battle-hardened general.

Rachael knew that voice; it was the same tone Sabrina'd used when explaining to her why her treasured brother Ethan had run off to Spokane with the strange group of friends he'd met at a bonfire on Pacific Beach. It was the tone that said she knew unpleasant truths that would derail any flights of fancy in which Rachael might be indulging.

She paused, teetering on one leather aqua pump, her bare foot hovering over the other. She grasped the back of the sofa and eased down onto her bare foot.

"Why? I don't have time to dress again—I'm going to be late!"

"Just trust me. The plum silk is what you need tonight."

Huffing and grumbling, Rachael clomped back into her bedroom and shed the aqua linen. She frowned a bit as the skirt whispered to the floor. The sleeveless tunic had shown off her honey-toned tan, light as it was, and the light blue hue had made her skin glow like pearls. At least, that's what Sabrina had said before she'd dashed off to the store for peanut butter and apparently sustained a head injury.

She had barely pulled on the plum silk before Sabrina barged in and began tugging and shifting. Before Rachael knew it, she'd been expertly accessorized, her hair pinned up in an elegant chignon and dressed with Austrian crystal butterfly barrettes, and her feet shoved into black matte leather pumps that showed a bit of toe. A glance out the window confirmed her suspicion that Sabrina had bonked her head or had gone suddenly insane: the wind howled around the apartment building and threw showers of rain against the windows.

"Sabrina," she ventured tentatively. "Open toed shoes and a silk outfit on a rainy night?"

"I'm just here to make sure you don't make an unpardonable fashion faux pas," Sabrina grumbled. And she would know—she had designed nearly every outfit in Rachael's closet that wasn't constructed of stretch cotton or denim.

She pulled on a lightweight trench coat and shouldered her portfolio, wondering just what had happened at the grocery store. And she was on the verge of asking Sabrina just that when her cell phone chimed.

"Rach—"

"Just a sec, 'Brina. It's Geoffrey."

"But—"

Rachael's attention had already turned away from her, however, and she let the conversation carry her out the door.

She met them at Bayview Manor rather than the restaurant, as Geoffrey's call instructed her to do. Parking close to the front entrance preserved most of her hair style, but many more trips through the rain was likely to have an adverse effect on her silk suit. Again she wondered what had possessed Sabrina, but the thought fled as soon as she closed the front door and saw Geoffrey detach himself from a cluster of people at the foot of the horseshoe staircase.

"Rachael! Finally!" He cupped a proprietary hand under her elbow and guided her toward the group he'd left. "How the wallpaper trip go?"

"Ferries," she said, and shuddered. "Water was choppy. It wasn't a pleasant trip as far as crossing the Sound goes. I brought samples though."

"Excellent." He sent her a sidelong look that turned her insides to mush. "You spent quite a lot of time with Riley, I hear." Riley was his personal assistant, and a bigger flirt Rachael had never met. "He's completely in love with you now, you know."

She chuckled. "Only until the next blonde, brunette, or redhead under thirty-five goes by. I'm sure I was thrown over within ten minutes of getting on the return ferry."

"I see I don't need to worry about you—you have his number."

"Yes, I do—he was sure to slip it into my planner," she replied with a wry smile.

"Smooth. Forget about Riley for the moment; there are people I'd like you to meet."

This was fairly obvious, as the small knot of people stood facing them, watching them approach with an air of measured patience. Lon Harris was there, listening politely to a small, dapper man who bore a sour expression and giving the impression of trying to edge away from the three women who completed the ensemble.

"Rach, this gentleman is Mr. Ray Hobart from Renaissance Flooring, a company in Bellevue specializing in matching period flooring with modern reproductions. Mr. Hobart, may I present Rachael Payne, my interior designer."

Rachael accepted Hobart's offered hand. His palm was clammy and he had a grip like a dead fish. She forced a smile onto her face at his lukewarm "Charmed."

Geoffrey wasted minimum time on the snobbish Mr. Hobart,

turning to the women. "My mother, Risa Windsor," and Risa offered her hand in a lady's handshake, more of a delicate squeeze than anything else, a tiny but seemingly genuine smile playing about her perfectly painted mouth.

"My grandmother, Heléne," and the oldest of the trio of women took Rachael's hand between both her own, squeezing tightly with a warm smile.

Geoffrey drew in a breath and moved from Rachael's side to stand next to the remaining woman, who was holding a bouquet of startlingly yellow daffodils. "And this is Sonia Stockwell." He paused. "My fiancée."

Shocked, Rachael's eyes flew to Geoffrey's for a fleeting second. He seemed to have dropped some sort of shield that masked all emotion. Sonia offered her hand, her own expression assessing but friendly. Numbly, Rachael shook it, firmly and briskly as she would any man, and managed a natural smile. Being able to do so helped her regain her composure.

"Any friend of Geoffrey's," Sonia murmured.

"Is to be regarded with suspicion," Rachael finished without thinking, and everyone, even the ever-so-restrained Mr. Hobart, broke into laughter.

Sonia Stockwell was tall—at least five-feet, ten-inches—possessed of an exquisite figure draped in a sage linen pantsuit, and moved with the easy grace of money. While not classically beautiful, her features were delicate and her lips firm and full. Rich dark hair framed her face, just touching the collar of her suit jacket and feathering to a point along her jaw. She was elegant and sophisticated and she was Geoffrey's fiancée.

Fiancée. She wondered why Geoffrey hadn't told her. She remembered asking him who Sonia was at least three times, and each time he had waved it off as unimportant.

"These are for you, Rachael. Geoffrey wanted to show his appreciation for all you've had to put up with so far." Sonia thrust the bouquet into her hands and laid a gentle hand on her arm, interrupting her reverie. "Darling, you won't mind if I borrow Rachael for a moment, will you? I'm dying to know what's going on the walls in the ballroom." Without waiting for Geoffrey's approval, she expertly guided her quarry away from the group and toward the ballroom.

"Stepped on your own sticky strands, did you?" Rachael heard Heléne murmur to Geoffrey, and then Sonia pulled her out of earshot.

The next forty minutes passed quickly and remarkably free of discomfort. Sonia, while looking every inch the heiress to a fortune that she was, had an easy way about her and a truly wicked sense of humor, which she displayed in her retelling of their encounter with Sabrina in the store.

The only anxious moment came when Sonia leaned casually against one ruined pillar and surveyed her through the gloom — they were just beyond the reach of the work lights Harris had turned on for them.

"He didn't tell you, did he?"

Rachael fiddled with the cellophane wrapper around the daffodils, but through monumental effort was able to offer a natural smile. "No, but then we've hardly had any opportunity to exchange social credentials. This project seems to be plagued with an unusual number of disasters."

Sonia smiled back, but she seemed troubled. Rachael was troubled too. What made a man hide a fiancée even after he'd been asked directly about the woman in question? She could think of no good reason.

༖

Sitting across from Rachael at dinner with Sonia to his left and constantly touching him was absolute torture. The only thing worse than having both women at the same table, he mused over his wilting salad, would be any mention of the Manor.

Rachael proved to be a natural hostess. When awkward silences fell upon the table, she stepped in smoothly, filling the voids with questions or comments designed to spark conversation. Even Sonia, notoriously reticent, appeared at ease and answered her questions at length and without hesitation.

Thankfully, they made it through the salad, soup and main entrée before anyone mentioned the Manor.

"So tell me, Rachael," Sonia began, her fork pausing midway

between her mouth and the cheesecake on the plate before her. "Do you know the history of Bayview Manor?"

The tiramisu Geoffrey had just spooned into his mouth suddenly tasted like sawdust, and he swallowed it with difficulty, chasing it with a hefty slug of chardonnay. He pushed his dish away.

Rachael hastily swallowed her bite of mud pie and dabbed her napkin over her lips. "Of course. This area wasn't settled until just a decade or so before Bayview was constructed. It was built in 1861 by Nathan Fotheringham, who made his fortune in lumber on the east coast. The family continued in the lumber industry after moving here, and eventually expanded into shipping. Michael moved north to Seattle, a logical choice for shipping, what with Puget Sound, and left the lumber business in the care of his son, Jonathan."

"I've heard...things," Heléne inserted tentatively. "*Strange* things."

"Oh, you mean about the house being haunted." Rachael smiled. She shot a glance at Geoffrey, who was sure his wan color warred with the smile plastered to his face.

He drained his wine glass in one convulsive gulp when Risa remarked off-handedly, "Oh, the Manor is haunted?"

"I don't believe in hauntings," Rachael assured her confidently, fixing him with a gimlet eye before turning her attention fully on his mother. "But there are always rumors of it around old, large houses, especially Gothic Revivals."

"Geoffrey said he heard that the house was found fully constructed on the Fotheringhams' land, so they just moved in." Sonia interjected. "If you don't believe it's haunted, how do you explain the rumors about the strange occurrences, lights seen in the windows, those kinds of things?"

It seemed to him that Rachael missed a mental step, but her voice was steady when she answered. "The work was constructed in secret, and then the forest cleared from around the house. Rumors sprang up from there, I suppose, about the house having been there all along, that Nathan just came along and occupied it since it was on his land." Her fork carried another chunk of mud pie to her mouth, and she chewed slowly while reflecting on what she knew of the Manor.

"And then with what happened in 1945, I can see where rumors of hauntings took hold so strongly."

Sonia's brow creased, and she and Risa exchanged a puzzled glance. "What happened in 1945, Rachael?"

Geoffrey coughed politely, sipping his coffee. "This is a very good blend," he commented out of left field. "Is it specially made?"

Rachael ignored his feeble attempt to change the subject, spearing him with a quelling look. "There was a murder-suicide at the Manor that year. The rumor mill went wild after that. It always will in small towns, especially after a scandal."

Risa and Sonia exchanged a concerned look. Heléne simply narrowed her blue eyes, her chin lifting a fraction as if her worst fears had just been confirmed.

"What happened?" Sonia queried.

"No one knows." Rachael's brow creased. "Supposedly Jonathan Fotheringham killed his wife, his sister, the nanny, and then himself. No one knows why; he left no note, no journals, nothing to indicate there was trouble of that nature. It was rumored he planned on leaving his wife and taking the kids. It was also rumored he was having an affair with the nanny, but just as many people have refuted that, so the truth on that subject is a little murky."

"Well, one does not go about murdering without a reason," Heléne commented reasonably. "I'm sure it relates to the portraits in the gallery."

Risa sighed and covered her eyes with her hand, Sonia cleared her throat delicately, and Geoffrey stifled a laugh. The look on Rachael's face was priceless.

"I beg your pardon?"

"The portraits," his grandmother repeated with exaggerated patience. "You only invite trouble when you have your portrait painted. All kinds of spirits can inhabit your likeness and steal away your soul."

To her credit, Rachael acted as though nothing was amiss with Heléne's reasoning. "Oh, yes, that superstition can be traced back to several early cultures. Some primitive cultures today still believe that."

"Exactly. Is it any wonder that mansion is plagued with spirits?"

"Gran, Rachael doesn't believe in ghosts, remember?" Geoffrey said gently. His grandmother shot him a dark look. "Well, she doesn't."

"I did not say *ghosts*, did I, Geoffrey? I said *spirits*. There is a difference."

"Not much," he muttered.

"Actually, a great deal of difference," Rachael put in unexpectedly. "The term *ghost* is traditionally used in connection with the spirit of a deceased person that has not 'crossed over,' as the occultists put it. Now the term *spirits* is used more broadly, to define the unseen beings around us. One third of the Holy Trinity is a spirit. Angels are referred to as spirits, as are demons."

Sonia pushed her cheesecake away, only half eaten. "That's very interesting, Rachael. Are you a theology student?"

Rachael smiled. "No. My father was a pastor when I was small. He remained very faithful in his beliefs even after he resigned his pastorate."

"What does he do now?"

Rachael's smile faltered. "He died two years ago."

Sonia looked stricken. "Oh, I'm sorry. I always put my foot in my mouth."

"It's okay. You couldn't have known."

Risa changed the subject with a silencing look sent in Sonia's direction. "Could the so-called ghost hauntings actually be demonic activity?"

Geoffrey fumbled his coffee cup.

"It could," Rachael agreed reluctantly, watching the brown stain spread on the snowy linen. She had spent so much of her life attributing the stories to overactive imaginations that it was clear she'd never considered the darker possibilities. While ghostly hauntings could be easily dismissed, given her spiritual beliefs, demonic activity was another matter entirely. Geoffrey wasn't sorry to see her so neatly backed into that corner. Maybe she would listen to him now.

"Well," Risa declared firmly, "As interesting as all this is, I'm sure we've nothing to worry about. Demons or ghosts, whatever they are — they'll simply have to leave."

Sonia chuckled. "I'm sure they'll pack immediately and head out at first light."

"That has to be the easiest exorcism ever," Rachael agreed, and joined Risa and Sonia in their laughter.

Geoffrey and Heléne didn't share their amusement, but exchanged an uneasy glance. He watched Rachael laughing, and beneath her carefree manner he thought he could detect apprehension.

Finally.

(Excerpt from an instant message conversation between Kimberly Schaefer and Taryn Ackerlin, April 6, 2009)

TARYN THE TERRIBLE: I'm glad you're feeling better.

KIMANDA: Me too. Bad one. Thanks for watching the munchkins.

TARYN THE TERRIBLE: No prob. Me & Dimetapp, world's best babysitters.

KIMANDA: You did not! LOL

TARYN THE TERRIBLE: Nah. I did swab their gums with numbing throat spray.

KIMANDA: That stuff tastes terrible. :-(

TARYN THE TERRIBLE: They didn't seem to care. They're piglets; they thought it was food.

KIMANDA: They take after Aaron. Another bottomless pit.

TARYN THE TERRIBLE: Speaking of Aaron... Will you do me a favor?

KIMANDA: Taryn, not now.

TARYN THE TERRIBLE: Will you go see Doc Jacobs?

KIMANDA: What for? It was just a headache.

TARYN THE TERRIBLE: You've had three in the last month. Don't think I didn't notice. The last time you had them clustered like that, you were pregnant.

KIMANDA: Doubtful that's the reason.

TARYN THE TERRIBLE: But what if it is? What if this time he comes home too late and you've hemorrhaged to death?

KIMANDA: I guess then he won't have to file for a divorce.

TARYN THE TERRIBLE: Not funny.

KIMANDA: Not meant to be. :'(

SANCTUARY
Wednesday, April 15, 2009

Kimberly sat in the middle row of the small church, letting the sounds of chatting fellow worshippers wash over her. With a couple exceptions, her circle of friends seemed to be extraordinarily busy this evening—so busy they had no time to stop and talk.

But she didn't mind; she didn't particularly want to be bothered with well-meaning inquiries, such as where she'd been the last couple weeks and where was Aaron tonight. The sound of human interaction was soothing after the silence of her home, but she had no desire to take part in it.

"I'm going to go get coffee, Kim. Do you want a cup?" Taryn hovered protectively at her elbow, seeming to sense something in the atmosphere that Kim herself was unable to. Wrapped in her cocoon of misery, Kim saw only the happiness around her— happiness that had eluded her since Melody Olmstead's visit.

"That would be fine," she said with a faint smile. With a last worried look at her, Taryn hurried off toward the beverage table set unobtrusively in the corner of the sanctuary.

Feeling eyes on her, Kim looked up and around, catching the gaze of a couple who had faithfully visited her every week while she'd been confined to bed during her pregnancy. They both looked away uncomfortably, and Kimberly finally realized that something was terribly wrong. Her eyes moved away and caught the trim figure of Melody Olmstead across the small room, chatting animatedly with a group of ladies Kim regularly enjoyed coffee with at the diner. Several cast glances her way; when they saw her gazing back, they quickly looked away.

Ah, that was the lay of the land. Now came the gossip mongering, the choosing of sides, the judgments from one side of a mouth while the other side expressed concern for her and Aaron.

And how long had this been a favorite topic of discussion at the Mills Church of Christ? Was this why Aaron had stopped coming, why he had given Taryn a flat look of disinterest when she said they were going to church and would he like to join them?

Someone slid into the chair beside her and laid a hand on her shoulder. Expecting Taryn, she turned with a frown to ask if her friend noticed it too, this cold front aimed in her direction. But it wasn't Taryn; Leon Witter, the church pastor, sat beside her, his expression filled with benign concern.

"May I have a word, Kimberly?"

"Certainly," she agreed amicably, but inside she recoiled in horror. She should have known; rumor was bound to have made it through the ranks to the ear of the pastor. Now she would have to issue disclaimers, refute gossip, exonerate Aaron while turning the laser beam of blame onto herself...for who else could be blamed for the ruins of their marriage? She had leveled it with the most destructive accusation available, and it didn't matter that the evidence pointed to its truth. What mattered was that she had not even heard Aaron out, had not given him the benefit of the doubt, had turned away from his plea for trust.

"There have been some...curious subjects racing through the grapevine," he began with a kindly smile. Kimberly relaxed slightly; it would be all right. He would simply offer to mediate as a counselor and advise her not to pay attention to rumors. Maybe he would even preach a stern sermon about the injurious, evil nature of gossip. Perhaps —

" — Aaron and Melody Olmstead?"

"Excuse me?"

Leon Witter looked stricken. "I'm sorry — I thought you were aware of the — oh dear."

"Aware of what, exactly, Pastor Leon?" Kim asked evenly. "That Melody Olmstead started a rumor that she's having an affair with my husband? Perhaps you should be having a discussion with her about whether deliberately trying to destroy a marriage is condoned in scripture."

"Ah —" he stammered. He closed his eyes, drew in a breath, and seemed to gather his wits. "I thought perhaps to put an end to the gossip...you could address the issue in service tonight. That way it's from the horse's mouth, so to speak."

Kim's mouth fell open. "You want me to stand before the entire congregation and acknowledge the trouble that woman has caused, as though I'm not humiliated enough by her lies? By refuting it publicly, I would only be turning the attention on her, which is what she wants. I see no reason to air my dirty laundry to stop a bunch of viperous tongues from wagging."

"Kimberly," Leon admonished.

"I will *not* turn the spotlight on Melody Olmstead."

"If you would just say a few words—even just deny the rumor. We must do something to stop the gossip! The whole situation is shameful!"

In a sudden moment of clarity, Kim realized that Leon—that probably everyone—believed the gossip. Leon wasn't trying to ease the burden on her because he thought her husband innocent; he was trying to clap a lid on a kettle of shit about to boil over because he didn't want to deal with the mess.

A fine tremor of fury thrummed through her body. "Remove your hand from my shoulder and get out of my way."

"*Please*, Kimberly, I don't want you to go away upset. I'm just trying to maintain order and respectability—"

She flung up her arm in a violent move that sent his hand flying off her shoulder. "If you want to restore order and respectability, you should start over there." She motioned to the other side of the sanctuary, where the gossiping hens were still clucking.

"I thought you would be the reasonable one!"

"You already spoke to Aaron about this?" No wonder he had refused Taryn's invitation to come to church with them.

"Yes. When the rumors started and you two weren't in church for the last couple weeks, I approached him about addressing the issue before the congregation. It's your duty to put an end to the gossip by coming forward with the truth!"

"Our *duty*?" Kim repeated, stupefied. Her brain spun its tires for a frantic moment, trying to find traction in some small bit of logic, but there was none in the whole sorry situation.

"How about this: why don't you preach your sermon on gossip

and aim it at the mongers rather than the victims? And while you're at it, perhaps you should preach something about sanctimonious pseudo-pastors who—"

A hand fell on her other shoulder, and from behind her Taryn said rather loudly, "I think it's time we blew this Popsicle stand, whaddaya say? I don't want that coffee anymore; I could go for a cold beer and some conversation that's a little less on the hypocritical side."

Her mouth compressed into a forbidding line, Kim snatched her purse from under her chair and stood. Her fury had attracted the notice of several people nearby, who tried to watch without appearing to watch. More fodder for the rumor mill. Leon stood up, his placating hands held out before him.

"Kimberly, *please!*" He looked worried. Kim suddenly wondered if what he was really concerned about was her going home and telling Aaron about this. She suspected Leon's conversation with her husband had gone less smoothly than his with her; she wished she could have heard exactly what Aaron had said to him.

"Get out of my way."

"Kimberly—"

Kim shoved her chair back into the empty row behind her, providing a clear path to the aisle. At the commotion, all eyes had turned their way and silence descended on the sanctuary. Her face blazing with anger, Kim made her way to the foyer, pushing through the crowd to the front doors. Once outside in the parking lot, she sucked in a huge breath, turned her face up to the April rain, and smiled for the first time in weeks.

"I never liked this church anyway."

Taryn laced their arms together and tugged her toward the car. "Me either. We should've stuck with the Baptist one around the corner from the high school. They have rocking worship. C'mon. I really *would* like a cold beer, and we really need to have a talk."

"I don't want to talk about Ron." Kim opened her mouth, letting the rain splatter on her tongue. Its salty taste reminded her of the ocean, and her smile faded as thoughts of the sea brought Bayview Manor—the Wyckham House—to mind.

"You don't have to. We can talk about Denny Wallace instead of Aaron Schaefer."

"Ah, Taryn." She turned away from the rain and leveled a sympathetic look at her friend.

"I'll live. C'mon, the tavern has a new band."

Kim's step faltered. "Oh, I don't know…"

"It's pop, not country," Taryn said quietly. "It doesn't even look like the same place, Kim. But even if it did…well, Scott saved your life; he'd want you to live it."

"I'm sure he'd rather have lived himself."

"Undoubtedly." Taryn sighed, and tugged her toward the car. "Come on. I'm getting cold and the natives are getting restless."

Kim glanced over her shoulder, seeing the knot of anxious — or was it anticipatory? — women who were prodding each other across the parking lot toward them. She sent a glare their way, and in case that wasn't enough to deter them, she let Taryn lead her away. Anger warred with sorrow as she realized the one place she had been certain would give her sanctuary from her living nightmare had turned its back on her.

The tavern parking lot overflowed, reminding Kim of the days it ran under Schaefer ownership. Ron wasn't particularly a people person, but his brother Scott had been the very definition of extrovert, and Scott's band boasted quite a following.

The latest owners had affixed corrugated metal siding to the log-cabin structure and painted it to give the illusion of rust. The name had been changed as well to *Bayou Baudelaire*. The Baudelaires were relatively new to Mills; childless and trendy, they'd carved their niche in the party crowd and brought their own flavor of fun with them from New Orleans. Kim had found herself avoiding locations and situations that would bring her into contact with them, for she'd seen them with Melody Olmstead on several occasions. There wasn't room enough in any crowd for both Melody and her.

"Busy tonight," Kim offered as she followed Taryn from the car to the door. Taryn sent her a look over her shoulder.

"Not really. It's worse on a Friday or Saturday night.

Wednesday they have karaoke, so that brings out all the twenty- and thirty-somethings."

"Karaoke?" Kim repeated, dismayed. Scott would have been mortified. On more than one occasion she'd seen him in a tee-shirt that proclaimed *If it ain't live, it ain't music!*

"Kim?" Taryn prodded, concerned. Kim had stopped ten feet away from the door. "Are you all right?"

Was she? For the life of her, Kim couldn't answer that question. Her marriage lay in tatters, the victim of her own impetuous nature; Mills' troubles hadn't appeared to have ended with the demise of the Circle; and the tavern had morphed into some alien structure she would expect to see on the banks of a Louisiana bayou.

But that hadn't caused her step to falter. When she walked in the door, would she see Scott in every minute detail? He had lived passionately; it had to have left an indelible mark somewhere other than on her heart. And Aaron…Aaron had built the tavern, driven it to success despite his introverted nature. By the time she had met him, his presence had leeched into the very molecules of the building. She had found friends and family, had fallen in love, all in this place. Could she bear to see it transformed into a techno-karaoke bar?

"I'm fine," Kim said as Taryn opened her mouth to prod her. She drew in a deep breath. "I'm perfectly fine."

Taryn didn't seem convinced, but she pushed open the heavy oak door, unveiling the Bayou Baudelaire.

The country atmosphere had been replaced with a sleek urban décor that seemed cold and impersonal despite the many clusters of friends gathered at the tall metal tables crammed between the stage and the bar. Stainless steel seemed the main element, from the new back bar to the sensual curve of the new, smaller bar. Neon framed the back bar, flashing insistently, the refracted light multiplied by the many reflective surfaces. The warm-toned carpet had been replaced with large, shiny tiles in metallic tones, and the leather bar stools had been replaced with tall, steel, ladder-back chairs. She wondered to where Ron's prized mahogany bar had vanished.

Taryn motioned to the bar and two empty stools on either side of a short, slender man with a ponytail. Kim arched a brow as Taryn slid onto the left stool and pulled the man's hair. He jumped, startled, then grinned and gave her a one-armed hug. Taryn looked over her shoulder at Kim and motioned her forward.

"Kim, this is Trent Baudelaire. Trent, Kimberly Schaefer."

"*The* Kimberly Schaefer?"

Warm color flooded her cheeks. "Ah—"

"I got somethin' for ya," Trent said, sliding off the stool. "Come in back, *cherie*." Kim sent Taryn a helpless look, and Trent seemed to sense her discomfort. "Taryn, you too, *s'il vous plait*. You gonna like this."

"Sure."

Trent led the way, his bouncy step betraying his excitement and enthusiasm. Kim couldn't fathom what he could possibly want to show her or what he had meant by "*the* Kimberly Schaefer," but she followed him and Taryn into the kitchen behind the bar.

Nothing much had changed in the kitchen; the chipped tiled floor had been replaced, as had the steel service door the werewolf had ripped from its hinges. The nameplate on the office door now simply read *Knock Before Entering*, and the break room, their destination, had undergone a serious overhaul. A new microfiber sofa provided comfortable seating, and the 1970's shag carpet had been exchanged for restaurant-grade Berber.

But that wasn't what held Kim rooted to the floor. Trent had preceded them into the room and with a magician's flourish swept a white sheet off a large piece of furniture: Ron's mahogany bar, polished and ready to be pressed into service.

"I wondered—" Her voice cracked, and she cleared her throat. "I wondered where it had gone."

"Beautiful bar, she is," Trent remarked, sweeping an appreciative hand over the smooth, gleaming surface of the bar. "I was gonna auction it off, but it didn't seem right."

"How much do you want for it?" Kim asked numbly. Taryn gave her an odd look.

"I couldn't sell it, Miz Schaefer—you mind if I call you Kim?"

"Feel free."

"All right. Kim, I couldn't sell it. Like I said, it wouldn't seem right. But you're free to take it."

"I'm sorry?" She was certain she hadn't heard him correctly. Had he just said —

"You're free to take it. Or I can have it delivered wherever you like."

"But...you *do* understand how much this bar is worth, don't you? It's an antique; Ron salvaged it from a pub in Philadelphia just before it was razed to the ground."

Trent grinned. "I know. But it'd be like selling the souvenirs of someone's love affair. It belongs to you two."

Kim chewed her lower lip. Obviously she couldn't leave it here; surely Trent would like the space back. And she didn't want to take it home yet; it would have to go in the barn until it could be installed somewhere in the house, and the barn was Aaron's domain. She wasn't going to give him a gift of this magnitude while they weren't speaking; it would feel like an attempt to buy his forgiveness.

Taryn sighed expressively. "Oh, all right! You can store it in my garage. Are you going to save it for your anniversary? His birthday? How about Father's Day?"

"Father's Day will do." Her eyes narrowed on her friend's face, telling Taryn her ploy had not escaped Kim's notice: a deadline for her to make things right.

"That's settled, then," Trent said happily, rubbing his hands together in satisfaction. "I'll make arrangements for it to be delivered to your house, *cherie*. Now, we got more serious things to talk about." He rapped on the wall between the break room and the office. "Just summoning my better half. This will take a woman's touch, I think. Go ahead and make yourselves comfortable. Do you want a drink? Martini, margarita, beer?"

"A beer will do," Taryn piped up. Kim still reeled from his gift of the bar and his lightning fast change of subjects, so Taryn added, "And one for her, too."

"No, a glass of water will be fine, thanks."

Trent disappeared to fetch their beverages. As soon as he had gone out of earshot, Kim turned on Taryn.

"Did you set this up – this little chat?"

"I swear, Kim, I have no idea why he would want to talk to

you." Taryn frowned sternly. "You're getting paranoid in your old age. Are you sure you don't have a hormonal imbalance?"

"Ha ha." But Kim let the subject go.

Trent returned a few minutes later with a slightly chubby dark-haired woman he introduced as his wife Caitlyn. She shook Kim's hand with both of hers, beaming happily.

"I've heard so much about you! I'm so pleased to finally get to meet you. I wish it were under happier circumstances."

Kim's smile faltered, and she shot Taryn a questioning look. But Taryn looked just as puzzled. "I'm afraid I don't understand."

Trent moved a couple of comfortable chairs from the break table and positioned them facing Kim and Taryn on the sofa. Caitlyn settled into one and leaned forward, bracing her elbows on her knees.

"I hate to be so indelicate about this, but we need to talk about Melody Olmstead."

Kim felt her face freeze. Her polite smile felt plastic. "I'm afraid I've run out of time. I must be —"

Caitlyn interrupted. "You've run out of time, all right. That woman's conjuring the devil and sending him after you."

(Article from Seattle Post-Intelligencer, November 16, 1944)

Seven-year-old reported missing in Heron Bay, WA
by Eric Delaney
Staff Writer

HERON BAY, WA — Seven-year-old Emil Szilágyi was reported missing on November 15 by his parents, Katalin and József Szilágyi. The boy had been playing with friends on Blue Heron Beach when they discovered a cave several yards up the bluff.

According to his friends, Szilágyi made the trecherous climb to the cave without incident and went inside to explore, where he subsequently vanished.

Authorities investigated the cave and located a tunnel on the back wall, leading to a dead-end. Several deep shafts branch off the tunnel. It is feared Szilágyi may have slipped and fallen into one of these. No evidence of him was found in the cave.

THE HOUSE THAT EATS PEOPLE
Saturday, April 11, 2009

Traffic was light on the 101 as Geoffrey headed toward Hoquiam. He'd watched Sonia, Risa, and Heléne drive away from their hotel, waving from the parking lot. The thought of spending the dreary, misty day in his hotel room was singularly unappealing, but the idea of tracking down this mysterious Michael St. Claire held such appeal that he climbed into his car and aimed it south. Even if he couldn't find the gentleman in question, he would at least be out of the oppressive town of Heron Bay and wouldn't have to go to Bayview Manor.

The latter was such a benefit that he slowed the car to five miles under the speed limit to savor it. Traffic picked up as he approached Hoquiam. He knew the address of his general contractor's office, but finding it was another matter, especially with cars crawling bumper-to-bumper through town so that changing lanes was a near impossibility.

But at last he made it, and there his plan ran aground. Greg Flanders had flatly refused to give any more information about Michael St. Claire, including where to find him, but Geoffrey was no mental slouch. He figured the best places to start asking around were diners and taverns, and just a few blocks away from the general contractor's office was a bar and grill—an excellent location for the mysterious Mr. St. Claire to have waited to get one of Harris's workers alone and deliver his warning.

Six bars later, he made his way into a shabby hole-in-the-wall, drawn by the neon POOL TABLES sign. Dim and smoky – the non-smoking law was being ignored in full-force in this establishment – and with a palpable air of tension, it seemed a haven for quiet, dangerous men.

The bartender sent him a glance of studied indifference as he strolled in; the patrons didn't even turn to look, confident they would be capable of handling whatever had blown through the door. The muted crack of pool balls came from the only bright corner across the room, where a gruff-looking man in his seventies watched a younger man break and run. The older man didn't appear to be concerned about either Geoffrey or his opponent, who was steadily clearing the table with a lot of luck and little finesse. He adjusted the eye patch covering his left eye, his good orb indifferently watching the young man's carom net him a lucky sink.

Geoffrey approached the bar, mentally preparing himself to be stonewalled when he asked after Michael St. Claire because…well, probably because he'd seen it happen in so many movies. But the bartender simply tipped his head toward the old man playing pool and went back to shifting glasses from a dishwasher rack to the back bar.

St. Claire must have heard him asking, for he was already handing his cue to a waiting player. He snagged his beer from a table littered with empty bottles and met Geoffrey halfway across the room.

"You looking for me, *mon ami*?" He seemed friendly enough. His fading Cajun patois instantly transported Geoffrey to the south Louisiana bayous.

"I am if you're Michael St. Claire," Geoffrey admitted. He extended his hand, and was once again surprised when his quarry shook it with alacrity.

"Me, I'm guilty as charged." St. Claire snagged the back of a chair and hauled it out from under a table so he could sit. Geoffrey took this as an invitation and did the same. "You found me faster'n I expected."

So much for catching the man off guard. Sometimes being well-known was a detriment.

"You know who I am? And knew I'd come? How?"

"Greg Flanders, he's much better at bein' honest than he is at keepin' his trap shut, him. I knew he'd blab." He waved a dismissive hand. "It's all right. If I din't wanna talk to you, I wouldn'ta been where you could find me."

Indeed. "You gave Flanders a warning about the mansion I just bought. How do you know about the house?"

"That's no house," St. Claire said. "That's an opening right into hell itself. You mebbe want a drink, Mr. Windsor. Dis a long story and you'll want somethin' what to wash it down with."

Geoffrey tipped his head toward St. Claire's beer, and the man signaled the server—a hard-looking woman Geoffrey was sure could bounce him off the floorboards without raising a sweat—and pointed at his beer. A moment later she rapped a bottle of Deschute's Black Butte in front of him, and he clutched it like a security blanket, dreading what St. Claire had to say. What was he doing here anyway, stalking a superstitious Cajun who'd reportedly been raised by a Louisiana voodoo queen to talk about his from-hell house?

"Do you think some people can see the other realm?" St. Claire asked, his casual tone belying his careful, watchful expression.

"What other realm?"

"The realm angels move through. And demons."

Geoffrey considered the question seriously. He had already made up his mind that his two-million-dollar mansion was possessed; it wasn't a far stretch to believe that some humans were allowed a glimpse beyond the veil that separated the human realm from the eternal one.

"Sure, I guess so. It seems to me it explains some people being able to see what they call ghosts."

"Interestin' way to word it," St. Claire observed. He adjusted his eye patch, easing the fit over his eye socket. He looked like a pirate come ashore for a drink.

"I have a friend who doesn't believe in ghosts, but she believes in demons."

"Smart friend. But Rachael Payne's belief in demons don' protect her from 'em. Best to keep her outta that house, you."

"She's in danger, then."

"We're all in danger, always. That's why we gotta be on our guard. But there's nothing the devil likes better than a challenge, and a devout Christian woman is definitely that. She won't be the first Christian to stand against that house, and she won't be the first to fall, either."

"How do you know so much about Bayview Manor, Mr. St. Claire? Did you live in Heron Bay?"

The old man spun the beer bottle between his hands, watching its precarious revolutions until the bottle wobbled to a stop. "Me, I'm one o' them can see the other side. Been seein' it since I was a little kid, three, mebbe four years old. I lived the first six years of my childhood in terror, and the rest of my life with the devastation those beings can bring into our realm."

He fell silent for a while. Geoffrey didn't prod him, sensing that the man was not so much sifting through the details and deciding he could tell than he was reaching inside himself to find the courage to talk about his experiences.

"My sister, she was four when it happened. I was six. Everything went crazy, and our parents and some others ended up dead. I'd seen the beings around them, spurring them on, encouraging mayhem and worse — murder, even. I saw it for months. My mother had brought in a psychic, wanted to 'reconnect' with our older sister who'd died two years before of bacterial meningitis. The man was swarmed by these beings."

"Beings," Geoffrey repeated. "You mean demons."

"I do. But demons aren't all that was trapped in our house."

"What do you mean?"

"Servants. The servants of Satan, having failed him in one way or another. They couldn't get out, see. There are no doors or windows for them. That house, it eats people."

"Eats people?" Geoffrey felt a little sick.

"I asked one. He was always there with my mother and her psychic, him. Always at their little 'gatherings' — séances is what they really were. Séances, talk about!" He shook his head wonderingly at either their naïveté or their stupidity. "Never saw him arrive, never saw him leave. So I asked him 'bout it. He said 'Boy, there are no doors or windows in this house. I can't get out.' Then he told me to go mind my own business 'fore he decided to kill me. He was there to the end. There *at* the end."

Geoffrey took a long swig of beer and studied his companion through the gloom that seemed to hover over their table. "I heard it said you were raised by a voodoo queen in Louisiana. How'd you end up there?"

St. Claire shrugged. "The aunt who was to be our guardian, she died too. Only remaining relative was my mother's sister in N'Awlins. Completely batty, but she wasn't no voodoo queen." He snorted derisively, and then added fairly, "Though she did know an uncommon lot about the subject."

"Hoquiam seems a long way from New Orleans."

"After my folks died, I asked God to take away that sight. Didn't wanna see that other realm no more. God, He's a gentleman, Him. He won't force you to do nothin' you don' wanna do. So I lived through my teens, my twennies, my thirties, didn't see a thing outside the norm."

"Must've been pleasant."

St. Claire guffawed. "Woulda been, 'cept I grew a conscience. Was I given the gift o' sight, shouldn't I a-been warning people of what was around 'em?" He shook his head. "Aahhh, *bon Dieu avoir pitié*, no?"

"So you heard about this house, came to see what you could see because of your experiences in your childhood home?"

"I only wish it'd happened that way. You're mebbe dense, but you're okay. So lean close, Mr. Windsor, and I'll tell you my secret in plain terms."

Geoffrey obliged.

They talked for another two hours, and St. Claire's revelations stayed with him the whole drive back to Heron Bay from Hoquiam, driving deep into his bones a chill even the car's heater, cranked as high as it would go, could not dispel. So now he knew the truth about the Fotheringhams, the truth about the Manor. The wipers beat a steady rhythm, a metronome that kept time with the thought that circled continuously in his head: *Good God, it's worse than I thought.*

He stopped at an internet café in Amanda Park to pump some hot coffee into his system, finally allowing himself the thought that he'd been reluctant to consider, because it meant a huge financial loss: he had to shut down the project, couldn't allow anyone else — least of all Rachael — back into that house.

The rain had worsened while he was in the café, now pouring down in icy sheets. He ducked into the car, shaking the water from his hands, and aimed to car toward Heron Bay. It didn't matter what anyone thought; the most important thing was to keep everyone safe. He'd be damned — literally — if he let them wander with carefree abandon through a house full of devils.

He drove at a steady sixty-five miles per hour, Michael St. Claire's confession spurring him on when doubts clouded his resolve and his foot eased up on the accelerator.

Our names were changed when we went to live with our aunt in New Orleans. She thought it best, the only way to leave behind the scandal. My real name is Joshua Fotheringham.

❧

The rain drove her from her apartment — the rain and her depression. She'd slept poorly, her slumber stalked by unsettling dreams and emotions, and had awakened to Sabrina's note on her night table, propped against the lamp: *Gone to coffee with Sonia Stockwell. She likes my designs, can you believe it?! See you this evening.*

She couldn't help the bloom of resentment toward Sonia Stockwell. Wasn't it enough that she had Geoffrey; did she have to take Rachael's best friend as well?

And then she felt a rush of guilt, for she truly liked Geoffrey's fiancée. There was only one thing that could drive her out of a blue funk on the rare occasion she fell into one: work. So she headed toward the Manor, ignoring her cell phone when it rang because she knew it was Geoffrey.

An unnatural quiet hung over the house when she slipped inside, pocketing her keys as she closed the front door behind her. Usually on a Saturday she could hear a couple guys working elsewhere in the house, calling out to one another above the whine of their electrical tools. Today the house lay utterly silent, and the still air seemed thick and oppressive.

From the marble-floored foyer she took the hallway on the left, the one the work crew had dubbed The Forbidden Corridor. The gallery lay behind the locked French doors, an unseen mystery behind papered mullions.

She stared at this feeble barrier for a long moment, then reached out and ripped the paper from her side of the door. Decades of dust lay thick on the panes of glass between the mullions—those that were still intact, that was. The pane nearest the door handle had been broken long years past, and it was small effort to punch through the paper on the other side and unlock the door. Obviously, only respect for Lon Harris had kept people out.

Following the beam into the gloom of the gallery, Rachael stepped over dark shadowy debris. She stopped to shine the light around the ruins of the once-magnificent corridor. The decaying remains of heavy velvet drapes hung from tarnished brass rods just under the high ceiling. The brackets of some had broken free from their moorings, spilling velvet puddles on the ruined parquet floor. Some had fallen from only one side, the drapes obscuring filth-caked oil portraits on the walls behind them.

Her toe caught a fallen rod, sending her stumbling. She clutched at the wall to catch her balance and tripped over the pooling curtain at her feet. Grabbing for whatever she could find to keep her balance, a rending tear as she tumbled painfully to the floor told her she had found the least effective stabilizer: a rotting velvet curtain. The flashlight spun away and came to rest aimed at the wall. She could almost hear Geoffrey: *Are you one of those people things tend to happen around?* and had to chuckle.

The chuckle died as she looked up and saw what was now visible at the edge of the beam of light: the gilt corner of an ornately carved mirror.

"Cool!" she exclaimed happily, climbing to her feet and brushing dust and debris from her jeans. Her knee throbbed painfully, and she must have whacked her face on something because her cheek felt swollen and bruised.

She picked her way across the wide corridor to the mirror. The light behind her came from one side, so she was able to see herself more clearly than if it had been directly behind her.

The silver backing had been corrupted by time and neglect, leaving her with a splotchy visage. Rachael didn't mind; she could see enough of her face to wipe away smudges of dirt and check for damage to her cheekbone. Other than a splotch of rosy red and the corrugated imprint of the curtain rod with which she had made impact, she appeared to have sustained no serious injuries.

"What are you doing in here?"

The voice echoed through the wing as a hand fell unexpectedly on Rachael's shoulder. Rachael screamed and whirled to find a stranger looming behind her. A gaping hole in the wall—a door-sized portrait of the fair-haired Fotheringham patriarch swung carelessly open on silent hinges—showed how he had snuck up on her.

Lon had warned her about traipsing through the Manor on her own. Geoffrey had made her promise not to. She had honored neither, and now found herself facing the very trouble over which they had worried. Panicked, she pressed against the crumbling plaster wall behind her, seeking an escape that didn't exist.

He stood mostly in shadow, his back to her flashlight, but she thought an impatient scowl marked his features. "I'm not going to hurt you. No one is supposed to be in here. Lon Harris has the door locked for a very good reason." He gestured at the debris strewn across the floor of the gallery.

"I know," she replied with a rueful grimace.

Careful footsteps brought him closer, and he stepped around her so the reflection of the flashlight beam lit his face. He was old enough to be her father but handsome nonetheless, his black hair holding glints of silver, crow's feet just beginning to appear at the corners of his ice-blue eyes. He looked familiar.

"I thought I knew everyone working at the house, but I don't believe we've met." Rachael cast a nervous glance at the door behind him. She had not failed to notice he had placed himself between her and her only avenue of escape.

"I'm off-hours security," he said easily. "And you are...?"

"Rachael Payne, the interior designer working on the house."

"Ah, the famous Rachael Payne," he murmured with a broad grin. "Yes. I've heard of you. My name is Alexander. You can call me Alex."

"Geoffrey didn't mention hiring off-hours security."

"He didn't. Lon Harris arranged it."

"He didn't mention it either."

"Nevertheless, here I am. And here you are, clearly trespassing where you shouldn't be, which means I haven't done my job very well. What brought you here tonight, Rachael Payne? Curiosity or sheer defiance of Geoffrey Windsor's orders not to explore alone?"

"Why should I be defiant?" Rachael lifted a shoulder in a casual shrug. She glanced over his shoulder, gauging the distance and the amount of debris between her and the door. She could run for it; she might make it…if she didn't trip over something.

"Perhaps the unexpected introduction to a fiancée you didn't know he had," Alexander said slyly. "You hid it well; I don't think anyone but Geoffrey noticed. And me, of course."

"You were watching?" Her humiliation was complete.

"Sometimes I can't sleep because of all the banging and whizzing and whirring. I use the servants' passages to move around so I'm not seen, because Lon didn't tell anyone about hiring me. He didn't want anyone laughing at him; they don't think anyone would come into the Manor to steal anything because of its reputation."

"And what do you think?" Rachael took a casual step away from the wall. If she could move slowly and carefully under the guise of exploring, she could pick her way to the door and be off like a shot through the vacant foyer.

"I think you'd fall on your face before you made it three steps, Rachael. If you'd like to leave the gallery, I'd be happy to escort you safely to the door. You don't have to run from me."

Color flooded her cheeks. "I wasn't…I meant…"

"You *were*, and I know what you meant." He smiled indulgently, like a tolerant uncle catching a favored niece in a harmless lie. "I think they're right. No one would steal anything from the Manor. No one wants to come here — even the workers are reluctant."

"I'm not reluctant."

His smile bloomed, radiant in his handsome, weathered face. "You are the rare exception, my dear. Now, you shouldn't be here — but since you are, would you like a tour of the rest of this wing, or would you rather I escort you to the gallery door?"

She cast a longing glance toward the darkened end of the gallery, and then glanced at the door to the foyer. "Geoffrey's going to be really angry when he finds out, isn't he?"

"Yes...*if* he finds out. But if you'll promise me you'll never come into the gallery again, I'll promise I won't tell him you were here. I can fix the paper and no one will ever know of your transgression."

"I should go back to the foyer." He was, after all, a stranger, and a dangerous looking one. But her eyes strayed again toward the unexplored wing.

"But you don't want to," he guessed. "Then I say in for a penny, in for a pound. You might as well satisfy your curiosity and take my offer for the tour. You have my word you are safe."

Rachael arched a brow. "The word of a stranger? I wonder how many similar assurances were given by Robert Yates and Gary Ridgeway."

His smile faltered. "And how many Washington State serial murderers have you heard of named Alexander?"

"None that I can think of, but it's impossible to research at the moment."

"Suit yourself." Alexander shrugged. "If you'll stay here, I'll get your flashlight for you and you can be on your way."

He picked his way across the room and stooped to retrieve her light. Rachael sent a wistful look at the dark wing beyond him.

"A tour, you said?"

"Yes."

"Of the hidden passages as well as this wing?"

"That can be arranged."

He aimed the beam at the dark floor between them, lighting her way, and offered his arm. Rachael walked into the darkness to take it.

(Correspondence from Cody Schaefer to his wife, Renée)

Date: April 17, 2009
To: Renee Schaefer [renee_schaefer@msn.com]
From: Cody Schaefer [encrypted]
Subject: (blank)

Renée,
I am writing this from the SeaTac airport—I am on my way home. My flight leaves about an hour. I wish I could say this is a good thing, but I can't. I will explain when I get there.

I will have a short stop at the office for debriefing—Carlos is expecting me—and then I'll be home.

I love you.
Cody

THE TEMPTATION OF CODY SCHAEFER
Wednesday, April 15, 2009

Caitlyn shot an apprehensive look at her husband and rushed on. "As I said, I don't mean to be indelicate, and with all the stories circulating about your husband and Melody, I don't blame you at all for feeling defensive and humiliated. I'd like to help with the situation as much as I can."

"No one can help."

Trent made a move as though to reach out to her, evaluated the expression on her face, and reconsidered. "We understand why you feel that way. But you don't believe the rumors, do you?"

"No," Kim replied woodenly. She wanted to be anywhere but here, even back to that March day on her porch, hearing Melody spill her vile news. "But it doesn't change the fact that it's Aaron's word against hers, and since she's the most vocal about it, people believe her."

"Not everyone. Not even a lot of the people she runs around with." At Kim's arched brow, Trent added, "She's not in our circle of friends. You may have seen her talking to us on occasion, but it's because we have some mutual friends, and we didn't want to be rude."

Caitlyn made a face. "I think her husband's death might have knocked a screw loose. She came in the bar a couple weeks ago. To Trent and me, it seemed she was feeling us out to see if we knew anything about voodoo."

Taryn barked out a laugh and clapped her hand over her mouth as all eyes turned to her. "Sorry. But I don't think Fred's death knocked her screws loose. I think *he* knocked her screws loose with his heavy hand."

"Abuse is not a laughing matter, Taryn," Kim admonished.

"And after what happened in this town, you know black magic is real."

"I know. I'm sorry. But...Melody Olmstead, a voodoo queen? Please."

"Barney Bellamy said he saw her coming out of her and Fred's old house out by the old logging road," Caitlyn put in.

"Could be reminiscing," Taryn stubbornly responded.

"She hated Fred," Kim reminded her. "He beat her, drank all their money, let her and Jared live in poverty. No, it's not reminiscing."

"Revenge?" Taryn wondered. True, Ron wasn't responsible for the death of Melody's son, but the reversal of the death spell against Ron's brother had claimed Fred Olmstead's life.

"What?" said her companions in unison.

"Revenge," Taryn repeated. She flicked an uneasy glance at Kim. "I don't know. I could be way off target. And I don't know if I'm supposed to say anything about it—well, at least he didn't say I couldn't," she said, more to herself than to them.

Kim felt the knot of anxiety—that new constant companion of hers—tighten, and she wanted to yank the words out of her friend's mouth. *What now, what-freaking-now?* She didn't think she could stand any more surprises where that woman was concerned.

"She came in to the greenhouse a few days ago, wanted to talk to Ron but he wouldn't talk to her. Her whole demeanor was more like a shakedown than a stalking. I don't really think it's about...you know...being with him. I think it's more about revenge for what happened five years ago."

Trent and Caitlyn exchanged a mystified glance. "I don't understand," Trent said.

"Melody's husband was part of a black magic circle that my husband's family had a hand in disbanding. Fred Olmstead died as a result of the investigation. She blames Ron for the death of her son Jared because Jared was dating the daughter of one of Ron's close friends, and Ron's disapproval of that relationship made them seek out secluded areas to be together. A...wild dog attacked them both, and Jared was killed."

Caitlyn's eyes went wide. "Oh, how awful!"

"So much for leaving Louisiana to get away from the witchcraft," Trent grumbled.

Taryn's brows shot into her hair, but she only said, "The Circle is no more. A bunch of people were arrested; others conveniently converted to Christianity. It's not a problem here anymore."

"Now you're wrong there," Caitlyn said seriously. "Just because it's been rooted out once doesn't mean it can't spring up again, especially if people aren't on their guard against it."

"Melody's been seen collecting certain...herbs and wild plants," Trent put in. "And apparently she has quite a garden."

"At her apartment?" Taryn interjected, puzzled again.

"No. She's been going out to some old shack in the woods, across the river and some distance back in the woods from the old mills. She's resurrected a garden at some old house there. I followed her one—Kim, are you all right?"

Kim took several deep breaths to banish the spots that suddenly danced before her eyes. Trent's voice seem to come from a long way away.

"Sarah Bennett's cottage," she murmured, more to herself than to the Baudelaires or Taryn. "I can't believe I never asked about her—I never even *thought* about her."

Taryn's hand pushed at the back of Kim's head, trying to force it between Kim's knees. "Put your head down. I think you're going to pass out."

"No, I'm okay," Kim said faintly, ducking out from under her friend's hand. "Sarah Bennett—what happened to her?"

"It was assumed she left with Caleb, or that she became one of his victims," Taryn answered. "Funny...I hadn't thought of her at all since Scott's funeral."

"Yes, funny," Kim mused uneasily. "I hadn't thought of her either until just now. Not once. It's as though she ceased existing with the Wyckham House."

"But the Wyckham House didn't cease existing. It's over on the Washington coast."

"Wait, wait!" Caitlyn called out. "Are you saying someone secretly moved an entire *house*?"

"It appears so, but I do wonder..." Kim left the thought

hanging and turned back to Trent. "You said you followed her to a shack in the woods. Did you go through a clearing before you reached the shack, a clearing with a stagnant pond nearby?"

"Yeah!" Trent exclaimed excitedly, and then amended, "Well, there was a clearing, but I didn't exactly go through it. I went around it, keeping to the cover of the woods so Melody wouldn't see me. I—call me crazy, but I didn't want to walk through the clearing. It seemed like I would be too exposed, too noticeable, and that seemed...dangerous somehow. It was kind of creepy; no grass grows there, and there weren't any animals around."

For a terrible minute her breath froze in her chest and vision grayed. She thought if any more blood left her face, she would become transparent. Her eyes closed, and she offered up a silent plea. *Oh, it can't be! For the love of everything holy, it can't be!* She stood abruptly.

"I have to go."

Trent and Caitlyn looked alarmed. Taryn simply looked resigned.

"We didn't mean to—" Trent began, worried, but she barely heard him.

"Thank you for the bar, and thank you for talking with me."

She shook their hands, all the while leading them toward the break room door. Her mind had already abandoned them, however, and had flashed forward to what she had to do. She had to go, had to see for herself...

Taryn trailed behind, making apologies and muttering dark opinions about brain damage caused by hormonal imbalances. When they reached the truck, Kim held her hand out for the keys.

"No way. Not until you tell me what you're up to."

"I'm going to the Wyckham House."

Taryn threw her hands up in exasperation. "The Wyckham House is *gone*, Kim! You can't live in the past anymore! What happened was terrible, horrible, scandalous, but it is *over* and you need to get over it now!"

Kim grabbed the front of her coat and yanked her forward, her voice a vehement hiss. "Don't you understand, Taryn? It is *never* over. The Wyckham House didn't go anywhere, because whatever lives in it is everywhere, all the time. And the shack in the woods behind it — it's Sarah Bennett's. And Sarah Bennett...oh God, why didn't I remember? Sarah Bennett is the devil."

A helpless look of incredulity claimed Taryn's face. She could tell her friend didn't want to doubt her but could find no way to believe her.

"*The* devil?" Taryn repeated cautiously.

"*The* devil, *a* devil, what does it matter? The point is, I didn't remember. No, it's not even really that; it's like the knowledge was there, but just...too unimportant to consciously think about it."

"I know that was a very frightening experience, Kim, but - "

"You weren't there, Taryn. Caleb made a bargain with her - with *it* - and I was the price. But I escaped." Her voice dropped to a whisper, her mind hurtling back to the awful day Caleb had abducted her, the awful day Scott had died. "And so he paid the price."

"You're scaring me."

"Give me the keys."

"No! No one's going anywhere in the dark. If what you're saying is true, there's nothing that can be done tonight. It can keep until morning." Kim opened her mouth to argue, but Taryn held firm. "I mean it. And if I have any inkling you'll try to go tonight, I'll tell Ron."

Her jaw clenched. "That's a low blow."

"I'll do what's necessary to make sure you don't break your fool neck. What about those babies, huh? What about your husband — if something happens to you, you're going to leave him mired in guilt and regret? Why not just stab him through the heart right now, Kimberly? It'd be kinder!"

Kim sucked in a shocked breath, but the ferocious look on Taryn's face stopped her words on her tongue. Her hand drifted to her temple, trying to rub away an impending migraine. A rolling wave of nausea made her release Taryn and rub her hand across her stomach. Anxiety always took her in the gut; she didn't think she'd had a nausea-free day since Melody's Olmstead's visit.

"All right," she gave in wearily. "All right. Just take me home, okay? I don't feel so well."

Taryn looked suspicious of her sudden capitulation. "We'll go tomorrow. I promise."

Kim nodded, but she couldn't keep her worried gaze from straying in the direction of the clearing the Wyckham House had occupied.

Not again, she prayed. *Dear God, not again!*

ℭ

Cody made the drive back from Port Townsend after a not-so-pleasant ride on the ferry, troubled to his soul. His meeting with Geoffrey Windsor had been enlightening only because it gave him a good idea of Windsor's state of mind and opinion of the mansion he'd purchased. It also had given Cody a glimpse of occurrences inside the house that he might otherwise never have heard about. Man-sized bat-like creatures, indeed.

It had been more than a week since he'd left his message in the dust for his brother, a message he doubted would be answered. Did he truly believe Caleb lived in the attic of Bayview Manor? Truthfully, he didn't know what he believed anymore.

As he rolled into Forks proper, he slowed and started to turn into the parking lot of his motel. Making a split-second decision, he suddenly goosed the accelerator and shot past the parking lot entrance, heading the car toward Heron Bay. The only way to get the answers he wanted—needed—was to go to Bayview Manor and see for himself.

Darkness had fallen on the town—as well as a frigid spring rain—and only the glow of a work light left on by one of the construction crew lit the Manor. Cody thought he might have a problem gaining entrance to the house, but a careless worker had left the kitchen door unlocked. He stepped noiselessly inside, drew in a deep breath to steady his nerves, and crept deeper into the maze of rooms.

The stairs creaked under his feet as he climbed one side of the horseshoe staircase. Onward and upward, he followed the yellow beam of the compact flashlight he always carried with him. Down dark corridors, up stairwells filled with coalescing black shadows, and finally up the attic steps into the stygian room beyond. His beam cut a narrow swath through the unrelenting gloom, but

Cody's step did not falter as he sidled through the cramped aisles of clutter to the steamer trunk.

He had never hesitated to do what he must no matter how frightening the situation, and he did not vacillate now. He raised the beam and shone it down at the flat top of the uppermost trunk.

Dust lay in the lines and curves of his words like snow in old footprints. But the reply below was sharply etched, as though he had arrived only moments after his brother had left his mark.

TOO LATE FOR ME. GO HOME. PLEASE.

The trembling in his hand transmitted itself to the flashlight, and the beam wavered, making the words appear to dance. A stealthy footstep broke the hush, and Cody whirled, the flashlight beam held strategically at eye level, nearly blinding the girl who had edged up behind him. She held an arm up before her eyes as a shield, but didn't seem to be alarmed.

"Who are you?" he demanded. He crossed the small distance between them and grasped her arm, yanking it away from her eyes. She didn't flinch, but smiled engagingly.

"Emily."

"Denny's Emily?"

Her eyes narrowed, and her smile slipped. "I'm no one's Emily," she said coldly. "But I met a young man named Denny. He was interested in the attic, too."

"What are you doing here? This is private property."

The fullness of her smile came like the sun. "What are *you* doing here?" She giggled. "I believe Denny and I played this game too. Let's save valuable time, shall we? I heard about the house, I came in to see what it's like. Unfortunately, I have nowhere to stay, so I simply hid up here until everyone left. Now it's your turn." And she waited expectantly, her eyes bright and expectant.

"I'm a federal agent, and I have permission from the owner to access the house any time I deem necessary."

She chuckled. "My story is much more bohemian and...well, interesting."

"The truth is rarely glamorous," he replied.

Emily chuckled despite his veiled insinuation that she had lied. She backed up against the support pillar behind her, her hands clasped at the small of her back. The motion served to make her flowered print dress stretch snugly over her graceful curves. She wasn't the first one to try to use her body to distract him from his duty, but he'd never been in such a situation in so secluded a location. Secluded meant dangerous.

"As you know, I'm Emily. And you are...?"

An idiot, Cody thought, but he said politely, "Nice to meet you," and moved away from the steamer trunk to leave.

As he passed her, Emily stepped directly in front of him. His momentum brought him into full-frontal contact with her curvaceous body; he felt a jolt of shock like electricity and took an immediate step backward. Emily followed.

"Do you have a name, Mr. Federal Agent?"

"Cody," he replied, swallowing over a lump in his throat. He took another step back, and again she followed. "No closer, Emily. This is highly improper."

She pouted, and he thought he'd never seen more alluring lips. He was in serious trouble.

"Awww, are you afraid of me, Cody?" Emily grabbed the lapels of his coat, tangling her hands into the fabric.

"This is against our code of conduct, and I'm a happily married man."

"Oh, they *all* say that."

She had backed him against a large armoire. Cody wondered how she'd managed it; he always knew his ground, never made a move without it being carefully calculated and flawlessly executed.

"Let go of my jacket, Emily." But he didn't sound commanding; he sounded desperate.

She chuckled again, and he became suddenly aware of how very close she stood. Her breath fanned his face, smelling of spearmint. Her body pressed close, speaking volumes on desires fulfilled and fantasies incarnate.

"Tell me no again, Cody, but say it like you mean it," she murmured against his lips.

He brought his hands to her hips to push her away as she sucked his lower lip between her teeth. A wicked lust reared its dragonish head, stealing breath and honor alike. Emily sensed his capitulation and pressed against him like a second skin, her mouth a fountain of poisonous passion, a carnal narcotic that drugged him and dragged him toward a yawning abyss of ruination and despair. Cody grasped at reason, that stoic rope of salvation, and found only the tenebrous veil of his momentary, wanton craving.

Timeless moments later, how long he would never know, a polite cough from the shadows delivered him from Emily's sorcerous embrace. He wrenched himself away from her, drinking in sanity like air, horrified by this unheralded turn of events. *Renée...oh God, Renée!* He covered his face with despairing hands. Vicious triumph filled Emily's smile, and he had the sudden certainty that if she showed her teeth, they would be pointed like the fangs of a viper. She sidled a pace closer.

"That's enough."

With a mutinous pout, she backed away from Cody. "He could have said no at any time," she responded curtly.

"I think you know he didn't stand a chance."

"No, he didn't," she agreed with a malicious smile of satisfaction. "They're so fun to play with."

"Leave us alone. I have things to discuss with my brother."

Petulance stamped her features, but she backed even farther away from Cody. As she melted into the dark shadows behind her, he could have sworn he saw her shift to an amorphous shape his brain couldn't quite grasp.

"Caleb."

"No joyful reunion scene, please," came Caleb's dry rejoinder. "And no thanks necessary. She's only one of the lesser demons; you should have been able to ward her off yourself."

"It was an unanticipated move," Cody admitted.

"But aren't you supposed to be constantly on your guard?" Caleb's voice held the impression of a sardonically arched brow.

"Yes. I failed, all right? Come out of the shadows and let's talk face-to-face."

As urbane as ever, his brother replied drolly, "And get within reach of you? I don't think so." He let a pregnant pause grow between them. "How did you know I was here?"

"Kimberly has seen you in her dreams."

"Ah yes," Caleb murmured. "The beautiful dreamer. I do believe she harbors an element of attraction to me—like most women toward a dangerous, forbidden man. She lets that attraction convince her I have some redeeming qualities."

Cody frowned. He'd always detested Caleb's circular way of discussion. "Why is that such a misguided belief? I've always believed you could be redeemed."

His brother barked out a full-throated laugh of genuine amusement. "I'm so far down the road to hell there's no redemption for me now. That's why I told you to go home. You're wasting your time."

"I'm not here to evangelize you," Cody snapped.

"Then if you're here to bring me to justice, Mr. Federal Agent, you're equally wasting your time on that venture. I am both captive and jailer in this godforsaken house. There are no doors or windows for me to exit."

Cody took a step closer to the voice in the shadows, keeping the beam of his flashlight respectfully lowered. "You expect me to believe you can't leave?"

"Yes, it's one for Ripley's, isn't it? Go home while you can; you can neither save me nor stop what's been set into motion. The battle for a soul."

"Geoffrey Windsor's."

Caleb laughed harshly. "You *are* priceless, Cody. No, not Geoffrey Windsor's. He already belongs to them by the mere fact of his indifference to God. The fight is always for the believers."

"Rachael Payne," Cody whispered, appalled.

"She's special, that one," Caleb murmured almost to himself. "Her faith is strong but she's untested. She should be relatively easy to break."

"Maybe you're underestimating her strength."

"The curse of an optimist: always overestimating. At any rate, Cody, you can't stop it. We're like chess pieces on a game board, moved by dark and light. Sometimes it's just easier to fade into the blackness than fight for the light."

"You choose condemnation over redemption because it's *easier*?"

"If I came to Him with the blood of my victims on my hands, do you honestly think He would take me in?"

"Yes."

Caleb fell silent for so long Cody feared he'd slipped noiselessly away. Then his voice came again, quiet and deep, the voice of a forsaken soul on the brink of a vacuous eternity.

"I'd like a favor." Cody had the impression of movement in the shadows, as though Caleb had raised his hand to his face, and heard an inhaled breath. "Tell me about Kimberly."

Cody stiffened, his head cocked warily. "Why? I know you had a fascination with her. Do you think you're in love with her?"

"Do you honestly believe I have the capacity to love anyone?" Caleb asked wearily. "I ask because I could swear I sensed her here. Do you believe the dream world is so close to the waking world that one can reach out and touch any moment in time, any soul in the world of slumber?"

Again that odd motion, as though he moved something in his hand to his nose. "Lilacs," he murmured, not waiting for Cody's reply. "I always remember her when I smell lilacs. And I smelled them in here just the other day."

Cody watched his brother's silhouette, as much as he could see of it in the dim glow. Defeat slumped Caleb's shoulders, and a visible aura of fatigue lay over him like an iron cloak. The truth came to him, incredible but undeniable: perhaps Caleb didn't harbor any affection for Kimberly, but something she had said or done lay heavily upon his soul, had changed something inside him, possibly resurrected some dead part of his conscience.

"She's well," Cody said quietly. "She married Aaron and they have two children — twins. She still dreams — prophetic dreams, I mean." He paused. "She is happy."

Caleb stood with head bowed for a long moment, and then he stepped from the shadows. "That's good. But she should have pleasant dreams, not dreams of me."

Cody reached out a hand to grab his brother's arm. At the touch of their flesh, an electrical shock buzzed up his arm, throwing him backward. He rubbed his other hand up his arm, soothing the persistent, painful buzz along his nerve endings.

"Go home, Cody," Caleb whispered. "Go home to Renée and Aaron and Kimberly. There is nothing for you here but devastation and sorrow. You can't save me, and you can't save Rachael Payne. That leaves only you to rescue."

"I can't run out like a coward."

"Do you think Emily is the worst that is planned for you? Save yourself, Cody; you're the only one you *can* save." His ice-blue eyes shifted to look over Cody's shoulder. "And you'd better do it now."

Cody turned with trepidation and beheld a positively harrowing sight. The grappling shadows disjoined and became moving beings, individual but alike, androgynous, silhouettes of caliginous light, exquisitely repulsive and hideously sublime. Fear gelled in his veins. He'd spent his life bandying about the word "demon" but had never completely understood what it meant.

The sin-seekers coiled around him. The pull of their enchantment was a tug at his soul a million times stronger than any temptation he'd ever experienced.

"Oh my God," he said weakly.

The demon who'd worn Emily Matthews' appearance laughed mockingly. "You'll have to do better than that," she hissed.

But although his voice was faint, his faith proved infinite. Reality blurred, time sluiced, and Caleb's sorrowful face swirled away. Spat out of Bayview Manor like phlegm, Cody lay in the numbing rain on the lawn outside the devil's mansion, sobbing his relief and shame into the ruined lawn.

April 8, 2009

Dear Ethan,

It finally happened — I met someone that I could love. He's The One — the one who makes my heart both race and skip a beat, the one whose smile steals my breath and blinds my eyes to every other man.

There's only one catch: he's already engaged to be married to someone else. When we were kids and you always told me I would find a wonderful man who would adore me forever, you forgot to mention that love is difficult, full of deceit and selfishness and obstacles. Maybe you didn't know.

I don't know what to do anymore. I like his fiancée very much. She's very lovely, a little on the quiet side, and very friendly. So that makes for difficult choices: fight for him and hurt a woman I like and respect — or walk away and shatter my own heart.

I need you, Ethan. I need my big brother here, not in some commune or wherever you are, where they don't let me speak to you, where you feel you must return my letters unopened. Family should be together. Haven't I been alone long enough? Haven't you?

Please…I'm begging you. Come home.

Your loving sister,
Rachael

TANGLED WEB
Saturday, April 15, 2009

The skies had opened and let loose a malicious deluge. Geoffrey cruised into Heron Bay at the sedate speed of twenty-five miles an hour, and even that seemed reckless as the car bogged through deep puddles of rain water that had collected in the dips in the road.

The crawling pace of the car gave him the time he needed to decide which way to go: left, up ahead a mile or so, would take him to Bayview Manor, where he stood an excellent chance of finding Rachael even though it was the weekend; straight ahead would take him to her apartment; a right two blocks up would take him into Heron Bay proper, where he was reasonably sure he could find the Church of Christ and Rachael's pastor, Hugh MacGregor. He didn't know whether MacGregor would consent to exorcise his house, but it never hurt to ask.

Exorcism. He wanted to laugh, wished desperately that he could. It sounded ludicrous. But there was no doubt in his mind that what walked in the Manor was far worse than ghosts or poltergeists.

He cranked the wheel to the right, heading into the town center. A spreading puddle where the street drain was clogged made the car weave and swerve toward the curb. He clutched the wheel tightly and wrestled to keep the car in his lane. A gust of wind threw rain onto the windshield in a thick shower and he braked, slowing to fifteen miles per hour. He was beginning to wonder if he should start building an ark just to be on the safe side.

Ah, there, up ahead—a whitewashed chapel, complete with steeple and bell, a sign at the street proclaiming Geoffrey had reached his destination: Heron Bay Church of Christ. One car squatted in the parking lot, a late-model Ford station-wagon that he hoped belonged to his quarry. He parked beside it and dashed up the steps to the double doors. Once inside, he hesitated, dripping on the carpet in the lobby. What *did* one call a pastor when one wasn't indoctrinated into the church?

He only had a moment to contemplate that question before footsteps sounded in the hallway to his right. He turned to find a white-haired man approaching and recognized him from Rachael's description. He was somewhat surprised to find the man of God in faded blue jeans, scuffed sneakers, and a sweatshirt with the Ghirardelli Chocolate logo emblazoned on the front.

Reaching into his pathetically limited knowledge of theology, Geoffrey gestured to the shirt and remarked, "The spirit is willing but the flesh is weak?"

MacGregor glanced down, startled, and laughed. "Actually, how can one *not* believe in God after having eaten chocolate?"

"I see you share Rachael Payne's affection for it."

MacGregor nodded. "Oh yes. Rachael and I alone could keep Godiva, Ghirardelli, and Lindt in business. You're Geoffrey Windsor." He offered his hand.

Geoffrey shook it. "And you're Pastor Hugh MacGregor?"

"Guilty as charged. Was there something in particular I could help you with, Mr. Windsor, or were you just checking to make sure God really *did* say He wouldn't destroy the earth with water again?"

"Did He? That's a comfort," Geoffrey said sincerely. "I didn't come about floods, but I *do* have a particular question. And while we're at it, please call me Geoffrey."

"All right, Geoffrey," MacGregor said agreeably, guiding him toward another set of double doors. "Let's have a seat in the sanctuary, and you can tell me all about it."

The pastor seated them in the front, near the raised dais where the pulpit stood. Strategic planning, no doubt—the distance would be intimidating to one's flight instinct, and the pastor's Bible lay open on the dais at the foot of the pulpit, within easy reach should he need it for reference.

MacGregor got them coffee and claimed a chair to Geoffrey's left, leaving one seat in between them for comfort.

"I believe we are ready for serious discussion, Geoffrey. Let's have it."

"I want you to exorcise my house," Geoffrey stated bluntly. MacGregor choked as his coffee went down the wrong pipe.

"I beg your pardon, Geoffrey. I thought you said you want me to exorcise your house."

Geoffrey's jaw clenched. "You heard correctly."

MacGregor rubbed his chin thoughtfully. "I think we should take this discussion into my office. It's rather delicate of nature."

Geoffrey agreed, and followed the pastor through the church to his office. MacGregor left the door open so he could hear if anyone who came into the church.

"Let's start from the beginning. In order for an exorcism to be warranted, you first have to determine there is demonic activity."

"I think that could be determined."

The pastor sighed. "It isn't as easy as saying 'People have said it's haunted for decades', Geoffrey. And you must understand, exorcisms are mostly a thing of the past. It's a rarity to find anyone who will do one these days, regardless of the circumstances. Which brings me to the heart of the matter: what *are* the circumstances?"

Geoffrey told him everything, and when his words dried up, MacGregor looked visibly shaken.

"After speaking with Michael St. Claire, I figured you — being a man of God and all — would be the best person to bring this to."

Hugh MacGregor's expression was momentarily horrified before he caught himself and arranged a carefully neutral expression on his face. But Geoffrey had already seen, and he wasn't comforted. If MacGregor wouldn't — *couldn't* — deal with Bayview Manor, what was he going to do?

"It isn't as simple as going into the house and sprinkling holy water here and there, praying in Latin. And it isn't something I would be able to do alone. I would have to call in the whole congregation for corporate prayer. I may even have to call in all the churches in our area to pray. When you go up against the enemy, Geoffrey, you can't go off half-cocked, or he'll chew you up and spit you out."

Now it was Geoffrey's turn to look horrified. "I don't exactly want to be known as the weird rich guy who had his house exorcised."

"Bad for business, yes, I know," Hugh commented expressionlessly.

Geoffrey waved off that comment with a slight frown of irritation. "I don't care what people think of *me*. Knowing how the world is today, it would probably drive business to me in droves. But the circles my mother and my sister move in would be vicious."

"I understand. But I can't just go in and utter a magic phrase and expect it to work. There has to be awesome prayer covering, confession, repentance, faith." He paused. "I know you believe in the possibility of demons, because you're here telling me you do. And I know if you believe in demons, you must at least entertain the possibility of the existence of God."

"I always have."

"But that's not the same thing as faith, and it's not the same thing as salvation."

Ah, here comes the pitch, Geoffrey thought with a good measure of cynicism. He had been through it with Rachael once; she had brought up the subject of his salvation — or rather, lack of — with a charming combination of candor and tact, and as quickly and casually she had brought it up, she had dropped it and moved on to something else, leaving him wondering if he had just been the victim of some weird kind of hit-and-run evangelism. She hadn't brought it up since, but he hadn't forgotten the things she had said, either.

"I'm not sure how successful we'd be, Geoffrey. Frankly I would be more comfortable with this if I could walk through the house first."

"How about right now?"

The pastor checked his watch. "Wish I could, but I'm taking my wife to lunch. Maybe we could meet at the Manor in a couple of hours?"

"Sure," Geoffrey agreed, rising to his feet and shaking Hugh's hand. "That should give me just enough time to convince Rachael that she shouldn't be in that house."

MacGregor snorted. "If you think so, you need more than an exorcism, my friend. You need a reality check."

ᚼ

"The gallery isn't the only thing in this wing," Alexander explained, his voice taking on the instructional tone of a tour guide, "although many people believe it is. The gallery actually is a long, wide corridor with doors leading into the hidden passages."

"And the passages were used by servants to move through the house unseen?"

"Yes. But not only the servants used them. The family and guests used them as well, usually to engage unseen in...er...liaisons."

She grinned at his attempt to tastefully explain. "Can we go in them?"

"Yes, but we'll save that for last." He smiled at her eagerness to explore the forbidden wing. "If you look at this wing from the outside, you'll see long, narrow hallways with windows that run the length of the gallery but really have no function. The Fotheringhams used them as sunrooms for exotic plants. I hear there were so many plants packed into them that at one time they were barely passable."

They reached the other end of the gallery, capped with a set of French doors. These weren't papered over. Years of grime clouded the few remaining panes of glass and the ruined floor at their base bore a sprawling stain of bloody history.

"It never comes out," Alexander said, his eyes following hers to the stain. "The floors were refinished when the last tenants moved in. Within a week the stain was back. That was when they moved out."

"So they believed in ghosts," Rachael deduced.

"No. They believed in worse."

He nudged the doors open and motioned her through. "This is the most interesting wing of the house, so it's a shame Geoffrey Windsor isn't working on it. It's much less practical, however, so I can't fault him his decision."

"Less practical? How so?"

"There's a sunroom, a library, a conservatory, and a swimming pool. All recreational space but nothing necessary."

"A swimming pool!" Rachael exclaimed. "I didn't know the

Manor had a pool."

He smiled at her enthusiasm. "The Manor has a lot of things you don't know about," he murmured mysteriously. "Shall we?"

The pool, naturally, was on the main floor at the back of the wing, surrounded by floor to ceiling windows that had once let in the sunlight and provided a magnificent view of the gardens and the ocean beyond. The sunroom ran the length of the wing between the pool and the gallery with an open ceiling to all three floors. Treacherous wrought iron staircases wound their way upward, and iron catwalks provided access to the many plant hooks suspended from the ceiling for those brave enough — or stupid enough — to risk their dilapidated moorings.

The library and the conservatory sat side-by-side across the hallway from the sunroom. The library ladders had fallen into disrepair, rungs hanging by rotting dowels or missing completely. The once lustrous paneling was stained and warped, and the shelves bore no evidence of the books they once held.

"Upstairs are guest apartments, but the stairs are impassible — a supporting column has collapsed, so I don't want to take you up them. It's too much of a risk to your safety."

Rachael was disappointed but not overly so. The forbidden wing had already revealed wondrous secrets to her eyes alone — and, of course, Alexander's.

"It's marvelous. Once Geoffrey has the work completed here, this will be breathtaking."

"Indeed," he replied. "Now for the best part — the passageways. We can reach the upper floors using them." He strode unerringly to a wall of shelves and pushed on the outer frame. To her surprise, it gave an inch or two inward, and then sprang back out. He swung it open on noiseless hinges. She guessed he had oiled them so he could move about the house undetected.

"Stay close to me so you can see the light. It's pitch-black in here without it." He stepped into the passageway, and Rachael followed unhesitatingly.

"We'll go this way, through the closed wing. We'll end up in the gallery." He started forward, catching her hand as he went. "I've cleared away most of the debris but it's still a little dusty. I don't exactly have a vacuum cleaner and the electricity to run it."

"It's fine. I don't mind."

The passage ran the length of the gallery, with doors leading into the gallery, conservatory, the library, and the pool room. At either end, narrow staircases provided access to the second and third floors. Rachael had no idea how long they explored the guest apartments on the top two stories. Each unique layout intrigued her, and she longed for a sketchpad.

At length, Alexander regretfully informed her they'd explored the very last suite and it was probably time he showed her to the gallery door. As they stepped back into the hidden hallway, Rachael noticed the outline of a door where the passage dead-ended.

"What's in there?" She stepped to the wall, tracing the outline of the door. It fitted into its frame so tightly she guessed it had either been pounded in or the wood had swelled to wedge it tight. Either way, they would not be gaining entrance today; there was no door knob, and they had no tools to break in—not that she would anyway without Geoffrey's permission.

"I'm not sure," Alexander said with a frown. "It looks like a doorway that's been blocked, but there's nowhere to go from here; we're at the end of the house. Maybe the builders used scrap to finish the passageways and had to fit a piece in."

"Perhaps so." No stranger to construction, Rachael knew this was a likely scenario. The passageways were hidden and for use mainly by the servants; the highest quality materials would not have been used to finish them.

She tagged behind Alexander down the hidden halls and narrow stairs until at last they stepped out from behind the portrait of Nathan Fotheringham. He escorted her to the door, a hand lightly cupping her elbow to catch her if she tripped.

"You've a cobweb in your hair," he said, reaching up to remove it.

"Oh. Thanks." She blushed.

"It was a definite pleasure, Rachael, and I hope your curiosity is satisfied. It would be best if you didn't venture in here again—if you were to be hurt, Mr. Windsor would be very unhappy."

"Yes, the insurance claim alone would give him nightmares,"

she replied drolly. She thrust out her hand and surprised, he shook it. "The pleasure was mine, Alex. Thank you for taking the time to show me the wing."

"Good day, Rachael," he said gently, and pulled the door closed behind him. She heard the rattle of paper and saw he was making an attempt to repair the damage she had done.

The squeak of the front door opening brought her head around, and she had taken a tentative step toward the concealing shadows of the room when Geoffrey stepped inside. He caught sight of her and stopped.

"Rachael, I need to talk to you." He glanced around, and then narrowed his eyes on her. "You're here alone?"

"I'm perfectly safe." With a nervous glance at the forbidden hallway, she swerved around him, heading to the front doors. He caught her arm and checked her forward motion.

"I need to talk to you, Rach. It's about the house."

"I really should be going, Geoffrey. I...have things to do."

"What things?" he challenged.

"Just...things."

His grip tightened, his fingers digging into her flesh. "We can't be in the house anymore. It's not safe."

She huffed out an impatient breath. "Please, let go of my arm. We shouldn't be here, all right—not alone."

He didn't seem to hear her. "I went to Hoquiam again today, tracked down a guy who'd warned one of Harris's crew not to have anything to do with this house. Guess who he is?"

"Geoffrey—"

"He's Joshua Fotheringham—one of the Fotheringham children who were in the house the night of the murders. Rach, he said—"

"You spoke to Joshua Fotheringham," she repeated flatly.

"Yes, I just said that. But get this—"

"He said he was Joshua Fotheringham, and you just believed him?"

"Well, why shouldn't I? Who would make up something like that?"

"All sorts of people."

He frowned. "What's wrong with you?"

"Oh, I don't know. Maybe it's the rain. Maybe it's crazy stories about missing heirs living in Hoquiam."

Rachael couldn't stop the bitchiness dripping from her tongue even as she was completely appalled by it. Geoffrey's eyes were wide in astonishment. He let his hand drop slowly from her arm.

"Or perhaps," her mouth raged on, even as her brain was frantically trying to find the emergency OFF switch, "it's that I asked several times who this mysterious Sonia was you kept mentioning, and you waved off the subject like it was a bothersome insect. Your own fiancée!"

Brilliant color flared along his cheekbones. "Now just a minute—"

"And then I find out when you introduce her. And after—after—"

"After what, Rachael?" His voice was dangerously soft.

Her own cheeks burned with color, and she said inanely, "I like Sonia. In fact, I like her a lot."

"So do I. Obviously."

She let out a growl of frustration. None of this was going well. She wanted to be smooth, sophisticated, the very picture of unconcern, but instead she sounded like a jealous shrew—and a delusional one, at that.

"I understand you're angry," Geoffrey said carefully, "although I have no idea why. That doesn't matter right now. What matters is this house. There are—things here, things that live here, things that belong here. And we don't. We have to abandon the project. We can't work here anymore."

Sudden fury blazed through her, consuming her patience and self-control. So it didn't matter why she was angry, did it? Perhaps it also didn't matter *how* angry she became. She rounded on him, and he recoiled from her fury.

"The house, the house, always the house! *There is nothing wrong with this house!*"

"Maybe you just can't see it!" he shouted back. "You're blind to it! You can't see the danger, and you won't admit someone else can."

"Danger?" she scoffed. "*What* danger? You have a case of the screaming meemies in the attic, hear a few hysterical stories, and that must mean the house is haunted."

"Oh, I see," he rejoined sardonically. "You're right and everyone else is wrong."

"Of course I'm right!" Her voice rose a dangerous octave. The anger flared like a wildfire in a strong wind, unreasonable, unwarranted, and beyond her ability to tame. "I'm not going to be banned from this house over a bunch of crybabies afraid of the boogeyman!"

"The job is over," he said coldly. "I will, of course, pay you the full amount of the contract. But I don't want you to set foot in this house again."

"Ban me and I'll sue you for breach of contract."

"You can't if I pay you."

Stop, Rachael! Just stop it! Get a grip! But that was the logical part of her mind speaking, and almost immediately her blazing anger silenced it. She stepped toward him, fury burning her vision red. Her finger stabbed at him as she spoke through clenched teeth.

"I'm going to finish this job, Geoffrey, and you're not going to stop me. So you'd better just stay out of my way."

"What the hell is the matter with you? Have you completely lost your mind?"

He caught her hand in mid-poke. She twisted her wrist, trying to free herself, at the same time he gave a sudden jerk on her arm to subdue her. The motion spun her around and smacked her against him.

The heat of his body against hers ignited a veritable firestorm of desire inside her. She crushed her mouth to his with bruising force, skipping the tentative exploration of a first kiss and going straight for clothes-removing passion. Explosive, inescapable, her need for him drove her farther and farther away from the moral bulwark Sonia Stockwell should have presented. She didn't care anymore about wrong or right; there was only longing, an insatiable yearning for this particular man.

Geoffrey's heart pounded frantically against her chest. His arms slid around her, anchoring her to him, his lips pressing frenzied kisses down her cheek to her throat. Rachael's head tipped back, her eyes opening to half-slits.

Alexander watched from a pane in the French door. His expression, hovering somewhere between disappointment and sorrow, was like a bucket of icy water dashed across her passion. Abruptly coming to her senses, Rachael wrenched herself from Geoffrey's arms and stumbled several paces away from him, covering her face with trembling hands.

What was she *doing*? Her bitter anger vanished instantly, and shame coursed through her in nauseating waves. Her gaze sought the forbidden hallway, but Alexander had gone. Paper neatly covered the glass; he had left no evidence that he'd been watching.

"Rachael... I'm sorry. I don't know what...I'm so sorry." He sounded as shocked as she felt.

Numb, Rachael shook her head.

"We have to talk about this," Geoffrey pleaded.

"No. I can't... I have to go."

She left without turning, flung open the front door, and dashed into the icy rain. Unable to face anyone, Rachael headed the car south toward Pacific Beach, barely able to see through her tears but wanting nothing more than to put distance between herself and Geoffrey Windsor.

(Correspondence from Taryn Ackerlin to Dennis Wallace)

March 29, 2009

Dear Denny,

I guess now is the moment when I have to admit I've read only your latest letter. Why? I knew if I read them all as they came, your words would bring you to life in my mind and then I would never have the strength to do what I have to do.

You know I love you. I think I always have loved you, ever since we were kids. Do you remember the mud fight when we were seven or eight? We'd gone fishing with Ron and that other kid — I can't remember his name; he only stayed in Mills for a year, I think — and when Ron splatted me right in the face with a mud pie and made me cry, you challenged him to a duel? I knew then that you were my champion, and no fair maiden could have loved her gallant knight more than I loved you at that moment when you stood toe to toe with your best friend, both of you covered in mud, and you threatened to put out his lights.

Despite this, I cannot, and will not, leave Mills — not even for you. I'm needed here. Or perhaps it's not "despite this," but rather "because of this." One of us must remain here, a testament to what we were, to what we could never be out in the great wide wonderful world that you think I'm afraid of. And Dennis, sometimes I do envy you, all the places you get to see, the adventures you live without me — adventures you can't ever tell me about because they're "classified." Your drugs are adrenaline and euphoria; with the Circle defeated in Mills, you've had to find other sources to satisfy your cravings, which takes you farther and farther away from me.

The job is your wife; to even consider making that commitment to me is to consider bigamy. You're already married, Denny. You speak of your calling with a lover's tone, and I see now that I'm not the love of your life and I never will be, not as long as your mind and body are capable of "doing the job".

And so I say, with grief so deep I can barely fathom the

pain…goodbye. You will miss me as you would miss a casual friend or a faithful pet, but you will not miss me as a man who has lost half his soul, and that is my greatest sorrow.

Always,
Taryn

SECRET GARDEN
Thursday, April 16, 2009

When Kimberly stumbled into the kitchen with a wailing Evan, her face ashen and creased with a grimace of pain, Aaron's concern for his wife's health deepened. As angry as he had been since she accused him of having an affair with Melody Olmstead, he wasn't so angry he'd failed to notice her weight loss and lackluster appetite. It also had not escaped his attention that she had been supplementing the twins' diet with formula, which meant her poor eating habits were interfering with her ability to produce breast milk.

The fact that he noticed these things but hesitated to speak up spoke volumes on the state of their marriage. He silently took the baby from her, longing to embrace her as well, wishing he could help alleviate her headache as he normally did by pinching the nerves in the web of flesh between the thumb and forefinger of each hand until her migraine medication began to work. He had read about it on a migraine website shortly after she'd become pregnant the first time; the dramatic change in her hormones had kicked off a series of headaches so severe he had feared she would suffer an ischemic stroke.

Kim gave a wan smile of gratitude, avoiding his gaze, and stumbled back upstairs. Ron knew within seconds she'd have the dark, heavy draperies pulled over the windows to block the spring sun and earplugs stuffed into her ears to muffle sound. He eyed the stairs and contemplated swallowing his pride and following after her. The breach could be healed; he knew it could. But he couldn't bring himself to apologize for something he hadn't done, and so he turned away instead, soothing his child while he prepared a bottle with one hand.

He'd barely finished feeding and changing Evan and rocking him back to sleep when Tia woke. He began the whole routine over, this time adding in a bath since Tia had soiled herself to the tops of her tiny socks. Once he had her back asleep, he called one of his part-time employees to fill in for him. As he hung up, he looked out the kitchen window in time to see Taryn pulling into the drive. He sighed; it seemed it was going to be one of those never-ending days. At least Taryn would be a help with the children and entertaining company for the day.

He met her at the front door, shushing her cheerful "hellooo!" as she came up the flagstone walk. "Kim's down with a migraine."

Taryn nodded wisely. "I wondered. When I dropped her off last night she was looking undeniably ill, even though she insisted she felt fine."

"Coffee?" he offered as she hung her fleece jacket on the coat tree inside the front door.

"Love some. Er…did *you* make it?"

He scowled. "Yes, as a matter of fact I did. You'd be surprised how good my coffee is."

Taryn considered. "I'm sure I would be, if I were adventurous enough to try some."

"I make very good coffee now," he protested. "Kim trained me well."

He clenched his jaw and turned away, busying himself with the coffee. A strange need inside drove him to mention his wife almost compulsively, as though speaking of their relationship would ensure it remained intact. Most times he was able to squash it, but on the odd occasion it was out of his mouth and vibrating the eardrums of those close to him, who were too respectful of his privacy to ask probing questions.

Taryn had been polite for as long as she planned to. Even the formidable expanse of his broad back didn't intimidate her into silence.

"Are you ready to end this silly battle with your wife?"

"Taryn, don't." He slammed the lid onto the coffee grinder and pressed the button, drowning out her reply. But he couldn't grind the beans forever, and she was prepared when silence descended again.

"Ron, you're letting Melody win. You didn't need to sleep with her for her to drive a wedge between you and Kim; all you had to do was get angry at your wife for considering the possibility that you were unfaithful to her."

"So it's all my fault, is it?" He banged the kettle onto the stove and gave the burner knob a violent twist.

"No," Taryn replied with waning patience. "That's not what I said. And for someone with a migraining wife upstairs, you sure are noisy."

Ron drew in a breath and let it out slowly. "All right. Fine. Now could we talk about something else, like what you're doing here at such an ungodly hour when it's your day off."

"Just came by to hang with Kim," she said casually. "Guess that won't be happening now."

"Mmm," was his noncommittal reply. "You, miss a day of sleeping in until ten? No way."

"Believe it or not, genius, the fact remains I'm sitting here, bright-eyed and bushy-tailed, and it's quarter to nine."

"So what were you going to do today that you don't want to tell me about?"

Taryn smiled serenely as he set her coffee in front of her. She gave it a cautious sniff and sipped experimentally. "Not bad," she admitted.

"You might as well tell me," he said, claiming the chair across the kitchen table from her. "I'll find out anyway. If you tell me beforehand, I'm less likely to be angry afterward."

She held his gaze for a long moment, then looked down into her coffee. "What do you know of the Baudelaires?"

Ron shrugged. "Trendy, yuppie couple." He paused. "Are they still called yuppies these days?"

"I don't keep up with current slang."

"They run a little more enthusiastic bar than I did. I've only met them a couple of times—I think they hang with Melody, so I've avoided them."

"They say they don't, that she has some friends in common with them and that's all."

"Doesn't matter. They aren't my type of people to choose as friends. Other than that, I'm neutral. Why?"

"Kim and I...ah...left church early, and swung by Bayou Baudelaire for a drink." He opened his mouth and she held up an admonishing finger. "Don't get all uptight. Kim didn't drink; she just had a glass of water."

"I wasn't concerned about that." He wasn't; he rather suspected she was unable to breastfeed at all, and that the twins were solely on formula. "I was going to ask why you left church early."

She fidgeted in her chair. "Yes, well. All I have to say on that matter is you either need to find a new church or a new pastor. And your wife should be congratulated for not socking him in the eye."

"Uh-huh."

"That doesn't matter. We can talk about church later. While we were at the Bayou, Trent and Caitlyn Baudelaire tried to talk to Kim about Melody. They think she's delving into witchcraft again. They...said something that made Kim believe the Wyckham House isn't really gone."

Ron jerked involuntarily. Coffee sloshed across the table. "Impossible. I've been there. It's gone."

"You've been there?" she repeated, green eyes wide with surprise.

"About a month before Kim and I were married. And two months ago after she had a particularly bad dream."

"Why did you go?"

"I had to be sure the house was really gone." He slid his chair back, careful this time to not make any unnecessary noise, and found a towel to mop up his mess. "It wasn't easy."

"I'm sure it wasn't."

He sat back down, staring down at his hands clasped around his mostly-empty coffee mug. "Are you saying you and Kim were going into the woods where the Wyckham House used to be?"

"Yes."

"Why?" he asked bluntly. He could see no reason for Kimberly to ever venture there again. To his knowledge, she had not been there since the October night his brother died. She would not want to be reminded of the hours she had been at Caleb's mercy. She would not want to be reminded of what lived there.

"Trent and Caitlyn said Melody has a garden growing at Sarah Bennett's old cottage in the forest behind the Wyckham House clearing. Kim started to talk some craziness about how she had never once thought about Sarah Bennett after the house vanished, and she said Sarah was the devil, literally. Or at least, a devil. She wanted to go to the clearing to make sure the house was still gone."

Ron stared at her, struck speechless.

"I, of course, don't believe Sarah Bennett was the devil, but it's indisputable that the Wyckham House is gone."

"And Melody?" he asked with obvious reluctance. "Does she really have a garden at Sarah's old cottage?"

"I don't know. I haven't been there."

He mulled this over silently, and at last heaved a weary sigh. "Well, all I can say is at least you two were going during daylight hours."

She squirmed in her chair, looking distinctly discomfited. "Um, yeah, about that… She wanted to go last night after we were done talking to the Baudelaires, but I wouldn't let her."

Again he was stunned into speechlessness. For Kim to consider going to the clearing at all was troubling, but for her to contemplate going at night was a whole other kettle of fish.

"Tell me everything the Baudelaires said last night." He scooted his chair closer to the table, leaned on his elbows, and fixed her with a warning glare. "And don't leave anything out."

Taryn complied, leaving out only Trent's gift of the mahogany bar. When she was finished, Ron paced the kitchen, one finger rubbing his upper lip as he evaluated her information.

"Do you have the number of that high school girl who babysits for the Nelsons? What's her name—Louise? Lucy?"

"Lori," she corrected dryly. "Yeah, I've got her number. Why?"

"I can't leave the twins with Kim. She won't be able to function enough to take care of them with the migraine, and her medication knocks her out for hours."

Taryn plunged a hand into the depths of her disorderly purse, searching for her cell phone. "Where are you going?"

"*We*," he corrected, his blue eyes gleaming, "are going to the

Wyckham House."

CR

"It's not going to be there," Taryn grumbled, pulling the collar of her fleece jacket higher up around her ears.

"Just humor me, all right?"

She huffed out an impatient breath but stopped trying to convince him. She, like most everyone, believed the house to be gone simply because when the FBI searched for it five years ago, it had vanished completely. She guessed he would need to reassure himself – by seeing for himself that the house was gone – for the rest of his life.

They'd left his truck at the gate that blocked the old mill road. The splintered ruins of the previous gate had been removed, and the new gate did not open to allow vehicle access, so they were forced to walk the rest of the way. It would take about half an hour, but it was quicker than taking the path through the woods — if they could even have found it. With the Circle disbanded, no one travelled the forest path to keep it clearly defined.

Ron didn't speak much as they walked. He grunted cursory replies to her questions and ignored anything said about his wife. She nearly broke through his restraint when she remarked, tongue in cheek, that perhaps Kim was right in saying Scott should not have taken her bullet. He stopped dead in the middle of the road, fixed her with such a smoking glare she expected to burst into flames, and then shook his head and continued on.

They passed the old abandoned mills, which were looking decidedly worse for the wear. The Circle had been careful to maintain the buildings structurally while letting the outside deteriorate to mask their use. Since the Circle had disbanded, no one bothered with even simple maintenance. The roofs sagged and Virginia creeper covered much of the exteriors.

Ron hesitated at the head of the path leading over the land bridge, drew in a steadying breath, and marched stolidly ahead. Taryn followed like a faithful dog, her teeth worrying the inside of her cheek. What if Kimberly was right? What if it was starting over again? Taryn didn't think she could bear it. The town's brush with evil had claimed the lives of two of her best friends and broken the bond between her and the love of her life. Victory had been costly.

Ron pushed through the brambles at the edge of the clearing and stepped unhesitatingly out of the cover of the forest.

The clearing was empty.

Taryn breathed a sigh of relief. "Can we go now? I'd like to be sitting in your nice cozy kitchen eating a huge slice of cheesecake and finishing that cup of coffee."

He didn't answer. As though he could see something where the Wyckham House had stood which her own eyes could not discern, he stared without blinking for a long time, his indigo eyes crawling over every inch of the ground.

At last he shook his head. "It's not here."

She raised a brow. "I could have told you that...oh, I *did* tell you that."

He acknowledged that with a wry quirk of his mouth. "Trent said he tried to cross the clearing?"

"No. He said he didn't want to walk through it for some reason."

Ron considered this for a long moment, and then straightened his shoulders resolutely.

Taryn grabbed his arm. "Oh, no you don't! If anything happens to you, Kimberly will skin me alive."

He smiled. "If the house isn't here, what's there to be afraid of?"

Shrugging out of her grasp, he strode purposefully toward the clearing. Without understanding quite how it happened, he was suddenly circling at the edge of the woods. He stopped, perplexed, and looked across the clearing at Taryn.

"Did I cross, or did I circle around at the edge of the trees?"

She raised her hands helplessly. "I...don't know. I thought I was watching, but..."

He motioned her forward. "Come across to me."

"Uhhh..."

"Just do it."

Shaking her head and muttering imprecations about crazy people, Taryn headed toward the middle of the clearing. A moment later she found herself walking at the edge of the forest. She stopped, bewildered.

"Did you watch me?"

"I thought I did, but I don't remember how you got over here." He frowned, troubled. "All right, that's a little odd, to say the least. My greater concern, at least for the moment, is Sarah Bennett's cottage."

Taryn waved a dismissing hand. "So what if Melody is tending a garden there? What's it matter?"

"It matters because, like Kim, I never once thought about Sarah Bennett after the Wyckham House vanished. That's as strange as the House disappearing."

"She was just an old woman," Taryn grumbled. "You don't really believe she was the devil, do you? Kim's overly emotional when it comes to this particular subject."

"Not without reason," he pointed out. "And yes, I believe. I saw her change, like a human form was a costume she wore. Sarah Bennett was definitely not human. And if Melody is involved with her – with it – she's buying more trouble than she can handle. That's why I want to see the garden."

She sighed but willingly followed him into the thicket. "How do you even know where to find it?"

"You said Trent Baudelaire indicated it was behind the Wyckham House. I'm going behind the Wyckham House."

She gritted her teeth and said with feigned patience. "The Wyckham House—"

"Is gone," he finished. "Yes, I know."

But he continued his headlong trek through the woods, following the faintest of trails. She didn't worry they would become lost; Ron's sense of direction was infallible. She did, however, worry that he was chasing a fantasy—a dark, terrible fantasy borne of his wife's terror. But there was little—if nothing—Ron wouldn't do for Kimberly. Except, apparently, talk to her about their current marital situation.

Ron moved through the shrubs and trees with very little noise, but Taryn managed to step on every imaginable twig. The woods filled with the snap-crack-crunch of her progress, and he sent a wry look over his shoulder at her. She knew what the look meant: *A good thing we aren't trying to sneak up on anyone.*

"I never said I was an expert in stealth," she grumbled, shoving her way between two closely spaced filbert bushes, yanking her jacket from the clutches of clinging branches. The chilly air was making her nose run.

"Good thing too," he replied without looking back. "Everyone between here and Perdix can hear you coming."

At last they came upon another clearing, this one smaller with a garden laid out in what seemed a haphazard fashion. A well-tended garden. Taryn tried to remember when she had first seen it looming ahead of them, but it seemed as though it had just appeared before them with no warning. A dilapidated cottage stood at the center of the garden. Since she could see no door on this side, she assumed it must be on the other.

"Is this it, then?" Taryn asked, her voice falling to a hushed whisper. She couldn't define her sudden unease or give reason for drawing closer to Ron, taking refuge behind him. There was something to be said for the security of a strong, broad-shouldered man.

"Yeah."

He stood near the gate but made no move to enter the garden, staring at the cottage with a narrow-eyed gaze. Taryn's mind reeled; she remembered Kimberly's description of her dreams of this place, of her dream-conversations with Sarah Bennett, of the cottage with no door, but she had thought it just that: dreams.

"What kind of garden is this?" she exclaimed, peering around him to look over the weathered picket fence. "I see things we'd be popping right out of our beds before they could spread. Like that Shepherd's Purse—that stuff will take over if you don't watch it. And aren't those mushrooms poisonous?"

"Helpful herbs alongside killing plants," Ron murmured. "A witch's garden."

"Melody's?"

"Trent said he saw her come here. That doesn't mean it's her garden."

Taryn sucked her lip between her teeth, debating the wisdom of asking the question that hovered on her tongue. He was apt to be angry with her.

So she phrased it carefully. "Ron...why do you defend her? She's spreading lies around town about you and her, and people believe them. She's caused a rift between your wife and you, and yet you defend her."

"I won't blame anyone without concrete evidence. And Melody didn't cause the rift between Kim and me."

"Ron—"

"We'll be fine," he interrupted. His gaze never left the bizarre garden. He was well-versed in the world of botany and named several toxic species of plant, the dreaded belladonna not the least among them, the very plant his uncle had used to drug Kimberly five years ago.

And mayapple—also called the devil's apple in certain societies but more commonly known to those outside the world of herbal medicine as the umbrella plant—occupied an inordinate amount of space near the fence. The rhizome was extremely poisonous but highly beneficial in proper doses as an anticancer agent, a laxative, and as treatment for intestinal worms. Ron could offer no benevolent purpose for having so much mayapple in one home herbalist's garden.

Growing cheek-by-jowl with the mayapple were clumps of valerian and skullcap, herbal sedatives both; tall spears of foxglove; and the highly toxic black henbane. The shift of the light spring breeze brought a faint whiff of the henbane's noxious odor. Taryn wrinkled her nose in distaste.

"And those mushrooms," Ron went on, not bothering to check to see if she was interested in his botany lesson, "are the same species that killed Lorna Mulberry's daughter twenty-five years ago."

"I thought so. Ron, can we leave now? I have the heebie-jeebies."

He didn't move, his eyes still scanning the garden, picking out the good from the bad. The beds were laid at odd angles, some tiny triangles from which smaller species such as thyme and chives spilled over their river-rock borders. The layout made absolutely no sense, but she didn't see anything sinister in it. She wondered why it held his interest.

"Yeah," he said, spinning abruptly on his heel and heading back to the forest. "Let's go."

"Can you find the way back?" she asked dubiously. The trail, as overgrown and hidden as it had been, seemed to have all but disappeared.

Ron spared her only a brief, cursory look in response and waited for her at the edge of the brambles. Feeling safer plunging headlong through the forest with no trail than staying in the clearing with the bizarre garden and abandoned cottage of Sarah Bennett, Taryn followed.

They skirted the Wyckham House's clearing, coming close enough to the algae-ridden, stagnant pond for its vile stench to make breathing a chore. They had crossed the land-bridge and passed the decaying mills before Ron spoke again.

"I think it's best if you don't tell Kim about this right away."

Taryn thought it best there were no secrets between this particular man and his wife with the present issues at hand, but just as she had promised Kim she wouldn't tell him about the mahogany bar Trent had gifted her, she promised to keep their trip to Sarah Bennett's garden to herself.

"I don't understand something, though," she said as they climbed through the brush beside the gate blocking the mill road. "It's only April; why is the garden growing so well?"

He tipped a slanted smile at her. "That's why I want you to keep this under your hat for a while. The foxglove should not be blooming yet; it shouldn't until summer. And the Shepherd's purse has already gone to seed — why is it blooming in April?"

"And check out the layout of that garden." Taryn paused before getting into the truck. "What's with all the weirdly shaped beds?"

Ron shook his head, his expression troubled. "I don't know, but something about it bothers me. It's as though I've seen the pattern somewhere before, but can't quite grasp it because I can't see it as a whole."

"What are we going to do, Ron? If Melody is cultivating that garden, she has to be stopped. From what you said, there are some very dangerous things in there that she shouldn't be messing with."

He grinned coldly but didn't correct her assumption that Melody was the tender of the witch's garden. "I'm going to take a plane ride."

"Oh? Where are you going?"

"Brad Harrington has a small Cessna. I'm sure if I pay for the fuel, he'll fly me over Sarah Bennett's cottage. I want to see that garden layout from the air."

"Can you find it again? From the air, I mean?"

"I can find it." He wrenched open his door and climbed in. Taryn followed quickly, still creeped out by the venture. Her flesh seemed frozen in permanent goosebumps.

Ron didn't start the engine right away. Instead, he half-turned in his seat to face her, his blue eyes inscrutable. "Will you tell me what happened at church last night?"

She raised her shin a fraction in challenge. "Will you tell me why you wouldn't go with us?"

He considered her request for a silent moment and nodded.

"Pastor Leon cornered Kimberly and asked her to publicly refute the rumors about Melody and you. She refused. Leon gave us both the impression that he believes what's being said. She called him a sanctimonious pseudo-pastor and told him his time would be better spent preaching about gossip to the gossipers rather than blaming the victims of such gossip."

A ghost of a smile curved his mouth. "That's my girl," he murmured. "I got much the same request—at least it was carefully couched as a request but it was more a demand. Leon and I had some words—mine were rather harsh—and I made it clear I'd not have any part in my wife's public humiliation. I also made it clear that I'll be talking to the church board, and he might want to delve into scripture and refresh himself on the subject of gossip."

"Have you told Kim?" His eloquent look was answer enough. "Ron, you really should—"

"Ready to hear my advice about you and Denny?" he asked, rudely interrupting.

Taryn bristled. What could he possibly know about the situation? How could he possibly understand her reluctance to leave the only home she'd ever known for a man who would be gone eighty percent of their marriage, off fighting darkness like a modern-day knight?

"I thought not. Perhaps when you're ready to talk about Denny, I'll be ready to talk about Kim."

"This is silly! Your male pride is going to cost your marriage!"

"It's not about pride," he replied, a definite wintry chill in his voice. "It's about trust. Now, would you like lunch at the diner, or just a quick sandwich at my house?"

"The diner would be good," she muttered, slumping into her seat with a mutinous glare at him.

"After lunch I need to go talk to Brad about that flight. Will you stay at the house with Kim and the twins?"

"Sure."

He sighed, facing forward, his hand reaching for the keys swinging in the ignition. "I appreciate everything, Taryn. I hope you know that."

She let go enough of her irritation to grin at him. "I know. But I'll give you the same warning I gave your lovely wife: my patience is not infinite."

He turned the key over, gunned the engine, and headed the truck toward town, his quiet "Neither is mine" almost lost in the noise.

Taryn sent a last glance over her shoulder as they drove away. The gate to the road seemed like the gate to hell, and she felt certain that Kim was right, that the devil's mansion—and the devil with it—had never really left Mills.

November 30, 1944

Our Thanksgiving banquet was rather bizarre. Jonathan was most displeased to find our dinner guests were none other than Kassandra's séance group, with the exception of Boldo Pattin.

They were, for the most part, polite and conversant, yet I could sense a certain smugness in their demeanors. I suspect they revel in their secrets, derive pleasure from deceiving Jonathan.

But I don't think Jonathan *is* deceived...especially where Alexander is concerned. As host and hostess, Jonathan and Kassandra sat at opposite ends of the long, formal table. To Kassandra's left sat Alexander, and to say they acted very much familiar with one another would be an understatement.

He is a very courteous man, gentlemanly to his last action, but something about him fills me with fear and revulsion. When he pulled out my chair at the table to seat me, his hands brushed my shoulders. I swear they were as cold as death, and at their touch I saw such things in my mind as I never want to see again.

I fear the devil walks with Alexander. Worse, I fear that Alexander may *be* the devil...

ALEXANDER THE GREAT
April 17, 2010

Geoffrey left the Peninsula the next morning with Sonia, Risa, and Heléne, early enough to catch the first ferry from Port Townsend. He didn't say goodbye.

Sabrina followed shortly after, her little car packed with sewing supplies and half of Rachael's business wardrobe. Sonia had commissioned her to design her fall wardrobe, a chance of a lifetime for Sabrina. Not wanting to spoil her friend's excitement, Rachael didn't tell her of the incident with Geoffrey, and she hid her depression and shame beneath of façade of enthusiasm.

Now she sat on the beach alone, turning a whole sand dollar over and over in her hand, the hood of her windbreaker pulled over her head against the dismal rain. The rain ensured that Rachael had the beach to herself, but she would have wept even had she been in a throng of people. The piercing shrieks of the gulls wheeling overhead drowned out her sobs.

She jumped, startled, when a shadow fell over her. She had no idea how long she'd been here, but the dismal grey day had given way to grey twilight. She swiped her eyes and looked up at Hugh MacGregor. Fresh guilt flooded her eyes.

"Ah, Rachael," Hugh murmured kindly. "A fine day to have a good cry on the beach. Is there room for two in your pity party, or should I take mine elsewhere?"

She laughed in spite of herself, blotting her wet face on the sleeve of her jacket. It was rather like trying to mop up a flood with a saturated sponge.

Hugh sluiced most of the water off the driftwood log next to her and sat down, tugging the strings of his wide-brimmed hat a little tighter against the wind.

"Whatcha got there?"

Rachael held up a sand dollar, a near-perfect round with a flower-like design on the top, completely intact. "The gulls missed this one somehow. I'll have to find a place for it to dry out where Marmalade can't get it. He loves anything fishy."

"It's lovely." He paused for a moment, letting the crash of surf on the sand and the cry of the gulls carry away the inane thread of conversation. "I heard Geoffrey Windsor closed down the job site."

She nodded, sniffling.

"So he left this morning? I thought I saw him driving north with Miss Stockwell."

She burst into fresh sobs, burying her face in her drenched hands.

"What are you doing, Rachael?" he asked gently. She shook her head, unable to answer. "This is a tricky situation. I don't want to see you hurt."

"I didn't know, Hugh!" she burst out. "I didn't know until he introduced me to her at the Manor Friday evening."

"A bit deceptive, wouldn't you say?"

She shrugged. "Why should he have told me anything? I'm just the interior designer working on his house. Other than that…"

"I believe he genuinely cares for you, Rachael," Hugh disagreed. "That's why I've been worried, especially since his fiancée came down. You're going to get your heart broken."

"Too late."

"Well," he remarked, obviously struggling for something positive to say. "He's not married yet."

Her mouth fell open in shock, and she laughed before she could stop herself. "I couldn't do that, Hugh. I really like Sonia. I wouldn't hurt her that way."

"You don't have to do a thing, Rachael, but be yourself." He tipped a crooked smile at her. "Will he marry her, do you think?"

"Why shouldn't he? She's everything I'm not: glamorous, wealthy, sophisticated."

"Is he a snob, then? He didn't seem so."

"He's not. That's not the way I meant it, either. There's just a big difference between Sonia Stockwell and me. She fits into his world;

I'm an outsider. There's no reason for him to…well."

"What—is he blind and stupid?" She offered a glum smile. "Come on, let Gina and I take you to dinner."

"Oh, I wouldn't want to intrude, Hugh. I'm sorry company anyway."

"We don't mind. Friends are for the times when you're feeling low as well as the times you're riding high. I won't take no for an answer. Now come along; perhaps Gina might have some solution to your man trouble."

"Cyanide?" Rachael quipped.

Hugh chuckled. "You're incorrigible. You'll be all right, no matter what happens. Let's go. I'm chilled to the bone and would dearly love some clam chowder."

"Okay," she murmured, capitulating. "I'm all right."

I'm all right, she repeated silently, *I'm all right*. If only she believed it.

Clam chowder did little to alleviate the hollowness Rachael felt, but she put on a good show for both Hugh and Gina. It was a relief to take her leave and not have to force smiles and pretend that she wasn't drowning in sorrow.

How had this happened? She couldn't remember ever feeling such an emotional connection to a man, and to learn he was otherwise committed was a devastation she didn't think her heart could survive.

She pulled off the road and parked on the shoulder across from Bayview Manor's long drive, wondering if she'd be able to talk her way into the house. Maybe she would get lucky and Harris would have cleared out, although that seemed like wishful thinking to the extreme. It would take his crew several days to wrap up, and as long as he was onsite he would never disobey Geoffrey's orders to not let her inside.

Making a reckless decision, she yanked the wheel to the left and stomped on the accelerator, shooting the car across the road and into the Manor's drive, narrowly missing a battered pickup as she crossed oncoming traffic. The driver blared his horn at her, but she paid him no mind, intent on reaching her goal as fast as the road—

and her aging Civic — would allow.

Her hunch was proved out when she parked in the cul-de-sac and darted through the remaining workers on the job, who were busy carrying out hand- and power tools of varying sizes and types. Harris had stationed one man at the front door to keep out those who had no purpose in being there — such as Rachael.

But while she didn't have a purpose anymore, not since Geoffrey had shut down the job, she had a need, an overwhelming desire, to be in the cocooning embrace of the Manor, witnessing the room-by-room transformation to its former grandeur. She flashed a charming smile at the guard, who had stepped into the center of the double entry, blocking both her way and that of the two men behind him who were carrying a heavy saw table between them.

"Sorry, Miz Payne. Owner's orders: no one goes in, and all equipment is cleared out by the end of next week."

"I left something in the third floor bathroom that I need to retrieve. Just two minutes, Emory, all right?"

"Will you two move it out of the way?" one of the men behind Emory grumbled. "This isn't exactly light."

Emory snagged her by her coat sleeve and pulled her out of the way, letting the men pass. "No can do, Rach. Sorry. Your tools and whatever else you've left here will be returned to you once we clear that floor."

"But—"

"Answer's no. You might as well go home. The job's over. Thank God," he muttered. "Not a minu—"

A crash from one of the work vans distracted him, and Rachael ducked under his arm and darted across the foyer. Emory realized his mistake too late to stop her, but surprisingly, he didn't chase after her. It was Harris who caught her, entirely by accident as she rounded the corner into the ballroom. He marched her back to the front door, amusement warring with exasperation for control of his face.

"Criminy, Stevens, can't you keep one woman out of the house?"

"Sorry, boss," Emory said, sounding anything but apologetic. "I'll do my best, but if they get past me, I'm not going after 'em.

That was our agreement: I don't have to go any farther into the house than this."

Rachael groaned. "Not you too, Em?"

"Just callin' 'em like I see 'em, Rachael. Go home and relax and think of how you're going to spend all the money you're getting paid. Windsor should be back next week to pay us all. Well, he'll be in Hoquiam, anyway. He may mail yours."

Harris flashed a sympathetic look her way, and Rachael felt herself tensing up. Great, did the whole crew know she'd entertained romantic thoughts about Geoffrey Windsor? Now she could call her humiliation complete.

"I know how much you wanted to finish the house," Harris said quietly. "You invested yourself personally in this job. It's okay, it happens. Your passion will let you do great things in people's homes. But this isn't the house to do it in. This place…it's bad, Rach. Nothing good will ever come of it. Don't waste your time wishing to finish it. Just go on and find another job to spend your passion on."

"I wanted to finish *this* one," she snapped. "Instead a bunch of ninnies with the heebie-jeebies have shut it down."

Harris frowned, exchanging a sidelong glance with Emory, who appeared just as surprised to hear her waspish tone. The foreman took her by the shoulders, turned her toward the entryway, and forced her outside. The wind threw a spray of rain onto the porch, making them both shiver.

"This place is not good for you. You've changed, and you can't even see it. Do yourself a favor: go home, have a hot cup of tea, relax, and start planning an ad campaign. Geoffrey Windsor will give you good references. Just stay away from here, Rachael. I'm afraid of what will happen to you if you don't."

"Nothing will happen!" Rachael flung up her arms in frustration. "I'm perfectly safe!"

Harris stared her down. "I've had to send two guys to the emergency room already today. One nearly cut his finger off with a saw. He said it bit him. The other managed to put a drill bit through his palm and skewer himself to the floor. It was pretty bad by the time we got to him—he was on the third floor. He might lose the hand. He said the drill turned itself on."

"Oh, *come* on—"

"And the battery was not installed at the time."

"He just thought it wasn't."

"I saw it myself, running with no juice. Are you going to say I just have a case of the heebie-jeebies? Well, I can't say you're entirely wrong about that, but nevertheless, I know what I saw. No more, Rach. We can't afford it. It's dangerous, both physically and spiritually."

She stared at him, feeling betrayed. How could he side with Geoffrey when Geoffrey was caving to hysteria? With one last smoking glare aimed Emory's way, she turned on her heel and went back to her car, her stride telegraphing her anger to anyone who cared to look.

This place isn't good for you. You've changed.

What a load of crap. She hadn't changed one iota; she was simply the only one who hadn't succumbed to mass hysteria. Perhaps it was because she was the only one who didn't participate in the campfire horror story exchange.

She aimed the car back down the long drive, ignoring Lon Harris's farewell wave. There was more than one way to skin a cat.

The construction crew didn't clear out of the Manor until after six-thirty. Waiting by the memorial in the ruined gardens, Rachael observed the last truck bouncing down the potholed driveway at a less-than-prudent speed, and allowed another half an hour to pass before she crept around the small marble building to the entrance and slipped inside. She needn't have bothered with the subterfuge; none of the crew wanted to be in the house after dark, so there was no one to witness her trespass.

She took care going down the treacherous stone steps, but once at the bottom she broke into a light jog, chasing the bouncing beam of her flashlight into the stygian darkness of the lava tunnels. A small pack holding her planner and her graph pad rhythmically thumped her back as she ran. Her wallpaper and tools were still in the third floor bathroom—she hadn't lied about that. She figured she could have the room papered by midnight.

Geoffrey would thank her in the end; if she completed the portions of the job that were ready for her touch, it would be all that much less he would have to have done once he got over his crazy idea that the Manor was inhabited by ghosts or demons or whatever the hell he thought they were.

She slowed as she approached the underground cemetery, and picked her way across the room, pausing to lean against a blank stretch of stone wall to catch her breath. The ceiling here was tall enough to allow her to stand at full height, which struck her as odd; everywhere else, the ceiling arced down to the floor as it reached the walls except where another cavern branched off. She wondered if there was another cavern on the other side, an air bubble in the lava flow that caused this anomaly.

There was no time to contemplate this possibility; she had limited time to work, and every minute counted.

Down the short tunnel to the sub-cellar, up the rickety stairs to the cellar, and finally, up the cellar stairs to the kitchen on the main floor. She remembered Geoffrey catapulting himself out of this very door, making a beeline for the back door with undue haste after something had spooked him. He had changed the subject when she asked about it, and she hadn't pressed the point. She remembered the moment not with nostalgia but with a burning resentment that made her want to go back in time and trip him on his way out of the pantry door, just for spite. She still couldn't believe he'd closed down the project; to learn he'd given specific orders to keep her out of the house like she was some sort of common criminal was downright humiliating.

The beam of her flashlight cut a swatch of warm yellow light through the utter blackness in the house. Rachael passed through the kitchen, circumventing the new appliances that would be loaded and transported God knew where sometime this week. Across the foyer, up the right side of the horseshoe staircase, down the hallway to the right, up another, less grand set of stairs to the third floor.

The work crew hadn't begun carting things off this floor yet, so the work light she'd borrowed from Harris was still there. She turned it on, flooding the room with light. She had no fear it would be seen from the window; this room faced the bluff. The chances of anyone from the crew being on the beach at this time of night — and in the driving rain, no less — were next to nothing.

The floor had been restored to its original small white octagonal tiles with occasional black accents. She had chosen a design for the walls that picked up the accent color in a sparse Chinese floral pattern. The stark black and white theme was clean and sleek, yet obviously vintage. The house would wear it well.

By eight-thirty she had all the pieces mapped out and cut, and had booked the first pieces to be hung. A blue streak of chalk cut a brilliant line across one cheek where she'd lost control of the plumb-bob. Other than that, she worked neatly and efficiently, her movements economical and confident. She had papered half the room and was booking a piece to go around the window when a discreet cough behind her made her jump.

"Miss Payne. Working late?"

Rachael sighed in relief. It was only Alexander. "Yeah. I want to get this room done."

"Mmm," he said noncommittally. She checked her watch and lifted the sheet of paper to the wall. "I was under the impression that Mr. Windsor closed down the job site."

She scowled at the wall, and brushed the air bubbles from under the paper with perhaps more force than was necessary. "That doesn't mean my work isn't done."

"I see." His eyes bore into her back as she slipped the next rolled sheet into the water tray; she rather suspected he saw quite clearly.

The paper had to soak for a few minutes, so she rocked backward off her knees and onto her backside, turning toward him. "Are you going to tell me I shouldn't be here, too?"

"Should I?"

"Everyone else seems to have an opinion. Why should you be any different?"

"Why indeed," he murmured. "I'm not everyone else."

The tension left her in a rush, and she was able to smile naturally. "No, you're not, are you."

He smiled back without comment. His eyes moved from her to

the half-finished wall behind her, to the finished alcove where the commode sat.

"It looks very nice, Rachael. Not precisely as it was originally, but very close."

"I couldn't match the pattern exactly, but this was similar. Not too busy."

"The company that manufactured the original paper has been defunct for decades now," he said offhandedly. "You'll never match it exactly. I like this better; it's less complicated, makes the room look less cluttered." He caught her pleased grin and chuckled. "You do good work, I don't think anyone can argue that point."

"No, but I'm sure they'll argue others."

The topic moved to her education and job history, to her teen years, to her childhood, to her plans for her future. She worked while they talked, methodically hanging and brushing and soaking and booking, and hanging and brushing some more. He sat in the doorway, propped against the jamb, and only left when she shooed him out so she could relieve herself.

Rachael noticed that he deflected questions about himself with a careless ease, not bothering to hide the fact that he was avoiding answering them. The first few times he did so caused a vague uneasiness to ripple through her, but when she cracked a joke about his reticence, it made him laugh and remark, "Listening to a young woman's dreams is much more interesting than hearing about an old man's regrets."

"Old man indeed." She had him pegged in his early fifties. While old enough to be her father, certainly not old enough to be an old man. A memory randomly flitted through her mind — Agent Schaefer of an unnamed government agency, telling her his dangerous, fugitive brother had a thing for much younger women. She smiled inwardly. A good thing she was here with Alexander rather than the agent's lecherous brother.

She completed the bathroom at half past one in the morning — later than she had anticipated, but she hadn't planned on Alex's welcome presence and engaging conversation. They stood side-by-side and surveyed the room, she with a satisfied smirk; he with an approving smile. When she swayed on her feet, he caught her under one elbow to steady her.

"You should go home and sleep, Rachael. I'll walk you to the door."

"I should go back out the way I came in." At his blank look, she explained, "I came in through the sub-cellar. There's a tunnel that leads out to the memorial."

He looked troubled at this news, but only asked, "Where did you park?"

"There's a trail that goes through that little patch of woods north of the gardens, comes out at a scenic overlook. I parked there."

"That's quite a dangerous route altogether. I'd rather you come through the front door."

Her anger piqued again, she said sharply, "I can't exactly do that, can I? Windsor banned me from the house and padlocked the doors."

"I can manage to break you in," he said, a bit arrogantly. "Don't come before darkfall; the workers don't leave until dusk. Although once they've cleared out their equipment, it will be much easier. There's no security here but me; no one else will be here at night."

"Don't you get frightened? Everyone else seems to be afraid of this house."

"Yes, I get frightened," he admitted, "but not of the house. Not of being here alone, either. Now let's clean up and get you gone."

He helped her clear away the evidence of her transgression, packing her wallpaper tools into a tidy pile, and then escorted her to the front door.

"It's about a quarter of a mile longer to go down the driveway and walk to your car along the highway, but infinitely safer. I'd walk you there, but I can't leave the house. Park behind the Manor tomorrow when you come; the kitchen door will be open."

She opened the door to wind howling through the trees, flinging rain with abandon onto the wide front porch, promising a miserable walk to her car. She didn't mind. The work she had accomplished was worth it. She sent a look over her shoulder to where he stood off to the side, out of the elements.

"Why are you helping me? If you're security, you should be

keeping me out."

He smiled a bit grimly. "I've always been a rebel. Goodnight, Rachael."

She smiled thoughtfully, then walked back to him and bounced up onto tip-toes to kiss his cheek. "Thank you, Alex. Goodnight."

The trek down the driveway was as miserable as she had expected. She tightened the drawstring on her hoodie to keep the hood from blowing off and lowered her head, plowing forward against the wind. Once she reached the road, she looked back toward the Manor, but she could see nothing through the driving rain but the looming outline of the house. If Alex still stood there watching, she couldn't tell. She rather thought he did; that would explain the sensation of being watched, and the warm feeling she had inside of being safe.

She would be all right as long as Alex was watching out for her.

(Excerpt from the progress report of Cody Schaefer, Director of Omega Team, to his superior Carlos Guzman, dated April 18, 2010)

"...Bayview Manor is exact in design and floor plan as the Wyckham House (Mills, Pennsylvania), Blessing House (Stamford, Connecticut), and Teufelhaus (Koblenz, Germany). The evidence at hand strongly indicates the same architect; the issue with confirming the architect's identity is that no one knows who built any of the mansions.

"The base construction of Bayview Manor and the Wyckham House appears to be basalt—igneous rock formed in intense heat. The oldest rock on the planet. It is dark grey in appearance, suggesting—against all evidence to the contrary—that it has weathered very little. The stones comprising the mansions' construction are large, of differing sizes, and polygonal, suggesting they were mined from columnar basalt deposits."

Handwritten in the margin below the text:

With all due respect, sir, I would like to put forth a theory. While the stone of the houses gives all indication of being basalt, I don't think it is. Igneous rock can be volcanic or plutonic—if you remember your high school science or college geology, plutonic rock is formed beneath the earth's surface.

I offer the theory that the house appears in so many locations because it comes from the earth itself, made from plutonic rock that resembles basalt but allows movement through the magma below the earth's crust. Only incredible supernatural power could allow that kind of travel.

It appears in several locations at once because time is not the same for their kind. This would explain my brother's presence in the Bayview Manor of today, and in the Bayview Manor of more than 65 years ago (under the name of Alexander, which you will remember from the Wyckham House case is Caleb's middle name). Although he is neither angel nor demon, he is in the custody of such beings.

After my experience in Bayview Manor, I can come to only one conclusion: we're hunting not just demons, but the very angels bound to the earth for mating with human women and teaching mankind of forbidden things.

I wish I could say I look forward to discussing this theory at length, as it's been long in coming together in any cohesive fashion. But I am afraid. For the first time since I began hunting evil with you, I am very, very afraid.

EN GARDE
Monday April 17, 2009

Cody Schaefer wanted nothing more than to lean his head against the wall and doze while he was waiting to see Carlos Guzman. But that wasn't the way things were done in the Omega Team. Weariness only meant that you were doing your job, and the fact that you were sitting in the waiting area of the office of the Director of the Schindler Project meant you were far from finished.

Or that you'd screwed up.

The Schindler Project (so named for the rescue and protection its various branches secretly offered their targets) was the umbrella agency for the Omega Team. Cody didn't know—at least officially—the names of the other teams or their functions, although he had heard a viable rumor about another shadow group called Limes. These fellows purportedly guarded from infiltration by foreign nationals the very cults Cody's team brought down. While it seemed at first to be a conflict of interest within the Project, he'd had long years to think about it and had come to the conclusion that the goals of each team were not so different. In essence, Limes protected the cults from being used against the United States by international invaders, and Omega dismantled them so they ceased to be a danger to anyone.

A limes, Cody knew, was a defensive border denoting a fortified boundary. It was not so odd for that particular team to be named after the Roman Empire's system of boundary markers meant to protect the borders. The very men of Limes were rumored to be swift, silent warriors, brutally effective and highly skilled at what was termed "resolution" but in reality was nothing short of assassination.

Guzman's frighteningly efficient receptionist looked up from her computer monitor and offered him a distant, polite smile. "Director Guzman is available to see you now, Agent Schaefer."

Cody nodded with a wry twist to his mouth. Although his own title was Director, no one but Guzman was addressed as such. Cody had served as the Omega Team's director for two decades but was still referred to as an agent.

"Thank you, Ms. Phillips. Am I outnumbered?" This was a code-phrase for "Is the Commander-in-Chief present?" Carlos Guzman reported to no one but the Vice President or the President himself. In fact, the Schindler Project had been put into effect by executive order in 1983. If either venerated man was present, Cody could look forward to an uncomfortable session in the hot-seat.

Ms. Phillips' plastic smile warmed considerably. "No, sir. You're being debriefed by Director Guzman only."

A measure of tension drained away, leaving a vague sense of relief behind—vague because despite the failure of the mission, facing Guzman would be infinitely easier than facing Renée.

Carlos Guzman sat in one of a cluster of comfortable armchairs, casually sipping from an insulated travel coffee mug while he read hastily scribbled notes on a yellow legal pad. Cody's backside had barely touched the cushion when Ellen Phillips—but always Ms. Phillips to the agents—set an identical mug on a small table beside him. He smiled his thanks, leaned back in his chair, and finally relaxed.

"All-in-all, not a good month, eh?" Guzman tossed the notepad aside and fixed Cody with a dark, piercing stare.

"No, sir."

"You look like you expected to be put before a firing squad, Schaefer."

Cody managed a tiny grin. "I certainly expected one of the top men to be present."

Guzman shrugged. "We can't win them all, and you've won more than your fair share. A failure every now and then is simply realistic. Care to tell me what happened?"

"Not particularly, but I will anyway."

The simple truth, laid out in blunt terms, was the enemy had found a weakness in Cody's armor, a weakness he'd never even suspected existed. He had never had any difficulties remaining faithful to Renée; he loved her deeply, desired her unequivocally, devoted himself to her completely. To have stumbled so easily when tempted at Bayview Manor shamed him to the bottom of his soul.

Carlos Guzman listened without interrupting, saving his questions until the end of Cody's monologue. He would not forget any; his mind had a peculiar bent that allowed him to file and organize information and recall it instantly. This ability had catapulted him into the Executive Directorship of the Schindler Project before his forty-seventh birthday.

It was also, Cody reflect ruefully, the quality that made all the agents fear a one-to-one debriefing. Guzman didn't forget anything said, didn't forget any questions he meant to ask, and always analyzed with razor-sharp clarity the series of mistakes that led one to fail a mission. He knew Guzman would find a flaw — either in his methods or his character — that had allowed the demon to breach his integrity. And Guzman would be accurate in his assessment.

When he finished speaking, a hush fell over the office while the Executive Director considered the information. Guzman rubbed a finger along the side of his nose as he analyzed and made his conclusions.

To Cody's surprise, he didn't immediately offer feedback. Instead, he rose and opened a cupboard, revealing a small wet-bar, and poured them both two fingers of Lagavulin scotch — neat, the way Cody liked it. The smoky aroma filled Cody's senses as he accepted his glass, and the scotch was warmth against the cold dread of facing his wife.

Guzman sipped his own glass for a few silent moments, and then shook his head. "I can't see where you could have done anything different."

Stunned, Cody set the scotch aside and leaned forward. "Sir, I failed miserably, and within a very short amount of time."

"Tell me, Cody," Guzman murmured, his dark eyes keenly scrutinizing his subordinate. "Have you ever before come face-to-face with a demon?"

"No, but —"

"We fight against their work all the time, yet you've never been face-to-face with one."

"No, sir. I was unprepared. And perhaps a little over-confident in my infallibility."

"Is that the way you see it." Guzman didn't voice it as a question, and Cody didn't take it as one. He waited for his superior to continue, outwardly calm but squirming inside.

Guzman finished his scotch and went to pour another. He held up the bottle in silent offering, and Cody shook his head. He drank only rarely and never much; his wits were his best asset in doing his job, and alcohol clouded his instincts.

"You've been an agent with the Schindler Project since its conception twenty-six years ago, and the director of an elite rescue team for twenty of those years. The purpose of your team is to extract people from dangerous cults—cults in which the worship of Satan is quite often practiced. And yet you've never before seen a demon."

"No, sir."

"Have you considered the implications of why you faced one now?"

"I let down my guard."

Guzman swirled his scotch in his glass, sending the ice cubes clinking against their crystal confines. "I don't think the fault lies with you."

"Sir?"

"Why do you think I sent you when I could have sent someone who isn't as busy? You have thirty agents under your command, Cody, and not all of them are on missions. I felt the situation warranted the best I had, so I sent you and your young protégé.

"Do you think the enemy has failed to notice your success in dismantling much of their hard work? They've come at you before through more subtle means—such as the attack on your son in 1993 and the knifing in Chicago in 1994. Human-executed actions guided by demons."

"So why did I see the demons this time?"

"Because you are a formidable opponent, and they knew nothing less than showing their faces would break you."

"It worked."

"Did it?" Guzman wondered. "I would say it showed you a weakness in your defenses of which you were unaware, but it didn't break you, Cody. What will you do now that you know of that weakness?"

Cody considered the question, rubbing a finger across his upper lip. "I'll be on my guard for a similar attack."

"Your opponent has given you valuable insight about yourself, and you are going to use it to bring about that opponent's defeat."

"It doesn't save my marriage," Cody wryly pointed out.

Guzman nodded. "Yeah, good point. But how many women have thrown themselves at you over the years, my friend, either trying to distract you or simply because you're a handsome, powerful man?"

"A few," Cody replied. The answer was more like "many," but Guzman didn't need to know that.

"And how many have succeeded in convincing you to be unfaithful to your wife?"

"None."

"See? You're too strong for their subtleties, so they threw at you what they had left: otherworldly enticement. They went face-to-face with you. You stumbled but you did not fall, Cody. That is a victory, not a failure."

"And do you think Renée will see it as favorably as you?" Cody asked ironically.

"Have some faith in your wife's ability to understand — and in her trust. Now before you go home to face the music, tell me why you put conditions on Wallace staying in Heron Bay."

"He's been in the house and met the same demon I met. He was prepared to take her off to lunch when she just vanished."

"That's not like him. What's going on with that girlfriend of his?"

"Dear John letter," Cody said neutrally. He'd vowed to stay out of it; he couldn't fix everything, and he had his hands full with Bayview Manor.

Guzman gave a low whistle. "Poor son-of-a-gun. What's he going to do?"

"I don't know. I'm staying out of it."

"Should I order him home?"

Cody shook his head. "I considered it, but he's actually won over the Historical Society and gained access to their records. He may be able to learn more about the Manor there than by going to it, but I've no idea what good that knowledge may be. I think the town is too far gone; there seem to be more sell-outs than hold-outs."

"That bad?"

"Psychic parlors, metaphysical shops, occult groups."

"And the risk to Geoffrey Windsor?"

"I worry more for his interior designer than for him," Cody admitted. "Windsor hates the house, admits it creeps him out. He told me he was going to ask one of the local Christian pastors to exorcise the Manor. And then something happened to make him shut down the job site, but I didn't have time to talk to him before I came home."

"What did you tell him about the exorcism?"

"I wished him luck. Everything is teetering there – the whole construction crew was on edge. Several walked off the job and wouldn't return even to collect their tools. Windsor won't go in the house unless absolutely necessary. Only Rachael Payne seems immune to the demonic presence."

Guzman considered. "Angelic protection?"

"Or demonic beguilement, which is more likely, in my opinion."

"One last question and then you can head home."

"Take your time."

"You're not a coward, Cody."

"The jury's still out on that, sir. I've never had to face Renée with a confession like this." Cody reached for his scotch, savoring its scent and flavor. A pleasant after-taste lingered behind, peat and smoke and butterscotch, providing the only enjoyment in the day Cody was likely to find.

"You say your brother is trapped there. Do you think he's dead?"

"I'm not sure. I don't think so, but I don't understand it myself."

"Could it have been another demon, putting on the face of your brother like the other one put on the face of the Fotheringham's nanny?"

"It could, but I know my brother well. It felt like Caleb. Do you understand what I mean?"

"As much as I can." Guzman finished his drink in one swallow and set his glass aside. "Do you think you can handle Blessing House in Connecticut? I convinced Ben Cummings to come out of retirement to have a look at the property, but he said he wouldn't investigate indefinitely."

"I'm sure Belinda's not happy about it."

"You have no idea. Will you take it on?"

Cody closed his eyes, his finger resuming its nervous rub across his upper lip. "The Wyckham House, Bayview Manor, Blessing House. They're all the same house, sir. There's even one in Germany that Todd Garrett found. Same layout, same problems. I'm not so sure I'd be any more effective in Connecticut than I was in Washington."

"I beg to differ, but it's up to you. Think on it for a week or two and let me know. Ben wants to wash his hands of the investigation by the end of the month. He says he values his marriage more than the extra income.

"In the meantime, you're on a one-month leave of absence once you've submitted your written report. Mandatory, so no arguments." Guzman held up a hand to halt Cody's immediate protest. "Take your wife on a cruise, go camping, go skiing, go to Italy, whatever, but for God's sake do not go home and sit in your study brooding over what's happened."

"Yes, sir. You'll have my report no later than Wednesday."

"You're dismissed, Agent Schaefer."

"Thank you, sir."

Cody left his glass on the bar and reluctantly headed home.

The clock had just edged past noon when he approached his house. Set on a private forest road barred by a stout wrought-iron gate that required biometric identification to open, the stately farm house provided sanctuary and security. Anyone thinking the gate could be bypassed and the Schaefers taken unaware would be laboring under a dangerous misconception. The grounds were wired with infrared surveillance cameras operated by a sophisticated computer program that could determine whether an intruder was human or animal. If identified as human, the computer triggered an alarm system that put the house into lockdown, electrified the perimeter fence, and summoned local law enforcement.

Cody flipped open the protective Plexiglas covering and pressed his thumb to the biometric scanner. The gate motor whirred to life and granted him entrance. He guided the car up the curving driveway and parked outside the garage. He could put the car away, but he might need it soon in the event Renée did not respond well to his news.

Birds called to him from the forest and an unseen squirrel chattered its alarm at his intrusion. The front door was open, letting in the warm spring day, and a bag of potting soil, a flat of empty pony packs, and two magnificent hanging pots cascading with alyssum, lotus vine and vibrant pansies gave evidence of his wife's activities. Curving beds stuffed with plants both uncommon and ordinary surrounded the house and flanked the edge of the woods, leaving sweeping expanses of lush green grass to cool the property. Renée worked hard to give him a beautiful, comforting home, and here he came to wreck it.

The security system would have alerted her that he had come through the gate, but she didn't meet him at the door. He heard her voice from the back of the house, and since no cars but his own were parked in the drive, he assumed she was on the telephone. He navigated through the comfortable country décor and followed her voice through the back door to the deck.

She lounged in an Adirondack chair in the spring sun, the phone to her ear and a glass of iced tea close at hand. She waggled her fingers at him and rolled her eyes at the phone. He claimed the chair across from her and waited.

"I understand, Belinda. I wouldn't like it either. But it's only a temporary assignment, and the extra income will be nice." Renée cocked her head as she listened to the reply. Cody was mildly surprised at who she was talking to. "Hang on a minute, will you?" She pressed a button on the phone to mute the transmitter and let out an aggravated growl.

"Belinda, I presume?"

"Your ex is in a snit."

"She's not my ex," Cody replied automatically. He'd never actually married Belinda, as she'd left him practically on the eve of their engagement for his brother, but their brief relationship had resulted in his oldest son.

"She's going to be ex something if she keeps calling me to gripe and whine about Ben going to Connecticut. She blames you, you know."

"I didn't send him."

"You're the team leader, therefore you're at fault."

"If she's waiting to chew my hide, she'll need to take a number and stand in line."

Renée arched a brow and thrust the phone at him. "You talk to her."

"Why me?"

She huffed out an impatient breath. "I love Aaron and I'm thankful I got to raise him, but I am not dealing with his mother."

"Well, all right." He tipped a smile at her and took the phone. "Belinda, what's the trouble?"

"Renée said you weren't home."

"I just came in. Did you need something?"

"My husband," she snapped.

"So I gathered."

"You have thirty agents, Cody," she went on as though he hadn't spoken. "Why did you need to drag Ben out of retirement? We're happy not being involved in that morass anymore."

"It wasn't my decision. And the situation in Connecticut needed an expert. Just sit tight and wait a couple weeks, Bee, all right? I'm on a leave of absence right now and then I'll be taking over at Blessing House."

Renée's eyes widened but she showed no other sign of surprise.

"A lot can happen in a couple of weeks, Cody, and you know it." Now she sounded close to tears. He gave a mental sigh of fatigue.

"Has something gone wrong at Blessing House, Belinda?"

"No. I just...I just don't like the feel of this."

"Nor do I," he admitted. "But I'm sure everything is fine or I'd have heard about it. In the meantime, why don't you fly out and visit the kids? I'm sure they'd love to have you, and you can see the babies before they aren't babies anymore."

Belinda drew in a breath, obviously making a collected effort not to bite his head off for changing the subject. "We're coming in July, Cody, as you well know."

"If money's an object, you know we'd be happy to—"

"I just want my husband home," Belinda interrupted, dissolving into tears. Cody was at a loss; while not possessed of the same strength of spirit as Renée, Belinda had been more or less a government wife just as long. Her thirty-year-long relationship with Ben, although they'd been married for only five of those years, should have prepared her for his absence.

"Two weeks, Bee, that's all I ask. Two weeks and I'll send him home."

"Promise?"

He closed his eyes. Promises like this were ones he tried rather hard to avoid. He couldn't guarantee an agent would come home. The work was risky, the danger high. He hadn't lost a man yet, but that didn't mean he could promise he never would.

"I'll do what I can," he assured her.

"That's not what I asked."

"You know that's all I can give."

"Well, all right," she accepted tersely. "Just let me know when you're done playing cloak and dagger so I can have my husband home safe."

"Bee—"

"Goodbye."

She hung up, and he gritted his teeth as he set the phone aside.

"Well, that was fun."

Renée grinned. "Wasn't it, though? Now tell me, husband dear, why I'm just now finding out about Blessing House?"

"I just found out myself in my debriefing this morning."

"What happened to the house in Heron Bay?"

"Yeah, about that." He grimaced and pulled in a breath, hearing Guzman's words in his head. *You aren't a coward, Cody.* Right. "I have something to tell you."

She took it well, all things considered. Better than he had expected, anyway. She had listened to his halting confession with a gradually hardening expression until finally she sat before him, blank-faced and emotionless. He offered no excuses but so many apologies that she finally help up a hand to stop his words.

"I am going for a walk," she said, her voice remarkably steady. "When I come back we'll talk." She went to shut down the security system in the area she intended to walk, and left without another word to him.

That had been an hour and a half ago. He was starting to get concerned; a fence surrounded their property so he knew if she got lost she could make her way to it in any direction and then follow it until she came to the driveway. However, there were several deadfalls he never had the time to clear away and a couple of streams. She could have fallen while crossing a deadfall, maybe landed face-first and unconscious in a stream....

Stop it! She would be back when she was ready to talk. This was always her way when he had to tell her unpleasant news. Thankfully he'd only had to do so a couple times in their marriage. The first had been when the paternity test came back naming him as Aaron's father. While clearly relieved at the nearly invincible weapon paternity handed them in their custody battle for Aaron, it had been no less of a shock to her that her husband had fathered a child with another woman, even though that relationship had ended long before he had met her.

Her walk that day had been four hours.

A brief flash of sunshine yellow and the angry castigation of a startled squirrel heralded her return. A moment later she stepped from the forest trail and into the yard. From this distance she looked like a teenager: trim and athletic, her yellow shirt accenting her tan, denim capris showing shapely calves and dainty ankles. She strode inexorably to the deck where he waited.

She passed him silently, sank into her chair, and unlaced her shoes, shedding them with a sigh of relief. He suspected she kept her trim figure by hiking out her stress; it was not easy being the wife of a secret agent.

Crossing her ankles under the chair to help her balance on the edge of the sloped seat, she leaned her elbows on her knees and stared down at her clasped hands.

"Has this happened before?"

"No."

She raised her brows. "Oh? Women have never made passes at you before?"

"This wasn't a woman, Renée."

"That's not what I asked."

He blew out an uneasy breath. "Yes, women have made passes at me. I've never accepted them."

Renée nodded as though he'd just confirmed her deepest suspicion. "I always knew that would happen if I married a handsome man," she said sorrowfully. "How did it happen? How did she get close enough to you to make it happen?"

"It," he said very deliberately, "distracted me. I never expected such a tactic. It had hold of me before I even suspected its intent."

"You must have been distracted," she murmured. "I remember how neatly you avoided the clutches of Marie DeLaCourt at the Christmas Ball two years ago."

Cody knew then that they'd be all right. She wouldn't bring up such a lighthearted subject if she were thinking of booting him out the door...or worse, shooting him with his own gun. She'd been nearly prostrate with mirth at Marie DeLaCourt's open pursuit of him; Marie's divorce had just been finalized and she made no secret that she was on the prowl. It didn't seem to matter to her that Cody was married. He'd spent the evening fending off her clutching advances and admonishing his wife not to leave him unattended.

"Don't remind me," he said with a grimace. "Renée—"

Her voice cut across his. "What concerns me more is what had you distracted. I know there are things about your job you can't tell me, but I think you owe it to me this time."

"It's not that I can't tell you. It's that I didn't want to tell you."

He scrubbed a hand over his face, already tired although it was only a little past two in the afternoon. "Caleb is at Bayview Manor."

Her hand clenched around her glass of tea. They'd enjoyed several years of a Caleb-free existence, although both were always on their guard for any unexpected homecomings. But Cody's brother appeared to have virtually vanished from the face of the earth and no such homecomings had occurred.

"How can that be?"

"It's been five years, Renée. It's not inconceivable that he made his way across the country undetected. It happens all the time."

"But why would he be in that house—a house identical to the Wyckham House?"

"I have a theory. But first, Renée, I need to ask your forgiveness. I don't know what—"

"Cody," she said softly, and he stopped talking. "Even had it been another woman—a human woman, I mean—I wouldn't divorce you over a momentary lapse in your restraint. You say you've always been faithful to me and I believe you. You were tricked, maneuvered, and I believe that's the only reason the demon got as close to you as she—it—did. Once she had you off-balance, well…. You can't be faulted for being human. You're not invincible, you know."

"The things I felt while…they sickened me, Renée. Sickened me, but I still wanted to do them. What kind of man am I?"

Renée slid from her chair and knelt before his, her arms sliding around him, her lips warm and soothing on his face. He held onto her tightly.

"You're my kind of man." A finger under his chin lifted his face to hers, and she kissed him fiercely. "You're mine."

"Yes," he whispered against her lips.

She tugged him from his chair, and he lowered her to the deck, her body warm and soft beneath his.

You didn't win this time, he thought with vicious triumph. *You tried, but you didn't win. Now I'm on my guard.*

And as he once again pledged himself to his wife, body and heart, he thought he heard the mocking laughter of his seducer in reply.

(Excerpt from Bayview Manor Journals (1943-45) appendix, written by Pastor Hugh MacGregor of Heron Bay First Church of Christ through May of 2012)

May 14, 2009

At what point does a soul begin to unravel?

The empty seat in the fourth pew from the front, left side, screams at me in alarm. Rachael Payne should be sitting there, where she has sat nearly every Sunday all of her life. Where she has not sat in more than a month. Her absence makes my heart cold, paralyzes me with fear.

Do I admit, now, here in this paper confessional, that I am glad Geoffrey Windsor left before we could go through Bayview Manor together? That I am relieved and grateful that I don't have to set foot inside that godforsaken house ever again? Is it cowardice to turn away from a battle you know you are going to lose? Or is it simply smart? Perhaps the distinction is in the reasons why you choose to walk away from the battleground.

I can fight for Rachael though — if only from a distance. She's a shadow now, a wisp. A beautiful, tragic myth. I glimpse her in the grocery store and hurry to catch up, only to discover she's already left, dodging me with a skill that leaves me cold and frightened. She doesn't answer her phone. She never returns calls. She's never at home; she's always at the Manor, as though she knows I don't dare cross the threshold and so she's safe from having to face me.

So I fight from afar with the only weapons I have: my love for a good friend's daughter, and God's love for His child. I know His love is unequaled in power and I should have faith in Him, the faith of a child.

But I am an old man, and I am afraid.

God be with you, Rachael.

UNDONE
Saturday, April 18, 2009

Sonia Stockwell lived part-time at her parents' house in Bellevue, a dwelling that could only be described as modestly palatial. Coming from money himself — although he'd seen precious little of his parents' assets since reaching adulthood — and having amassed his own small fortune, Geoffrey nevertheless felt like a poor street urchin skulking up the flagstone walk.

The front door opened as he approached; the ever-watchful, uber-efficient butler Sonia's parents employed stepped aside as Geoffrey entered, and then moved forward to close the door behind him.

"May I take your coat, Mr. Windsor?"

"Well, Paul, that depends. Is she inside or at the dock?"

"At the dock, sir."

"Then I think I'll keep it. It's a bit brisk out today."

"Very well, sir. Do you know the way?"

Geoffrey sighed inwardly. Of course he knew the way; he'd grown up with Sonia Stockwell, and had been in this house — with the same attendant butler — hundreds of times.

"I know the way."

And he proceeded along "the way" while the butler hurried in another direction to do whatever butlers did when not in immediate service. He himself didn't employ such an entity; his household was managed by a housekeeper, and if she didn't answer the door — which she often didn't — Geoffrey did it himself.

French doors led from the spacious sunroom to the patio — or lanai, as Sonia had called it since their first trip to Hawaii when they were preteens. He stopped on the lanai, taking in the furnishings. The patio set had changed over the years — usually every year. This year's model, still covered in shrink wrap and bearing the shipping receipts, appeared to be chunky teak with wrought iron vines and deep, comfortable cushions in a floral pattern. To his left was the pool house, with its ingenious removable walls that came down as soon as the weather turned warm; that wouldn't be until early July, most likely. He'd spent many hours in that pool over his lifetime.

He forced himself to move on, noticing little details as he moved across the lanai and into the grounds. Last summer's broken cobblestone, which he'd tripped over and nearly severed his tongue, had been replaced. A section of the yew hedge surrounding the ornamental garden had been replanted; several of the shrubs hadn't seemed very healthy by the end of August. It looked as though the gardener was excavating a new plot on the other side of the pool.

His mind noted these things carefully, totting them up on the list titled *What the Hell Do You Think You're Doing? You're Giving Up All of This?* And indeed he felt the lure of the familiar, that bewitching song of inertia inviting him to stay where he was known, where he was comfortable.

He knew what he was doing; he was deliberately cataloging all the things he would miss if he walked away from Sonia, all the things he had grown up around, the familiar, the aggravating, the beloved. What was he doing here, anyway, preparing to break a lifelong connection for some wisp of a girl who was probably never going to speak to him again?

Maybe it's not about Rachael at all. Maybe it's really about you, and Rachael is just an excuse you're using as a shield.

There was that, too.

He sat down on a stone bench slick with rain and gazed out over Lake Washington. Below him, down a slightly sloping lawn, he could just make out Sonia, clad in jeans and a windbreaker, cleaning out her boat. Sonia, whom he had promised to love forever. Sonia, whom he loved in every way but the one that gave meaning to the ring on her finger.

It didn't matter how long he sat here, prolonging the inevitable; this would still be unpleasant. And sooner or later Sonia would notice him on the bench and wonder why he was sitting in the rain in her parents' garden. So he swallowed his dread and made his way down to the dock, where she'd pulled her boat out of the covered boathouse and was methodically restocking it with all the items she'd taken out of it last October. She heard his footsteps on the dock and poked her head out from under the boat's clear vinyl cover.

"Geoffrey! I didn't expect to see you until dinner."

He stepped off the dock and into the boat, bending to kiss her offered cheek. "I wanted to talk to you."

She stood very still, staring at him with solemn eyes for several seconds. Finally she drew in a bracing breath and said, "I can't pretend I'm surprised."

"What do you mean?" Had he been that obvious? He had tried to keep his growing affection for Rachael away from prying—and knowing—eyes.

Sonia sank onto a pristine white seat, clasped her hands, and rested them on her knees. He sat opposite her, his own hands dangling between his knees, and avoided looking at her for as long as he could.

"Why don't you tell me what's going on in that mind of yours?" she suggested.

In her tone he thought he heard understanding and gentleness, which made him feel worse. How could he do this to her? And why should she be so gracious as he did it? He chanced a look at her, and was surprised to find amusement in her expression.

"I think—" he began, and his voice cracked. He cleared his throat. "I think we've gone as far with this as we can go."

"Mmm," she murmured. "Is it Rachael Payne?"

Hot color flooded his cheeks. "It's more than Rachael. But she's part of it." He squirmed, and as her amusement deepened made an effort to sit still. "It's not that I don't love you, Sonia. You know I do. It's just—"

"Not the right kind of love," she finished quietly. "Yes, I know all about that."

She played with the charm bracelet on her wrist, waggling her hand and watching the charms glint in the grey afternoon light. He watched her watching her charms swing, and suddenly wondered, not for the first time, if there was someone else Sonia yearned to be with but had put aside because she hadn't wanted to hurt Geoffrey.

"You've been trying to tell me that for some time, haven't you?" he deduced. "But I'm a stupid man, and subtlety is lost on me."

"It is indeed," she replied, and the amusement was back. "I think we just wanted to make things work. It made sense. We grew up together, everyone was expecting it, it just seemed natural. But it doesn't work anymore, Geoffrey. I'm glad you think so too."

"It seems a shame, what with all the wedding preparations we've made." He slanted a crooked smile at her. "I will, of course, reimburse you for those god-awful expensive invitations you ordered last month."

"Don't be silly, Geoffrey," she laughed. "I didn't order them; I only told you I did."

"So you knew as long as a month ago."

"What, that I wouldn't be able to go through with marrying you? I knew longer ago than that. I was just waiting for you to catch up."

He chuckled. She fiddled with her Pandora charms. There seemed to be more of them than she'd had before, like the silver heart set with a red crystal. He was reasonably sure it hadn't been there last month, because he'd bought her a new charm for her birthday and had put it on for her.

His gaze moved to the items on the deck, waiting to be put away. More than what she alone would need. He looked up to catch her gaze on him. His eyes moved to the pile of supplies, and then very deliberately to the red heart charm.

"Would you have told me before you went off on your...trip?"

She followed his gaze and flushed slightly, fingering the heart. "I would like to think so," she whispered, "but I can't say for sure."

"Does he make you happy?"

"Insanely."

"Well, that's good, then."

He fidgeted again, not sure what he was supposed to do now, and finally stood. His eyes fell on the supplies, neatly piled nearby, and he suddenly started laughing. Sonia gaped at him, obviously thinking he'd lost his mind.

"And to think I had all this guilt over kissing Rachael once."

She stood up too, an impish grin curving her mouth. "And so you should have, being engaged as you were." Her grin faded. "I'm really sorry, Geoffrey. I didn't plan it, it just—"

"It just came along when you least expected it. Real love did, I mean."

"Exactly."

She twisted the engagement ring off her finger and held it out. He took it after a moment, and folded it back into her hand.

"Keep it. Give it to one of your kids."

"I don't have any kids."

"You will." He bent and kissed her cheek. "Goodbye, kiddo."

She closed her eyes as his lips lingered against her cheek. "Silly Geoffrey. We'll see you next Saturday for dinner."

"I can't swear by that. I made rather a mess of things with Rachael; I may not survive trying to patch things up."

It was her turn to chuckle. "You really *are* silly. Why don't you take her check in person? A contrite man coupled with a hefty check is a hard combination to resist."

"You're so wise," he remarked, meaning *You're such a wise-ass.*

"Someone must be," she countered, meaning *You're so hopeless, Geoffrey.*

She was still grinning when he left her, and he didn't think that she was simply staving off her tears until he was gone. It sort of stung, actually, to have her give in so graciously and quickly, with no tears and another man already waiting in the wings. Well, more like *hiding* in the wings, because, from all appearances, there had been precious little waiting going on.

But it didn't sting as much as knowing Rachael was probably never going to speak to him again, and he'd just walked away from his only other source of companionship and comfort. Maybe not completely—they'd always be friends—but he rather doubted Sonia would be as readily accessible as she had been as his fiancée.

Why don't you take her check in person?

Why not, indeed?

ଓଃ

The sound whispered through the house, unfamiliar,

unwelcome, painful to the ears that heard it. Music. Not just music, but music about faith. Music about *Him,* sung in a sweet contralto, the tone more true than the voice was talented, saturated with reeking faith and stinking devotion.

They didn't watch from the shadows; they *were* the shadows. They gathered in corners, in darkened rooms, in the spaces between walls and the far reaches of high ceilings. They permeated the mansion like a foul odor, crowded around the solitary worker, drinking in the dark thoughts her songs of faith belied. Had they been of earthly substance, the woman would not have been able to move.

But she could not see them, could not sense them. Her movements methodical, mechanical, she plowed on through her task, applying a chemical stripping agent to the wallpaper, waiting, peeling, applying, waiting, peeling, and again, and again. She moved with dogmatic determination, not noticing the exhaustion that dragged at her limbs, completely unaware that she had been working without pause for fourteen straight hours. When she ran out the last of her energy, they gathered around her, held her upright when she started to fall, lifted her arms when she could not, driving her closer to collapse with every second that passed.

Alexander watched from outside the room, unable to disperse them, unable to interfere, unsure that he wanted to. Torn, always torn. Evil battling to silence good and always winning, always, because evil was like a shiny object full of wonders, flash and fire, and good — well, good had its purpose but not here. Not in this house.

And so he simply watched, as he had through the decades, through the centuries, because time was a fluid thing, a changing thing, a circle surrounding him, and he, at its center, could walk into any moment in any year and see someone like Rachael Payne being slowly driven mad by the beings that engulfed her, clung to her, grasped her with greedy, filthy hands and whispered greedy, filthy thoughts into her unsuspecting mind.

He had never interfered. He had never wanted to. Until now.
She's my friend.
And why would that be? Because she trusted him, liked him?

Because when she saw him, her smile lit up her entire being? She was not trying to please him to gain favor or to escape his brutality. She simply enjoyed his company, unaware that he worked in the darkness, *with* the darkness, eradicating her faith, destroying her moral underpinnings, crumbling the very foundation that made her the Rachael Payne he called his friend.

He stepped forward unconsciously, and the wall of shadows turned as one and hissed at him in warning. Defeated, he melted back into his corner. He had done his duty and done it well. Too well. Comfortable in the Manor, trusting of her "security guard" friend, certain there was nothing in the mansion but bad memories and the ghosts of rumors, Rachael Payne was coming undone.

His sorrow and regret were too vast for words.

A clatter from the bathroom brought him forward again, and this time the shadows scattered and allowed him entrance. She swayed on her feet, dark circles of exhaustion beneath her eyes, her hair lank and sweaty and disheveled. Her stomach rumbled; they'd not let her pause for food or drink.

Her legs trembled. He caught her under her arms just before she hit the floor, and he eased them both down to the tiles. She blinked at him.

"Alex?"

"The one and only," he assured her with a warm smile. He wanted to cry instead.

"I think I overdid it today. How long have I been here?"

"Too long."

"I'm hungry."

"You should probably go home, eat, and get some sleep."

"Too tired." She slumped against him, sliding on the tiles until her head rested on his thigh. In seconds, she was asleep.

Too late for me, he'd told his brother. And now it was too late for her. He cursed everything he touched, like that mythical king who turned everything and everyone he loved to gold. Only instead of gold, his touch turned their lives to ruin.

He leaned against the wall, Rachael Payne curled against him like a small, trusting child, and tears of shame and grief flowed unchecked down his cheeks.

(Correspondence from Dennis Wallace to Taryn Ackerlin)

April 7, 2009

Dearest Taryn,

I can't believe you would wait until I'm three thousand miles away to decide this can never work and sever the tie. We've been together a lifetime; is this how forever ends—a Dear John letter while I'm on assignment in a town that feels more like hell on earth every day?

You think my love for my work and my love for you are irreconcilable. And as long as you're unwilling to compromise, you're right. Perhaps I'm married to my job because I'm not married to you. I'm willing to bet you never thought of it in those terms.

I refuse to believe this is the end of us. I can't even fathom how you could walk away so easily, so I'm praying that there's nothing easy about it. If every step you take away from me is a struggle, if your heart breaks over and over every time you think of me, then you are wrong; it's not the end. This is not the way it's supposed to be.

Yours,
Denny

AMAZING GRACE
Saturday, April 18, 2009

Denny Wallace contemplated the new limitations of his mission as he guided his car north toward La Push. Mist dotted the windshield, not rapidly enough to justify the wipers being on even at their lowest setting, but enough to cause diminished visibility and annoyance. Almost as much annoyance as the last directive from his boss had caused.

Cody had delivered his final instructions as he packed, studiously avoiding looking Denny in the eye. *Continue your research to the fullest extent possible without going into the house.* Cody had been adamant on this to the point of obsessive. *Do not, under any circumstances, enter Bayview Manor. Ever.*

The fact that Cody had been reassigned in the middle of an investigation was just short of perplexing. Denny had an inkling that something had happened while his boss had been in the Manor, something that had seriously shaken him. This intrigued him more than it scared him; anything that could shake the ordinarily unflappable Cody Schaefer was worth looking into. He doubted he would have an opportunity to enter Bayview Manor again, regardless; Geoffrey Windsor had closed down the job site and reportedly secured the mansion against unauthorized invasion. It wouldn't stop someone with Denny's resources, but his respect for Cody would stand in the gap and keep him out.

After some gentle interrogation disguised as idle chatter, with a good deal of charming flirtation thrown in for good measure (which, given the Dear John letter he carried in his pocket, gave him no small sense of guilt), he'd managed to extract from Anne Quequesah the name of an unofficial historian on all things Bayview Manor. Not only that, Anne had confided with a surreptitious glance around the Historical Society's library to be sure no one was eavesdropping, Grace Markham had played with the Fotheringham children and had been in the Manor during its glory days.

Denny wondered just what kind of glory days the devil's mansion had enjoyed; it was an edifice of torture and misery, infecting all who came into its sphere of influence. And after everything he had learned so far, he wasn't sure he wanted to know more.

But knowledge was power, and his talisman against the evil of the Manor was knowing its history. In the thirteen years he'd worked with the Omega Team, he had searched tirelessly for a pattern, for a mistake that would allow evil to be vanquished. He had yet to find one. The fallen had enjoyed the benefit of eons to cover their tracks; Denny had worked for a mere decade to expose them.

At sixty-seven years of age, Grace still walked several miles every day along Rialto Beach in the early afternoon, and had reportedly retained all her mental faculties. And best of all, except for the fourteen years she attended boarding school in Boston, had never been away from the Peninsula, which had made her a popular source for writers, researchers, and gossips alike. Or so said Anne Quequesah, and he had no reason to doubt her.

He missed Grace at her home, but as Mora Road deposited him into a parking lot on Rialto Beach, he caught a glimpse of fuchsia pink in the distance and deduced he'd found his target. *When I am old, I shall wear fuchsia*, he thought randomly. He stowed Taryn's letter—always with him lest he forget her words and feel the need to drive them into his heart so it would accept that she was gone—in the glove box, not wanting to risk it to the capricious weather or an accidental dunk in the sea.

He was grateful he'd planned ahead today and had worn jeans, sneakers, and a hoody. Jogging on the wet sand allowed him to gain on her rapidly, and he was barely winded when he stopped at a respectful distance and called out to her.

"Mrs. Markham!"

Grace Markham stopped, her hand clenching on the strap of her tote bag for several seconds before turning around to greet him. Her face, weathered by a lifetime of ocean air, bore an expression of resignation.

"Agent Wallace. I wondered when you would get around to hunting me down."

"I should hope you don't feel as though I'm hunting you, Mrs. Markham," Denny replied with a disarming smile. He didn't bother asking how she'd heard about him; he knew all about grapevines in small towns.

Grace Markham sighed and tilted her head down the beach. "Let's walk, shall we? You could offer me your arm, as a gentleman would."

Her brow arched expectantly and Denny complied, his smile widening. Her grip was light, arthritis-gnarled fingers resting submissively on his forearm. They started down the beach toward her original destination, a cluster of sea stacks rising from the sand like granite sentinels.

"I played there when I was a child," she remarked, nodding at the stacks. "This place—the Peninsula, I mean—has always held a special place in my heart, even when I lived back east."

"So you didn't live in Heron Bay proper? How is it you came to know the Fotheringham children?"

"Oh, back then we lived in Heron Bay," Grace replied easily.

They plowed through a cluster of gulls huddled on the wet sand, waiting for the surf to bring sustenance. The birds scattered, a few taking flight and landing back where they'd started after the humans had moved on.

"This beach was my father's favorite one, probably because it's a reasonable distance from Heron Beach. He was not a fan of anything Heron Bay, couldn't wait to get us out of there."

"Seems he did a good job in that regard," Denny observed. "The east coast is just about as far away as he could get you and still remain in the United States."

"He did what he could," she replied. Her fingers tightened on his arm a fraction. "Only what he could."

"I'd like to talk to you about Bayview Manor. I've heard that you were a playmate of the Fotheringham children. Do you remember anything about your time spent in the mansion?"

Grace didn't answer for a long time. The sea stacks had come into clear view when she finally spoke again.

"I remember a very little bit. I was quite young when I was there, four years old when we left the Peninsula."

"Pretty young to be a playmate," he ventured.

"I came as a package deal with my brother. A tag-along, if you will." She smiled faintly, and suddenly stopped, turning toward him. "You've been in the Manor, Agent Wallace?"

"Yes."

"What impression did you have?"

He considered her question very carefully before building an answer. And build it he did, of half-truths and fleeting impressions and outright evasion.

"It's a very grand old mansion," he said. "And very unnerving. A man could get lost in there."

Judging from her expression, she wasn't fooled by his circumspect reply. "And many have. Let's sit for a moment."

She veered off the wet sand, and he let her guide him to a cluster of driftwood, where she settled on a low log. He straddled the log beside her, facing her.

"Agent Wallace, no good is going to come of your investigation. This town has gone too far into the darkness."

"We're not here to discover the deep, dark mysteries of Bayview Manor or Heron Bay," Denny said, although it wasn't quite the truth. He suspected that the deep, dark mysteries might even be more important than Caleb Schaefer. "We're just looking for someone."

"So I've heard. I guess now is where you show me his photograph."

Denny grinned. "I was saving it for a little farther into the conversation, but if you insist…"

He fumbled his badge wallet from his back pocket and slid out a photograph of Caleb Schaefer. Grace Markham took it and stared at it for several minutes before handing it back.

"His name was Alexander. No one knows from where he came, and no one knows to where he went when the dust settled. "

"He just vanished, you mean?"

"Vanishing would imply that someone had previous knowledge about him. People in the town knew *of* him, of course, but only those who'd been to the Manor ever saw him firsthand. No one knew his full name, so when the list of the missing was compiled after Kassandra Fotheringham's last séance, he was a giant question mark."

"The last séance — that was the night of the murders?"

"So the story goes. I myself was quite small at the time, so my own knowledge is sketchy. I only know what I've pieced together from others' accounts. Eleven people went into the Manor that evening, and none were ever seen again. When the authorities were alerted and the Manor searched, Alexander was gone and the only other person who knew what had happened was dead."

"Kassandra Fotheringham," he deduced.

"I've often thought that perhaps she she asked for what she got. You shouldn't play around with things like black magic."

"She deserved to die, you mean."

Grace was silent, staring into the ocean beyond the surf. When she spoke again, it seemed her words came across the distance of half a dozen decades, her memories dusty with age, blurred at the edges, full of dark capering things best glimpsed from the corner of one's eye because to face them fully meant looking into the cavernous maw of insanity.

"She invited them into the house. Or perhaps they'd always been there, and she simply invited them out of the shadows and into the light. Where she embraced them. And where, once she was firmly in their grasp, they drove her mad."

A chill crept through him at her low, powerful words. "Are you talking about ghosts, Mrs. Markham?"

She turned her head to stare at him blankly, as though wondering how she had come to be sitting on this splintery driftwood log with this young man who asked questions about the painful past.

"No, Agent Wallace. I'm talking about demons."

ભ

The French doors were opened at either end of the gallery,

funneling a breeze from an open window or door elsewhere in the Manor that loosed the velvet curtains from their staid, upright posture and made their skirts dance.

Her measured steps took her past the ranks of oil portraits that stood as sentinels in this elegant corridor. She barely noticed them; they weren't what mattered. What mattered was the man waiting at the other end, leaning negligently against the jamb, a stylish figure in a crisp tuxedo and pristine black shoes.

She was no less fashionably dressed, her sleeveless, beaded flapper dress—rescued from a trunk in the attic and updated by a local seamstress; even the Fotheringhams were feeling the pinch of the war—swirling around her calves. Her buckled heels tapped rhythmically on the polished parquet floor as she steadily closed the distance between them.

He was handsome, Alexander was, but not as young as he appeared from a distance. She didn't mind; she already knew he was a suave, sophisticated man teetering on the cusp of middle age, but he was still lean and attractive. His ice-blue eyes watched her approach, showing no emotion. They never would, she knew. Plenty of physical passion but a heart of ice. Her arm snaked around his neck, her flesh white against his raven hair, and she pulled him down to her, their lips melding.

And then she drew away, shock propelling her backward. He moved fast, anchoring her to him, his grin eloquent and ironic. Her beautiful flapper dress was gone, as was her desire for the man who held her. She pushed against his chest to force space between them, her plaid-flannel incongruous against his tuxedo.

"Why, Kimberly, I didn't know you cared," he drawled.

That voice, at once comfortingly familiar and violently hated, washed over her like rich whiskey, intoxicating with false reassurance. She tried to breathe, to speak, but his eyes held her paralyzed.

"But of course you don't," he went on smoothly. He stared intently into her eyes as though searching for something. She glared back, and finally he exhaled heavily and released her.

She found her voice. "I knew you were here."

"Of course you did," he agreed with no hesitation—and

surprisingly, no mockery. He reached out, his hand skimming along the curve of her cheek without touching her. "Beautiful dreamer."

"Rachael," she remembered suddenly. "Who is Rachael?"

His face darkened, and his body tensed. "She's my friend."

"I'm glad you have one," she replied, surprised that her own voice held no mockery. She looked around at the gallery, which now lay in ruins, the tattered velvet curtains pooled on the floor, broken curtain rods sticking up like iron branches. He stood on a dark stain on the parquet floor.

"You should leave this house, Caleb."

"There are no doors, my dear. And no windows."

"You can make your own."

"It's too late for me. Remember? You were here that day, weren't you?"

She ignored the question, even though it shook her. It had been a dream; how could he have sensed her dreaming of him?

"It's never too late for forgiveness."

"Still determined to see some redeeming qualities in me?" He smiled sadly. "I'm too far gone, Kimberly. Too deep in sin. I've murdered, I've raped, I've stolen, and I've lied. I've given my allegiance to darkness, and there's no going back now."

"I don't believe that."

"Why not? I do. Everyone else does." He offered an elegant shrug.

"Because if you were too far gone for forgiveness, I could not have forgiven you."

He straightened, startled, now watchful and cautious as he moved closer. "You're a very dangerous woman." His head bent until their foreheads touched. "Leave and don't come back, not in real life and not in your dreams. This is a cursed house, Kimberly, and you're too good to be in this filth."

"Letting me go again, Caleb?" she whispered. "You did once before, even if you won't admit it."

"Goodbye, Kimberly."

"I'm not going anywhere."

"I think you are."

He was right. She was somehow insubstantial, like a gossamer veil in a high wind, fingers of air grasping at her, tugging her away. She thought he closed his eyes and inhaled deeply, but then the gallery had swirled away and vanished. Her eyes opened to her darkened bedroom, curtains closed against migraine-taunting rays of light.

Tears glittered on her cheeks. Kimberly left them there to dry, in bereavement of what she had lost to Caleb Schaefer, and in honor of what he had given back.

(Correspondence from Rachael Payne to her brother, Ethan)

April 27, 2009

Dear Ethan,

   More and more I feel that I'm writing these letters into a void, as sort of a diary. But when I try to write in my journal, I simply stare at the blank page and can't summon the memory of even the simplest thing I did today.

   Geoffrey Windsor has closed down the job at Bayview Manor. Sabrina went to Seattle or Bellevue or somewhere in that direction; it's the opportunity of a lifetime for her. But more and more I feel alone, isolated, disconnected from my world. Is that how you feel, so far away from home and family? Who listens to you when you're lonely, when you're sure that you've lost your mind and just need to connect with someone to be sure you're real, that you exist? Are these feelings the reason you left with those strange people from the beach and moved so far away from me?

   I think I'm losing my mind, Ethan. Please, I beg you, write back to me! Let me know, at least, that you're safe. Let me know that you still exist. That *I* still exist. Please, Ethan, I'm desperate.

Your loving sister,
Rachael

INTO THE VOID
Friday, April 24, 2009

The firemen had put out the flames before anything other than his office had caught. The police had come and gone, taking with them his statement and leaving with him the uncomfortable suspicion that they thought he was behind the vandalism. He had, after all, just thrown a few million dollars at a house no one would ever live in and no one would ever buy.

His insurance adjustor had spun a small circle, surveying the damage, and then went off to a private corner to call her office, solidifying his hunch that he was the main suspect of both the cops and his insurance company.

Geoffrey stared at the smoking remains of his office with an overwhelming sense of dismay, loss, and an impotent anger that shook him to his core. The outer office had sustained only smoke damage; the real damage had been confined to Geoffrey's area alone. The antique executive desk he had found for a steal in a second hand shop seven years ago had taken the brunt of the fire; its top lay in cinders between the burnt-out hulls of the drawer compartments.

To add insult to injury, the exquisite surrealist paintings he had purchased from a Spokane gallery, created by one of the gallery owners who was every bit as exquisite as her work, had been set fire to as well. Several valuable pieces of bric-a-brac had been toppled from their shelves and shattered on the floor. A globe in a handsome cherry spindle frame had been freed from its moorings and rolled through the flames. Scorch marks had obliterated much of the territory from Alaska through Australia, and a smudge marred the otherwise snowy surface of Antarctica.

This was just the latest occurrence in a mysterious chain of vandalism that had plagued Geoffrey over the last two weeks, the first of which had been the wrecking of his immaculate gardens at his home on Orcas Island. While his house didn't boast an eight-figure price tag, it was still a gorgeous property, and he had hired a Japanese master gardener to create and maintain flowing beds of flowers and emerald lawns. He had not lamented a single penny spent, either. His gardener had been inconsolable for days and was still prone to bursts of outraged Japanese imprecations at random moments while clearing away the wrecked debris of cherished shrubs and rare perennials.

And three days following the destruction of his garden, someone had smashed out all the windows of his car — from the inside — and shredded his tires.

The next day, his wallet went missing, and he'd had to cancel all his bank cards and spend four torturous hours at the Department of Motor Vehicles, also known as hell on earth, to get a new driver's license. Later that afternoon, his key ring had vanished, and he'd spent a small fortune for the local locksmith to change out the locks on house, automobiles, and office. If he didn't know better, he'd think a vandal with a grudge was following him, wreaking havoc for some imagined insult or slight.

But he did know better, and chalking up these instances as a string of bad luck or the work of an angry grudge-holder didn't explain the odd feelings he sometimes had of not being alone, of being watched, stalked, and the glimpses of movement he often caught from the corners of his eye. It added up to something he didn't dare put into spoken words, not to anyone, but which clanged in his mind incessantly like an alarm: something had followed him from Bayview Manor, something he could not see except in glimpses, but something that did not want him to return.

His hands clenched at his sides, the swell of anger pulling him in so many directions. He wanted to run to the Peninsula and take Rachael forcibly from that hell house. He wanted to rage at heaven, screaming for solace and sanctuary. He wanted hurtle into battle, shrieking with fury, and annihilate the enemy. Mostly he wanted to huddle in a corner and cover his eyes and ears and pray for them to leave him alone.

She's in the Manor, working.

He didn't know how, but he knew this was true. And he knew there would come a day when she would try to leave, and they would not let her. The house would claim yet another life.

That house, it eats people.

He forced himself to take a calming breath and let his hands relax at his sides. When he thought he could walk without shaking and lurching, he turned his back to his ruined office and made for the door, where he paused and looked back with burning determination.

"I'm going after her. And you're not going to stop me."

He left quickly, stiffening at the sounds of further destruction, but he didn't look back, and he didn't stop.

God be with me. Please, God, be with me.

ᴄʀ

The small sledgehammer made quick work of the plaster walls. Rachael was pleasantly surprised at how much damage the small tool caused. Chunks of plaster rained down on her, coating her in white dust. This was the fourth room she'd demolished in the last two weeks; she struck the plaster off the lathe and knocked the lathe from the frame and whacked the two-by-four studs from the stone.

She couldn't believe that she'd once been so eager to slap up paint and wallpaper, never dreaming of the lovely stone beneath the lathe and lime covering. Her hand stroked the rough block.

A sibilant whisper hissed through the house, a stirring of the air that signaled she was no longer alone. She wasn't afraid. Alex was here, somewhere, always watching if not right at her side. He had rarely left her alone in the last several days, and lately he seemed nervous and afraid.

She wasn't nervous, nor was she afraid. She felt none of Geoffrey's misgivings, shared none of his silly superstitions. Because she loved the house, the house loved her and welcomed her.

"Rachael!" exclaimed a shocked voice behind her. "What the hell are you doing?"

She lurched around, the sledge hanging at her side. "Geoffrey."

He strode forward and yanked the sledgehammer from her

hand. She let it go without a fight. "You aren't supposed to even be in here, let alone be demolishing the interior!"

Her vision wavered and she saw two of him. Just as suddenly, the two Geoffreys merged into one. She swayed on her feet, and he reached for her, his anger turning to concern. Her upheld hand stopped him, and she sank down on a folding chair, scattering bits of plaster from the seat.

"I'm all right. I skipped lunch." She frowned, thinking back, as he flicked a glance at the ice chest of food she'd brought, which sat against the wall just inside the front entrance, forlorn and forgotten. "Breakfast, too, I think. And to answer your question, you wanted the house restored. I'm restoring it."

"You're *destroying* it," he corrected, his anger flaring again. "How did you get in here?"

"There are more ways in than through the front door," she replied, circumspectly. "I'm restoring the house to its original condition."

"Oh, it came with holes in the walls?" he shouted.

"You don't even like it; what do you care? You won't live here, and you won't sell it so no one else can live here. If there are holes in the walls, who is going to see?"

He spun in a circle, arms thrown up in frustration. She didn't care. He could be as frustrated as he wanted but it wouldn't change the facts.

"What are you doing here, anyway?"

He stopped spinning and shot her a look over his shoulder. "I own this house."

"No one owns this house."

"But to answer your real question," he went on, ignoring her remark. "I came to bring your final payment."

"You could have mailed it. Probably should have. Now, if you don't mind..." She retrieved the sledgehammer, hefted it up, and struck another large hole in the plaster wall before he could stop her.

But he didn't try to stop her this time. He simply stared at her for a long moment, and shook his head.

"I think I should just tear up the check," he commented to no one in particular, eyeing the growing damage to his million-dollar mansion. He shook his head again. "Why don't you let me take you to lunch? You need to eat."

A protest automatically sprang to her lips, but her stomach chose that moment to betray her with a loud growl. To be honest, she couldn't really remember the last time she'd eaten. She'd put in so many hours on the house, and the work went so quickly that time flew faster than she could keep track.

"All right. Lunch would be good. And then will you go away?"

"Only when I can be sure you're not coming back into this house. Don't you understand, Rachael? There's nothing good here! You're standing in a piece of hell itself!"

With no forethought, she flung the sledgehammer at him. He ducked just in time, his eyes wide with shock. She felt a little shocked herself; she'd never raised a hand in violence to anyone, not even her brother when they were growing up. And she was more than a little confused; it had felt like her arm had swung back and hurled the hammer of its own volition.

"Rachael!" he shouted, sounding stunned and suddenly afraid. "What the hell?"

But she paid no attention to him. The hammer had hit the marble floor with tremendous force—more force than it should, having been wielded by a 120-pound woman on the brink of exhaustion—and had exposed a swatch of rust-colored stone beneath the broken tile. She dropped to her knees, unmindful of the shards of marble that cut her knees, and brushed away the broken stone.

Geoffrey forgotten, she reached for the sledgehammer, raised it, and crashed it down on the edge of the shattered tile. Cracks rippled through the floor. She hammered again, and bits of marble flew into the air as the tiles broke apart, revealing stone of rust, green, and grey beneath.

Beautiful. She'd never seen anything more beautiful. She raised the hammer, let it fall, raised it, let it fall, again, again, until a sizable portion of the marble had split open and pulled away from the stone. She reached for a floor scraper, and jumped in surprise when a hand fell on her shoulder.

"What do you think you're doing? Are you insane?" Geoffrey's face, an inch from hers, bore a mixture of rage and worry as he pried the floor scraper from her fingers and tossed it aside. "I'm getting you out of here. You'll be able to think more clearly once you're out of this house."

Rachael pushed him away, but he came at her relentlessly, clutching at her arm, dragging her across the foyer toward the front door.

"Let me go! STOP TOUCHING ME LET ME GO!!"

He was ripped away from her in an instant. His fingers clutched at her desperately, leaving behind welts that would later bruise, and then he was flying across the room, landing on his backside and skidding through the debris of broken tile. He hit the wall beside the door and lay without moving, the breath knocked from him.

Rachael watched dispassionately, unable to quite remember who he was to her, as his eyes widened and his mouth formed a rictus of horror. The front doors swung open wide, and he was unceremoniously tossed outside. The doors slammed, and she was alone once more.

She stared at the doors for a moment, trying to comprehend just what had happened. She reached for the sledgehammer. Her arm rose and fell, rose and fell, and for hours the only sound in Bayview Manor was the echo of shattering marble.

(From the journal of Kimberly Schaefer)

April 30, 2009

I dream of him all the time. Caleb Schaefer, I mean. There is something different in his demeanor now, something that tells me that if he were here, I would have nothing to fear from him.

Remorse... From where does it come? And why, after a long life of crime and sin, does he suddenly find it within himself? For remorse is what he feels; I know it as surely as I know my own name. He let me go at the Wyckham House, I am convinced of it. And for that he is paying a terrible price. Perhaps that is why he's befriended this mysterious Rachael.

I have to go there, to that house in Washington State where Caleb is imprisoned. While Rachael is his friend, she hasn't known his dark side like I have. I have to convince him to find his way out of that house, because when he is free of it, I will be free of him.

And Aaron...oh, Aaron will blow a gasket, despite the fact we have barely spoken in weeks. I can't ignore the pull on my soul that Caleb Schaefer has; I try to, but then I remember lying on that cold stone altar in the Wyckham House, awaiting my death at his hands, and instead finding the keys he'd "accidentally" left behind when he went to investigate a mysterious sound only he heard.

Mercy. That's what he'd shown me, against all odds. Can I do any less for him?

I don't think I can.

ASHES
Monday, May 4, 2009

Kimberly paused on the shoulder of the road, stooping to tie her cross-trainer. The March weather had given way to April storms, and she now enjoyed the respite of warm, early May days — as much as she was able to enjoy anything lately.

Aaron spent fourteen hour days at the greenhouse, preparing for the summer planting season. She tried not to think about how in previous years he had hired extra help so he could keep normal hours. Kim ate by herself before he came home and left him a prepared plate in the refrigerator, which he consumed alone in the kitchen while she pretended to work in the sunroom. Hiding was what she was really doing, hiding so it would be too troublesome for him to ask her to leave. They shared the care of the babies, and it seemed all the love that had been hers he now lavished upon Tia and Evan. She felt irrationally jealous of her own children.

She straightened, ignoring a sudden rush of nausea. It was nothing new; nothing worse than she had expected. Fate was a cruel lady, giving her one last gift from the broken shards of her marriage. Paul Jacobs had imparted the news to her with a marked lack of enthusiasm just three weeks ago.

"I thought we discussed the dangers of you becoming pregnant again, Kimberly."

"It wasn't planned, Paul," Kim said faintly. She felt a very real fear; every day she expected Aaron to come home and tell her he wanted a divorce. Now she had to somehow tell him another obligation chaining him to her grew in her womb.

"Are you all right? Do you need to lie down?" Paul asked with concern.

Kim shook her head. "No, I'm fine. Paul...please don't say

anything to Ron yet. He'll put me in bed again immediately."

"And you think I won't?" He leaned forward on the stool. "At the first sign of weirdness, Kim, you're on bed rest again."

"I know," she replied, holding up a placating hand. "Please. I promise I won't overdo it. Aaron's just so busy this time of year; I don't want to make him feel as though he has to be home worrying about me all the time."

"He loves you. It's his right to worry."

She smiled wanly. "Still," she began.

Paul cut her off tersely. "Is everything okay with you two, Kim? I've heard things – "

"We're fine, Paul. Just busy. And you know what a mother hen Aaron was when I was pregnant with the twins. I could use a little time without being stifled."

Paul squeezed her shoulder reassuringly. "I understand. Aaron meant well, you know. He was very frightened when you lost the baby two years ago, and he had reason to be. You almost died."

"I know," Kim murmured. She rather doubted Aaron would worry now. His anger at her was a palpable entity, hovering in the air between them, coloring even mundane actions such as passing the salt.

"All right," he said dubiously, obviously not believing her but loath to intrude where he wasn't invited. "You can keep on taking your walks but no farther than the end of your driveway and no more than one a day. I'll write you a prescription for prenatal vitamins. If you experience any bleeding or cramping, call me immediately."

Kim had accepted the prescription, had it filled in the pharmacy, and kept it hidden in her purse. Every day she tried to find a way around the almost visible barrier between them to impart the news, and every day she found a hundred excuses not to.

Such as this morning when she came into the kitchen to find him still home, eating breakfast. She'd risen earlier than usual, unable to sleep, and the silence in the house had given the impression he'd already left. He passed the orange juice silently, and as she took it she opened her mouth to say the words, but she couldn't force them past her lips. It should have been a simple thing to tell her husband she was expecting their child, but the forbidding set of his expression made her awkward and afraid. Then he slid out of his chair and went out the back door without a word, leaving her alone with her secret.

Kim started walking again, fighting down the nausea. She sank so deeply into her reflection on the five-week cold war in her home that she didn't at first notice the niggling pain low in her abdomen. She cast a glance behind her and discovered she had walked farther than she should have. To mark the distance equivalent to their driveway, she had tied a red ribbon to the split-rail fence running along the side of the road. The ribbon fluttered in the breeze, barely visible in the distance. She turned immediately to start the trek home. Ripping pain screamed through her abdomen, dropping her to her knees.

Bad news.

She fumbled her cell phone out of her pocket and dialed the house number, trying to calm her panic as the cramping swelled in intensity and strength. Taryn was sitting the twins and undoubtedly preparing their afternoon meal. She had been spending more time of late with Kim, who couldn't fathom if she knew about the Schaefers' marital troubles or if she only sought to forget her own. Kim didn't care which; Taryn's regular presence kept the crushing loneliness at bay.

"Okay," Taryn answered the phone without a greeting. "Do you want butterscotch chip cookies, or peanut butter? Last time I think I made peanut butter —"

"Taryn," Kim cut in, gasping as pain clenched through her uterus. "I need...help."

"Where are you?" No-nonsense Taryn could always be counted on to immediately gauge the situation and not fritter around. The comforting sounds of action came over the line as Taryn began the considerable task of getting the babies ready to leave.

"Down the...greenhouse road. Past the red ribbon."

"What happened? Did you fall?"

"No. Bring....my Explorer. Car seats. Keys are —"

"Got 'em," Taryn sang out. "I'm on my way. Don't hang up."

With a fainting kind of relief, Kim heard her Explorer start. She huddled on the shoulder of the gravel road, the open phone line the only thing keeping her from screaming her despair to the sky as a hot rush of blood soaked her jeans. She already knew from bitter experience the outcome; she was losing the baby, and no matter how skilled of physicians Paul Jacobs and Reggie Spaulding happened to be, they would not be able to stop it.

She was barely aware of the Explorer stopping beside her, Taryn careful not to spray her with gravel.

"Oh, *Kim!*" her friend murmured softly, kneeling beside her. The blood spoke for her, the spreading stain down her thighs an unspoken confession of her secret.

Taryn lifted her and guided her to the open passenger door; the pain as she straightened to climb into the Explorer was excruciating. Kim curled into a ball on the seat, barely aware of the SUV moving or of her infant twins fussing in the back seat.

And then more hands lifted her from the Explorer and onto a gurney. Reggie Spaulding hovered over her for a surreal moment, his anxious brown face the last thing she saw.

"Kimberly."

She shrank away from his voice, wanting to stay in the soothing embrace of slumber. In her dreams her marriage was intact and her womb full with their child. But his voice coaxed her, beckoned her, and when had she ever been able to deny him anything?

A cool hand against her cheek brought her eyes reluctantly open. She stared into pristine pools of deepest blue, and then he blinked and drew back. Kim closed her eyes again.

"Kim, wake up. We need to talk."

Her eyes came open with utmost reluctance. Aaron had pulled a chair close to the side of her bed, where he sat wringing his baseball cap between his knees. His raven hair stood out in spikes, sweat dampened from work and rumpled from worried fingers. He didn't break eye contact as he spoke.

"You were hemorrhaging badly. Reggie...oh boy." He blew out a breath. "Reggie had no choice. He had to do an emergency hysterectomy."

Kim, insulated in a morphine-induced haze, didn't comprehend. She stared silently at her husband and wanted nothing more than to go back to sleep. His words...well, it didn't matter what he'd said. She could make no sense of his words anyway. Her eyes drifted closed.

His hand against her cheek woke her again what seemed like seconds later. But he had showered and changed his clothes, so she knew it had to have been hours. She felt more lucid, aware enough to realize her abdomen hurt badly.

"You can push the button in your hand for a dose of morphine," Ron said quietly, "but don't do it yet. Please."

Kim's thumb slipped away from the button. She returned his solemn stare, and in his eyes she thought she saw accusation and recrimination.

"You were pretty out of it earlier. I guess I tried to talk to you too soon."

Kim remembered him saying something vague and nonsensical. Now wild fear raced through her veins; had he been trying to talk to her about the state of their marriage?

"Do you remember what I told you earlier?" She shook her head. "You were bleeding heavily. Reggie had to do an emergency hysterectomy."

No more babies. No more...anything?

Kim squeezed her eyes shut, dislodging the tears that pooled in them.

"Did you know you were pregnant, Kim?"

"Yes."

He inhaled sharply. "For how long?"

"Three weeks." She knew he wasn't going to like the answer, but she was unprepared for the intensity of his reaction. Deep color burned up his neck and through his face, and his jaw clenched so tightly she thought he might break his teeth.

"I see. And were you planning on telling me before the baby was born?"

Kim flinched, his harsh words grating across the rawness of her loss. "We weren't exactly speaking, but yes, I would have told you soon."

"I'm assuming you believed you had a good reason not to say anything before now?"

"I didn't want it to be the only reason you stayed."

That shut him up, Kim thought with grim satisfaction. Aaron stared at her as though seeing a stranger, words utterly failing him for several interminable minutes.

"Tia and Evan are reason enough."

His words went through her heart like a sword. After the first shocked seconds, she turned her face away, blinking rapidly to hold back her tears.

"Kim, I didn't—"

"Please go," Kim interrupted. Her thumb jabbed the morphine button.

"Kim—"

"Just *go*."

The sweet oblivion rushing through her blood stole his reply, and when she woke up again he had left. He didn't come back.

Taryn took her home from the hospital four days later. Kim had been expecting Aaron, and her surprise and hurt must have shown on her face when Taryn came through the door, for her friend rushed into an explanation.

"Tia's running a fever, and she only stops fussing when Ron holds her."

"A fever?" Kim exclaimed, moving gingerly off her bed.

"Just teething, I think. Nothing to worry about." Taryn flashed a smile as she picked up the plastic bag holding Kim's personal effects. "Let's get you home. The twins have missed you, and I'm sure Aaron would like to see you home. He's been enduring TV dinners."

"He knows how to cook." Kim didn't care if he'd been forced to eat dog food, not after what he'd said. If she'd harbored hopes that her marriage could be saved, she'd let go of them the instant those words had left his mouth.

Taryn shot her a questioning look, but Kim didn't elaborate. If she talked about it, she would cry, and she might not stop for a thousand years.

She had a dangerous moment in which she nearly lost her grip on her iron control when Aaron coolly informed her that he had moved some of her and the twins' things into the spare bedroom on the main floor so she wouldn't have to go up and down the stairs.

"That's convenient," Taryn said brightly, disappearing down the hallway with Kim's things. "That way you're forced to obey Reggie's discharge orders."

Kim felt as though Aaron had just reached into her chest and ripped out her heart. He started to say something more, but she turned abruptly and followed Taryn into the spare bedroom, away from him, away from the ashes of her marriage.

March 20, 1945

I fear we've waited too long to leave. We should have been gone before the spring equinox. Neither of us even considered that Kassandra would have a séance tonight. While on one hand it will keep her occupied while we leave with the children, I fear that those beings — and Alexander — will know our intentions and will tell her before we can make our escape.

I am packed and ready, my journal the only thing remaining to be secured. Jonathan is packing, and my and the children's luggage is already hidden in the pantry; it is doubtful Kassandra will discover them as she never ventures more than a step into the kitchens, and that's only to order about the staff. If the creatures keep silent, that is. Please, God, keep them silent. Hide our intentions from them.

Jonathan has arranged safe passage for me to San Francisco; I will stay with my sister until I can find another position. He intends to take the children to Boston to stay with his sister, who arrived unexpectedly last week for a surprise visit and who remains unaware of our escape plan, as she will until the moment to leave arrives. He has a servant ready to pack her belongings in an instant. If she were able to keep a secret, we would have a sounder plan, one that would make me easier in my mind. But since she has no sense of discretion, we cannot risk her letting anything slip to Kassandra.

Kassandra...she watches me with strange eyes now, eyes that seem to look at me from the brink of madness. It's as though she believes she knows my heart, and finds its desires amusing. She would be wrong; I have no designs on her husband. He is a kind man, attractive in physique and personality, but he is not for me, nor I for him. My heart belongs to a soldier who is, at this moment, somewhere in Germany.

But the children...how I wish the children could remain with me while Jonathan makes arrangements for Kassandra's admittance to the asylum. However, the attorneys say their custody must be legal and binding, and only family is acceptable. I shall miss them, but I long more to be free of this house.

And soon, I shall be just that. Free.

SHOULDA KNOWN BETTER
Tuesday, May 5, 2009

Spring weather on the Olympic Peninsula was capricious, and this spring proved no different than any other. From the moment Geoffrey had pulled himself out of the muck into which the incessant rain had turned the Manor's cul-de-sac, the sky had begun to clear of the heavy rain clouds. By the time he had showered and changed into clean clothes, rays of sunlight had broken through the gloom.

He had stayed two days, determined not to leave the Peninsula without her. His calls to her cell went unanswered and unreturned. His three attempts to gain entrance to the Manor again had been dismal failures. Hugh MacGregor had gone with him the first two times, but neither of them had been able to even approach the gate. Hugh had been troubled and more than a little frightened at Geoffrey's persistence, especially when he suggested they try climbing through the cave from the beach and gain access through the tunnels.

"She's in the company of demons, Geoffrey," he'd said, his voice shaking and holding a note of incredulity. Geoffrey couldn't quite believe it himself, and he'd been face-to-face with one. All the more reason to rescue Rachael as soon as possible.

Access through the tunnels from the beach proved impossible. Although he was more than up to the task of climbing the cliff face to the cave entrance – and managed without mishap – it became obvious twenty feet inside the dank cave that only a small child would be able to wriggle through the tunnels, if in fact the right tunnel could be identified. Four yawning holes offered possibilities. Of the four one was a straight drop down, so deep he was sure it ended below low-tide sea level, too deep to see the bottom, although he thought he caught a flash of white against dark volcanic stone.

White like bleached bones.

Somehow he had made it back down the cliff face to the beach without mishap, although he had stayed too long and the tide was coming in. He spent a few tense moments fighting the suction of the sea as it withdrew from the beach, and then he was clambering up the rough stone steps hewn into the cliff side to the parking lot, where he sat in his car, soaking in the solar heat. His dashboard clock said his sojourn had taken three hours. Geoffrey was sure he'd only been gone an hour, at most, an hour-and-a-half – ten minutes to scale the cliff face to the cave, twenty minutes investigating, twenty minutes to climb back down and wade through the incoming tide.

So now he knew the cave led to the house, for where else would time cease to exist except in their realm? But the knowledge was useless; it didn't help him get to Rachael.

After stopping at the sheriff's office to report the possibility of a body in the cave, drawing a quick diagram for the skeptical deputy, Geoffrey headed up the 101 toward Port Angeles and the ferry that would take him back home. The sky was blue and blameless, and the sun shone bright and unsympathetic.

He thought it should be raining. In fact, it should rain forever, a reflection of the state of his heart. Fear and gnawing worry, underscored by growing panic, became his constant companions. The sunshine somehow made it worse, brought out into clear view the severity of this situation: the house had won. Somehow, during his absence, it had gained the upper hand and managed to claw its way so deeply into Rachael's psyche that she had turned on him.

But perhaps that was ignoring the facts. If he were completely, baldly honest with himself, the house had sunk its talons into her from the first moment she walked in the door. Her captivation had been complete, her surrender inevitable. She had flung herself into the heart of hell without a backward glance or a moment's doubt, never seeing the danger, never suspecting the truth.

She was lost, and he was paralyzed with fear and heartbreak.

Putz! his conscience spat at him. *Coward! Get off your yellow ass and DO SOMETHING!*

But every time he thought of returning to Heron Bay, a wisp of smoke rose from the scorched globe, now reunited with its spindle frame, and all thoughts of heroism died a swift death. This was greater than him, more powerful than him. How could he hope to win? He couldn't even go into the Manor, and Rachael, from all evidence, never left it. She'd even brought her own food; he'd seen the box of non-perishables next to the red Coleman cooler by the front doors.

Maybe you can't go back to Heron Bay, he thought, *but you can call someone who's already there. You can call Hugh McGregor —*

Smoke drifted across the room from the direction of the globe. Geoffrey refused to look.

— or Agent Wallace. He's still there. He could probably get into the house, force Rachael to leave. He's a trained bad-ass, after all.

A flicker of orange caught his eye, and he turned his head. Africa had burst into flames.

On second thought, I'll just stay right here. I don't need to make any phone calls. I'll just have another gin-and-tonic, and pack for my business trip to Olympia tomorrow. ONLY to Olympia. And when I'm done in the capitol, I'll come right back here to Orcas Island and try to forget all about Bayview Manor. And Rachael Payne.

The flame guttered and abruptly extinguished.

He sat at his new desk, a cheap replacement for the one he had lost — just in case his demonic stalker decided to incinerate his office again — and doodled mindlessly on a legal pad, forcing his mind to stay blank. If they divined none of his thoughts, there would be no destructive warnings, no dangerous retribution. His hand made looping circles on the yellow lined paper, over and over.

A dark shadow moved at the corner of his vision. He stared with obsessive concentration at the notepad. His heartbeat quickened, thudded, hammered. His flesh rippled as all the fine hairs stood on end. *Don't look, don't look, DON'T LOOK!*

He'd seen them at the Manor the day Rachael had thrown the sledgehammer at him, when he'd grabbed her arm and tried to drag her from the house. The second she'd screamed at him to let her go, the veil had dropped between his dimension and that of the unseen beings that inhabited Bayview Manor. At last he could see their invisible companions, the true owners of the mansion. They were the shadows that clung in dim corners, glimpsed only from the corners of one's eye; the forces that stole tools and left them in random locations; that turned on drills and impaled men's hands. That swarmed Rachael and imprisoned her, working her to exhaustion, driving her to madness.

They had presented a wall of supernatural power between him and Rachael that day, shielding her from his rescue. One had risen before him, terrible in its rage at his interference, beautiful beyond this world, its eyes a kaleidoscope of jewel-tone colors floating on depthless black voids, its wings unfurled to block his path. Lips curled back from sharp teeth in a snarl, long-fingered hands reached for him, and then he was flying through the air. Chips of razor-edged marble had cut him through his jeans; more had bruised him when he hit the floor with tremendous force. He was amazed the impact hadn't killed him.

It had come for him again as he lay stunned, trying to move and unable to, knowing he must at all costs get to Rachael. It had lifted him effortlessly, flung open the doors, and heaved him outside into the muddy cul-de-sac. He landed face-first, sucking mud. By the time he had cleared his mouth and eyes, the house had sealed itself against him. He stared in dismay at a giant edifice bare of windows and doors.

His love and fear for Rachael had propelled him to his feet and up the crumbling front steps, but the closer he came to where the door should be, the thicker the air became, until it was like trudging through tar. And then he had hit an invisible, impenetrable wall, as though the air had turned solid. Whispers sighed on the wind, a chorus of discordant bells: *get out go away she's ours she's ours SHE'S OURS!!*

The echoes built to a thundering crescendo until he thought the sound would drive him mad. He staggered down the steps to his car and fell inside, jamming down the locks although he knew it would not keep them out. He gunned the engine and floored the accelerator, barely able to keep the car on the road as he bounced through potholes and squelched through mud, certain that just as he reached the huge iron gates at the head of the drive, they would swing shut and he would crash into them at sixty miles an hour and no one would find him for God knew how long.

But they let him leave. As the car skidded onto the wet blacktop and he raced north toward Forks, the iron gates slammed shut with a clang that echoed all the way to hell and back.

He'd limped into his motel room, showered and changed into clean clothes, and on impulse had reached for the phone to call Hugh MacGregor. The phone had glowed orange, and an acrid stench filled the room as the receiver melted onto the console.

No matter. There was still his cell phone. But when he reached into his jacket pocket, he had found it in pieces, damaged beyond repair from his impact with the floor.

He got the message, loud and clear. And the message had not changed over the last week. *Hands off, leave her alone, don't interfere, she's ours.*

She's ours.

No, that wasn't right. She was God's. She had been God's all her life; she had simply lost her way. Got lost inside the house. Was led astray.

The globe caught fire, the flames high enough to scorch the ceiling. Geoffrey cast a disparaging eye at the fire sprinklers that, for the second time, failed to come on in the event of a fire, and then he lumbered to his feet, grabbed the extinguisher that went everywhere with him now, and doused the flames.

A calm, still thought made its way through the cacophony of panic. *Go now. You can't worry about what will happen while you're gone.*

He stared at the smoking remains of the globe—damn, that had been an antique!—and dropped the extinguisher. A quick sweep of the room showed no visible sign of his otherworldly stalker. He fished his keys from his pocket and headed for the door.

"Burn it down. I don't fucking care."

He slammed the door behind him, not caring if he came back to find his office burned to the ground, not caring if his house was likewise destroyed. They were just things, big things containing smaller things. And things didn't matter anymore.

Five hours later, he rang Hugh MacGregor's doorbell. The look on the pastor's face when he answered the summons told Geoffrey that his absence on the Peninsula had been appreciated by more than just Rachael Payne and her horde of protectors.

"I'm getting Rachael out of Bayview Manor, and I'm going to need your help," he said without preamble.

Hugh seemed to slump in resignation. "I was afraid it was going to come to this. When do we go?"

"Daylight," Geoffrey replied, casting an eye at the night sky. No way he wanted to be in that house after dark, although he didn't think it mattered what time of day he entered. Those creatures were always there, always waiting.

"Pick me up in the morning, then," Hugh said, and closed the door before Geoffrey had taken a full step away from it.

She came to him at midnight, the witching hour, accompanied by a soft breeze and an inky blue sky scattered with stars. Her quiet knock summoned him from slumber, and from the moment he laid eyes on her, he was unable to deny her.

"The stars are incredible tonight, especially from the beach. You want to...?" She gestured vaguely in the general direction of Heron Beach and smiled, seeming more like the Rachael who had so captivated him from their very first meeting than she had in weeks.

Which is how he found himself on a dark beach, walking close enough that their arms bumped. The stars *were* incredible, but he could see nothing but Rachael. He caught the apple fragrance of her shampoo over the stronger scents of ocean air and wet sand, and for what seemed like the millionth time, he had to make a conscious effort to calm his heartbeat and curb the persistent desire to wrap himself around her, lose himself in her, take them places they had no business going.

She stopped at the edge of the surf, shoes dangling from her fingers, and stared out across the ocean. "It's beautiful in a primitive, barbaric way," she remarked, breaking a long stretch of companionable silence.

"Yes, it is."

He was looking at her, not at the ocean. Over the course of the last six months, without his even being aware of it, she had transformed from girl-next-door pretty to compellingly, hauntingly beautiful. And barbaric? Certainly, if her chucking the sledgehammer at him was anything to go by.

"I'm sorry I threw that sledgehammer at you," she said, as though reading his thought. She cast him a glance over her shoulder. The moon gilded her face in silver, reminding him of the cold beauty of a marble statue. "I don't know why I was so angry that day."

"No worries." He shrugged it off, and was surprised to find he meant it.

She turned back toward the water. "Did I ever tell you about my brother?"

"You mentioned him once or twice, but nothing in particular."

"We lost Dad two years ago. A heart attack, out of the blue. He'd never shown any indication of heart trouble. Dad left the house to me, with the stipulation that I always give Ethan houseroom. Or if I sold the house, I had to put half the money in trust. Ethan was never the most responsible, made some reckless choices. I think Dad always knew Ethan would flake out if anything happened to him, so he made sure there were stipulations to his inheritance."

"Rather wise of your father."

"I've heard the saying 'A wise man knows his father.' I think an even wiser man knows his child."

And what would the late Mr. Payne think of his daughter tonight, if he could see her standing here at the water's edge, the wind blowing her jacket open and plastering her shirt to her chest? What would he think, seeing his daughter fresh from a house of demons?

"My father was a pastor, did you know that? He resigned his position when my mother died—that's how we got Hugh MacGregor. I was six, Ethan was almost eight. His heart would break if he could see where Ethan is now."

Geoffrey scuffed his feet, kicking up wads of wet sand. His feet were freezing. The obvious question, at this point, was *And just where is Ethan?* All things considered, he rather thought that her brother had to be in a better place right now than Rachael herself.

"Where—"

"Somewhere in Spokane," she answered before he'd finished asking.

"That doesn't sound so bad. It's a nice city."

She laughed without humor. "It's not the city Dad would object to, but the people Ethan left with. Strange people who only came to the beach at night. He's tried to access his inheritance several times, but I've managed to block it through court order because of his behavior."

"You think he left with some kind of cult?"

"I think so. I was going to use one of those organizations that specialize in extraction, but my attorney said I could be charged with kidnapping. So Ethan's on the east side, Dad's dead, and I'm here all alone. Sometimes I really think that I'm losing my mind."

"You need some sleep. Why don't we finish this talk tomorrow? I'll take you home."

"I'd rather finish our talk, but somewhere warm. Do you have any wine?"

"No. I have some Sprite, though."

A half smile curved her lips. "That will do. Let's go."

The warmth of his motel room was almost painful after the stinging chill of the beach. Geoffrey stripped the bedspread off his bed and wrapped it around her, pushing her down into the chair beside the bed, and went to get them both a can of Sprite from the fridge in the kitchenette. The motel had only one vacancy when he rolled into town, a suite with an extra bedroom and a kitchenette.

He took a few minutes to compose himself, unsure what to make of the strange thrum vibrating the air between them but knowing he was treading dangerous ground.

Bracing himself with silent admonitions to be on his guard, he grabbed two cans of Sprite and went back into the main bedroom. He stopped short, the cans slipping from his hands and rolling across the carpet. His mouth worked silently to voice words his brain couldn't seem to form, as it had gone utterly, blissfully blank.

She had shed the bedspread and left it laying on the floor by the chair. She had shed most everything else, too. Her shirt was draped haphazardly over the back of the chair; her jeans had been kicked off and shoved beneath it.

"Rachael," he managed to say, his voice cracking. "What ..."

Her steps carried her around the end of the bed, closer to him, and though he knew he should back away—he should, in fact, be running out the door as fast as he could—he stood rooted to the spot, unable to move even when she stopped before him, her hands coming up to snap open the front closure of her brassiere. The scrap of Lycra and lace dropped out of sight.

"Rachael," he said again, his voice cracking again, but this time it was an expression of need rather than one of alarm.

"Geoffrey," she echoed his tone. She reached for him, one hand snaking around his neck, the other sliding over his cheek, cupping his face, urging him to lean down into her kiss. *A gentleman always obliges a lady.* Even when the lady stood naked in front of him, urging him toward wanton, sinful acts?

Yeah, even then.

Her mouth was still cold from the night air. Her icy tongue sliding over his made him shiver, but he didn't pull away. Instead, he gathered her against him, her bare skin igniting his hunger. Although he had made a concentrated effort to keep their relationship within acceptable confines, God knew he was no choirboy, and the feel of her in his arms burned through propriety with supernatural speed.

She was too thin; her collarbones stood out in sharp relief, and he could feel every one of her ribs, confirming his suspicion that she wasn't remembering to eat. He wondered if the demons of Bayview Manor drove her so hard to demolish the inside of the mansion that all other thought fled, even those concerning her basic human needs.

But he didn't want to think about the demons right now. She was out of the Manor; that had been his goal. And she was here with him, mostly naked, completely willing, and that *hadn't* been his goal—not a short-term one, anyway—but he wasn't one to look a gift horse in the mouth. She was safe, and she was his.

He shrugged out of his tee-shirt, flinging it aside; he'd find it on the TV later. Her fingers began an exploration of his bared flesh that left him shaking and gasping for air. Her palms and fingers were rough with the remnants of blisters that had raised, broken, and healed; the scrape of her callused skin was somehow erotic. The button on his jeans refused to give, and for a frustrating moment he struggled with it, finally slipping it free. He kicked his jeans off his feet and out of the way; he'd trip over them on his way to the bathroom later.

They tumbled onto the bed. Limbs tangled, mouths sought, fingers explored, bodies arched, and even as they crashed through the last barricade, a part of Geoffrey watched the proceedings with horrified dismay, wondering where his self-control and moral code had gone.

But he knew where. He'd shoved it into a dark closet and locked it in; he'd regret it later. Right now he held his heart's desire in his arms, and there was no room for reason or judgment.

A very long time later, physically exhausted and emotionally spent, they slept.

She was gone when he woke, leaving behind a bloodstain on the sheets and the fragrance of apples on his skin. He viewed the former with shame, and inhaled the latter with the kind of sick dread a man experiences when he has lost something of intrinsic value.

He should have known better; he saw the trap now that it was too late. How could she have known he was in Heron Bay and where he was staying? She couldn't have. But *they* knew he was coming for her and that he was bringing Hugh MacGregor. She had been sent to head him off at the pass, and the cost they had extracted — intangibles that, in their eyes, were expendable — was her virtue and his honor.

A formidable price and a victory for their cause.

(E-mail from Aaron Schaefer to Dennis Wallace)

Date: May 7, 2009
To: Dennis Wallace [encrypted]
From: Aaron Schaefer [gardenplans@stoneridgenursery.com]
Subject: I am stupid

When are you coming back? Advice is welcome, although I sometimes think you're the last person to be giving it. But who am I to point fingers when I think I just killed my marriage?

SHATTERED
Thursday, May 7, 2009

Ron studied the aerial photographs of Sarah Bennett's garden, taking advantage of his wife and children taking an afternoon nap. It had taken two weeks to connect with Brad Harrington and arrange a time to go up in the Cessna, and then another week to get the photos back from the developer. They weren't the best quality — no one would ever hire him as an aerial photographer — but they served the purpose.

From the sky, the pattern of the garden was clear, thanks to the unseasonable growth of the plants and the neat, well-tended gravel paths. It triggered something in his memory that he couldn't quite bring to full realization. He didn't think he'd seen this pattern so much as he'd experienced it, as though he'd walked it, perhaps. But he had no recollection of having been to Sarah Bennett's cottage, and he rather doubted that Caleb had taken him there when he'd hidden him at the Wyckham House when he'd been a toddler; there had been no reason to. He hadn't needed a healer, and the relationship between Caleb and Sarah had not been one to invite casual visiting. To his knowledge, no one had ever enjoyed that sort of intimacy with the mysterious herb woman in the woods.

She said Sarah was the devil.

He sifted out a photo with a particularly clear image of the garden pattern, and set its duplicate off to the side. With a red Sharpie, he drew lines along the paths. The lines intersected, creating triangular sections and long rows of irregular boxes. His eyes blurred as he stared down at it, trying to force the memory to the surface. It wouldn't come. He cast a glance at the untouched duplicate, and on inspiration made the lines of the paths bolder.

There it is! You can see it clearly now!

But what "it" was still wasn't certain. His subconscious fought to shove the memory to the surface, and his fear beat it back relentlessly. There was still so much he couldn't stand to remember, so much he wished he didn't know about himself.

Coward. You won't face what happened to you, just like you won't face the part you played in the destruction of your marriage.

He scrubbed a hand over his face and eyes. It was right in front of him, what he sought; why couldn't he see it? And he had glimpsed it the day he and Taryn had gone to the cottage, when he'd first walked up to the gate and beheld the haphazard layout of Sarah's garden. Maybe if he went back and approached the gate with his eyes closed, and then opened them suddenly, it would become clear…

But he didn't have to do that. He had the photographs, and those were much safer than venturing into the woods again. One hand covering his eyes, the other holding up the photograph on which he'd traced the paths with the red marker, he took in a huge breath, let it out slowly, and dropped his hand.

And understood.

The paths were corridors, the planting beds were rooms, the curving paths that converged and joined at the gate formed the horseshoe staircase — he was looking at the blueprint of the Wyckham House.

He took the photos into the sunroom and ran them through the scanner, and then sent them to Denny's e-mail. It felt strange not to send them to Cody first, but his father had given strict, if not cryptic, instructions that he was not to be bothered while he and Renée were in Italy, and if it were something to do with Bayview Manor, he was not to be bothered at all. Ron didn't know what had happened, but it was bad enough that his father and stepmother went abroad without coming to see him before they left.

Everything seemed to be falling apart. And perhaps that was why, when he saw the document on the taskbar with the tantalizing title "Journal," he clicked it and began reading, his heart hungry for the thoughts of the wife who seemed further out of his reach every day.

It took precisely twenty seconds to deeply regret his impulsive decision to snoop into Kimberly's private thoughts.

All I know is when I dream, I dream of him. I feel his longing, his sorrow, his regret...and I feel drawn to help. Is that God — or is it insanity? I don't know the answer to that question, either. And Aaron...oh, Aaron will blow a gasket, despite the fact we have barely spoken in weeks. I can't ignore the pull on my soul that Caleb Schaefer has.

The saliva vanished from his mouth, leaving his tongue and throat parched. He felt faint with shock. No wonder she'd had no trouble shutting him out. A heart divided could not be loyal. And to think she had dragged him over the coals for his fictitious infidelity.

He diminished the document and left the sunroom through the door leading to the deck, where he slumped into an Adirondack chair badly in need of paint. His mind reeled, jumping from denial to suspicion to paranoid certainty in a vicious circle. Finally he accepted his suspicions as fact, and he sat silently, hands gripping the arms of the chair convulsively, flaking paint chips cutting into his palms and fingers, his burning anger building to a volcano of fury.

൭

He found the book on the stacks in the corner of the used bookstore, stuffed onto a bottom shelf between two larger volumes and nearly obscured. A fraying string from the hand-laced binding caught his eye, and he spent several minutes wresting it from its spot. His fingers shrank from touching the cover; it was presumably leather although he couldn't define exactly what animal it had once been. It felt...gross. He laid it on a small table in a cramped alcove nearby, shoving aside a stack of paperbacks another shopper had left behind.

Cramped though the alcove was, it was brightly lit with a banker's desk lamp. Denny adjusted the shade so that the brightest light fell squarely onto the book. Now he could see the symbol etched on the front. His finger traced it, and his stomach did a somersault. He wasn't ordinarily squeamish, but the feel of the leather made his flesh crawl.

He peered closer at the symbol, and realized it wasn't etched but burned into the leather, a strange arrangement of triangles and irregular squares. Something niggled at his subconscious, as though he'd seen the symbol before in some other context.

The pages were thick and irregular, made of what he was sure was papyrus. Ink, dark brown with age, traced its way across the pages in nonsensical forms. It was no recognizable language, so he assumed it was a book of illustrations. But what they meant was a mystery. The symbol on the front was repeated on the final page in smaller form below a uniform block of symbols. A signature, maybe.

His smartphone made a discreet sound, alerting him that he had received an e-mail. He had trouble dragging his eyes from the strange book, and once he did he felt as though he had awakened from a dream. A tap of an icon brought up his e-mail on the small screen; another tap opened the new e-mail from Ron. No doubt another appeal to come save him from drowning in the estrogen pool.

And then the pictures loaded. Denny felt the ground spin out from under him. The red lines Ron had drawn on the photograph of Sarah Bennett's garden paths were an exact match to the symbol on the front of the book he had just found. He scrolled to Ron's notes below the photos. The words—*the garden layout is the Wyckham House's floor plan*—propelled him from the alcove, the book in hand. His skin broke into gooseflesh. He stopped at the register, fishing a credit card from his wallet and laying the book—with a silent sigh of relief—on the scarred wooden counter. The shopkeeper stared at it blankly.

"That's not our book, sir."

"What do you mean? I found it on a shelf in the back corner."

She raised her gaze to his with what seemed like great effort. He remembered his own difficulties looking away from it, and his unease doubled.

"I own this shop. I know every book we have, and every book is tagged with our price stickers." She pointed at the cover, free of any markings except those burned into the leather—and free of price tags. "That's not our book."

"Maybe I should leave it here, then. Someone may be coming back for it, not realizing they left it here."

"No," she said, a strange note of panic in her voice. "Please take it. I don't...I don't want it here."

He gazed at her for a long moment, wondering if she was pulling a gag, but her expression was deadly serious. "May I have a bag? I don't mind paying you for it."

She took a small plastic bag from under the counter. Revulsion twisted her expression as she shoved the book into it. He thanked her and turned to leave.

"Get rid of it," she said before he had taken more than three paces from the counter. Her voice was low and passionate. "Drop it down a mine shaft, anything, but get rid of it where no one can find it."

He came back to the counter. "Why? What do you know about this book?"

She was staring at the bag. Denny grabbed her wrist, squeezing until the pain made her look away.

"What?" she asked blankly, and then realized he had her arm in a painful grip. "Hey, that hurts!"

"Why did you tell me to get rid of this book?"

"What are you talking about? I don't care what you do with it." She twisted out of his grip and backed away several steps, eying him with considerable — and justifiable — suspicion. Denny realized she hadn't been aware of speaking at all.

He left the shop, the bag with the book dangling from his hand, its weight like an anchor dragging him down into unknown depths. He had never been one to believe in coincidences, and he didn't think this was one. That Ron had sent him the pictures with the exact symbol drawn on one as he had found in a book the bookstore insisted wasn't theirs reeked of orchestration. But whose?

Not daring to look at the book again, he opened Ron's email and studied the strange symbol of lines and shapes. He needed an occult expert, but he had no idea where he would find one schooled in obscure and heretofore unknown languages. Hugh MacGregor might be able to tell Hebrew from Aramaic, but Denny rather doubted this was either. He'd seen both languages, and this looked nothing like them.

Aliens.

Before that thought had fully formed, he was already pushing it away. While he believed in an unseen world beyond the reach and understanding of humans, he didn't believe in beings from other planets who were able to travel to this one across a vast universe or more.

An unseen world. Otherworldly. Angels.

Demons.

And he knew who he must ask.

୧୬

She watched them from a distance: the pixie blonde and her ardent suitor, envy burning along her nerve endings like acid. She didn't know them, had no desire for either of them, but she longed for the touch of her husband more than she thirsted for water or craved air.

The man wound his fingers into the woman's hair, his thumb stroking a silken lock. Their breath came harsh and gasping, through their noses because their mouths were melded tightly together. His other hand explored, its meandering path designed to elicit passion and encourage the shedding of inhibitions. Three times she rebuffed his fingers as they sought intimate areas. The fourth time, she offered no protest.

Kim stepped forward in alarm. She had no idea why. She'd never seen them before. But she knew she must stop them, and stop them now.

They didn't notice her, even when she stopped and leaned down to the woman, her lips a mere inch from her delicate ear.

"Remember Rachael," she whispered. The words surprised her, because she had no recollection of thinking them.

The pixie started, wrenching her mouth from her lover's kiss.

"What is it, Sabrina?"

"Did you hear that?"

"Hear what?" He was valiantly trying to capture her mouth again, but her hand on his chest impeded his progress considerably—she was pushing him back.

"You didn't hear someone whisper?" Sabrina extricated herself with some difficulty from his full-body embrace, looking around. The man collapsed backward against the overstuffed cushions, groaning in resignation.

"All I heard was you."

"I heard someone say 'Remember Rachael.'" He snorted, and she bristled like a cat. "I'm serious, Riley."

Kim, who had backed away a step as Sabrina fought her way into a sitting position, leaned in again. "Go home. Now."

Sabrina stood up abruptly, her face pinched with fear. "I have to go home."

"*What?*"

"I have to go home," she said again, impatiently. She looked at a slim gold watch strapped to her wrist. "If I leave now, I can make the last ferry to the Peninsula."

"Home to the *Peninsula*? I thought you meant to Sonia's." His petulance was tempered with good humor. Kim suspected that, despite his sexual frustration, he didn't mind the interruption, didn't even mind Sabrina's rebuffs.

"Something's wrong—something with Rachael. I have to go home."

She was rushing around now, gathering her purse, a sweater, her cell phone. Her fearful, worried thoughts telegraphed to Kim as though shouted aloud: *Did I just have a paranormal experience? The voice sounded so real! An angel? Oh God, I hope Rachael's OK. I haven't even called her in two weeks! I haven't even* thought *about her since I started seeing Riley! I'm a terrible friend! Oh God, please, let her be all right!*

"I'll come with you, drive you down," Riley said unexpectedly, getting to his feet.

"You don't—"

"I know I don't have to. You've got me freaked out now. I like Rachael too."

The blonde's frightened expression softened and she opened her mouth to reply. Kim didn't hear what she said because the room spun away, the couple was gone, and she opened her eyes to her guest bedroom, staring into the crib that held her sleeping son. She sat up slowly, brushing her hair off her sweaty face. That had been strange, like the dream she'd had of Caleb in the ruined gallery of Bayview Manor. Beyond strange, and outside the scope of her normal precognitive dreams. She cast a glance askance toward the heavens.

"When I said I wanted my gift back, I didn't mean with extra measure."

Of course there was no response. She slid off the bed, adjusted the blankets over both the babies, and tiptoed out of the bedroom, stopping off in the bathroom to wash her face before heading to the kitchen for a snack. Her body clamored for nutrition at the same time her stomach rebelled at the thought of eating; she had been force-feeding herself since she'd come home from the hospital, ignoring the sometimes violent protests of her turbulent tummy.

Two paces into the kitchen, her step faltered. Aaron sat at the table, leaning on his elbows. His blue eyes had been trained intently on his hands until she walked in, and then they flashed to her face like lightning. And like lightning, the expression in them sent a buzzing shock through her. Fury, betrayal, the need to lash out—all flared in those blue depths before an icy chill submerged them.

"I need to talk to you," he said coldly.

Dread squeezed her heart. *Here it is, the moment you've been praying would never come. His next words will be 'I want a divorce.' You can handle it. You've been expecting it. But oh God, this is going to hurt.*

She edged into a chair, warily returning his stare. "All right."

He breathed in sharply through his nose, as though seeking strength from the air around him. "What really happened with Caleb while he had you at the Wyckham House?"

This wasn't the question she had been expecting at all, and she suddenly felt wrong-footed. Wrong-footed and insanely hopeful.

"I told you."

"What you told me does not even begin to explain your continued fascination with him and your inability to let him go."

She blinked. "What the hell are you talking about?"

"I had to scan some photographs to send to Denny."

She didn't hear the rest of what he said. She understood perfectly now. Her computer was hooked to the scanner. Her journal had still been open because never once in their marriage had he ventured into her private writings.

"You read my journal," she interrupted and felt the first stirrings of anger.

"It was open."

"It wasn't on the screen. You had to click on it. You deliberately read my journal."

"Probably a good thing I did," he snapped back. The chill vanished from his eyes, melted by a blazing fury. Kim recoiled. She didn't think he would strike her, but she had never—*never*—seen him this angry.

"I understand now why you thought the worst of me when Melody came to see you. The guilty often project their guilt onto someone else."

She flinched inside. "I told you what happened with Caleb."

"You told me he didn't rape you. You never said anything about having sex with him willingly."

Kim stood up, her body shaking with a rush of anger-fueled adrenaline. "Do you have to work hard at being such a son-of-a-bitch, or does it just come naturally? Oh wait, you don't have to answer that. You *are* blood-related to Caleb, after all."

She strode out of the room, her legs weak and trembling, his accusation like a spear through her chest that made it impossible to breathe. Down the hall, out the back door, and into the garden. Her emotions jumped from fear to fury as her feet carried her down the paths on autopilot until she reached the edge of their personal garden. She stopped at the gate, staring through the drizzly, grey day toward the greenhouse across the fields of herbs and lavender, and then made her way to a bench a few paces away. She slicked the rain off it with one hand and sat, huddled into herself, shivering.

How dare he? How dare he snoop into her journal and then take it all out of context? How dare he justify his own actions by trying to pin unwarranted accusations on her?

But...hadn't she done the same thing to him in March? Hadn't she worried for years about his reaction to the truth of those eight hours she'd been Caleb's captive? Her journal was full of her guilty maunderings, and there was no sense denying it. He'd already read it.

The crunch of rapid footsteps on the gravel path gave her a second's warning before he came into view. Rain glistened in his hair like jewels, and she felt a rush of longing that rivaled her anger. God, she loved him so much. How could this be happening to them?

He unlatched the gate and swung it open, only seeing her as he stepped through and turned to close it. He froze, his cold stare chilling her across the distance between them, and then he took a few angry steps back toward her.

"How could you sleep with him and then marry me without even a word about it?"

"I—"

He interrupted. "You should have been honest with me. You know how I feel about him. It would have changed everything."

"I didn't—"

"You know how much I despise him."

"You don't understand!"

"*I UNDERSTAND PERFECTLY! YOU WERE HIS WHORE!*" he shouted, and in his rage she saw the shadow of his uncle, the man who had held her in chains at the point of a black stone knife.

"At what point do you think I screwed him, Aaron?" she screamed back, jumping to her feet to close the space between them. "Would that be while he was chaining me up to an altar covered in my friend's blood? Or would it be when he made me lie down in her blood? Or perhaps it was when he was telling me all the things he was going to do to me before he killed me. What the hell do you think happened in there? Eight hours waiting for him to kill me — *eight fucking hours!*"

He blinked, opened his mouth to speak, but she plowed on, rage driving her across the space between them. She jabbed her finger into his chest.

"Do you want to know what saved me? It wasn't *you*, that's for sure. Lemon bars," she said, and he blinked again at the apparent non sequitur. "Lemon bars saved me. Because how could he not like someone who liked lemon bars?"

She was crying now, which made her angry, so she balled her fist and pummeled him where she had jabbed him. He stepped back, grabbed for her flailing hand and missed. She struck him again, her voice rising to a banshee shriek.

"And yes, I dream about him! I can't seem to stop. I can't help it. Because I like lemon bars, he liked *me*, and he let me go. He's a prisoner in that house because of me. I can convince him that he can be forgiven, and I *have* to do it, because until he's free I can never be. Do you know what that's like? *Do* you? To have to go to the man who told you for hours every detail of how he would rape you and then how he would murder you, *every detail*, and offer forgiveness?"

"Kim—"

"But no, how *could* you understand when you were God knows where doing God knows what while I was counting down the minutes of my life?" She gestured violently toward the gate. "Go on, go. Go to your little white-trash piece of ass. We both know this is over."

His eyes widened in shock, and then the wintry chill was back. He grinned cruelly.

"Don't wait up."

He spun on his heel and crashed out the gate, slamming it behind him. It bounced off the latch and creaked halfway open. When he reached the lavender field, he broke into a jog, steadily eating up the distance to the greenhouse.

She stumbled blindly back to the house, arms wrapped around herself to keep herself from flying apart. The twins were still asleep, so she crept off to the shower, where she turned the water so hot it scalded her skin red. The tears came in a ferocious squall, and she huddled on the floor in the corner of the shower, sobbing until she had no voice left, the water beating down on her in a fury of blistering heat.

(Correspondence from Ethan Payne to his sister, Rachael)

May 3, 2009

Dear Rachael,

It pains me to have to write this letter, but your persistence leaves me no choice. Please don't write to me again. No good will come of it. There can be no reconciliation of what's left of our family. You're there, and I'm here, and if I had my way, there'd be a hell of a lot more distance between us.

I'm sorry. I miss you too. But it's better this way. And it's the only way it can be.

Ethan

DANGER AND DARKNESS AHEAD
Wednesday, May 6, 2009

Hugh MacGregor knocked on his motel room door at just past eight-thirty in the morning. Geoffrey had showered but hadn't had time to straighten the room, wasn't sure he could have had he had enough time. His mind was in turmoil. He should have been on his guard, should have seen her ploy before it had gone too far. But he had sailed blithely past the point of no return, unable to focus on anything except his bone-deep desire to be with her in any capacity.

The pastor took in the wreckage of the room: Geoffrey's clothes, scattered across the room; the two cans of Sprite on the floor, kicked aside on one of their trips to the bathroom in the dark; the bed, which was not so much rumpled from sleep as annihilated from sex. He frowned as he scooted into a chair just inside the door, picking Geoffrey's discarded tee-shirt from the TV and tossing it onto the bed.

"Well, this complicates things."

Geoffrey flushed but didn't pause in his task of tying his sneakers. "I admit I didn't see it coming."

"Pun intended?"

"Pastor, I'm shocked."

Hugh barked out a laugh. "I'm a pastor, not a monk. I'm well aware of the ins and outs of sex. Pun definitely *not* intended," he added as an afterthought.

"I love her, if that makes any difference."

"That makes all the difference in the world," Hugh assured him. "Do you have any cans of Sprite that haven't been abused?"

"Yeah, in the fridge. I need to use the bathroom, and then we can go."

Geoffrey dashed into the bathroom as Hugh vanished into the

kitchenette to grab a can of soda. The pastor was lounging against the wall just inside the kitchen, sipping his Sprite and staring at the wrecked bed thoughtfully when Geoffrey reappeared.

"We're not going to obsess over this, are we?" Geoffrey asked, sending a pointed glance at the bed.

"Hmm?" Hugh looked at him blankly, and then gave himself a shake. "Oh, that. No, not at all. I'm actually very pleased. Now if we can just get the girl away from that devil house."

"You're pleased," Geoffrey repeated. "Despite the fact that Rachael and I aren't married?"

Hugh smiled serenely. "You are now. At least as far as God is concerned. Washington State may have a different take on it, but I admit I don't consider the State the ultimate authority." He pushed away from the wall. "I thought we could go by Rachael's apartment first, just to be sure she isn't there before we go through all the trouble of fighting our way into Bayview Manor."

"That sounds like a good idea. I wouldn't put it past that house to pull a trick like that."

"Past the house, eh?" Hugh cocked a brow at Geoffrey, waiting while he checked his pocket for his motel room key and closed the door behind them.

"Well, the things in the house, anyway. I haven't told you what happened to me the last time I was there. Or what's been happening to me ever since."

"I have a good idea it hasn't been pleasant. You can tell me about it on the way."

Geoffrey held him to the offer, filling the car with his story the whole drive to Rachael's apartment. Hugh didn't interrupt except to ask for clarification, and when Geoffrey fell silent, the pastor's troubled demeanor intensified. Hugh was scared; Geoffrey could read it as clearly as if the man had taken out a billboard advertisement. He guided his Buick into the gravel lot outside Rachael's small apartment complex, shut off the engine, and shifted to face Geoffrey.

"You're saying you saw a demon."

"I'm saying I saw what *I* think is a demon. Of course, I can't be sure, but it makes sense, considering the history of the house and the events supposedly occurring inside it."

"And they are guarding Rachael."

"Yes."

"And she threw a sledgehammer at you."

"I was shocked, too."

"And then she came to your motel and seduced you."

"I was an easy conquest."

"Because you love her."

"Because I love her," Geoffrey agreed. A completely inappropriate goofy smile wanted to claim his face, but he managed to hold it in check.

"She's still at the Manor, isn't she?"

Geoffrey sobered, all humor vanishing along with the spit in his mouth. He'd never in his life felt fear so great, so consuming, an avalanche of anxiety that suffocated and bore him away on a tide of powerlessness. The fear drove him on, toward the house of devils, toward spiritual peril and physical jeopardy, the singular thought of Rachael the only thing that kept him from flying apart and dissolving into a heap of hysterical gibbering. Rachael couldn't see the danger, was blinded to it, seduced by the beings invisible to her eye but to whose whispers her heart paid heed. Something more precious than physical life hung in the balance: her eternity. He would storm a thousand evil castles to rescue her soul, and joyfully lay down his life doing it.

"Someday they won't let her leave," Geoffrey whispered. "And that day is coming soon."

Hugh popped open his door and stepped out into the misting rain. Geoffrey followed suit, hunching his shoulders against the weather. A steady breeze covered them with an icy blanket, the chill cutting through them like millions of frozen razor blades.

"Good news," Hugh said, motioning to a small Honda. "That's Sabrina's car."

Geoffrey remembered the faerie-like creature whose beauty had poleaxed him in the grocery store, and he hoped he wouldn't make a fool of himself again.

They took the steps two at a time to the upper apartment Rachael and Sabrina shared. The wind howled around the corner of the building, buffeting them with rain so cold Geoffrey was sure it had come from the iciest reaches of the Arctic. The surf crashed to shore beyond the apartment, the ever-present cries of the gulls ominous instead of soothing, foretelling danger and darkness ahead.

It was old news to Geoffrey.

Sabrina answered the door on the fourth knock, and even Hugh sucked in a shocked breath. Dark circles underscored her summer-blue eyes, and her chic, shag-cut hair was pulled into a messy ponytail. Her face was scrunched with lines of worry and fatigue. An acidic odor wafted through the cracked door around her.

"You'd better come in."

She opened the door wider and let them in. The stench hit them, a physical assault that made eyes water and sinuses burn. Cat piss. They followed her to the kitchen, where she pulled on a pair of yellow rubber gloves she'd discarded to answer their summons. The fridge stood open, and while they watched she grabbed items and tossed them into a waiting garbage can with barely a cursory glance.

"Sabrina, what in God's name—" Hugh started.

She interrupted, her eyes flashing and her voice cold. "She came home a little while ago, but luckily I got here yesterday. Something just felt...wrong." She started to say more, then frowned and shook her head. "Good thing I did, too."

"I smell cat piss," Geoffrey said.

She blew out a breath. "I'd never have thought it of her, would never have believed she was capable of..." She broke off, wiping her brow with her sleeve. "I don't know how long since she's been here, but he ate through what was left in the bag of cat food in the cupboard—and luckily he was able to get the cupboard open. Thankfully she left the bathroom door open so he had water. Otherwise..."

"Marmalade," Hugh said, and Geoffrey frowned in confusion.

"He even ate the bananas that were on the counter—there were peels vomited up all over the place." Her eyes welled. "He could barely move when I got here."

Geoffrey broke in. "Marmalade is her cat? Is he dead?" She

burst into tears.

"Sabrina, where is Marmalade?" Hugh demanded, clutching her arm.

"The mobile vet took him yesterday. I—I lied and said he'd run off and had come back in this condition. I couldn't bear to tell him that Rachael had abandoned him while she lived in that hell house. He's at the animal hospital. The vet isn't sure if he'll make it."

They were stunned to silence. And in the silence, a sound that he had previously dismissed because it was so normal, so ordinary, penetrated his consciousness. The shower.

"You said Rachael came home last night? Is that her in there?"

Her eyes met his, trying to gauge whether he was angry or desolate. Geoffrey himself didn't know.

"You should see this before she comes out."

She led the way out of the small kitchen to a closed door across the room. Without a word, she opened it, moving out of the way. Geoffrey stepped inside, surveying the wreckage. It looked as though someone had thrown a colossal temper tantrum. Clothes littered every surface, bric-a-brac lay in shattered pieces on the carpet along the baseboards. The heavier pieces had punched holes in the drywall. The bedding had been ripped from the mattress and flung pell-mell all over the room. He peered at the floor lamp across the room.

"Is that a shoe in the lamp?"

Sabrina's perfect mouth twisted. "Her favorite pair. Black and ecru pumps that I won't let her wear with anything." Her eyes traveled the room, glazed and shell-shocked, pausing on the fragments of a knick-knack. "I bought her that in Germany."

"What the hell happened?"

"I don't know what happened. She came home in a fury, raging about how 'he didn't understand' and 'how dare he' and a lot of other things that didn't make sense. I admit I thought she was talking about you." She speared Geoffrey with a narrow blue look. "But when she went to town on her bedroom, she seemed to be talking to someone named Alex, telling him to do a lot of things that are anatomically impossible."

"Rachael?" Hugh said, shocked.

"Rachael," she confirmed, and explained to Geoffrey, "She wouldn't say 'shit' if she had a mouthful."

"Did she talk to you at all?"

"Geoffrey, I don't think she even noticed I'm here. I've been cleaning up Marmalade's mess since I came home. Riley came with me, and he helped for a while. He volunteered at the vet clinic today to help pay off the bill. It's going to take a tank full of Stink-Free to get rid of the smell. Our landlord is going to flip when he sees the walls in her room and smells the carpet. I don't know when she last ate, because everything in the fridge is in various stages of penicillin development, and there's nothing in the cupboards. I don't know what the hell is going on, but that—that—" She closed her eyes, and her voice lowered to a conspiratorial whisper.

"That person in the shower is not my best friend. I don't know who she is. Or *what* she is."

The shower stopped. The screech of curtain hangers on a metal shower rod made them jump. She started humming, an indistinct tune they couldn't make out. A moment later the bathroom door swung open and Rachael shuffled out, her thin frame encased in a fluffy bathrobe, a towel wrapped turban-like around her head, accentuating the harsh angles of her face. She walked past them as though they weren't there, opened the sliding door to the minuscule balcony and stepped out into the night.

"*Maaarrrrmalaaaade! Here, kitty kitty kitty!*"

Geoffrey exchanged a disbelieving look with Hugh. Sabrina began sobbing. The pastor wrapped an arm around her.

"I don't know what to do! I want to be here for her, to help her, but I'm afraid of her."

"I'm sure she would never..." Geoffrey let the thought trail away. She had thrown a sledgehammer at him. Who knew what else Rachael would do these days? He was certain the fiery seductress who'd thoroughly compromised him last night had not existed when he met her, either.

"You can't stay here with her," Hugh said, quietly but firmly. "I think...I think it might be dangerous if you do. I don't think she's alone. Pack a bag and you can come stay with Gina and me."

"Oh, I don't know—" Sabrina protested, while Geoffrey said,

"What do you mean, she's not alone?"

Rachael came back inside and closed the sliders before Hugh could answer. Her gaze landed on them, and she stared dully for a moment as though surprised to see them - and as though she wondered who they were. Then her eyes shifted to Sabrina, and a tiny smile played around her mouth. A nasty smile. She disappeared into her room, closing the door behind her.

"I'll get that bag," Sabrina said decisively and headed down a short hallway on the opposite side of the living room from Rachael's bedroom.

Geoffrey was certain that Rachael would pop out of her room and try to stop them from leaving—a thought no doubt caused by watching too many horror movies—but they escaped the apartment with no interference.

The ride passed in complete silence. Hugh dropped Geoffrey off at his motel with a thoroughly eloquent look as his only farewell. He watched the car vanish into the grey day, and tried to reassure himself that at least Rachael was out of that damned house.

But when he went into his room, he closed the curtains and locked the door, and vowed not to answer any summons, no matter how much he wanted to. There was love, and then there was just plain foolishness.

May 2009

To me, the word "magic" does not refer to mysterious wonders and inexplicable phenomena. To me, it speaks of love, of trust, of the utterly indescribable feeling you have watching your child grow and learn. It speaks of golden moments, bright spotlights shining on the amazing highlights of a life lived in joy and serenity.

The only real magic I've known was watching Jared grow, watching him climb his way from babyhood to manhood, to see him turn away from his father's beliefs and instead embrace the good and the magnificent, building up others rather than destroying lives. There are no words to describe the desolation of seeing such a life cut short, winked out in an instant by his own father's insane creation.

And yet I've embraced that insanity, crossed over into the black void where love and reason do not exist, where Power is wielded against others for personal gain. Power, not magic, because in Power there is nothing good and nothing righteous, only might and the subjugation of the innocent. Power.

I fear the blackness creeping in, closer every day to obliterating all I once believed in. Bitterness and hatred are consuming me. I must see him. I must know if I can still love, if I can still feel shame and regret. And if I can still love, there is still time to turn away from the Power. To be redeemed.

THE BATTLE IS OVER, BUT THE WAR GOES ON
Friday May 15, 2009

He made it through the selling floor of the greenhouse to his office without giving away his emotional turmoil—or so Aaron Schaefer thought. Something in his greeting to Taryn Ackerlin caught Melody's attention; a strained note that fairly shouted he was on the edge and moments from hurtling into the abyss.

Taryn had heard it too. She excused herself as politely as she could from the elderly couple with whom she'd been chatting, handing them over to one of the part-time employees, and followed him to the back of the building.

Melody followed too, at a discreet distance. Taryn hadn't known she was there; she hadn't gone out of her way to greet anyone. As Taryn opened the office door to let herself inside, Melody saw him in the room beyond, pacing frantically, his hands raking through his hair, then grabbing handfuls of it as he spun a circle, as though he sought to keep his head from exploding.

She ought to have been pleased. This was what she had wanted, after all—the total ruination of Aaron and Kimberly Schaefer's marriage, and the utter devastation of Aaron Schaefer himself.

But when he dropped to the thick area rug in front of his desk and rolled himself into a ball, rocking back and forth on his knees, his arms wrapped over his head, every movement, every line of his body screaming anguish, all she felt was shame and regret.

An eye for an eye makes the whole world blind, Gandhi had said. She didn't necessarily agree—there were some cases where the line between vengeance and justice was so thin it was nearly indiscernible. But this wasn't one of them.

Taryn looked up and saw her peering through the crack in the door she hadn't quite closed behind her. Her face suffused with fury, she advanced on Melody with grim aggression.

"What the *hell* are you doing here?" Taryn seized the edge of the door to slam it closed in the other woman's face.

"Please." Melody held up an imploring hand. "I'll make this right, I swear I will."

"If you come near either one of them again, I will kill you myself. Get out, and don't come back."

The door slammed in her face, puffing air into Melody's eyes and making her blink. She backed away a step, bracing herself to face the spectators of her humiliation. But when she turned, no one was watching. No one had even noticed anything amiss.

She forced her numb legs to carry her through the greenhouse and to her car, where she sat for a long time, watching the storm clouds gathering for a renewed assault on the town. Rain splattered the windshield, blurring the world outside, so she didn't see the man approaching the car until he had knocked on the driver's window. She rolled it down.

"You all right, Miz Olmstead?"

The new constable, Nicholas Something-or-another. She couldn't remember. He had the accent-free voice of a westerner. Rumor had it he'd come from the Pacific Northwest, where he'd somehow crashed and burned his career as a major crimes detective. His wife, purportedly much younger than him, was still out west overseeing the packing and final details of their relocation. Or so she thought. She couldn't recall all the details, meted out over coffee with the gossip crowd from church after Nicholas Something-or-other had assumed command of the safety of Mills.

"Yes, I'm fine, constable. Thank you." He looked skeptical. Not only skeptical, but genuinely concerned. It had been so long since Melody had been the recipient of genuine concern that, to her horror, tears filled her eyes. His expression slid from concern to alarm.

"Ma'am?"

"Have you ever done something you're ashamed of, but you don't know how to make things right?"

Understanding claimed his face. Not only understanding, she thought, but pity as well. He'd only been in town for a week and a half, but already he'd heard the rumors—rumors Melody herself had spread.

"A simple 'I'm sorry' usually suffices, Miz Olmstead."

Sorry. Such a tame word for the wild regret coursing through her. *Sorry.* She couldn't see herself approaching Kimberly Schaefer and offering that simple word. Neither could she see Aaron Schaefer accepting it as reparation in full.

"I'm afraid the deed goes deeper than a simple apology will fix, constable."

"I'm a good listener. I'd be happy to listen over a cup of coffee at the diner."

Melody considered. He was a very attractive man, not break-your-heart handsome like Aaron, but rugged and manly, with kind grey eyes. But hadn't bad decisions like this gotten her into this mess to start with?

"Thank you, but no. You're married, and people would talk regardless of how innocent it was."

His smile bloomed. "Then I'd say you've learned from past mistakes. Have a nice rest of the day, Miz Olmstead."

He disappeared into the rain. Melody watched him go until he was nothing but a blur in a khaki uniform, hunching down into the police cruiser. She wondered what he would have said had she accepted his offer. She started the car and edged it out of the parking lot and onto the rain-flooded street, driving slowly to compensate for the torrential downpour.

Her heart felt lighter than it had in months. And while she held to her belief that no apology could ever be adequate to repair the damage she had done, she knew there was something she could do to speed the healing of the rift she had caused between Aaron and his wife.

୧

The babies woke while Kim was toweling herself dry. She took only enough time to drag a comb through her hair and slip into her jeans and shirt; if left too long, their howls would rival a starving wolf pack. Evan, the more patient of the two, calmed as soon as she came into the bedroom, but Tia's wails ululated like a hurricane siren until Kim plucked her from her crib and plopped her on the bed to change her diaper. Her howls rose again when Kim put her back in the crib so she could change Evan, but both were rolling and scooting, those precursors to crawling, and Tia had a penchant for heading right for the edge of the bed and had to be corralled.

With a baby on each hip, Kim headed for the kitchen, buckling them each into a high chair and losing herself in the soothing routine of the mundane. When both twins had consumed rice cereal that looked to Kim like papier-mâché, she coaxed half a jar of applesauce into each. Neither cared for it; they much preferred pears or bananas, and they made extraordinary faces that usually made her chuckle.

She didn't think she would ever laugh again.

The minutes ground by like a laboring machine on the brink of breakdown. She played with the babies, changed them, bathed and dressed them, always with one eye on the clock, dreading closing time at the greenhouse. Dreading not that he would come home, but that he wouldn't.

An idea began to form around two o'clock, and by two-thirty it had become unshakeable. Her marriage was over, lying in irreparable ruins around her, ripped to shreds by her lack of trust and Aaron's bitter anger. They couldn't be saved.

But others could.

The children went down for a nap. Kim went about her preparations in a haze of numbness, not thinking about what her decision meant to the lives around her, keeping her focus only on the two people she had the power to help. At three-thirty she called Anna Malone, who arrived half an hour later to watch the children while Kim ran undisclosed errands.

She kissed the twins, laying her hand along each of their cheeks in turn, breathing in their fragrance, committing to memory their silky skin. A moment of panic clawed through her heart—how could she leave her children? How could she even consider it?—and she resolutely beat it back, locking it into the vault inside her mind where she had once locked all thought of Caleb Schaefer.

In the drawer of the nightstand beside the guest bed, where she'd been sleeping since her miscarriage, she left a letter, her cell phone, and their wedding rings. Her purse she stashed between the bed and the night table where it wouldn't be immediately visible. It would mess things up if Anna caught on and alerted Aaron in time for him to stop her. Not, she acknowledged, that he was likely to make the effort.

She went in jeans and a tee-shirt, topped with a flannel shirt she'd filched from the boxes in the attic labeled SCOTT'S THINGS. It fell to her knees and she had to roll the sleeves up. A fleece-lined zip-up hoodie ensured she would stay at least marginally warm. Her driver's license was tucked into her back pocket; in the event she was ever found, she didn't want to become a Jane Doe in a state grave. She didn't want him to always wonder.

Her Explorer held the car seats for the twins, so she took Aaron's pick-up and left it at the barricade at the end of Willow Road, thoughtfully turned back toward town and the keys locked inside. He'd be able to retrieve it with little trouble.

Her recent surgery hadn't left her in any condition to vault over the barricade, so she climbed through the rails, staggering a little as she regained her footing on the other side. She kept her mind blissfully blank as she walked through drifts of leaves the seasons had left on the old road. The Circle was no longer here to maintain it, and the town thought it best to let the forest reclaim this area, including the two abandoned mills that were now falling to rack and ruin. These Kim passed, one after the other, with barely a cursory glance, distantly noting that it wouldn't be long before they collapsed under the weight of the Virginia creeper draped over them.

She reached the end of the road and stepped without hesitation onto the footpath that led a short distance to the river. It took some effort to follow it this time; the intervening years had seeded it with wild grasses and scrubby flowers. But the forest had not yet repaired the breach carved through it, and she navigated by the winding gap through the reaching branches of the trees until she came upon the land bridge across the river. She walked across without pause.

Through another gap in the trees, following a path long lost to people but not yet forgotten by the forest. Storm debris and a thick cushion of autumn leaves showed that the forest was, at least, attempting to heal the scar jagging through it.

At last she came to the edge of the woods, and she stopped, hovering at the perimeter of the empty clearing. Her abdomen ached, her incision a line of fire in her belly. The Wyckham House had been so massive that it had been impossible to tell its dimensions or its shape. With it gone, however, she faced a small clearing of irregular shape, with strange points and jags, large enough to hold a small mansion but not nearly large enough for one the size of the house.

Didn't I tell you? This is a magical house.

Freed from their confines, the memories of her abduction and eight-hour imprisonment at the hands of Caleb Schaefer ricocheted around her head like bewitched boomerangs. There was no help for it; the mysterious vault inside her mind, where she held all things too painful to remember, was only so big, and she had lovingly entrusted Aaron and the children into those confines.

The woods were devoid of sound: no bird chirps or squirrel chatter. Even the breeze seemed loath to intrude. The gentle patter of rain came from far away, as though it feared to alert the house to its presence.

But there was no house. The clearing was empty. It was a dilemma she hadn't considered. She had assumed, if she came willingly, it would show itself and allow her entrance. It did thrive on sacrifice, after all.

She pulled the collar of the flannel shirt to her nose. Aaron had packed away Scott's clothes without washing them, and the shirt still retained a trace of Scott's scent. Not aftershave, but soap. *Lever soap*, her mind supplied, *for all his two thousand body parts.* She smiled faintly. *If he could throw himself in front of a bullet for you, you can throw yourself into the mouth of hell to save someone else.*

A deep breath, and another, and she was ready. She stepped from the tree line, but could go no further. The air, like sludge, held her at the edge of the clearing. She closed her eyes and breathed in Scott's scent again.

"I've come willingly. Let me in."

For a moment she stood, waiting, certain that she had wasted her time. There would be no way in but to go to Bayview Manor itself. She had been so sure that the houses were connected, and if she could enter one, she could skip through others until she finally came to Bayview itself. To Caleb.

The air rippled, shimmering like dark heat waves, and then the weathered grey stones of the looming mansion appeared. Kim took an experimental step and found her way was no longer blocked. She had not faltered once since she had made the decision to come, but now her legs trembled and fear made her heart hammer in her chest. She forced herself onward, and when she reached the battered, rain-swollen wooden door, it creaked open and allowed her entrance.

Without a backward glance, Kimberly Schaefer walked into the welcoming embrace of the damned.

(Found scratched into the mirror in Geoffrey Windsor's hotel room)

NO ONE CAN HELP YOU NOW.

(The engraving was filled with Rachael Payne's blood)

ENCHANTMENT
Thursday, May 7, 2009

His phone rang at 2:33 a.m. Geoffrey knew because he stared at the clock uncomprehendingly for several seconds until the last three flashed to a four. He groped for the phone, dropped it on the floor, and groaned as it fell silent.

He had fallen back into a doze when it rang again. This time he clicked on the lamp, hung his arm over the side of the bed and scrabbled for the phone, and just managed to catch the call. He didn't want to miss it again — the display told him it was Rachael.

"Rach?"

"I'm sorry to call so late." She sounded weary and depressed.

"It's all right. I don't mind." He didn't. "What's wrong?"

"I don't know..." She hitched in a breath; she was crying. "I don't know what happened to my life. I'm missing pieces of time. I don't even know what day it is. And my cat is gone. Who would steal someone's cat?"

He closed his eyes, falling back against the pillows. "No one stole the cat, Rach. He was sick, so Sabrina took him to the vet clinic."

"He was just missing me, that's all. She should have told me."

"You didn't exactly talk to her."

"She didn't stay long." Geoffrey didn't reply. "Where is she? Did she go back to Seattle?"

"She's staying with a friend for a few days. Rach, what do you want me to do?"

"Will you come over?"

"That's not a good idea." But his heart sped up to an enthusiastic beat.

"Can I come over there?"

"No."

"Don't you want to see me?"

More than anything. "Rachael, what happened the other night...it shouldn't have happened. It can't happen again, not the way it did. It was wrong. And it never would have happened if you'd stayed out of the house like I asked you to."

Her sharply indrawn breath ended in a sniffle. "Will you stop harping about the house? Everything I've done has been my decision. The house had nothing to do with it." Her irritable tone softened. "Please, Geoffrey. We have to talk about this. It isn't something that we should talk about on the phone."

"I agree. But I'll see you in the morning at the diner, say nine o'clock? It's more appropriate."

"Why don't you just open the door?"

"You're *here*?" Fear battled euphoria, both wanting to be his dominant emotion.

Her voice dropped to a seductive pitch. "No, Geoffrey, you're *here*. Open the door and come in."

And to his horror, he saw he stood at the double-door entry to Bayview Manor, and his hand was already turning the knob.

(Excerpt of correspondence from Kimberly Schaefer to her husband, Aaron)

May 15, 2009

… I am sorry I ever gave Melody any benefit of doubt. I was wrong. I knew it all along. I was simply too much of a coward to ignore your anger and apologize. The current state of our marriage is completely my fault. I hope that someday you can forgive me, not for my sake but for yours, and for Tia and Evan. And maybe when they grow up, you'll tell them that their mother loved them very much, but she had to do something for someone else…

THE CONDEMNED
Friday, May 15, 2011

She answered his knock with a weary, resigned expression that reminded Denny of when he'd tracked her to the beach.

"Agent Wallace. I mean no offense, but I'd hoped I'd seen the last of you."

He wasn't offended. If people had to talk to him, it usually meant there was trouble. Bad trouble.

"I'm sorry, Mrs. Markham, but I found something that I need help with. Do you know anyone from Boldo Pattin's family? I think they might be the only ones who can answer my questions."

"They're all seers and soothsayers," she replied sharply. "You don't want anything to do with that family. They're not even welcome in their own clan, from what I've heard."

"Roma?"

"No, some obscure Hungarian clan. The other Gypsy clans call them Merries, but I don't know why. From what I know of them — which isn't much — they're just as strange as the Pattins. And good luck finding any of the Pattins, by the way. They scattered after Boldo disappeared."

"Damn." Denny swung a look behind him at the rain-washed road, wondering where he could go next. The town of Heron Bay was littered with psychic parlors and palmistry rooms, but he doubted any of them were as steeped in the occult as he would need them to be to tell him what the book was. What the symbol on the book was, more to the point.

"May I ask what you found?"

"I'll get it from the car." He dashed down the walk to the sedan, flinching as icy raindrops smacked his skin, leaned in through the passenger door and grabbed the bag off the back seat. She watched him with dread as he ran back to the porch.

"I found it in a bookstore, but the shopkeeper said it wasn't hers. It had no price tag. She wouldn't let me leave it there, said she didn't want it in the store."

He unwrapped the book, careful to leave a layer of plastic bag between it and his skin. When he held it out for her to see, her face blanched.

"Do you know what this is, Mrs. Markham? Have you seen it before?"

She didn't answer, but stared at the cover as if in a trance. Her eyes moved, and he realized with chill that they were tracing the lines of the symbol over and over. He pulled the plastic back over the book, and she blinked.

"Mrs. Markham, this is urgent. Do you know what this book is? Have you seen it before?" he asked again.

"Where are you staying in Heron Bay, Agent Wallace?" Her voice was faint, distant.

"Heron Bay Lodge. Room 132."

"Go there. I'll call you."

"What do you know about this book?" he persisted.

"I have to check with…someone before I… Please, just go back to the Lodge and wait for me to call. This may take some time." She took a step back to shut the door, pausing long enough to say, "And leave that book in your car." The door closed in his face.

He huffed out a frustrated breath, dug a business card out of his wallet, and stuffed it through the mail flap in the door. "Call my cell phone!" he hollered through the flap, but Grace Markham didn't answer.

He stopped at the Pizza Palace in Heron Bay and got a take-out. The smell was tantalizing, but his stomach lurched at the thought of eating. The rain was hammering down by the time he reached the Lodge, and he dashed from the car to his room, splashing through icy puddles and soaking his shoes. He was thoroughly soaked by the time he let himself into Room 132; even the cardboard pizza box was dripping. But the pizza made it through unscathed and, his appetite suddenly restored, he ate four pieces in a sitting. As he stowed the rest in the mini-fridge, he realized he hadn't been hungry since he'd found the book.

She didn't call for three-and-a-half hours, and then it was only a terse, "We're on our way, Agent Wallace."

We? But she didn't give him time to ask before hanging up.

He braved the elements and retrieved the book from his car, leaving it wrapped in the plastic bag. Twenty-five minutes later, a knock on his door brought him out of a pizza-induced stupor. He bolted off the bed and flung open the door.

Grace Markham stood shivering in the howling wind, a man approximately of the same age beside her. He didn't ask for explanations, simply invited them in. His room was large enough to include a small seating area, with a small lodge-pole sofa, two matching chairs and a slender coffee table. He led them to this area, claiming a chair adjacent to the sofa, where they both sat, close together.

"Agent Wallace, my name is Michael St. Claire. Me, I have a story to tell, an' something to give you. But first, I wanna have a look at dat book."

"Sure." Denny motioned to the bag on the coffee table. "Feel free."

St. Claire pulled on a pair garden gloves with latex coating on the palm and undersides of the fingers, and gingerly unwrapped the book. His face, weathered and seamed from sun and age, offered no clue to his thoughts as he studied the cover and the symbol burned into it. He wondered about St. Claire's connection to Grace Markham; clearly he was from the Louisiana bayou country, although his Cajun patois had faded.

"Dis book, I seen her before. She belong to a man named Alexander. How did you get her?"

"Found it in a bookstore."

"Huh." St. Claire didn't seem surprised. "I grew up in the swamp. I seen a lot of things in my life. Things others can't see. Never thought I'd see dis book again, 'cause Alexander, he vanished wit' the others."

"What others?"

"The séance group. We was sent away, off to Louisiana. But Aunt Pearl, she thought mebbe I was too protective of my baby sister, too intense, so she sent Becca away to Boston, to her cousin. See, we was both s'posed to go to Boston, but our father's sister, she died that night too."

Denny frowned. The parallels, entirely too coincidental, were not lost on him. "Mr. St. Claire, are you telling me—"

"Be quiet now, Agent Wallace, and jus' listen."

He set the strange book down, felt around inside his jacket, and pulled out a leather-bound book that looked very old. He handed it across to Denny, who took it cautiously. But the book simply felt like leather, worn and shiny with age.

"Your agency can have that. It was our nanny's diary. She was a good woman."

Denny opened the cover. The name *Emily Matthews* was penned in calligraphic script, the ink faded. He looked up at St. Claire. "You're Joshua Fotheringham."

St. Claire's mouth twisted. "Your agency can have that book only on the condition it's never given to anyone else. No historical societies, no rare book museums, nothin' like that. Emily, she saved us. She deserves to be remembered as more than a superstitious hysteric."

"How did you get it?"

St. Claire's eyes travelled to the window, where a gap in the curtains allowed a glimpse of the raging weather beyond. The glass was sprayed with random raindrops the wind had blown under the roof overhang.

"The night she died, it was a night like dis, rain, thunder, lightnin'. The wind howled like a wolf outside, and Becca and I, we jus' cowered under the covers in Emily's room, where she'd moved us 'cause she was too afraid to walk to our rooms in the night.

"Father an' Mother were arguin' again, but dis time it was worse. He told her he was takin' us; she said she din't care. But he'd waited too long, an' the house, it din't wanna let us go. That house, it eats people. I told Geoffrey Windsor that, and he shut down the job. Wise, dat. Wait too long, an' it's too late; they won' let you loose."

He glanced at the book on the coffee table, its odd symbol still clear after seventy years of languishing God knew where.

"I dunno what changed things. Suddenly I heard Mother shriekin'. Emily couldn't bear not knowing what was happenin'. See, Father was her ticket outta the house, off the Peninsula. Without it, she'd'a ended up in Heron Bay, working for another fam'ly, prob'ly another occultist fam'ly. She took us with her, 'cause she din't dare leave us alone no more. Our parents were screaming in the gallery, so Emily hid us in the pantry and locked the door. She slid the key underneath the door so if the worst happened, we could get out. You know those doors, dey have keyholes on both sides. I always wondered why. Guess now I know.

"She gave me her diary, too, pressed it right into my hands an' said 'Keep it safe, Joshua. Don' let no one have it.' An' I never did, 'til now. I'm sure she'd approve."

St. Claire fell silent. Denny didn't push. The rain battering the lodge was a strangely cocooning sound, imposing such a strong feeling of isolation that he had to repress the urge to run to the window to make sure the world was still out there.

"I can't say exactly what happened. Mebbe the argument went too far an' he really did kill her. It don' seem true, though. He had no reason; he was already leavin', an' in those days, a rich man could get his children easy, even when the mother hadn't gone completely crazy.

"Father an' Emily, dey ran into the kitchen. Someone was chasin' them. Emily backed up against the pantry door, an' Father stood in front of her, tryin' to protect her. We could see their feet through the gap between the floor an' the bottom of the door. Father was beggin' for our lives, Emily was cryin' an' prayin'.

"Then Father fell, his forearms cut, his blood runnin' under the pantry door. Emily screamed, and then she fell too. Dat book" — he motioned to Denny's book — "was in her hand when she hit the floor."

"Do you think she took it from someone who killed her to get it back?"

"I think she took it from Mother after Mother had been killed. An' I think Boldo Pattin chased them an' cut them down in cold blood. He wanted dat book."

"Why?"

"It's a book of the damned. That symbol there...Alexander, I asked him once what the symbol meant when I seen him carry dat book around. He said 'It means The Condemned.' When I asked why he always had it, he said it was his ball and chain. Then he said to stop bothering him or he'd kill me. He said that a lot, an' usually I thought he din't really mean it, just wanted me to go away. But dat time, he meant it. So I never asked again."

"Emily died starin' into my eyes underneath dat pantry door. An' Becca an' me, we jus' sat there an' waited to die. Waited for the shadow people to come kill us. But they never came. Two days we sat in the pantry, eatin' what we could open with our bare hands, too scared to come out, before the police found us."

Denny shot a glance at Grace, who had remained silent throughout St. Claire's whole narrative. She sat as close as a lover, her fingers clutching his sleeve. Side-by-side, their faces told the rest of the truth, although his was worn by the Louisiana heat and hers by the coastal weather. Not as close as a lover, then, but as close as a treasured sister.

"Becca," he said to her. "You're Rebecca Fotheringham."

"Not for a very long time."

To St. Claire, he said, "The book I found — do you know what it's made of? Who it belongs to? I doubt Alexander made it."

"I only know what I heard, the once I heard Mother talking with him about it. According to him, the book is a grimoire made from angel skin."

Denny sat a little straighter, his heart pounding. "*Angel* skin?"

"Not one o' theirs. One o' the good guys. There was a war, remember, a war in heaven. I imagine it was brutal. Dat book, who knows what's written inside. No one can read it. It's no language known to man. It's a book of the condemned. *The* condemned. As in the angels cast from heaven after the rebellion, the ones who were subsequently bound to the earth for teaching enchantments and war. For mating with human women."

"The fathers of the Nephelim."

"Good, you know your scripture. The very ones. Dat house, she move through the earth, that's what Alexander said. It's no house at all, but the stone of the earth, a conductor for the fallen to move from place to place. 'Cause dey bound to the earth, dey move through the earth."

"Demons, you mean. Fallen angels. And Bayview Manor..."

St. Claire nodded. "Bayview Manor is their lair."

Denny didn't think he could take any more bad news, so when his cell phone rang shortly after Grace Markham and her brother left his hotel, he considered not answering. Michael St. Claire had been blunt: there was no winning in this town. It was best to just pack up shop and leave Caleb Schaefer to the damned. He had bought his way into their ranks, after all, and there was no sense bringing justice to a man already serving a sentence in hell. And oh, by the way, don't drop that book into a deep dark hole like the bookshop owner had suggested. That was only returning it to its rightful owners, who would simply send it out into the world through one of their human servants. Better to lock it in his agency's secure facility and check every day to make sure it was still there.

But his phone's display flashed up a name—BOSS—and Denny couldn't refuse. *You're already married, Denny. You speak of your calling with a lover's tone, and I see now that I'm not the love of your life.* And he could see it from her viewpoint now, so clearly he wondered how he could have been so blind. But she was wrong on one major point: the job was not the love of his life. It was his ball and chain, an anchor dragging him to the bottom of the ocean of lost opportunities and forsaken dreams.

He could let it all go, walk away in a heartbeat, leave the job for someone else to do. There would always be someone else; he was hardly indispensible. But there would never be another Taryn Ackerlin, and to walk away from her would take more strength than he would ever have.

He let the call go to voicemail.

The room was littered with notes, charts, photographs, photocopies. The job. The damned job. He was sick to his soul of the damned job. His cell rang again. Instead of answering, he began dismantling his war room. He did it neatly, methodically, conscious that organized records would be of use later. To someone else.

The phone on the night table beside his bed rang as he was

taking down the centerpiece of his battle plan: Taryn's Dear John letter. He kept it always visible to remind him what this job cost, to make him think about his choices, his options. His life.

The phone fell silent. A red light blinked on the keypad, signaling a voicemail. He slid the angel-skin book into a thick plastic sleeve and sealed the zip closure, stowing it neatly in his briefcase. His leather garment bag hung from a clothes bar outside the bathroom. He flopped it onto the bed, opened the dresser, and began packing.

The phone rang again. Denny closed his eyes. Whatever it was, it was bad, judging from Cody's persistence. He scooted around on the bed and grabbed the receiver.

"Whatever it is, I don't wanna know."

"One last mission, Denny. Please." Cody sounded frantic, his voice hoarse with a pleading note that Denny had never heard before.

He rubbed a hand over his eyes. How the hell had Cody known he'd hit the wall? His letter of resignation was in his metal attaché case, signed, sealed, and waiting to be delivered in person.

"I can't do it anymore, boss," he said quietly. "It's not the love of my life."

"Just one more."

"And then what? It'll be another mission, and then another, and then another, until Taryn becomes just a bitter old man's reminiscence. I want more than bad memories, Cody. I want a wife. I want kids. I want a *life*—"

"Kimberly's gone into the Wyckham House."

Yeah, it was bad. As bad as it could get. "When?"

"Sometime late afternoon is the closest we can pinpoint. She had Anna Malone sit the kids. Left a letter."

A letter, God love her. "There's nothing I can do, Cody. You and I both know it will be too late by the time I make it back to Pennsylvania."

"It's not too late," Cody snapped. Denny blinked. "She's gone to Caleb."

"The hell you say."'

"Rescue mission."

"Impossible. That would be suicide."

"Try telling her that. Up close and personal, preferably."

"Dammit, Cody!"

"You have to go into Bayview Manor and bring her out."

"I can't!"

"Otherwise, I don't know if she'll ever make it out. I don't know if she'll even try." The garbled sounds of a loudspeaker blared over the line, and Cody spoke in an aside to someone, his hand over the mic muffling his words. He came back on the line. "We're at the Florence-Peretola Airport, trying to get a flight back as soon as possible. It's faster than waiting for the agency to send a plane over to get us. At least, I hope it will be."

"Cody, you're not listening!" Denny shouted. "I. Can't. Do. This. Anymore."

Cody drew in a sharp breath. "This is Kimberly, Dennis. Your friend. Your best friend's wife. This isn't for the agency. This is for family."

He sat, holding the dead phone in his hand, long after Cody had hung up to beg, borrow, or bully himself onto a flight out of Florence. Finally he dropped the receiver into the cradle, and prepared to launch one last rescue.

(Excerpt from Bayview Journals, entry by Hugh MacGregor, July 2011)

Of the Heron Bay Pattin family, there is none who would speak to me of Boldo Pattin, the "seer" who vanished the night of the Fotheringham murders. You speak his name, and they make the forked sign to ward off evil spirits, and abandon any semblance of manners, simply walking away even as you're talking to them. They want nothing to do with whatever Boldo was involved in.

I asked one about the book Agent Wallace found. "The book, it is the names of the demons. A summoning book. It should be returned to the house. That it is out in the world, that is bad. Very bad."

But the book is gone, and so is Agent Wallace.

TORMENT
Friday, May 15, 2009

Sabrina had been at Hugh and Gina MacGregor's for three days when she noticed a pattern of odd occurrences, such as doors she was sure had been closed suddenly standing open, items in a different arrangements on the coffee table than what she remembered when she left the room, and personal possessions that seemed to vanish into the thin air for hours—or days—and then suddenly showed up in places she had thoroughly searched.

And then there were the movements she caught from the corner of her eye, shadows that seemed to move only in her peripheral vision. She often felt as though there was someone in the room with her even when she was clearly alone.

The worst thing, however, were the times when she woke out of a sound sleep, certain someone had just spoken her name right at her ear. After an occurrence like that, she turned on her bedside lamp and let it burning all night long, lying wakeful or dozing lightly until dawn.

She tried to call Rachael every day, but with one exception, Rachael never picked up. And that exception had done nothing to alleviate her fear for—and of—her friend. Geoffrey, likewise, had been incommunicado, and while his car was parked outside the Heron Bay Lodge, he didn't answer the door. The Do Not Disturb sign hanging from the door handle inspired an fierce dread that tied her stomach in cramping knots.

Sabrina came to dread the times when Hugh and Gina were both gone—and those were often. Her anxiety intensified until she was nearly paralyzed from it, although if someone had asked her, she would be unable to explain exactly why she was anxious.

On the sixth night at the MacGregors', she sat alone watching a muted TV, the seconds dragging agonizingly by while she waited for Hugh and Gina to return from a walk on the beach. Her dinner—lobster bisque from Catch of the Day Diner—churned in her stomach. Minutes ago, she thought she had seen movement at the edge of her vision, but when she had turned her head, the room was empty but for the shadows lurking in the farthest corners of the room, out of reach of the meager lamplight. She had turned on all the lamps afterward, and banished all but a small corner of darkness. She was afraid to look directly at that patch of darkness, because something about it seemed unnatural.

A glance at the clock told her enough time had passed that another call to both Rachael and Geoffrey would be construed as concern and not as harassment. She missed Rachael desperately, feared for her to a depth she hadn't known possible. She didn't know what she would do if something happened to her best friend. How could she possibly ever explain to anyone just what Rachael Payne meant to her? A friend, a sister, a savior.

They'd been sixteen when they became friends. Rachael had unexpectedly sought out Sabrina, braving the inclement weather of March in her prim skirt-and-sweater set and no coat. Sabrina had been sitting outside the school, contemplating ditching her next class—Economics, and who could really blame her for wanting to ditch that?—and truthfully was contemplating ditching life altogether, when the former pastor's daughter claimed a seat on the cold stone retaining wall beside her. Sabrina had looked up in surprise and after a moment asked what she wanted, with a few choice adjectives thrown in for good shock effect.

Rachael had simply smiled, ignoring the foul language and even fouler attitude, told Sabrina how much she admired her wardrobe, which everyone knew Sabrina designed and sewed herself, and asked how much it would cost for a special Easter dress.

Sabrina had gaped at her, then tossed out a figure that was at least twenty dollars in excess. Rachael only smiled again, offered her half in advanced payment for the necessary materials and notions, and took her leave.

Part of Sabrina wanted to design something so outrageous and shockingly revealing that the sheltered daughter of Heron Bay's former pastor would be utterly mortified. But something in Rachael Payne's parting smile had stopped her from doing so—perhaps a hint of challenge that Sabrina found she wanted to accept.

A week before Easter, Sabrina was in Rachael's bedroom for the first—and as it turned out, last—fitting. Rachael had done one slow turn before her full-length mirror in the frothy pale yellow silk dress that fit perfectly, had tucked two twenty dollar bills—twenty dollars more than was left owing on the dress—into Sabrina's jeans pocket, and invited her to stay for dinner.

Sabrina declined. No way could she sit across the table from a man of God when only two weeks earlier she'd terminated her seven-week pregnancy.

Rachael delayed her long enough that, as she made her escape out the front door, Patrick Payne was coming in. As he greeted his daughter's companion, he seemed not to notice the heavy makeup, black-leather clothing, and the gold ring piercing her left eyebrow, and insisted on seeing the dress Sabrina had designed. The next thing Sabrina knew, she was indeed sitting across from him at the dinner table, with no clear recollection of just how the two Paynes had managed it.

She and Rachael had been inseparable since.

In fact, it was Rachael who had found her seven months later when Sabrina had swallowed most of a bottle of Darvocet. It was Rachael who had been on her knees in the ER waiting room, praying ceaselessly while medical personnel pumped Sabrina's stomach. Rachael who had stayed by her bed the six hours Sabrina had been barely alive. Rachael who had prayed her back to life.

Rachael had brought in a post-abortion counselor, books and flowers, and church friends to visit. After the hospital, it was Rachael alone who had remained her friend, while everyone Sabrina had known virtually turned their backs on her and pretended not to know her.

"Best friend" couldn't even begin to describe what Rachael was to her.

She tried Geoffrey first, and the call went to voicemail, as expected. She dialed Rachael, and was stunned when she answered.

"Rach? I've been trying to reach you for days."

Two seconds of silence ticked by. "Who is this?"

"Sabrina." Cold fear trickled through her, icy tendrils that started in her heart and spread slowly outward like some sort of strange physiological kudzu vine.

"I can't talk right now, Sabrina. I'll call you later."

And Sabrina was left with a dead line and a sudden flash of anger. How dare Rachael blow her off like that after she'd been trying to reach her for days? She jabbed the redial on her phone, and listened to the first ring, the second ring, her anger growing, the third ring —

The phone ripped out of her hand and smacked her in the face. Sabrina shouted in pain and ducked, covering her face with her hands. Her head and hands took the brunt of the attack, the corner of the phone digging into her scalp and fingers, leaving round bruises. She tripped over the edge of the carpet and fell to her knees, crossing her arms over the top of her head to protect herself. The phone struck her neck, her back, her shoulders. She rolled away from it, pressing her back against the wall, her tears of pain rolling unheeded down her cheeks.

Thwack! against her knees. *Thwack!* against her shins. *Thwack! Thwack! Thwack! Thwa* —

"*Stop!*" she screamed, sobbing. "*FOR GOD'S SAKE, STOP!*"

The phone hurtled toward her face like a black-and-silver electronic bullet. She screamed and pitched herself to the side; it brushed through her hair as it whizzed by and smashed against the wall. Shattered plastic rained over the floor, and the battery bounced painfully off her foot.

Sabrina curled into a fetal position, blood from dozens of tiny wounds smearing into the MacGregors carpet, and cried until no more tears would come.

(Letter of resignation from Dennis Wallace to his supervisor, Cody Schaefer, found in his attaché case in his abandoned hotel room)

TO: Cody Schaefer, Director (Omega Team)
FROM: Dennis Wallace, Assistant Director (Omega Team)
DATE: May 14, 2009
SUBJECT: Official Resignation

I regret to inform you of my intention to resign my position with the Schindler Project, specifically in regard to assignment with the Omega Team, effective June 1, 2009.

I understand that should I desire to return to the Project, I will be required to undergo all mandatory background investigations to be reinstated, and that I might not be reinstated at the same security clearance as I enjoyed in my previous employment.

It has been a pleasure working with you, sir.

IN THE HOUSE OF THE DAMNED
Date Unknown

She existed outside of time, outside the universe, in a world where there was only an endless dark corridor dotted with countless iron-bound wooden doors, where the air was cold and stale, carrying on it a faint scent of blood and death and despair.

She'd heard it said that time was a spiral, and maybe it was for those who made the claim. But for Kimberly Schaefer, it was this never-ending, unremarkable hallway. Gradually, she noticed changes here and there: a subtle shift of light, the waxing and waning of odors, sometimes signs of occupation. She was moving through time, from house to house, era to era.

How would she ever find Caleb when she could travel this house from the twenty-first century to prehistoric times to the far future? There was no way she could anchor herself in the present.

She panicked and sprinted forward, and was soon running flat-out. Pain ripped through her belly. Her lungs seared. Her quadriceps burned. Nausea hurled onto the shores of her stomach like a bitter tide. Black spots danced before her eyes.

Vertigo swept over her, swirling her away, and the hallway fell away beneath her feet. She plummeted into darkness, spinning in violent revolutions. So those people had been right; time was a spiral, and she was caught in it, in a whirlpool of time, petrified that she would break free of the centrifugal force and spin out into the void.

The house had tricked her, and now she was lost.

She clutched at the blackness spinning around her, could find no purchase. With a primal scream of fury, she thrust out her arm, reaching through the veil of time ...

And someone grasped her hand.

Monday, May 18, 2009

"I don't understand how you could let this happen."

The ringing judgment hung in the still air of the kitchen. Aaron Schaefer, numb, let it wash over him, knowing the words held a sting but not feeling it. He hadn't felt anything after those first moments of sheer panic and terror after reading Kimberly's letter. *Knowing how the house works, I doubt if I'll return.* The words had killed what was left of his heart, because she was right. He would never see his wife again, and his last words to her had been filled with deliberate cruelty.

"Aaron? Are you even listening?"

"Cody, leave him alone." Renée's voice was sharp. "This has been a huge shock. It's not time for blame or judgment. We have to figure out what to do."

Cody's mouth opened, and Ron spoke smoothly into the pause, calmer than he should be, more reasonable than he felt. He wanted to storm the Wyckham House and rescue her, just like he had five years ago. But this time she didn't want to be rescued. She had gone of her own will, gone to Caleb, and he couldn't move his heart past that sticking point.

"We can't do anything. We could search the Wyckham House — if we can even find it — from top to bottom and we would never find a trace of her. Because she's right; the house is outside of time. If you want to find her, you'll have to go to Bayview Manor. And even then you might not succeed."

Cody's temper ignited. Ron had never seen him lose his calm in an emergency, not even when Scott had been killed. Then, he had been calm to a frightening degree, obsessed with bringing Scott's murderers to justice, fearsome in his cold, calculated wrath. Kimberly was the daughter Cody had always secretly longed for. And while Kim adored Renée and got along with her very well, it was Cody to whom she had bonded. Cody presented an unshakable, competent demeanor, and in her eyes he was the icon of trust and safety.

"So we just let her go?"

"She's gone to rescue Caleb. We can't stop her. We probably

can't even find her."

"She's gone to rescue Rachael Payne," Cody corrected him.

"You read the journal. She may tell us — and possibly herself — that she's going for Rachael Payne, but she's really going for Caleb. A mercy for a mercy."

"And you're just going to sit here and let her do it?"

Ron didn't answer. He existed in a vacuum, knowing his reactions weren't what they ought to be but unable to find the right emotions, the right words.

Anna Malone had waited until seven-thirty to call him. She hadn't been alarmed that Kim hadn't returned from her "errands," but had been uneasy that she hadn't taken her purse. Ron had been prepared to sleep on the sofa in his office at the greenhouse, but he had come home and relieved Anna of her babysitting duties. He tried calling Kim several times on his way home, jabbing the Send button so hard he was amazed he didn't break it as he redialed and redialed. She never picked up. He had sent Anna home with assurances that everything was all right. Once she had gone, he corralled the babies in the play yard in the living room and slipped into the guest room.

He felt like he was betraying her privacy once again as he dumped the contents of her purse onto the bed. Her migraine medication was inside, a full prescription. She hadn't taken any with her. That was when he'd felt the first twinges of real fear; she never went out without a dose in her pocket. Her driver's license was gone, but the debit card and checkbook were still socked neatly into their respective places. She had taken no money. *Errands, my ass*, he thought.

Her Bible lie on the night table, opened to 1 Samuel chapter 17, with parts of verses 34 and 35 highlighted. *When a lion or a bear came and took a lamb from the flock, I went out after him and attacked him, and rescued it from his mouth.*

And he knew then where she had gone.

The rest was a blur until Cody and Renée had arrived. He remembered yanking open the drawer of the night table so hard it flew off its tracks and landed on his foot, spilling her silenced cell phone, their wedding rings, pacifiers, a roll of Tums, and an envelope bearing his name onto the floor. Falling to his knees in the middle of the pile, he had ripped open the envelope, knowing it was bad news, knowing it was the decimation of the life he had built with her, knowing his heart would be in tatters after reading the words she had left behind.

He hadn't been wrong. He had called Cody at some point, but couldn't remember the exchange except for his utter relief when Cody had said "We're on our way. It will take some time to arrange a flight." The following twenty-four hours had been agonizing as he waited for his parents to hop a flight out of Italy. Taryn had seized command of the greenhouse and ran the part-time employees via phone and e-mail until Cody and Renée had arrived, staying with him not only to help with the children but to keep him from losing his mind completely.

She didn't tell him everything would be all right. She knew it wouldn't.

Cody's team had been waiting for him when he arrived in Mills, and had already begun investigations. They found Ron's pick-up at the end of Willow Road, parked near the barricade that restricted access to the old mills' road. They had followed the road to the trail that led to the land bridge across the river, and there they found the only trace of her passage: scuffs through the leaf layer where her feet had kicked up several seasons of fallen leaves.

They had turned back without crossing the land bridge; Cody had given strict orders they were not to approach the clearing. Ron hadn't condemned his father for that directive; it was pointless for anyone else to risk going to the Wyckham House, because Kimberly wasn't there.

He'll kill her this time. You know he will. So what the hell is wrong with you? Why can't you DO SOMETHING?!

He knew why, of course. He had reached such a high level of anxiety and panic that his brain simply refused to function. Four times this morning, he had gone into the kitchen to fix the twins a bottle, and had spent five full minutes trying to remember why he was there. Renée had taken over the care of the babies after that.

"I'll call Denny," Cody decided. "He's going to have to go into the house and get her out. Do you want to go to Washington State?"

Aaron stared at him blankly. Go to Washington State? And do what? Die with his wife, so his children could be orphaned?

"And who will raise my children if I do?"

"Aaron, I know you're angry with her, but you can't just let her—"

The dam inside him crumbled, letting loose a flood of emotion that, for a terrible moment, robbed him of speech and breath. Rage and fear battled to dominate him, and he lost control to both. Adrenaline coursed through him, making his heart hammer and his breath come short. He popped out of his chair.

"*Let* her? I'm her husband, not her jailer. And as if I could *stop* her from doing whatever she wants to do. She's reckless and impulsive, and this time she's gone too far. I can't help her. I doubt I can even *find* her this time. It will do no one any good—least of all my children—for me to go tearing off after her only to die with her."

"*DON'T SAY THAT!*" Cody roared. "*DON'T YOU EVER SAY THAT AGAIN!*"

"Cody!" Renée looked frightened.

Cody closed his eyes and sucked in a breath through clenched teeth. "She's not going to die. He let her go once—"

"And whatever lives in that house won't let him do it again."

Ron turned away, bleak despair clenching round his heart. He had to get away from them, had to be alone, had to come to grips with this awful turn of events before it destroyed his sanity.

"She's made her choice, and it wasn't me. Now I have to do what's right for my kids."

They didn't stop him when he strode out of the room. Cody was too angry, and Renée was diverted by the doorbell. Ron didn't wait to see who it was—probably just some guy in a black SUV, coming to give an update. He didn't need a useless update; they'd never find her, even if they spent the rest of their lives looking.

He let himself out the back door, heading for the barn, the wild flow of adrenaline giving him a jerky gait. His whole body trembled so hard he thought he might jitter apart.

The barn was a barn in name only: shaped like one and painted red. There the resemblance ended. This barn held gardening implements and workbench with tools hanging over it, neatly arranged on pegboard. The cement floor was pristine, and the building largely empty.

He'd wanted to raise chickens, have their own fresh eggs, but her miscarriages and high-risk pregnancy had put off those plans. Then when it was confirmed she carried twins, he knew she wouldn't have the time—or energy—to mess with chickens. She had asked for a puppy while she was pregnant, and he had cited the same reasons, promising they would get a dog when the twins were older and a little self-sufficient, possibly when they'd started school and could actually help train the dog.

He should have just bought her the puppy.

In the letter she'd written, she had taken the sole blame for the collapse of their marriage, but she was wrong. He knew full well that it was entirely his fault.

His legs refused to hold him anymore, spilling him onto the cold concrete. He wrapped his arms around the splintery two-by-four leg of his workbench and, finally, wept.

Date Unknown

She flew out of the spiral with a physical force that plowed her rescuer right off his feet. They landed in a heap of tangled limbs. The spiritual havoc of her hasty extraction from the vortex of time pinned her to the floor as securely as gravity. Her senses bombarded with stimuli, she could only stare at a grey mass before her, trying to sort it all out. Sound came from everywhere with no discernible logic. Vertigo flung her about on its violent amusement park ride, up and over, around and around. Her stomach heaved.

"It will pass in a few minutes. Just hold on and try not to throw up. If you throw up, the vertigo lasts longer. And don't close your eyes."

It took several moments to make sense of his words. His voice was familiar, but her insides were spinning with such force she couldn't keep her mind set to the task of tracking down the memory.

Time passed. How much, it was impossible to tell. She realized she'd finally understood his words. Don't throw up. Don't close your eyes. Just hold on. Okay. She could do that. Her eyes fixed on the greyness before her, she waited out the vertigo.

The violent revolutions gentled, like the calm waves of a sea after a furious storm. The grey mass in front of her resolved itself into a wall of huge stones, roughly hewn, and pitted with age. Her brain translated the sounds around her: the rustle of clothing as he checked out his wounds, the slight scrape and squeak of his sneaker against a littered stone floor, the whispers and sighs of the air moving through the house.

The house.

She tried to bolt upright, but she was still pinned to the floor. Not gravity but his hand, forceful and impossibly strong.

"Not yet. You only *think* you're ready."

His voice, that velvet voice, smooth and rich as caramel. She almost had it...almost...

"What the *hell* are you doing here? I thought I told you not to come back here." Exasperation. Frustration. And, worse than either of those, despair as black as the heart of this house.

"Caleb," she croaked. "I found you."

He barked out a bitter laugh. "You didn't find me, Kimberly, *I* found *you*. And just by chance. You never know where the spiral will let you out. Worst one for me was at the top of a flight of stairs. Pretty sure I cracked a bone in my arm when I finished falling down them."

His hand eased its pressure, and he helped her sit up. The world gave one last gentle whirl, and all was still. Her stomach took another moment to realize the vertigo had passed, and then it, too, calmed.

"What would you have done if I hadn't happened to be there, if I hadn't seen your hand come out of thin air?"

"I guess I'd be stuck in the spiral, wouldn't I?" She smiled weakly.

He didn't smile back, only fixed her with a bleak glare. Kim leaned against the wall, closing her eyes. She didn't know how long she had fought to surface from the stream of time, but she was impossibly tired.

"How did you know you could get here from the Wyckham House?"

"A lucky guess."

"Lucky." He snorted.

The silence grew between them again, not precisely comfortable but familiar. Expected. The house whispered around them, sibilant echoes bouncing off the stones. She didn't look too closely into the shadows, afraid they might move. Like they had in the Wyckham House.

"What the hell, Kimberly?"

"I figured it might be harder for you to refuse to listen to me if I were here in person."

His eyes crawled around their space as though desperately seeking an escape. *There are no doors or windows for me.*

"Do you see them?" Caleb asked harshly.

"Who?"

"Not who. What. The doors and windows."

Kimberly looked around for the first time, realizing they were sitting at the bottom of the dilapidated horseshoe staircase. Heaps of plaster and lathe turned the floor of the foyer into a treacherous junkyard.

"Redecorating?"

He followed her gaze and frowned. "Not me, no." His icy gaze speared her again. "Tell me you can see the doors and windows."

She scowled. "I'm not leaving. You're here because of me, because you let me go. So I'm here to let you go."

Annoyance and exasperation turned slowly to disbelief, and then a dawning look of horror. So he finally understood. Good. Kim closed her eyes again. Tired, so tired. Her journey through time was nothing compared to the emotional wasteland she had walked through since March, but it had sapped what was left her will to keep going. So it was a fine thing that this was the end for her. The end of everything.

"Why?"

She didn't want to answer, wanted to just rest in the peace of the moment, where the turmoil of her shattered life couldn't touch her. But he would persist, and the peace would be ruined anyway.

"Why not?"

He digested this for a moment, but he was not the type of man to accept an answer like that.

"What happened?"

"What do you mean?"

"You're running. What happened?"

She drew in a deep breath, heaved it in a resigned sigh. The air was odd here, thin, with a bitter tang that coated the tongue.

"Melody Olmstead happened."

He started laughing. And he kept laughing until tears ran from his eyes and his breath hitched into his lungs in staggering gasps. His laughter erased years from his face, and not for the first time she wondered what his life could have been like had he not been seduced by the darkness.

"I'm glad you think it's funny. It's been rather painful from my end."

Caleb wiped his eyes on the sleeves of his shirt and fought to contain his humor. "He would never. And especially not with Melody Olmstead."

"I didn't say he did. I'm just saying she happened, and now everything is all messed up, and nothing can be fixed. And the best part is, I can blame no one else. It's all my doing, all my fault. So now the only use I can be to anyone is" — she gestured lazily — "this."

"And your children?"

"You almost sound genuinely concerned."

"Don't kid yourself."

"Still convinced you're just a bad guy?"

"Still convinced I'm not?"

He scooted around to face her, clutching her shoulders, his fingers biting deep into her flesh. She felt a swell of the familiar fear and couldn't help cringing away.

"I didn't let you go. The keys fell out of my pocket. That's why I'm here, unable to get out. Because I was careless, not because I was merciful. Do you get it yet? I have shown mercy to no one, not Elizabeth Peterson, not the child I fathered on her, not Tiana Michaels, not even you."

"But—"

"No one, Kimberly!" he shouted. "Not. One. Person."

" —Rachael—"

He closed his eyes. "Have you forgotten I chased after you when you escaped from the ceremony room? Have you forgotten that I shot at you and would have killed you if Scott hadn't jumped in the way?"

"That doesn't matter. And you didn't answer my question about Rachael Payne."

"You didn't ask one."

"Only because you kept interrupting," she said sharply. "You said she was your friend."

"She is."

"So—"

"I betray my friends all the time, Kimberly. I betray everyone."

She struggled for words, could find none. What had she been thinking? Or better yet, *had* she been thinking? So determined to see good in Caleb, determined to find whatever small piece of him that was redeemable, had she ignored the truth in favor of what she wished? And the truth was that he couldn't be redeemed, because he didn't *want* redemption. He wanted power, magic, and the kind he craved didn't come from God.

"I've done my job well. She trusted her good pal Alex." His tone was bitter, full of self-deprecation. "She's in the hands of the fallen, and she doesn't even realize it yet. And it still might not be enough to convince them to release me. I promised them you – and failed to deliver."

"You tricked her."

His hands fell away from her shoulders, and he looked away at her tone of terrible disappointment. "It's what I do."

Kimberly turned away from him, not sure what the sinking feeling in her belly was. Not fear; she was beyond it. Certainly not betrayal, because he had never hidden what he was or what he did.

"You wasted your time," he whispered. "You wasted your life. I won't be careless this time."

"I can't go anyway," she whispered back. "There are no doors or windows. There's no way out." Her mind groped for his words, finally drawing them out of the vault of her memory. "I made a bargain. It isn't the kind of bargain on which one reneges."

"I'll make it fast," he promised.

"They won't let you. And you wouldn't be able to help yourself, anyway."

"You finally understand."

"You have no sense of mercy."

"That's right." He watched her silently for a moment. "Are you going to cry now?"

"Never."

And as the last echoes of her answer faded away, she thought she heard him whisper, "That's my girl."

(Quotation used by Rachael Payne in a debriefing conducted by Cody Schaefer, Omega Team)

"But who can endure the day of his coming?
Who can stand when he appears?
For he will be like a refiner's fire..."

Malachi 3:2 (New International Version)

PURIFY
Friday, May 15, 2009

Rachael remembered Sabrina calling for about four seconds, and then she was lost in the endlessly repeating pattern of foliage on the reproduction wallpaper behind the sofa. The foliate pattern in golden brown-on-black formed diamonds like a chain link fence, with sprays of flowers in the centers. Her eyes followed these processions across the wall and back again, over and over, the mindless action calming the panic that had raged through her since Alexander had forced her to leave the Manor.

She had known something was wrong; he wasn't his usually charming self. But he slyly waited until she was leaving to tell her he didn't want her to return; he had blocked the entrance through the memorial and would not let her in through the back door again. Bayview was no place for her, he had said; she didn't belong.

And then the jerk had the audacity to ask her to give a book to the federal agent who had come to the Manor. She had stuck it in a mailing envelope but had no address to send it to, so it was…somewhere. She couldn't remember where she'd put it. It didn't matter; she had more important things on her mind, such as how she was going to finish stripping the Manor down to its original form. It was too large, too many rooms for her to do by hand. Besides, her hands were blistered, raw, and bleeding; she wouldn't be able to do much more manual labor.

She didn't stop to question why she had to complete the restoration of Bayview Manor. She only knew that she must. There had to be a way back into the Manor, and a way to complete her task, without Alexander being able to evict her.

Her eyes traced the interlocking diamonds, back and forth over gold-on-black, the pattern fading out of focus the longer she stared.

The gold diamond patterns blurred and danced like flames in her unfocused vision.

Flames.

And she knew what she must do.

(Quoted in a letter from Kimberly Schaefer to her husband, Aaron)

"Remorse is impotence; it will sin again.
Only repentance is strong; it can end everything."
– Honore De Balzac

REDEMPTION
Monday, May 18, 2009

Melody sat primly, rigidly, in the chair beside the fireplace, trying not to let her eyes crawl around the house. Her curiosity got the better of her, though, and occasionally she found her gaze sneaking surreptitious looks.

So this was where Aaron dwelled when he was not out in the world. The décor was comfortable and inviting, nothing like what she had expected from his California-transplant wife. But she had to admit, she had always sold Kimberly Schaefer short. It had to have taken a remarkable woman to bring Aaron out of his self-imposed isolation after the Circle had devastated his life sixteen years ago. She had never fully appreciated just how remarkable that woman truly was.

Kimberly's presence underscored everything in the room, from the family photographs on the shelves by the front door to the cluster of polished rocks and seashells arranged artfully on the mantle between a beaten copper vase of dried flowers and a hunk of petrified wood. Autumn tones dominated, giving warmth to the room, but Melody was cold to her core.

Cody had said very little since she had talked her way past his wife and laid before him her tools of a trade she no longer wished to ply. Across Kimberly's distressed-pine coffee table was strewn an assortment of leather-bound books, loose papers, and two envelopes: one for Aaron and one for Kimberly: her apologies. The latter had been ripped open, and Cody was currently reading, his face impassive, his attention focused, his eyes moving steadily through the cramped lines of handwritten text.

At last, he folded the letter and tucked it back into the envelope. Without a word, he reached for one of the leather-bound volumes and flipped through its pages.

"These were Fred's?" he asked. His eyes raised from the page and speared her with a searching look. She squirmed.

"Two of them—the one you're looking at is his. The rest"—she swallowed over a nervous lump in her throat—"are Caleb's."

He stared at her unwaveringly for another few seconds, but otherwise seemed unaffected by this news.

"I thought we had obtained all of Caleb's documents."

"He had Fred hide some away—the more dangerous ones."

His gaze pierced her again. "And you're just now coming forward with them, almost five years later?"

She licked her lips and squirmed again, and then admonished herself. She was here willingly, trying to make reparation. She had known there would be interrogation of some form, and as far as interrogations went, this wasn't the ordeal it could have been.

"I've already explained that. I wasn't sure what I wanted to do."

His eyes moved from hers to the scatter of books and papers on the coffee table. He laid them all out in a line and opened the front covers, studying the handwriting, and then laid aside Fred Olmstead's. Fred was dead, so Caleb's writings were more of interest to him. He rifled through the pages, skimming the text, and moved onto the next one, and the next. Partway through that volume, he stopped reading and held up the book, tapping an intricate symbol of lines and angles.

"What is this?"

Melody frowned. "I don't know. I've never seen it before."

"Fred never drew it on anything?"

"Not that I can recall. I didn't see it in any of his papers." She gestured to the table. "They're all here. You can look if you don't believe me."

"I believe you."

He dipped a hand into his jeans pocket, bringing out his cell phone. He snapped a shot of the symbol and laid the phone aside. His hand smoothed the leather cover, rested against it for long moment as though he was testing it for some reaction. His brow puckered.

"This must not be like the other book," he murmured.

"Other book?" Melody parroted blankly.

"A book my associate found across the country. It had this symbol on the front cover." He elaborated no further, leaving her with the impression that she was lucky to get even that much of an explanation.

She summoned her courage and said tentatively, "Could it be a symbol for...for the beings who gave the Circle power?"

When he looked at her this time, his eyes were narrowed, speculative. He was wondering just how much she really knew about the otherworld.

"The demons, you mean."

"Is that what they are?"

"Just a theory I have. But I've had confirmation recently that I'm at least very close to being right." He closed the book and set it on top of the others. "What do you want me to do with all of this, Melody? Why bring it to me?"

She shifted again, a fierce blush rising in her cheeks. "I don't know...I just thought...well, this is kind of what you do, isn't it?"

"I disband cults that have proven to be powerful and dangerous. I already disbanded the one here in Mills. Are you telling me that it's reformed?"

She shook her head. "No, nothing like that. Oh, the ones who aren't happy with how that all went down grumble about it and make plans to organize, but they can't ever seem to get it together. "

Cody leaned back in his chair, templing his fingers under his chin, staring thoughtfully over their tips.

"I admit they convinced me to...do things I swore I never would. I never approved of what Fred did, and I was terrified he would drag Jared into it and I would lose my son to them."

"It was a fear that proved true," he pointed out. "You did lose him, and they were responsible."

She didn't miss his underlying message: The Circle was responsible, not the Schaefers. Her vengeance had been grossly misplaced. She already knew that. It was why she was here.

"That's not what I meant. I meant that I would lose him to the Circle, that he would become part of them, choose evil." She looked down at her hands, which were wringing themselves in her lap as though trying to strangle each other.

"What kind of witchcraft did you use to split up my son and his wife? Can it be reversed?" Cody asked bluntly.

Her hands fell still and she chanced a look at him. "None." At his raised brow, she rushed on. "No, it's true. I didn't use witchcraft. In one of Fred's books, he said that sometimes a lie is better than magic to come between two people, because when people really love each other, magic doesn't give you an advantage."

"A lie worked admirably," he remarked.

"There was nothing admirable about it." Melody slid to the edge of her chair. "I didn't let myself think it all the way through. I just listened to all the people who said I should be blaming the Schaefers and taking my vengeance. And so I did, and I was real proud of myself until..."

"Until?"

"I saw him at the greenhouse, the day Kimberly left. I've never seen someone so close to losing his mind—someone that I drove to it. I'm so ashamed."

With absolutely no artifice, she began to cry. Cody offered no words of comfort or solace of any other kind.

"So I brought you these things, because I don't want them anymore. I don't want anything to do with magic again. Your agency should lock them up and hide the key. I packed my things into a U-Haul and I'm leaving Mills."

He didn't try to talk her out of it. "Where will you go?"

"I don't know. I thought I'd try Arizona for a while, some place so different from here that maybe I can deal with the memories."

"That might be wise." He hesitated, frowning at his steepled fingers. "It's wonderful of you to confess to both Aaron and Kimberly what you did. But this whole town is talking about what they think is the truth, and short of showing this letter around to everyone, Aaron and Kimberly have no defense."

"I left a letter at the church, with the secretary. Pastor Leon wasn't there or I would have talked to him personally as well."

"Pastor Leon won't be returning to Mill's Church of Christ,"

Cody informed her in a bland tone. "The board of directors was not very happy with a few things I had to say to them. It's very uncomfortable to have to defend your actions to an agency like mine."

She chanced a smile. "You're kind of like Captain America, aren't you, only on a Christian level. Captain Christian."

He surprised her with a genuine smile. "I was. I'm retiring as soon as this mess with Kimberly is resolved. Then I'll simply be a man who loves his God and his family."

"That's still some kind of awesome."

"You should go find yourself that kind of awesome, Melody. You don't have to replace your son, and your husband was no kind of prize, but you should have some happiness. Just choose better next time."

"I don't think I deserve a second chance, Cody. My choices – all the way back to marrying Fred Olmstead in the first place – caused all of this."

"Set the stage, maybe, but everyone's choices caused this. And everyone deserves grace. I know my daughter-in-law very well, and I have no doubt she would extend that grace to you."

"And your son?"

"Well, now," Cody said, rubbing a finger over his upper lip to hide a smile. "He's a stubborn man. But he's been given a measure of grace himself, so I doubt he'd withhold it from someone else."

"Will she come back? I know you don't want to tell me where she is, and that's okay. I wouldn't try to talk to her; I'd only make things worse. But I'd like to know if you think this can be fixed."

"I don't know. It's looking pretty bleak right now."

There seemed to be nothing left to say, so she rose, hoping her trembling legs would hold her. Cody stood as well, following her to the front door at a leisurely pace. She paused on the threshold for only a second.

"Thank you, Cody. Goodbye."

"Best of luck, Melody."

She didn't look back as she drove down the long, curving driveway. When you were looking backward, you couldn't see where you were going, and this time she was not going to run blindly into a future she would later discover wasn't the one she wanted. The only thing she knew for certain was that she would never return to Mills.

Date Unknown

The waiting was excruciating, and Kimberly could see no need for it. It was impossible to mark how much time had passed since they had last spoken; time was different here, suspended or at least so close to it she could not determine its passage.

So she stood, waited for the pins and needles in her numbed legs to pass—which told her she'd been sitting on the hard stone floor for a good long while—and brushed the dust and debris from the back of her jeans.

"Going somewhere?" Caleb asked. He sat against the wall at the top of the stairs, his knees drawn up and hands clasped loosely around them, eyes closed.

"It's time," she said quietly. He opened his eyes.

"So anxious to die?"

"Not so much, but the waiting is killing me slowly. You promised fast."

"A promise you know I'm incapable of keeping."

"Doesn't matter."

He got to his feet with seeming reluctance. "There's no going back," he warned. "No changing your mind."

"I know."

He blew out a breath, his nostrils flaring. "All right. Let's go."

Instead of leading her downward, he led her through the upstairs hallways to a flight of stairs to the next floor up. The house was infused with dim light, so they didn't need a flashlight. More magic, she supposed.

"The ceremony room is blocked off. We have to go this way."

"It's blocked off in all the houses?"

"No. Just this one."

"What happened? Earthquake?"

He sent her an amused glance, as though wondering why she was so chatty on her way to her death. She wondered why as well.

"I blocked it."

They walked on, down interminable corridors to another flight of stairs leading upward. Debris littered every corridor they traveled, making the way treacherous. In one pile, she thought she saw shreds of wallpaper in a black-on-white pattern. How could people ever have wanted to live here?

"Were you here the night the Fotheringhams died?" she asked suddenly. She had read extensively about the murders after she had dreamed of Caleb in Bayview Manor.

"Yes."

"Did you see everything? You know who killed them?"

"Killed who?"

"The Fotheringhams. Who else?"

"They had a séance group who all disappeared that night. They died, too," he said matter-of-factly.

"Did you kill them?"

"No."

He turned down a hallway with several rooms on either side, and that ended at a stout wooden door directly ahead of them. He opened the door. Stairs led upward into darkness. Instead of going up them, he swung around and sat on the third step. Kimberly sat beside him without question.

"Boldo Pattin, Kassandra's medium, was always on the edge of insanity, but that night he toppled over. In the middle of a séance, he started raving about how everyone present must die to preserve the secrets, to appease the spirits." He laughed a little, a humorless sound that fell flat in the stairwell.

"Well, the séance group didn't take that very well. There was chaos, running, screaming, fights. But in the end..." He drew a breath. "In the end, he had killed everyone but Kassandra and me. I got her out of the séance room, told her to get her family and get out of the house while I dealt with Pattin."

"But he got her first," she deduced.

"Yes. She might have made it, but she stopped in her room for her diary, and then stopped to rouse Jonathan's sister. I could have told her that was an impossible task. She was fond of absinthe, and too drunk to comprehend what was going on.

"Pattin cornered Kassandra in her sister-in-law's room—sorry, but I can't recall her name."

"Charlotte," Kimberly supplied quietly, bringing another of his strangely bleak smiles.

"Kassandra escaped, but Pattin killed Charlotte. Then he stalked Kassandra through the house."

"He was driven mad by the...the demons who live here?"

"It happens. They had their hooks into him so deep he was barely human. He caught her in the gallery. I found her too late; she was almost dead, bleeding out onto the parquet floor." He closed his eyes. "She made me take her diary and asked me to protect her children."

"I wouldn't have thought you had much concern for anyone's children," she remarked.

"No, but their deaths would have no purpose. I heard the screams from the kitchen, so I ran as fast as I could. But Jonathan was already dead, and Emily nearly so, lying in a pool of blood in front of the pantry door. Pattin was reaching for the door to the pantry where Emily had hidden the children."

"So you killed him."

"So I killed him."

"Yet you say you have no mercy."

"I don't. I just saw no purpose in killing the children." He scowled at her. "I dragged his body to the cemetery room Nathan Fotheringham had secretly constructed - Kassandra was not the only Fotheringham driven mad by the demons. Nathan chiseled the stone coffins with his bare hands, engraved them with the faces of the demons who drove him to insanity. When his work was done, he walked through the house, his hands dripping with his own blood, looking for his family. He'd made the coffins for them. But he fell dead from exhaustion in the front yard before he could kill them."

"Does anyone even know it's down there?"

"Rachael does. And Geoffrey Windsor. But I doubt it's a secret Windsor wants to divulge. Too many people would want access to it, and that's dangerous."

"I don't get why you hid their bodies. Why not leave them to be found, along with Boldo Pattin?"

"Do you know how many have come seeking them? And how many have left with a new perspective?" A demon's perspective, he meant. She understood. "Their disappearances have served as bait for decades. I'd've taken the others there, too, but the children were still alive, and I didn't want the fate of their parents and caregivers to plague them all their lives."

Kimberly mulled over his story, still failing to see how he had failed to show mercy to his lover's children. "Dead or missing, what does it matter?"

"Death is honest," he answered, surprised by her question. "To make them wonder when they can have the truth…well, that's just cruelty."

"It's what you did to Aaron, with Elizabeth."

"Yes, it is." And offered no explanation why he had done it.

"Do you still have Kassandra's diary?"

Another bleak smile. "I gave it to Rachael before I made her leave the house for good. So you see, your riding in to rescue her was pointless."

"I didn't ride in to rescue her. I rode in to rescue you, so that *you* will rescue her."

"Sounds complicated. You should have just concentrated your efforts on Rachael."

"Too late now. Let's go."

Up the attic stairs, through narrow aisles of human belongings. She knew the way from her dreams. He led her to the back wall and sprung the catch of a hidden door, stepping into a small, stifling room. Dark splotches stained the floor and walls: seventy-year-old blood.

Across the room to another door, and down narrow, plain stairs into what appeared to be an unfinished corridor.

"The hidden passages go throughout the whole house," he explained. "This one is blocked at the end, but it will be easy for me to get through."

It was. Rigged from this side to provide easy access, the blockade was easily removed, and then they were going downward again, through narrow corridors and down rickety staircases, until at last they ended in a cavern with rough stone walls, long-dead torches slung in brackets on the walls. The altar was a dark shadow in the center of the room.

"It looks smaller," she said.

"Time does that."

Kimberly paused halfway across the room, staring at the altar, fear finally trembling through her. Would it hurt to die, even if he somehow kept his promise and killed her fast? And Aaron...the children... She slammed the door on that thought. She would not think of them, would not taint them with this deed.

"No changing your mind," he reminded her.

"I know." She swallowed over a lump of fear and forced her shaking legs to carry her the rest of the way to the stone where she'd been chained five years ago by this very man. The hilt of his black stone knife crowned the head of the altar. She touched it tentatively.

"Will it hurt?"

"I don't know."

"Take a guess."

"Yes. Very much."

She took several deep breaths and turned to face him, her fingers going to the zip pull of her hoodie. She was startled to find him right behind her; she hadn't heard him move.

And she was even more startled when his hand covered hers, stopping her.

"No. You don't need to do that. There won't be any of that."

Relief swelled through her. She hadn't realized how much she was dreading that part.

"I should take off my jacket anyway, so you don't miss."

"I won't miss."

He didn't stop her as she shed the fleece-lined hoodie anyway. She dropped it on the floor, but he picked it up and draped it over the cold stone where she would die.

No mercy, indeed.

She hoisted herself up onto the stone, surprised again when she felt his hands against her back. He eased her down slowly, and then stared down at her as though uncertain what to do next. She settled herself more firmly, waiting, but he still didn't grab the knife.

"Get it over with, Caleb."

He searched her face. "What if this doesn't work?"

"Then you know what will. Pick up the damned knife."

He did, and brought it up to bear on her heart. He took several steadying breaths. Their gazes locked on each other as though if one looked away, neither would be able to do what must be done. Something shifted in his, their icy blue depths showing a glimpse of something she had never before seen in them. A soul.

And, incredibly, warm wetness splashed her face, once, twice, three times, rolling down his cheeks and off his chin to baptize her in his regret and sorrow. The salty brine of them seared her nostrils. The knife wavered. A sibilant hiss of disapproval shuddered through the air as he moved to lay it aside.

"I can't." His voice cracked, and something broke in his eyes.

"You have to."

Kimberly reached up, her hands closing over his, bringing the knife back to point over her heart. When he would have wrenched out of her grip, she wrenched back with incredible strength, unnatural strength, bringing the knife singing toward her chest.

(Found as an entry in Kimberly Schaefer's journal)

LEMON BARS

Ingredients

Crust:

- 1 cup butter, softened
- 1/2 cup white sugar (can use half brown sugar, half white sugar for richer crust)
- 2 cups all-purpose flour

Filling:

- 4 eggs
- 1 1/2 cups white sugar
- 1/4 cup all-purpose flour
- 2 lemons, juiced (or equivalent amount of bottled lemon juice)

Directions

Crust:

- Preheat oven to 350 degrees F (175 degrees C).
- Blend together butter, flour and sugar.
- Press into the bottom of an ungreased 9x13 inch pan.
- Bake for 15 to 20 minutes in a preheated oven, or until firm and golden.

Finished bars:

- Whisk together sugar and flour.
- Whisk in the eggs and lemon juice.
- Pour over the baked crust
- Bake for an additional 20 minutes in preheated oven. The bars will firm up as they cool.
- Cut into 2 inch squares.

THE END OF EVERYTHING
Friday May 15, 2009

He didn't know why, but Denny took the angel-skin book with him when he went to Bayview Manor. And because Bayview Manor was…well, Bayview Manor, he locked all the documents pertaining to the investigation in the stainless steel briefcase provided to all agents involved in the Schindler Project, and left it in his hotel room. Cody would be able to access it and retrieve the information in the event he didn't return.

Also in the event he didn't return, there was a letter for Taryn in the briefcase — all team members all had one written and ready due to the nature of their work, much like soldiers engaged in war. His was simple and to the point: *Taryn, you were right all along. I'm so sorry. I love you.* As the potential last words of his life, they were pretty piss-poor, but she would not doubt the truth of them.

He dressed in his typical extraction uniform: light-weight, charcoal-grey turtleneck and slacks; black, soft-soled shoes; no jewelry; no identification except the RFID chip coded with his serial number that was implanted on the inside of his right thigh. If he was found and the chip read, any search on his serial number would trigger an alert in the Omega Team system, and they would know he was captured or dead.

The gates at the end of the Manor's long drive refused to open, so he left the rental car there and scaled the wrought-iron spires, shimmying his way down the other side. The book, still wrapped in the plastic bag, was under his shirt. Even through the bag, it made his skin crawl.

He dropped lightly to the ground and walked along the edge of the driveway to avoid the more treacherous potholes. There was no need for cover; the inhabitants of the house knew he was coming, and they knew why. There would be no covert search-and-rescue, simply a snatch-and-run in true damage-control style. It wouldn't be his first. God willing, it would be his last.

From outside, the house looked like any other decaying mansion: windows dark and free of glass; splintered, weathered siding hanging askew. The right-hand door of the double-entry stood ajar as though waiting for him. He squared his shoulders and stepped through the door, into a blackness so thick it seemed to be a living entity. Otherworldly hands grabbed him, alien fingers greedily plucked at his shirt, trying to pull the tail from the waistband of his pants. They wanted the book.

He ran blindly, the absolute darkness erasing his equilibrium. And then he was spinning down into the dark, up and over, around and around, caught in a never-ending freefall.

Monday, May 18, 2009

He struggled against the downward thrust of the knife, throwing all his weight into stopping the point before it speared her chest. Its momentum halted as though it had hit an impenetrable force-field. The point punctured Kimberly's tee-shirt but sank no deeper. She yanked on his hand, but his strength was greater. He ripped her fingers from around his and threw the knife at the wall as hard as he could. It shattered, the shards of the black blade scattering across the floor.

A beat of absolute silence filled the ceremony room, and then he said hoarsely, "We have to go. Now."

Their fury would transcend anything known to mankind, and he didn't want to or experience it. She grabbed his shirt, pulling herself up onto her knees, her mouth twisted in a snarl of rage and despair.

"What have you done?" she screamed. Tears spilled from her eyes. *"You promised!"*

"I betray *everyone*, Kimberly," he reminded her. "What did you think, that committing a murder to free myself would help me find redemption? You know it doesn't work that way. And it's not the way to escape what's happened to your life."

She closed her eyes, dislodging more tears. "This isn't about my life."

He cast a nervous glance at the shadows behind her. "We have to go. They're coming."

"Then go. Maybe if they have me, they won't chase you."

She released his shirt and would have sank back down onto the stone, but he grabbed her by the front of hers and lifted her up.

"I'm not going without you."

"But—"

"Kinda shoots in the ass your whole reason for saving me if I won't leave, doesn't it?"

She blew out an impatient breath. "Why are you doing this? Just *go*."

He leaned his forehead against hers and whispered, "Lemon bars."

More tears spilled from her whiskey eyes, and he thought in that moment that if he was capable of loving anyone, he would have loved her unequivocally.

"I'm trading one prison for another, Kimberly," he said quietly. "But at least the next one will have windows. If I can do that, you can go home and fix your life."

He didn't leave her a choice; he simply backed up, his fist still tangled in her shirt, and dragged her off the altar. And then he stumbled backward, horrified, pulling her with him as he spun around to run, because they had gathered behind her, a wall of shadowy figures that undulated closer, coiling around each other, advancing inch by silent inch. He had been so lost in her that he had failed to see them.

Stone exploded around them, shrapnel stabbing into their flesh. Like sharks scenting blood in the water, they swarmed, shrieking and snarling. Kimberly screamed as their clutching hands ripped the flannel shirt from her back. The force nearly yanked her off her feet, which checked his flight, but Caleb recovered quickly, sprinting forward, hauling her up the stairs and into the attic séance room. The round table upended and whirled through the air as though caught by an invisible tornado. Caleb hit the floor, yanking her down with him. The table smashed into the wall and shattered, raining plaster and lathe and oak onto their backs. He scrambled to his feet, saw Kimberly climbing to hers, holding her back.

"Are you hurt?"

"I feel like someone took a two-by-four to my back and pulverized my kidneys." She took a step and winced.

"Can you run?"

"If my life depends on it."

"It does."

They picked their way over the debris and out the door. There was no running through the attic—it was too cluttered—but he sidled through the orderly rows of cast-off furnishings quick and lithe as a snake, Kimberly at his heels despite the pain in her back that twisted her mouth into a grimace with every step.

And from one step to the next, all light vanished, and they were left in the stygian dark of nothingness. He stopped instantly.

"Caleb?"

Kimberly's voice sounded far away, muffled. He wanted to scream in frustration. These demons and their little ploys. And this was, indeed, a *little* trick, not hard for them to do at all, employed to slow them down and separate them. A simple folding of the layers of time until he had passed through them into the world. Then they folded it back again, leaving Kimberly somewhere in their realm. He was well-schooled in the anomalies of the house, though; the challenging part would be reaching through the right layers to where they had trapped her.

"*Caleb!*"

There was a note of panic in her voice now; he had to hurry before she completely lost it, although he simply couldn't imagine it happening. She was fearless. She always had been. Fearless and reckless and impulsive.

He closed his eyes and felt the air in front of him. His fingers were sensitive after all this time to the feel of the different layers, the different times, and he knew at a touch which were which: this one, Hungary in 1241. Some bad shit had happened then, and he hadn't dared go back. The demons had been riled big-time, spurring on both the invading Mongols and the defending Hungarians, while one Countess Mariszka haunted these halls, so deeply immersed in the demons' power that she might as well have been one of them.

Next one: 1972 Connecticut. Beguiling the Manor's tenants and encasing them in stone statues was still the big rage, as it had been in this occurrence of the house since time out of mind. But they'd had good food, and he had visited often, usually in the still of the night when the occupants slept.

Next: an unknown year Before Christ, in what would become Romania. He had been there once, and what was happening then had scared the hell out of even him. The demons had discovered that biting humans caused the humans' DNA to mutate, creating the race that would eventually be called vampires. The mutations were blood-drinkers all; their morphed systems could not process any solid protein, and their hyper-metabolism made them constantly hungry. *Very* hungry.

Ah! At last, the final fold that was outside of human time. He reached through and grabbed her wrist, yanking her — kicking and shouting obscenities — into the present. She landed a lucky punch in his diaphragm, knocking half the wind out of him.

"Stop fighting, for God's sake. *Stop!* It's me."

"You scared the hell out of me!"

"Sorry. They separated us with layers of time. I had to grab you and pull you through."

"You could have said something."

"You wouldn't have been able to find me. I didn't want to risk you panicking more than you already were."

He could feel her glare even through the absolute blackness, but thankfully she didn't argue.

"Okay. Where's your hand, so we don't get separated again?" She groped around blindly, searching for his hand.

"Aahhh," he said, and took a step away from her. "That wasn't my hand."

"Where is your damn hand, then? And stop laughing."

"It's just hysteria. I've never been so scared in my life."

Her voice was suspicious. "Really?"

"Really."

He didn't elaborate that he wasn't scared for himself; he'd been a prisoner in this godforsaken, crazy house long enough to know what was in store for him, especially at the moment of his greatest betrayal. But they still wanted her; the current mess of her life was evidence of their orchestrations to get their hands on her again.

He felt through the inky void, found her arm and slid his fingers down it to catch her hand. "Don't let go, because if we get separated, I'll never be able to find you."

"What happened to the light?"

"We didn't need light outside of time. We're in the present—*our* present—now. There's no light here. I have a flashlight near the door, if I can *find* the door."

They inched their way forward. His hand swept the air in front of them to locate obstacles before he tripped over them, and to the side to identify the objects they were passing. He had a rough idea they were near the rows of steamer trunks where Cody had left his message. He also had an idea—or paranoia—that they were being stalked through the attic and the demons would let them get to the door...but not beyond. He didn't voice it; no sense giving them an idea if it hadn't already occurred to them, and no sense scaring Kimberly. He was determined to see her out of this house, and then—perhaps—that deed alone would be enough to free him.

His questing hand struck a hard splintery object: a supporting pillar. They had reached the main aisle that led through the junkyard from one end of the attic to the other. Thirteen pillars to the left, and then a blind grope for the door. He yanked her up on her tiptoes to whisper in her ear.

"When I say NOW, throw yourself to the left and drop to the ground."

She moved to whisper back, and the scent of lilacs filled his space. "Can't we go back outside of time?"

"No. I don't think they'll let us back out."

"But—"

His hand tightened on hers, and she hissed in pain. "Kimberly, do you understand what I've done? I've broken every bargain I made with them and twice refused to deliver you to them."

Her voice was cool. "I thought the keys fell out of your pocket on accident, Caleb."

"They did. But when I took that shot at you before you ran into the woods, I aimed high."

"How merciful of you."

"Think what you want."

"I always do."

"Don't I know it. Will you do something for me when we're out of here?"

Her wariness was a palpable presence between them. She was forced to rely on him, but she didn't entirely trust him, was reserving a healthy measure of doubt. Good.

"If I can," she answered finally.

"Only think of me when you're eating lemon bars. Not any other time."

She took several breaths and released them, stirring the air against his neck. "I can do that much."

He knew she'd never eat another lemon bar in her life. Satisfied that she would be able to break whatever strange tie bound her to him, however reluctant that binding was on either of their parts, he tugged her along through the lightless room, feeling for the pillars and counting them as they passed.

Twelve...eleven...

He felt them gathering around them, silent, stalking. Their presence stifled the already thick, heavy air.

...ten...nine...eight...

Cold sweat trickled down his neck and into the collar of his shirt.

...seven...six...five...

He gripped Kimberly's hand tighter, this time lacing their fingers together for strength; he didn't want her to slip from his grip at an inopportune moment. That she allowed it told him she felt the demons' presence around them.

...four...three...two...

Caleb took two steps past the last pillar and made what he hoped was a ninety-degree turn to the right. He secured his grip on her hand, lowering himself into a half-crouch, preparing for their attack.

Two more steps, and two more...

Shrieking and screaming, they came, swarming them like a hive of furious bees, clutching at their clothes, their hair, their limbs, not seeking to take them, for they could do that at any time, but to terrify, torment, and herd them.

"NOW!" he screamed, and threw himself to the floor to the left. Their arms went taut between them, testing the strength of their hold on one another, and then went slack as she threw herself in the same direction a split second after him. Her lighter body flew farther, her hip glancing off his shoulder. She slammed into the floor behind him, and he rolled toward her and covered her body with his.

The throng of demons hurtled past and crashed through the wall of the attic, still in pursuit of a quarry that had, amazingly, eluded them once again. Shredded plywood flew through the air like splintery missiles, and he took the brunt of the fallout. Gingerly, he pushed himself upright, blood from a dozen wounds oozing from his scalp, neck, and hands.

"Omigod omigod omigod!" Kimberly scrambled into a sitting position, pushing herself backward until he grabbed her foot to check her flight; he couldn't afford to lose her in here. There would be no chance of finding the flashlight now.

"We've have to move. They'll be back any second."

"How many were there?" Her voice shook, teetering on the brink of panic.

"Legion."

"We're never getting out of here, are we? It was too late the moment I walked into the Wyckham House clearing and told them to let me in."

"We'll get out."

She would, anyway. He knew now they would not let him leave; otherwise they would have let them move unimpeded through the house. But he wasn't about to tell her that, or she wouldn't even try. When she was out of their grasp and he was still trapped, she would realize he had once again bought her freedom with his.

But she could not say he had not warned her. He betrayed everybody.

He pushed to his feet and grabbed her hand, hauling her

upright, and yanked her along behind him, not bothering to be gentle because there was no time for it.

Out the shattered wall and into the attic entry, careful not to spear themselves on the jagged edges of the hole in the shattered plywood.

Across the open space, feeling the way to the wall opposite, and then groping for the door to the stairs.

Down the stairs, stumbling and nearly falling in their haste, and into the corridor beyond the door at the bottom of the stairwell.

A flat-out sprint down the corridor and around a corner into another hallway. Unable to see in the absolute blackness, they banged off the walls and stumbled over heaps of debris Rachael had left everywhere. He fell once, tripping over a pile of rubble that seemed to rise up out of nowhere, dragging Kimberly down with him. She tried to keep her balance, but his weight was like an anchor. She landed on his back, her elbow digging into his kidney. Their linked hands broke apart. He cursed fluently.

"Sorry." She scrambled to her feet.

"Don't move!" He got up, groping in the darkness.

"It's all right. I've already got your hand." Her voice came from several feet away and was travelling away from him, back into the depths of the house.

"No!" He ran forward, blind in the darkness, his hand extended in front of him. His fingers brushed her hair, tangled into it, yanked her head back.

"Let me go! Get off me!" She struck at him, landing a few good blows.

"You're going the wrong way! They've got you!"

He pulled her backward by her hair, and the demon pulled her forward by her arm, snarling and snapping and hissing. Caleb snaked an arm around her middle and yanked. The demon dug its claws into her flesh for a better grip. Kimberly screamed. Hot blood splattered his hand and wrist.

"She belongs to Him," Caleb snarled coldly, calmer than he felt. "It's pointless to try to keep her. She'd be just another martyr you can't turn."

It let go. She stumbled backward and would have fallen if he hadn't already been reaching for her. She pressed her face into his chest, drawing shuddering breaths, her whole frame shaking.

"No mercy."

"None," he agreed. "We're almost there." They weren't. They still had half a house to go, but she didn't need to hear that right now.

They went more carefully this time. He felt his way along the wall, kicking his feet in front of himself to find any obstacles before he tripped over them and seeking the next stairway with his hand.

Finally they were heading down, and he experienced a relief so indescribable he nearly wept with it. These stairs let out just mere feet from the top of the horseshoe staircase—which came up so suddenly and unexpectedly that he almost fell down it. Only Kimberly hesitating behind him, thus providing an anchor, kept him from tumbling down to the foyer and possibly breaking his neck along the way.

They were halfway down the stairs when they smelled it.

"Is that gasoline?"

"Smells like it." He inched carefully to the side, peering over the railing into the darkness below. To his surprise, he saw a lantern bobbing in the foyer, and then he heard the splash of liquid. The lantern came to rest, as though roosting in an unseen tree, and then the flame was turned up, illuminating the area immediately around it.

"Oh God." Kimberly's voice choked off. Caleb gripped the railing so hard his fingers went numb.

Lying at the base of the decrepit work table where the lantern had been set down, was Geoffrey Windsor. He looked catatonic, but it wouldn't have mattered if he'd been lucid and fighting for his life because he was surrounded and restrained by a slithering coil of inhuman beauty, demons with eyes like black voids filled with jewel-dust clouds. Eyes that were looking at Kimberly with undisguised, covetous greed.

Beside Geoffrey, a red plastic gas can lay on its side.

The lantern was hoisted up and held aloft, illuminating Rachael Payne. Her hair hung lank and lifeless around her gaunt face, her eyes black smudges. She had been dousing the piles of debris in the foyer with gasoline. She saw them on the stairs and a her mouth twitched into a grimace. Caleb started down the stairs again, moving carefully, cautiously, as though approaching a skittish animal.

"Rachael, what are you doing?"

"It's faster with fire, Alex. I can't do it by hand anymore." She held her hand up in the light of the lantern, showing raw, bleeding wounds that made his stomach turn over.

"That's..." He swallowed, his throat suddenly so dry he was afraid it might cause the spark that ignited the gasoline. "That's not a bad idea, Rach. But can you wait until we're all out of the house? Look." He pointed at Geoffrey. His hand was shaking. "Geoffrey's in a bad way. You don't...you don't want to kill him."

Down more stairs, closer and closer to the foot of them, Kimberly hovering on the step behind him, clutching the tail of his shirt to keep from becoming separated.

"This is the end, Alex. The end of everything."

They'd reached the bottom of the stairs and came within reach of the lantern's glow. Kimberly twisted out of his grip and edged around behind him, picking her way across the foyer to where Geoffrey lay. The demons scattered as she approached and knelt beside him. Rachael didn't seem to notice her. Caleb toed his way through the debris, not daring to take his eyes off Rachael as she set the lantern down again and picked up a box of wooden kitchen matches.

He stopped. She was only five feet away, but he was afraid to go any closer. "Rach, honey, give me the matches, okay?"

"It's the only way, Alex. The only way to finish the job."

She struck the match. Flame crawled up her hand, igniting the gasoline she had spilled over it, a blue-orange glove that engulfed her to the wrist. She screamed, waving her flaming fist in the air.

He saw it with crystal clarity in that fraction of a second, as though time had stopped and allowed him to see even the tiniest details: the match, flung away in desperation, tumbling end over end, a tiny spinning ball of fire falling toward the floor. He lunged, grasping—and missed. He checked his motion and grabbed Rachael, whose shriek has risen to rival a fire engine siren, by the front of the shirt. His other hand snagged Kimberly, who had a shoulder under Geoffrey Windsor's arm and was attempting to get him to his feet. He spun toward the front doors.

The doors that weren't there for him.

His remorse was too little for redemption after all, and came too late.

The match landed. Fire erupted around them, a roaring dragon of blistering greed, spread by the gasoline and by the destructive nature of the house itself. He fell to his knees beside Kimberly and yanked Rachael down beside him, engulfing them in a huddle, smothering the fire on Rachael's hand against his chest.

In their final moments, he was unable to help himself. He pressed his face into Kimberly's hair, breathing lilacs and smoke, and let the dam break inside him. He did love her, after all.

"God help us," he whispered.

The house exploded around them in a deafening shriek of grinding stones and rending wood. One desperate choice was left to him, and he seized it without hesitation: he reached through time, dragging them all through the folds of eons and away from the fire.

Around and around in the swirling dark, the odors of smoke and lilacs searing his nose, and then they broke from the centrifugal force, spinning out into the void, and there was the scent of rain, the brine of the sea, water splashing onto his face. He couldn't catch a breath. He coughed, tasting smoke and blood, and opened his eyes, staring into the grey sky above. Rain pattered onto his face, soothing the burns from the fire.

He'd lost hold of Rachael, and Kimberly had lost Geoffrey, but they had all made it out. He could see Rachael crawling toward Geoffrey through the grass, which was littered with debris from the house, a livid red burn covering most of her left hand. Kimberly lay half-sprawled over him; his hand was still clenched into the back of her shirt.

Rain splattered against her eyelids, into her open mouth, and she coughed, blinking the moisture away. She opened her eyes to stare into his, and then her gaze moved upward to the sky.

"You're out!"

She grinned and then laughed exultantly, pushing herself

upright. She beamed down at him, and her euphoria vanished in an instant. Her grin turned to a perfect O of horror. Her hands shook as she reached for him, pressing against the left side of his chest where the shattered end of a closet bar had punched through his lung.

But the blood flowed thick, too much of it. A mortal wound. Caleb didn't feel it; he was numb, cold, his only sensation the warmth of her hands, like hot coals moving over his chest, ripping open his shirt, trying to staunch the fatal flow of blood.

He wanted to reach up to touch her face, but his hand refused to obey his brain's command. It flopped onto the grass, splashing into a puddle. She hovered over him, her hot tears mingling with the cold rain, her bloody hands cupping his face, her lips forming words he could barely hear over a persistent buzzing in his ears. The day grew darker, as though heavy storm clouds had moved in.

"Kim."

His voice had faded to a harsh whisper. So this was what it was like to die: little feeling, distant sound, fading sight, the coppery taste of blood on his tongue, and the hot tears of a woman who should not cry for him because he did not deserve it.

"Kiss ..." he rasped.

Her face crumpled, but she leaned down to him, her lips warm on his cold ones, her salty tears trickling into his mouth.

The world exploded in blinding light, and Caleb committed himself to the white-hot brilliance with overwhelming relief.

Given the opportunity to go back in time and choose differently, I rather doubt Christ would say, "Sorry, the cost was too high. Not doing *that* again!" And when God let Satan take everything from Job that he held precious, did Job curse God? Not once.

So despite the fact that they cost everything I hold precious, I don't regret my choices, and I don't hate God for moving me to make them. The price of ransom cannot be measured too great when calculated in terms of mercy toward even one lost soul.

THE PRICE OF RANSOM
Thursday, May 21, 2009

The next two days passed in a surreal blur, barely registering in Kimberly's memory. She had gone to the Wyckham House fully expecting to die; when she hadn't, she had been thrown completely off-kilter. She felt strangely empty and wondered if that meant she was finally free of Caleb Schaefer.

Unable to gain entrance to the grounds, worried by Geoffrey Windsor's sudden disappearance and by his inability to reach Denny Wallace, Hugh MacGregor had watched the final moments of the human habitation of Bayview Manor. He told Kimberly that he had never seen anything quite like it, and hoped he would never see anything like it again. The house had spit out virtually everything that had come from human hands, and debris — flaming and otherwise — littered the grounds. It was Hugh who had called for emergency personnel, and when he had finally decided to scale the iron gates, he had found them suddenly unlocked.

Cody found her at Forks Community Hospital, where she was taken and treated for minor burns, abrasions, dehydration, and shock. The EMTs had been alarmed when they arrived at the scene; she had been feverishly working over Caleb, trying to revive him, and was covered with such a liberal amount of his blood that they were at first certain she'd been mortally wounded and was bleeding out. But other than a searing second-degree burn on her left forearm, a ring of bloody cuts around her wrist, and a whopping bruise on the small of her back, she was physically fine.

Once away from the house, Geoffrey Windsor made a rapid recovery with nothing more than a few scratches and a knot on his forehead where he'd hit a stone when the house ejected them.

Rachael Payne had sustained serious burns on her hand and

suffered from severe dehydration and malnutrition, as well as acute depression. Her mangled hands, already infected, would scar, but her doctors seemed to think she would still be able to ply her trade, although her range of movement might be limited. She could remember very little of the days since Geoffrey had ended the work on Bayview Manor.

Geoffrey staunchly insisted that an unstable boiler had been left behind, inadvertently still lit, which had exploded and caused all the damage. The fire inspector could scarcely debate this scenario as there was a mangled boiler on the front lawn and literally no signs of human habitation or vandalism inside the house. A discreet word from Cody — along with a flash of his badge — sent the fellow on his way with no further questions.

Denny Wallace seemed to have vanished altogether. His car was found at the gates of Bayview Manor, but there was no sign of the man himself. Cody retrieved his subordinate's belongings from the Heron Bay Lodge, and lapsed into a morose silence that Kim suspected carried a healthy amount of blame and disapproval.

"Are you ready?" Cody asked.

"I guess."

Kim eyed the custom black Bombardier Learjet 85 from the window of the Rite Brothers Terminal. There had been no conversation during the drive to the William R. Fairchild International Airport in Port Angeles, where two days ago, Cody — wielding his credentials like a club — had bullied his way onto the only runway in the vicinity that would accommodate his agency's private jet.

"Once we've reached cruising altitude, I'll fix us something to eat," he promised as they boarded.

"I'm not hungry."

"You need to eat, Kimberly. Starving yourself does no one any good."

For the first time, his voice carried a trace of concern. Kim felt the sting of tears in her eyes and fought them back. She waited until they were seated and buckled in to speak.

"I'd like to make a suggestion." He waited, head cocked and eyebrows raised. "Don't bring him back to Pennsylvania. Bury him in Seattle."

"Why would I do that? He was my brother, all else aside."

Her fingers clenched the arms of her seat, knuckles going white. He *would* have to argue over this.

"Rachael Payne was his only real friend. I just think he should be buried near her."

"Maybe she doesn't want that."

"She does. I asked."

"She doesn't realize what he was."

"What he was at the end was our rescuer. The rest is up to God to sort out."

He frowned at her. She could almost see the thoughts cycling through his mind, each weighed for validity and merit before being voiced.

"I'd like you to see the team's psychologist when we get back to Pennsylvania. I think..." He broke off, discarding what he'd been about to say, choosing different words. "I'm afraid of your reaction to all of this, of your weakness where Caleb is concerned. I'm worried that your recovery will be negatively affected."

"Oh, can't you stop being a federal agent for five minutes?" Kim snapped, losing her tenuous hold on her temper. "Just come out and say you blame me for Denny's disappearance, for the hell Aaron's going through, for Caleb's death. It won't surprise me, and trust me, you can't blame me any more than I blame myself."

He inhaled sharply through his nose, reminding her forcibly of his brother. "All right," he said easily, taking off his gold-rimmed glasses and folding them. His blue eyes speared her, the neutral mask he wore for his job dropping away.

Reckless walks hand-in-hand with regret, she had told Caleb five years ago, and she'd had no reason to change her opinion of that over the years. And once again, she had cause to regret her impetuousness.

"I love you like a daughter. Renée couldn't have any more children, so we never got the daughter we wanted. When you came along—the changes you caused in our family were nothing short of miraculous."

"Until your son died because of me."

"He died because Caleb shot him. That isn't your fault. You're lucky you didn't die that day too."

"He aimed high."

"What?"

"He aimed high. He didn't let me go in the Wyckham House, but he did at the edge of the forest. But somehow…somehow they made sure someone died."

He didn't ask who; he knew full well what they were dealing with. "Why would he let you go? He never let anyone else go."

"I don't know."

Cody waved the issue aside. "That isn't the important thing. You changed Aaron in ways I never thought I'd see. But despite all of your wonderful qualities, you're—in Aaron's words—reckless and impulsive. The price everyone else pays for it is astronomical. We can't do it anymore, not even for you."

"You take dangerous chances every day, too. Do we rake you over the coals for them? How is that any different?"

"It's different because it's my job to take dangerous chances. Everyone knows what I do is dangerous. You don't have to, and yet you do it anyway, and usually when everyone least expects it."

"What do you mean, when I don't have to? You think I gaily waltzed into the Wyckham House on a whim without a thought to what I was doing?"

"You had a choice. There were other ways to deal with what Caleb did to you - ways that wouldn't have left your children motherless or ripped out your husband's heart. The risk was too high for the potential cost to everyone involved."

Kim's heart took up a wild drum beat somewhere in the vicinity of her throat. "He wants a divorce, doesn't he?"

Cody looked surprised and then shrugged. "I don't know, Kim. Honestly, I don't," he insisted when she sent him a skeptical look. "What I *do* know is that you have two beautiful children—children you almost died to give life to. They deserve for you to respect their right to grow up with their mother, for you to take more care with your life. It's not just about you anymore."

She considered his words for a long time, her face burning with shame. He was mostly right, she could give him that. But he wasn't a hundred percent right.

"Sometimes you're moved to act on behalf of someone who doesn't deserve it, who you have every right to refuse to help."

"You got it into your head that it was your obligation to save Caleb because you thought he let you escape, that only you could do it. That's arrogance, Kimberly."

"Maybe. Or maybe it's what God wanted me to do."

"He could have killed you. In fact, it's what we expected. Aaron is a mess. Your father flew in from Germany. Beth is on her way from San Antonio."

Kim gaped at him, horrified. "You called *Beth*?"

"You disappeared, Kimberly!" he said, exasperated. "What would you have us do? We didn't expect to find you alive."

"I'm sorry to have inconvenienced you by not dying."

He glowered dangerously. "Do not ever say that to me again."

Her flush turned painful. "I apologize. And you're right, he could have killed me. I even gave him ample opportunity. But when it came down to actually doing the deed, he couldn't. He broke his stone knife and ran with me. I'm only alive because he refused to take my life. I can't ignore that."

"You put yourself in the hands of a killer and blithely expected mercy when he's never shown any before."

"I put myself in the hands of God and expected a miracle," she replied, an edge to her voice. "And I got one."

"He's —"

"Everyone deserves grace. Even remorseful murderers."

"He was not remorseful."

"It seems I knew your brother better than you did."

"That's doubtful, Kimberly. You only know what he was willing to show you."

"And yet what he showed me was mercy," she countered, arching a brow.

He held up a hand, conceding the argument. She didn't deceive herself he was acknowledging that she had won it; it was just pointless to argue over something on which neither would budge.

After a while, he said, "Taryn told Aaron about the bar Trent Baudelaire gave you."

"I figured she would."

"It was a very generous thing for him to do. Why didn't you tell Aaron about it?"

"It wouldn't have made any difference."

"Maybe it would have broken the ice." When she didn't respond, he opened his briefcase, rummaged around, and handed an envelope across the aisle to her. "From Melody Olmstead."

Her lips compressed. "I'm sure I'm not interested."

"If I were you, I would read it."

Kimberly turned to envelope over, saw that it had already been opened once and resealed with tape. She sent him a sidelong look. "This fall under government jurisdiction?"

He didn't flinch from her veiled accusation that he had been snooping. "We expected to find you dead in a house under federal investigation, at the hands of a man on the FBI's Most Wanted list. So yes, it fell under government jurisdiction. I had to know everything I was dealing with."

She blew out an impatient breath but didn't argue. Cody has his own opinions about what was his agency's business; that she felt her marital issues should be free from his intrusion was irrelevant to him.

The envelope taunted her almost as much as Melody's lie about Aaron's infidelity. She would have laid the envelope aside but for the challenge in her father-in-law's eyes. With barely concealed annoyance, she ripped it open and slid out the letter. *Dear Kim, blah blah blah bullshit bullshit bullshit...* But wait, what was this? *I lied. Aaron's always been very careful not to allow any opportunity for such a situation, not that he would have been tempted anyway. Since the day you arrived in town, every other woman in the world is virtually invisible to him.*

Her hand convulsed on the letter, crumpling the corner. Cody made a point of shuffling around the contents of his briefcase, trying to give her some semblance of privacy despite their close quarters.

I lost everything in such a short amount of time, the worst part of my life and the best part of my life. I had no idea how to handle any of it. And people kept telling me how the Schaefer family was responsible, until finally I believed it. Cody is too well-protected, too alert, so Aaron was the only one I could get to.

Her hand clenched again. She and Aaron were paying for something that Melody's own husband had caused? Neither Aaron nor Cody had been involved in the black magic circle that had created the beast that had killed seventeen-year-old Jared Olmstead. That had been Fred himself.

It was very unfair, and my blame was very misplaced. I can't tell you how sorry I am for the hurt that I've caused. I stole Aaron's wedding ring from the cash drawer at the greenhouse. I knew about your strange experience when he kisses you because I was hiding in the cutting field and eavesdropping on his and Taryn's conversation about it. Aaron has never been in my bed. He's never been in my house. He's never laid a hand on me.

Kim crushed the letter into a tight ball and tossed it into Cody's open briefcase. "Has Aaron seen that?"

"Yes. He had his own letter, much along the lines of yours. Poor excuses for bad behavior, but I believe the apology is sincere."

"Sure."

"Forgiveness is—"

"Very improbable at the moment."

He snorted impatiently. "You can forgive Caleb but you can't forgive Melody? Caleb tried to kill you!"

"And yet here I am, alive." She turned away. "I'm sorry, but I don't want to talk about it right now. I'd like a snack and then a nap after take-off. I have a lot of things to think through."

He didn't argue, just faced forward. When they had reached cruising altitude and the pilot informed him they could move around, he disappeared into the galley for a time, returning with a tray of sandwiches and a couple of bottles of water. Kim munched her way through three wedges of tuna salad—her personal favorite—and barely noticed when Cody cleared away the debris. He returned with a small plate and a couple of napkins.

"Lemon bar?" he offered, holding the plate across the aisle to her.

Kim stared at the plate for what seemed like an eternity, and then said softly, "No, thank you."

Her homecoming was nothing short of anticlimactic; Kimberly wondered if Cody had timed it for when he knew everyone would be away from the house.

The house was sparkling clean, fresh flowers in a vase on the mantle, cozy and inviting. But Kimberly felt like a stranger. Worse, like an *unwelcome* stranger. Her carry-all, full of the necessities Cody had purchased for her in Forks when she had been in the hospital, flapped against her back as she headed upstairs, looking for some sign of occupation. It wasn't that she looked forward to facing her husband, but—as it had in Bayview Manor—the waiting was killing her.

Their bedroom was as tidy as ever except for the rumpled blankets on the window seat. He was still sleeping there, then. She didn't know if that was a good sign or a bad one. A tee-shirt lay in a discarded heap on top of the blankets, drawing her across the room. The khaki cloth held the scent of lime, lavender, and sage, and her heart squeezed into a painful knot. She could almost see him in the herb field, the sun glinting red in his raven hair, sweat pearling on his tanned skin, white teeth biting into that sensuous lower lip as he worked.

"Was he worth it?"

His deep voice reverberated in the utter stillness of the house. Kim jumped, dropping the shirt, and turned warily. She had thought he wasn't home. He stood in the doorway, leaning against the jamb, watching her with cool blue eyes.

"Everyone is worth something, Aaron."

"He was a murderer, a rapist, a pedophile, neck deep in black magic."

"And at the end he was repentant, regretful, and saved our lives."

"So again I ask, was he worth what you gave up to save him?"

"What did I g—"

"WAS HE WORTH IT, KIMBERLY?" he roared, and she flinched. Down the hallway, one of the twins began to cry.

"Everyone is worth a second chance."

His mouth twisted. "I'll take that as a yes."

He moved into the room, yanked open the closet, and grabbed a duffel bag and a tote bag, both stuffed to the point of bursting. Her bags, filled with her things. She couldn't breathe as he dropped them at her feet and left the room.

Kim stared at them for a long moment, trying to will them away with the very force of her gaze. But they didn't vanish, and at last she picked them up and walked to the door, her pulse pounding in her ears, her heart perched on the edge of a precipice, hurtling toward a heartbreak from which there would be no recovery.

He stood in front of the open nursery door. Renée hovered on the top stair, drawn by his shouting, her face white. Kim stopped several feet out of his reach, mortified that her mother-in-law was bearing witness to her ultimate humiliation.

"Do you have the twins' things ready?" Her voice, polite and cool, was a stranger's.

Color burned along his cheekbones. "You willingly put yourself in the hands of the most dangerous, merciless man I know, the man who killed my fiancée and my brother, and you think I'm going to trust you with my children?"

Panic gripped her, and she took an aggressive step toward him. He straightened, squaring his shoulders, preparing to physically block her from the nursery. Tia's wailing raised in pitch, and was joined by Evan's. The sound pierced her heart, flooding her with helpless panic.

"This isn't funny, Aaron."

"I'm not trying to be funny. You're not taking my children."

His children. She saw now that she had been right; it was the end of everything. Without him, without her children, she might as well have died with Caleb.

"Aaron," Renée pleaded, tugging on his sleeve.

He shrugged her off, his eyes never leaving Kim's. "Please stay out of it, Renée."

There would be no reasoning with him, not today. He was determined to punish her, and keeping her from her children was the best weapon he had against her. She couldn't believe he would use it, but lately he had done a lot of things she couldn't believe he would do.

"I'll be the cottage." She raised her chin. "I trust that's acceptable?"

He was already dangling the keys to the rental cottage from one finger. She took them, careful not to touch him. If she felt the touch of those fingers, she knew she would fling herself to his feet and beg. And God knew she would not be able to bear his rejection.

Somehow her legs carried her down the stairs without incident. Wrapped in an insulating cocoon of shock and despair, she didn't hear Beth's words as she passed her, only saw her lips moving, felt her fingers clutching futilely at her sleeve. She barely registered her father's presence as he took a look at her face and then headed upstairs, his own expression set in forbidding lines. For a lingering moment, as her numbed feet carried her toward the front door, her eyes met Cody's, and she saw her pain mirrored there as though he felt every agonizing jab himself. Yes, he loved her as a daughter, but she *wasn't* his daughter, and she wouldn't make him choose between Aaron and her, would not divide his loyalties. He made a move toward her, but she flinched away and he backed off, torn.

She was out on the porch, the front door shut firmly behind her and muffling the shouting inside, when she realized she didn't have her purse, didn't have her car keys. She had nothing she needed, nothing she wanted.

The bags slid from her shoulders, thumping onto the wide boards of the porch floor, and she headed down the long drive, the key to the cottage clutched in her hand as though it were the only thing anchoring her to sanity.

The cottage wasn't far, only a half-hour's walk. She held on as long as she had to, waving at people who beeped their horns at her in greeting or called hellos out their car windows. And then she turned down Willow Road, away from traffic, into the woods where the only sounds were bird calls, squirrel chatter, the breeze in the leaves of the trees.

She let herself into the cottage and curled into an aching ball of misery on the carpet just inside the door, where Beth found her ten minutes later.

(Correspondence from Geoffrey Windsor to Anne Quequesah, Heron Bay Historical Society)

July 12, 2009

Dear Ms. Quequesah:

I appreciate your vision for the future of Bayview Manor as well as your concern for the fate of this historical landmark.

Unfortunately, your request to be allowed access to the grounds and to the interior of the Manor, as well as your request to conduct limited tours through the Manor, is not something that I, in good conscience, can honor.

The nature of the Manor is still unknown and deemed quite dangerous. As the house is still under federal investigation and therefore under federal control, I have forwarded your request to the appropriate governing agency. I expect their response will be much the same as mine.

Rest assured, however, that I will authorize the cleanup of the grounds by select individuals hand-picked by myself and by one federal agent, Cody Schaefer. And because I truly appreciate your heart for preserving the past history of Heron Bay, I have enclosed a check for the purpose of establishing and maintaining the Bayview Manor library at the Historical Society. I hope this will suffice in lieu of access to the property.

Regards,
Geoffrey Windsor

NO CURE FOR WHAT AILS ME
Thursday May 21, 2009

"He's here again, Rachael."

"Thank you, Matthew."

"Will you see him this time? He says he's not going away until you do."

Rachael sighed, glancing up from the book she was reading. "I'll see him."

The deputy stared at her through the open door of the cell as though hoping she would vanish. When she didn't, he heaved a sigh and went to bring Geoffrey Windsor.

After being released from the hospital yesterday, she had turned herself in for arson, although no one seemed to be cooperating with her. The fire inspector, try as he might, could find no evidence of a fire inside Bayview Manor, although there was plenty of evidence scattered across the grounds. Geoffrey was stubbornly sticking to his story that a malfunctioning boiler had blown up. Because of those two, the sheriff refused to charge her with any crime despite her confession.

But she knew her culpability, and she had refused to leave the tiny Heron Bay jail. Exasperated beyond belief, the sheriff had shown her into a cell and left her there overnight, door unlocked, with dinner delivered from Catch of the Day — but only because the jail was otherwise empty. And this morning, she had awakened to scrambled eggs with creamed cheese and chives, grilled ham, and hashbrowns and toast, with coffee and orange juice chasers. They were treating her like a visiting celebrity instead of a criminal.

A shadow fell over her, and then the mattress beside her dipped as he sat down.

"Thank you for seeing me. Finally."

She half-shrugged. "Ready to recant your silly 'it was the boiler' story?"

"No. I'm here to take you home."

"I'm not going home. I committed a crime, and by God, they're going to arrest me for it before I'm through."

"They may commit police brutality before you're through," he remarked sardonically. "Rach, you shouldn't be in a jail; you have serious injuries. You have a consultation at Harborview Medical Center for later today; they want to evaluate the burn and determine treatment. I'm taking you there."

Her hand screamed pain like all the fury of hell despite the painkillers she was faithfully popping. She had discharged herself from the hospital against advice and admonition, filled her prescription, and came directly to the sheriff's office. That she was in agony seemed justified.

"I'll go if you promise to bring me back here when you're done."

He huffed out an impatient breath. "I'm not bringing you back to Heron Bay at all." He scuffed his foot along the cement floor, flushing a little. "I thought maybe you would go to Orcas Island with me. To my house."

"How absolutely scandalous, Geoffrey." She looked at him for the first time, brow arched. "Don't think it sets a precedent just because we...we...."

"As my wife," he interrupted, glaring at her.

Her flippancy vanished. This had to be a joke. He had been gracious enough not to mention it when she had fallen in love with him, even while he'd been engaged to another woman. And he was stubbornly gracious even now after she had tried to burn his mansion to the ground. But this was going too far.

"You don't have to do that, Geoffrey. I'm fine. I'll be all right. Once my hand heals, I'll be back to work."

"Don't be so sure. There's no guarantee you won't need skin grafts. I talked with your doctor when I paid your bill."

She flinched. "I'll pay you back."

"Like hell you will." He grabbed the plastic chair the sheriff had left in the corner of the cell and scooted it closer, swinging onto it so he could face her. He caught her uninjured hand in both of his.

"I don't need a mercy marriage," she said quietly, looking away, trying unsuccessfully to tug her hand out of his. "I'll pay my own way."

"This isn't about mercy or pity, Rachael. It's about love."

She didn't dare look up. Didn't dare breathe. Didn't dare hope.

"That's a pretty serious word, Geoffrey."

"I'm a pretty serious-minded guy." He waggled her hand back and forth. "Will you look at me?"

"No."

"Why not?"

"Because I burned your house down and you're saying you want to marry me."

"The house is still standing. The insurance company has classified it as an accident caused by a malfunctioning boiler. They're paying the claim, and I'm using the money to clean up the grounds and maintain the house. It won't ever go back on the market. I won't ever let anyone live there again."

Unexpected tears prickled her eyes. She wasn't a weepy woman, so they surprised her. Her voice was small when she spoke, all flippancy gone.

"Geoffrey, I think I've done some terrible things. I...I don't remember much, but I remember a bookstore and leaving a strange book there, but I can't remember what it was or how I got it. I think Alex gave it to me. And that night I came to your hotel and we..." Her face burned.

"You have no choice but to let me make an honest woman of you."

"I do so have a choice, and so do you! You shouldn't want anything to do with me after all of that. I...I flung myself at you and seduced you, even though you're engaged to someone else. I didn't even ask if you wanted to — you know."

"Sonia and I agreed to a mutual severing of our romantic ties, which weren't that strong in the first place. As for the rest...I definitely wanted to," he assured her, amused. "I don't go to bed with just any woman who strips naked in my hotel room."

She sent him a look through her rumpled bangs. "Are there

many?"

"Naked women in my hotel room? You're the only one. I don't care what else you've done. I know why you did it; you weren't yourself. There were extraordinary circumstances. All I care about is I love you, and I want to be together for the rest of this life. And beyond, if it works that way."

"There's something seriously wrong with you, Windsor."

"Yeah, but there's no cure for what ails me." He ducked his head, forcing her to look at him, and grinned. "I have a surprise for you."

"Besides the marriage proposal? I feel spoiled."

"You should be spoiled. Don't move; I'll be right back."

He dashed out of the cell and came back a moment later with a nylon-and-mesh cat carrier. A huge mass of Creamsicle fur pressed against the mesh on one side, and a low growl warned of the cat's displeasure.

"Marmalade!" Rachael burst into tears. "I thought I'd killed him."

"I won't lie. It was close, Rach," Geoffrey said, sobering. "But he's good as new. And pissed as hell about being in there. How about we get out of here and get him somewhere we can let him loose? He's missed you."

She slid off the bed and put her arms around his neck, hugging him tightly, careful to hold her burned hand out of the way.

"I love you," she whispered fiercely.

"I know," he whispered back. "You said so when we made love."

"I did?"

"I thought you did. Maybe it was the angels who told me."

"They'd know. Let's go."

Man, woman, and cat left the jail, and headed out of Heron Bay for the last time.

(E-mail from Taryn Ackerlin to Aaron Schaefer)

TO: Aaron Schaefer [gardenplans@stoneridgenursery.com]
FROM: TAckerlin@gmail.com
DATE: June 1, 2009
SUBJECT: [blank]

You know I try to keep my nose out of other people's business. But how long are you going to let this go on?

I ran into your wife in the grocery store. She looks like hell. She is desperate to see her children. And speaking of the twins – you're having such a hard time with them because they miss their mother. They *need* their mother. And if you were honest with yourself, you need her too.

I'd give anything to be in your situation, Aaron, with the love of my life within reach if only I swallowed my own stupid pride. But he's gone, and only God knows if he's ever coming back. All I have are memories and regrets.

Life is too short and too uncertain to waste it on a fit of wangst. And before you fire off an angry reply to *that*, think over what I've said. I'd give everything I have to be in your situation, Aaron. Everything.

SHE LOVES ME, SHE LOVES ME NOT
Sunday, June 7, 2009

He lasted fifteen days before the silence — and his conscience — got to him. Yes, Kimberly had been reckless with her life, but the more Aaron considered the situation, the more he realized he had been reckless with so much more. Of the two crimes, his was the bigger betrayal.

But the inertia of fear held him in his chair. Would she even talk to him after everything he had put her through? When she checked on the children, she called Taryn, or Renée if she was in town. Cody had called her once about a week after they came back from Washington State, but they had only argued. Cody wouldn't tell him over what. It had upset his father enough to make him slam out the back door and disappear into in the nursery's herb fields for hours.

Speaking of his father… "Are you eating that mostaccioli or are you conducting experiments on how long the pasta can withstand being mashed around on your plate?"

Aaron looked down at the plate in front of him, smeared with massacred pasta in curdling Alfredo sauce. He had followed Kim's recipe with obsessive attention to detail, but it didn't taste right. He knew there was nothing wrong with it, compositionally speaking. That it lacked flavor only meant that it lacked Kimberly. She was a fabulous cook and loved to sing as she prepared every meal and sometimes danced around the kitchen. But he had sent her away, and now the house was missing her, missing her voice and her laughter and her love.

He dropped his fork onto the plate with a clatter, and pushed the plate away from him. The *house*, hell. *He* was missing her.

"When are you going to admit you were wrong?" Cody asked

quietly, dropping into a chair across the table. He moved a huge vase bursting with fresh flowers from between them. Determined to make the house cheerful in Kim's absence, Renée had plucked virtually every early bloom from his garden, and not a few from the nearly fields and roadside.

"Is that why you two argued, because you called her to tell her you were wrong?" He was satisfied to see Cody wince.

"You're annoyingly persistent sometimes," Cody muttered. "We argued because I was going to bring Caleb's body back to Pennsylvania once the coroner was done with the autopsy."

"And yet there he is, buried in Seattle."

"She has a way about her."

"Yeah." Ron laughed a little. "Yeah, she does."

Cody plucked a daisy from the vase and idly started pulling petals from it. "I can watch the kids for a while, you know."

Ron nodded at the daisy. "Does she love you or does she not?"

His father grinned. "Oh, Renée definitely loves me. Why, I'll never know." He yanked another daisy from the mass in the vase and tossed it across the table. "Give it a shot yourself."

The daisy seemed to mock him. He was even certain he could hear mocking daisy laughter. "No thanks."

"Coward."

Ron snatched up the daisy and began ripping the petals off. When one remained, he stared at it for a long time until Cody prodded an answer from him.

"Well?"

"How long did you say you could watch the twins?"

"As long as you need."

And that was how he found himself parking in front of the cottage, preparing to face the most frightening thing a man could ever face: a stubborn wife he had wronged and who was apt to shoot at him from the windows as he approached.

No one answered his knock, so he tried the knob and found it unlocked, which told him Todd was here somewhere. He'd been a constant bulwark between them, fiercely protecting his daughter from awkward and unexpected public encounters.

He called through the house, but no one answered, so he

continued on his way out the back door and across the patio. He was unlatching the gate to head toward the river when he heard a throat clear, unconvincingly casual. Ah. The Bulwark.

Todd was sitting at the metal mesh table which he had pushed out of the middle of the patio and closer to the shade-giving trees. The patio itself, comprised of carefully laid flagstones held in place by tufts of Scottish moss and purple alyssum, was scrupulously tidy. Kim's doing, no doubt. He was smoking, careful to tap his ashes into a terra cotta pot filled with sand so as not to litter the flagstones and incur his daughter's wrath.

"Your daughter know you're smoking?"

"She's not the boss of me," Todd replied, amused. "Have a seat, son."

"I'm actually looking for my wife."

"Let me be clear: before you talk to Kimberly, I'd like to talk to you. Man to man."

Crap. Ron hooked a chair out from under the table and sat. "Spit it out, Todd. I only have as long as Cody's patience lasts."

"An eternity, then."

"Not when it comes to your daughter."

"You have a point." Todd squinted at the cigarette smoke rising into the air. Once upon a time, he'd been the quintessential California beach bum, with boyish good looks that fell just short of handsome. There were secrets behind his amber eyes now, and shadows that drew his face into mysterious and compelling lines. "I just wanna know beforehand how bad this is gonna be."

Ron squirmed with guilt. "Aww, Todd."

"She's cried herself to sleep every night. She walks through the day like the living dead. So if you're going to make things worse, I need to be prepared, because to be honest, it rips the hell out of me to see my daughter suffer like this."

"I'm not going to make things worse."

Todd turned his squint toward his son-in-law, his eyes seeming to peer directly into Ron's brain. What he saw appeared to satisfy him. He made a motion toward the gate and the path beyond it. "I think I'm going to go see my grandkids for a while, chew the fat with your dad. Kim's down at the river. You know where."

"Yeah."

He made his escape with relief. Sunlight broke through the dense canopy of leaves, dappling the path to the river. A squirrel paced him, jumping from tree to tree and chattering loudly, ruining his stealth approach.

She sat on a flat boulder near the water, a small pile of skipping stones beside her, but she wasn't skipping them; she sat huddled into herself, watching the water rush past. Her jacket was zipped halfway, revealing the lace-edged camisole she wore beneath. It reminded him of before they were married, of a rainy night when she had come to his house at a thoroughly indecent hour, driven to the brink of hospitalization by the belladonna berries the cook at the diner—one of Caleb's cronies—had put in her blueberry pancakes. Five years later, he could still taste the rain on her skin and smell the lilac lotion she favored, as though his memories were actually a portal through time.

He navigated the rocks, claiming one near her, taking it as a good sign that she didn't flinch away from him or move farther out of his reach.

"Hey."

She glanced up, and huddled more securely into her own embrace. Her face was too pale, and she was still too thin.

"Hey," she replied. She reached for her skipping rocks with a shaking hand.

"I want to talk to you. Is that okay?"

Her fingers clenched around a rock. "I suppose. It can't be any worse than the last time you wanted to talk to me."

Ouch. "Yeah. I'm sorry for that." Her eyes flicked quickly to his face, and away again just as fast. "I just think we need to decide where we're at."

That surprised a humorless laugh out of her. "Where we're at? You're in our home with our children, and I'm living in our rental cottage, trying to dodge you at the grocery store."

"I'd like to change that."

"Bring the papers. I'll sign them."

"What papers?"

"Look, Aaron, I can't live in limbo for the rest of my life.

Just...finalize the details and let me know when I can see my children. I want..." She closed her eyes. "I *need* to see my children."

"I don't want a divorce."

"You give a good impression of it."

"I'm sorry for that, too."

"You made it quite obvious over the last three months that you don't love me anymore, so I can't see the point in continuing to drag me through hell."

"I can't think of you in terms of love anymore," he said quietly.

She flinched. "Well, that's pretty clear." She sounded as though the breath had been knocked from her. "Just go, Aaron. I don't think I can do this—"

He interrupted. "The children want their mother. *I* want their mother. So I came to ask if you would come home." He scuffed his feet through the marsh grass sticking up between the boulders at his feet. "Beg you to, more like."

She started crying, clapping a hand over her mouth to stifle a sob. Her nose turned bright red, and her eyes were flooded lakes of copper in her dead-white face. He thought she'd never looked more beautiful.

"I tried to make sense of everything, but I was looking at the whole situation through my anger. When I stepped outside of it, all I could see is that I'm no good without you. You refresh me, from my soul on out. I think you, I dream you, I breathe you, I live you. I feel alive with you. There's no word to describe all of that, so I use the catch-all 'love' even though it's just not adequate."

Kimberly was sobbing too hard to speak, so he went on, hoping this was a good sign. Women were like that, crying out their emotions, but a man could never really tell if it was in his favor or if he'd better duck.

"But we're going to have to do something about all of these other men wanting you." She barked out a laugh through her tears. "Caleb, Scott, even that little dink down at the market who bags our groceries."

"He's seventeen, for God's sake," she said, her voice thick with tears and nearly incomprehensible.

"Doesn't matter." His smile faded. "The worst thing about

Caleb was not knowing why you went to him. You said it wasn't sexual or romantic, but God knows he wanted you bad. It was obvious from the first time he saw you in my bar. It was more than just a desire to go to bed with you. It was a need to possess you. And..." He trailed off, choosing his words carefully now. She'd mastered her tears and was wiping her cheeks on the sleeve of her jacket, eyeing him warily. "I think, no matter what you say to the contrary, that you desired him on some level."

"He was a very attractive, charismatic man. Most women desired him. But he raised my hackles at the same time. Gorgeous and charming, but lethal. I never would have become involved with him because he scared me." She met his gaze for the first time. "If we're going to make this work, I have to tell you everything. Everything that happened in the Wyckham House, and everything that happened in Bayview Manor."

She talked for a long time, her face often burning with shame or twisting in sorrow. He held his horror inside, because it came with a large measure of guilt. He'd never speculated too deeply—or pushed too hard to get her to tell him—about what had happened in those eight hours she'd been at Caleb's mercy five years ago. He had been too afraid of how far their physical interaction had gone, and that she had been unable to free herself of him because of an emotional attachment.

But now he could see the way Caleb had twisted her by alternating charm and cruelty. And he could see, finally, that Caleb had not been the true target of her rescue mission two weeks ago. She had gone to untwist what he had twisted, had gone deep to root him out of her psyche completely. She had gone to rescue herself, cure herself of the poison, and the only way she could do it was with Caleb's cooperation.

When she had finished, he sat for a while, absorbing the true hell his wife had lived behind her smile for so many years.

"I just have one other question. Did you see Denny in the house at all?"

"Taryn asked me the same thing. I never saw him. But if he went into that house and never came back out..."

"Then he's still in there," he deduced, his shoulders slumping.

After a long pause, she asked, "Are you going to go after him?"

"No." He didn't explain his reasons why; she already knew the cost of ransoming anyone from that house was too high. She was lucky to be alive herself.

"Do you think she'll try?"

"I hope not. It's too dangerous. But we can't stop her if she does. Did Cody tell you they tried to put up an electronic perimeter fence four years ago to keep people from going into the Wyckham House clearing? The units burned out, every single one of them."

"You remember what lives there, don't you?"

"Yes."

"They're fallen angels. So if they travel through the stones of the earth to get from one point to another, there's no way to keep people from accidentally encountering them. You can't fence off where they are, because they're everywhere. He should've known better."

"It was a shot in the dark."

"She won't go look for him," Kimberly said quietly. "He left her a long time ago. She's finally admitted they're over. But it's going to be very hard for her. This is different than breaking up with someone when they live in another city. This is like losing someone to death."

A chill of dread crept into his heart. "Do you think he's dead?"

"No. But I don't think they're going to let him go without an epic fight. I'm sorry. It's my fault he's in there."

"No. He could've said no." He stood. "Let's go."

"Wait. There's one more thing." Her expression settled into determined lines. Uh-oh. Whatever it was, she wasn't about to let him say no. "I want a puppy."

"I know. Brad Harrington has a litter almost ready to leave their mom. We'll go look tomorrow."

The rush of the river faded into the distance as they walked the path to the cottage. A chipmunk raced ahead of them on the trail and dove into the cover of a patch of wildflowers. The woods smelled fresh and moist, cool, soothing. In another six weeks they would smell like hot pitch in the burning sun, one of his favorite smells on earth, but for now he breathed deep, feeling cleansed and refreshed. Their hands bumped, and he twined their fingers together. She let him.

"Your father went to see the kids," he said as she unlatched the gate and swung it open, casting a look toward the empty patio table. She cocked a brow. "We talked before I went down to the river."

"I see."

"He's totally on your side, you know," he joked lamely.

She smiled. "There are no sides. There's only what happened and how we're going to handle it."

The kitchen smelled of coffee left on a hot burner too long. She shut off the coffee maker, shed her shoes in the kitchen, and went to put her jacket away. He followed her down the hall and came up behind her as she dropped her jacket over the back of the desk chair. When she turned, she jumped a little, startled to find him behind her. Although he wasn't touching her, there was a buzzing along his nerve endings, as though he'd stepped into an electrical field surrounding her.

Without a word, he shed his hoodie, and then his tee-shirt.

Equally silent, she unbuttoned her shirt, her eyes fixed on the snarling scars on his chest, the legacy of the werewolf attack five years ago.

Shoes off. Socks off. Pants off. She stepped out of her jeans, holding onto the back of the desk chair. They stood like that, naked before each other, for what seemed like forever. His eyes travelled down her compact frame, over breasts that were still firm and sassy, a waist still trim, hips that flared slightly more than before the babies. Her flat belly was marred by a livid scar. She had her own reminders of her own battles, and he finally admitted that perhaps hers had been just as scarring as his.

"I want to lie down and hold you, skin to skin, but I'm not going to make love to you. I'm not even going to kiss you."

Her brow furrowed. "Why not?"

"I just want to be close to you for a while, alone, with no barriers, before we go home."

Her frown deepened. "I don't see why there can't be a kiss or two. Maybe ten."

His mouth twitched. "I think I've figured out what happens between us when I kiss you. We've always thought it happened to show us every aspect of each other, our very essence, so we would trust each other. But we were wrong."

"We were?"

"It's not about us. We're supposed to have faith in each other regardless, and to rely on that phenomenon alone to assure ourselves we can trust each other is actually showing a lack of faith. It gave them power over us, allowed them to influence our bad decisions."

"So what do you think it is, then?"

"It's being with God. It's how He sees us, individually. And how He sees us together."

He took her by the shoulders and guided her backward to the bed. When her knees hit the edge of the mattress, he slid his arms around her and tumbled them down. They bounced on the springs, and she laughed. Her laughter was the sound of eternity, his definition of absolute joy. He pressed his face into her neck and kissed the soft skin of her throat.

"Hey, you said no kissing," she murmured, breathless.

"We aren't kissing. I'm kissing you. Are you complaining?" He grinned and kissed her again, his tongue tracing a filigree pattern on her skin.

"No." She shivered and sighed. "No, not at all."

The hours passed in wordless sensuality, but he was true to his word. They did not kiss, and they did not make love. But there were languorous caresses, the almost unbearable stroke of fingers on hyper-sensitive skin, the touch of tongues on bare flesh and the exquisite taste of each other. Her hands were delicate butterflies moving over him, and her hair was silk in his fist.

He did not think that he could ever love her more than he did in those hours, as he lived her and breathed her and she refreshed his soul.

They dressed at dusk, in the blue twilight that matched the color of his eyes and, still in that wordless communion, went home to their children.

(Quotation used by Hugh MacGregor in the Bayview Journals, cited for the official government record by Cody Schaefer, Director of the Omega Team)

This day I breathed first: time is come round,
And where I did begin, there shall I end;
My life is run his compass.
– Cassius (*The Tragedy of Julius Caesar*), William Shakespeare

AND SO SHALL I END
June 2012

The wind blew in from the west, tangling warm fingers into the man's silver hair. His head was bent over a notebook on his knees. His posture was more one of self-protection than of protecting the paper, as if some unbearable pain tore away at his heart.

After a moment, his spine straightened perceptibly, and with a look of grim acceptance on his face, he put pen to paper. Still, there was hesitation.

To lay down on paper the last events of Bayview Manor — and his speculations about the nature of the house — was to lay himself bare for ridicule and pointing fingers. Unfortunately, he had opened his mouth before he thought and had told Anne Quequesah about Kassandra Fotheringham's diary, which he had found at Rachael's apartment when he had supervised the moving company as they packed her things, and of course Anne wanted to get her hands on it.

It had been difficult to keep the Historical Society from going after whatever they wanted, whether it was him for harboring Kassandra's diary or Rachael Payne for attempting to burn down one of the region's oldest structures. Hugh expected to be served court papers any day now.

A visit from Geoffrey Windsor had made the Society reconsider their vocal stance that someone needed to pay for the outrageous act of arson at Bayview Manor regardless of the fact that no fire damage could be found inside the house. Geoffrey wouldn't reveal what had been said in his first, last, and only meeting with Anne Quequesah, but the public cry for blood had ceased, and they seemed to have come across a large sum of money with which to expand the section of their library devoted to the Manor. In addition, the Historical Society would oversee the maintenance of the grounds on the condition that no one entered the house for any reason. Ever. Money talked, and Geoffrey Windsor could afford to speak very loudly.

Hugh scrubbed a hand over his face, wiping away the mist of salt water the wind threw into the air, despising this last chore regarding the Manor. But the Historical Society had vehemently insisted that he complete what he had started, that the full story be told; he rather suspected they were more concerned with driving in tourism than they were with revealing a decades-old mystery.

His head bent again, and his pen moved nimbly across the pages.

Was it Shakespeare who said "Here did I begin, and so shall I end," or something to that effect? I can't remember the quote exactly, nor the person to whom I should give the credit for having said it, but the idea remains the same: Here I began with Bayview Manor, and here I shall end – with Bayview Manor.

Hugh snorted impatiently. He had opened this can of worms himself by continuing the journals. He had felt they were incomplete, had felt compelled to finish them, more so after learning from Kimberly Schaefer the true events of the night the Fotheringham family was murdered. He had doubted the version Caleb Schaefer had given her, but Kimberly's unshakeable faith that Caleb had been honest about the events had swayed him, and he had laboriously reproduced the story in the blank pages following Kassandra's last entry.

I've said the Manor is still standing, God help us. Is the evil still present? Ah. Evil is everywhere, all of the time. This present darkness. The devil prods, his demons poke, their spurs dig into tortured souls. The house is theirs. It is of them, their vehicle through the earth to which they're bound.

But enough of waxing philosophical. Fairy tales have happy endings, this one no less so in spite of the tragedy that led up to it. And so I would like to end the dark era of Bayview Manor with a light of hope.

Sabrina Ketterick married Riley Grant. She led him a good chase and brought him to the altar twice in one year: once for the baptism and once for the marriage. Her shop is doing well, remarkably so. Backed by Sonia

Stockwell's money and reputation and Sabrina's talent, it could do no less than be insanely successful. Sabrina and Riley are expecting their first child in just a couple of days.

Hugh paused again, thinking of petite, sunny Sabrina. The Manor had taken its toll on her as well as on all the others. She had retained her wit and forward personality, but the wit was a little sharper and the directness a little more cautious. She hadn't forgotten being beaten by her own cell phone, wielded by an entity she could not see, simply for catching its notice while it had been attached to Rachael.

I still preach in Heron Bay. I can't bring myself to leave, mostly because of something Grace Markham said to me, about the metaphysical bookstores and psychics parlors that had popped up between Hoquiam and Forks over the last couple of decades. I have work here. The battle at the Manor is not the only one needing to be fought. Grace, regrettably, passed on last summer. Unlike the Fotheringhams before her, she is buried far from Bayview, in a lovely little green village cemetery in a small town outside Boston.

Rachael Payne married Geoffrey Windsor a mere two months after she torched his two million dollar house. I suppose if love can survive arson, it must *be true. They live on Orcas Island on a beautiful but not too ostentatious estate. Nanette and Greg Flanders occupy one of the guest houses. He fixes everything, and she plants beautiful gardens under the tutelage of Geoffrey's ever-watchful Japanese gardener.*

Rachael works from an office in their home; I tease her sometimes that she still *doesn't have a real office, but she is more comfortable working from her home and taking the ferry to her clients. Bayview Manor took a little of the extrovert out of her, but Geoffrey says she is getting better. She still dreams poorly but less frequently, and she's stopped associating the smell of gasoline with terror and despair. She no longer flinches when someone calls her name unexpectedly, and she now willingly – and with minimal uneasiness – ventures from the island to the mainland, something she wouldn't do in the first months after their marriage. The burn healed without the need for skin grafts, thank God, but her hands are scarred. Worse, her psyche is scarred, but her husband is certain that she will recover.*

Geoffrey has been the very definition of patience; he is good for her and to her. They have two beautiful daughters, light-haired bright-spirited

Pamela and dark, melancholy Serena. They show promise of growing into beautiful women in body and in spirit.

Neither Geoffrey nor Rachael have been to the Peninsula since that day in May 2009.

Neither will go.

The ferry horn sounded, and Hugh looked up. Over the railing, he could see the landing. Rachael was there, her tea-length summer dress rippling in the breeze. One hand held onto the straw hat atop her head, the other to a diminutive girl beside her. As the ferry docked, Geoffrey joined Rachael, carrying baby Serena. They waved, and Hugh waved back. He glanced back down at the journal.

Like it or not, I was chosen by the very nature of my profession to be the keeper of this lighthouse. I will, therefore, watch diligently. I will not abandon my post. I will know my times.

But this era is over. Thank God…it's over.

Hugh closed the journal and stuffed it into his leather portfolio. Gina was hovering a few feet away, obviously anxious for him to be done with his noxious chore. He shouldered the bag and took her hand, pulling her into the throng of departing passengers.

Two steps off the ferry, a man detached himself from the milling crowd, blocking Hugh's path. He wore a lightweight windbreaker over a crisp polo shirt, blue jeans, and Wayfarer sunglasses, but even so, his whole demeanor screamed "government official."

"Agent Schaefer. What a surprise to see you here."

"Just plain Cody; I've retired. I have the final details regarding Bayview Manor to wrap up, and then I'm ready for a life of leisure." He dipped his head toward Gina. "Mrs. MacGregor, I apologize for the delay."

Gina squinted up at him. "Hopefully it's the last one concerning that devil house."

"I believe so."

"Ever find Agent Wallace?"

"No. He's still missing. Listen, Hugh, I heard there was a journal discovered. I believe it belonged to one of the Fotheringhams."

"And if there was?"

"There are some things about this house that we would like to keep under wraps for various reasons. The agency is concerned about the unusual nature of the Manor becoming common knowledge." Schaefer reached into his windbreaker and took out a folded sheet of paper. Hugh saw the embossed seal in one bottom corner and sighed, pulling the journal from his bag. He didn't need to read the official order to know he had to hand it over.

"Yeah, yeah. Classified documents and all that."

Cody took the journal from him and slid it into his own bag. "I'm sorry. I have my orders."

"It's probably better this way. The last thing the Historical Society needs in their Bayview Manor section is Kassandra Fotheringham's delusional ravings."

"You're right, they don't need that. I won't keep you — Rachael is waiting." Schaefer touched two fingers to his temple in a lazy salute. "Be at peace, Hugh."

"You too, Cody."

Hugh watched him sidle into the crowd, and then turned to find the Windsors. Rachael's welcoming smile was like the sun, and shrugging off the dark past, Hugh walked gratefully into it.

CHÂTEAU DE MERVEILLES
Date Unknown

They had kept him moving from house to house, time to time, trying to create confusion and weariness so he would give them the book. They had many agents caught in the house — many who, for their freedom, would take the book into the world where it could beguile and trap others. So the book stayed hidden under his shirt, tucked into the waistband of his jeans. As long as he was outside of time, he didn't need rest, didn't need food, could remain vigilant in guarding it.

When they had failed to overcome him through confusion, they had trapped him outside of time, in whatever incarnation of the house he was now in, and they stood guard around him so that he couldn't make it to the spiral and back into his present. He wondered how much time had passed; it seemed like only an hour or two.

But he couldn't stay here forever. He was an unwelcome intruder in this house of the damned; his fight against evil had waged long enough that his faith was unshakeable. They could not sway him; he was tried and tested, seasoned, a warrior of God. Soon they would try to kill him and take the book by force.

It was time to go home, though, and he prayed his strength was enough to carry him into the present...whenever the present happened to be.

He stood, faced his demonic guard, and secured the book in its hiding place.

Taryn, I'm coming. Maybe I'm too late, but I'm coming home.

With no further thought on the pros and cons of the action, he sprinted forward and flung himself into their midst. They began their dance, the spin of chaos, whirling him away into a void of disorder and cacophony.

Corridors flashed by, faces swam into focus and just as quickly blipped past. Words came in many languages—German, French, Hungarian, Russian, many others he couldn't name—and faded before he could make sense of them. Whirling. Falling. Up and over, around and around, until he started to lose his sense of self.

The book loosened, sliding up his chest toward the neckline of his shirt. *No!* He clamped his arms over his chest, trapping it, inching it downward. He couldn't remember why it was important, just that he could not let go of it.

A sweet face pressed in close to him. Emily Matthews. *"Just give us the book, Denny, and you'll be free."*

No! But his arms loosened a fraction. *NO!* He tightened his grip, battened down his resolve. *You're a warrior of God. You're a warrior of God. You're of God…*

And with monumental effort, he ripped free of the spiral and tumbled into the present, spilling from thin air into the drawing room—and into the middle of a surprised gathering of women. He lay unmoving, anchored to the floor by the violent revolutions of vertigo, while the women hovered over him, speaking in rapid French.

At last he was able to make sense of the world, and he raised his head a fraction. *"Quelle est la date d'aujourd'hui?"*

One of the women blinked and drew back slightly. From the way the others deferred to her, he assumed she was the mistress of the house. *"C'est le 4 juin 2012."* The fourth of June, 2012.

"2012?" he repeated, stunned. He'd been gone three years? Oh God, *three years?*

"Oui, monsieur."

Denny rolled onto his feet, and the women scattered, chattering excitedly in French. He pushed to his feet, shaking violently. His impromptu hostess overcame her wariness and wedged her plump shoulder beneath his armpit to help support him.

"Puis-je utiliser votre téléphone, s'il vous plaît?" Denny inquired, gritting his teeth against the sudden nausea that came with standing upright. She started moving them toward the hallway, not at all put off by his halting steps.

"*Oui, monsieur,*" she said again; then, with a charming accent, "You are *un Américain,* yes? I speak English."

"Thank God." He was not fluent in French but could get by if necessary. What little he knew of the language was swirling in his head, a jumbled mass of nasal tones and accented vowels. "You aren't surprised to have me just appear in your house."

She blinked at the slight accusation in his tone. "But, *monsieur,* you are not the first. The *téléphone.*" A sallow hand waved at the telephone table in the hallway, just outside the drawing room between the two horns of the horseshoe staircase. The house was luxurious, festooned with fancy furniture, expensive rugs, and priceless tapestries, quite unlike the manifestation he'd just escaped.

"*Merci.*" A thought occurred to him as she retreated. "Wait! Where am I? What…what region in France?"

Her perplexed frown faded into understanding. "Bordeaux, *monsieur.* You are at *Château des Merveilles.*" And she hurried back into the drawing room.

He snorted. Castle of Wonders, indeed. But Bordeaux…at least the wine would be good while he waited for extraction. He dialed a number from memory, waiting for an answer at the other end. This was an emergency hotline, rarely used. He hoped it had not been deactivated, that the team had not been disbanded. A lot could happen in three years.

But the phone was picked up with a curt "Yes." Not a question, but a statement, as in "We know you're in trouble."

"Number 78394290. Bordeaux, France. Château des Merveilles. No documents." He hung up. Within twenty-four hours, he would have a passport, currency, and a plane ticket back to the United States. Unless his hostess decided to call the authorities.

He popped his head back into the drawing room. The ladies had gathered into their tight circle again, gabbling animatedly. One saw him hovering in the doorway and tapped his hostess on the arm.

"*Simone, l'Américain.*"

Simone hurried out of the room again, closing the doors behind her to keep their conversation private.

"*J'ai besoin d'aide, madame.*" She dimpled at his halting French, and he switched to English. "Within twenty-four hours, someone will arrive to help me. May I stay here until then?"

He'd had no idea he was uttering the magic phrase, but the floodgates of hospitality opened wide. He was fed until he was certain he could go a week without eating another bite and was shown to a luxurious guest room with a private bath. It would be all too easy, in his present surroundings, to forget what house he was in. But he was a highly trained professional; when he showered, the book went into the stall with him. And when he dressed, he tucked it back into his shirt. He sat on the bed, legs stretched out, back propped against a padded velvet headboard, but he did not sleep. Not here, not in the devil's mansion. Twenty-four more hours, and he would be rescued and could sleep all he wanted.

The extraction team arrived in four.

EPILOGUE

It seemed unfair that he should find it on a sunny summer morning. The discovery of your worst nightmare should be reserved for those dark and dreary days of winter, when you expected to be chilled bone-deep and were less likely to notice the frigid depths of your fear.

But once found, nothing can be *un*found. And so he stood silently, staring at the scarred and ancient wooden planks of an iron-bound door, mostly hidden behind a tangle of brambles and ivy. The door sat at the base of a tall bluff, and he felt a quivery sort of dismay that he had walked at the top of this very bluff dozens of times and had never realized what lay beneath.

Back then he wouldn't have known to what the door led, wouldn't have been able to recognize the danger, although perhaps he might have been spiritually astute enough to intuit the evil emanating from the area. Hadn't he always felt it, like the low hum of high voltage electricity zinging along his nerve endings? He'd never liked this place, never felt the peace of the dead as he walked among their ranks.

Would he have even found the door had he not spent the last three years training to recognize the signs? It was impossible to say. The fact remained that he *was* trained and had found the door; while he was untrained, he had not. Perhaps that was the answer in itself.

He made no move to go inside; that would be tantamount to suicide. Not that he actually expected to survive this extermination; none of his kind ever had. Instead, he turned and walked briskly away, feeling the malevolence lessen by degrees the farther he moved away from the bluff.

The time for planning had come. He must be clever and bold, a precarious mixture of courage and recklessness. An old saying flickered through his mind: *There are bold pilots, and there are old pilots, but there are no old, bold pilots.*

The same applied to assassins.

He sat in his truck for a long time, his hands clenching the steering wheel. It went without saying that he'd rather live, but he didn't lament his destiny. He would do what he could to ensure the hive was exterminated so that *she* would survive, but his own fate was sealed: he would die young to save her, to save thousands.

A fair trade.

ABOUT THE AUTHOR

Sharon Gerlach was in training to be a ninja, but a dismaying lack of physical grace and balance—not to mention the inability to keep her big mouth shut—ended her ninja career before it had really begun. Now she writes. She doesn't write about ninjas because that's obviously a sore subject. But she writes about other really cool things and figures someone else will cover the ninjas. Life's really not all about ninjas, anyway. Sharon lives on the dry side of the Pacific Northwest with her husband (who must really be fond of her as he hasn't left her yet despite her ninja failings); two of her three kids (none of whom possess ninja qualities either); and a Border collie who suffers the presence of seven cats. Yes, you guessed it—ninja cats!

Sharon lives on the dry side of the Pacific Northwest with her family, her six ninja cats, and a fat, lazy Border Collie. Subscribe at Running Ink Press (www.runninginkpress.com) to be notified of more releases by this author.

Blog:
sharongerlach.wordpress.com

Twitter:
@SharonGerlach

Facebook Fan Page:
www.facebook.com/AuthorSharonGerlach

OTHER RUNNING INK PRESS BOOKS

NEMESIS – N. L. Gervasio
After the last prince ran off without any notice, breaking her heart and their engagement along the way, Nemesis Mussolini swore off men and passed the time kicking ass and slinging drinks, something her mafia father would never approve of. But, when her boss Clancy ups his flirtations, it's difficult to remember she's not interested, especially when he gets that delicious evil glint in his eye that makes her melt.

OFFICE POLITICS – Sharon Gerlach
Malaria is nothing a good dose of quinine can't handle, thinks Frannie Freeman when her vile office manager Malia—aka Malaria—marries their boss Sam, whom Frannie has loved for years. When Sam suddenly confides that he believes he was roofied the night of his surprise Las Vegas wedding, Frannie prepares to battle for her man with a woman's three best weapons — a loyal heart, a willingness to fight dirty, and the strongest margarita money can buy.

THE SECRET DREAMS OF SARAH-JANE QUINN – Sharon Gerlach
Self-confidence and social skills have never been Sarah-Jane Quinn's strong suits. So when two men - as different as night and day - vie for her affection, she's both flattered and mystified. And then Sarah is brutally attacked by a violent stalker. In the aftermath, she must re-evaluate her priorities and decide which man reaches deepest into her heart - and let the other go forever.

MALAKH – Sharon Gerlach
He hunts, silent and unseen. The string of mutilated bodies points to a madman, but biological evidence yields no DNA—human or animal. Suzanne Harper had once been the lover of an angel. The murders point to him and tell a terrifying tale: he's working his way to her. Now she must reconcile her longing with justice and honor, and she must do it fast...for the next murder could be hers.

THE WYCKHAM HOUSE – Sharon Gerlach
The Wyckham House has stood for centuries, its origin unknown, its history black and bloody. When Kimberly Owens' father disappears in Aaron Schaefer's town, all evidence points to the Wyckham House. Only one man has gone there and returned alive.

But even if Aaron could remember what happened to him, he doesn't want to. For there are worse things than death.

www.runninginkpress.com

www.ingramcontent.com/pod-product-compliance
Lightning Source LLC
Chambersburg PA
CBHW030617250626
47154CB00006B/1818